Wings of Destiny

V.M. PIRE

EMBRACE YOUR WINGS, BEWARE YOUR HEART

All rights to Wings of Destiny copyrighted to V. M. Pire of Snow Pire Books, LLC, EST. 2024

All rights reserved.

No portion of this book may be reproduced in any form without written permission from the publisher or author, except as permitted by U.S Copyright Law. For permission requests, contact the author at snowboundpublishing@gmail.com

Any cultural references such as movies, books, or fictional characters from other franchises are strictly mentioned for relatability purposes and are not being claimed by V. M. Pire. Any individuals or names mentioned throughout the story are not based on actual individuals and are not meant to portray real individuals.

Published by Snow Pire Books, LLC

EST. 2024

Standard Cover Art designed and provided by Selkkie Designs

Special Edition Cover Art by @Luriusa

Special Edition Cover Formatted by Selkkie Designs

Formatting by V. M. Pire

Editing by Encantedauthorco

Line Editing by @maraseditorialservices on Instagram

Proofreading by @maraseditorialservices on Instagram

EPUB ISBN 979-8-9905485-0-3

PAPERBACK ISBN 979-8-218-36401-4

HARDBACK ISBN 979-8-218-40131-3

First Edition 2024

Content Warnings	IX
Dedication	XI
Writing Playlist	XIII
1. Erin	1
2. Erin	9
3. Erin	37
4. Erin	45
5. Erin	55
6. Erin	67
7. Seth	77
8. Erin	83
9. Erin	89
10. Seth	97
11. Seth	103
12. Seth	111

13.	Seth	121
14.	Erin	125
15.	Josh	137
16.	Erin	149
17.	Erin	159
18.	Erin	171
19.	Erin	183
20.	Erin	199
21.	Erin	209
22.	Erin	219
23.	Seth	229
24.	Erin	237
25.	Erin	245
26.	Seth	249
27.	Seth	257
28.	Seth	261
29.	Erin	269
30.	Erin	279
31.	Erin	289
32.	Erin	295
33.	Erin	301
34.	Erin	309
35.	Erin	315

36.	Seth	321
37.	Seth	329
38.	Erin	337
39.	Josh	343
40.	Erin	347
41.	Erin	353
42.	Erin	359
43.	Erin	371
44.	Erin	379
45.	Erin	383
Acknowledgements		393
About the author		395
Also by		397
Social Media		399

Content Warnings

Potential Triggers
Nonconsensual kissing & physical contact, kidnapping, violence, weapons, emotional trauma, character death, abuse, torture, sexual assault, cheating, alcohol consumption, cussing & vulgar language, like a lot of it. If you can't handle cussing or fiery characters, turn back now.
Before reading, please take these into consideration. As an author, a reader and someone who has struggled with my own mental health and trauma, your mental health is important.

Dedication

For the ones who had to grow up too quick, who's trust issues are out the ass, had their heartbroken, said fuck this and fought back against their demons.
For the ones who felt abandoned, forgotten about and left out.
Never anyone's first choice.
You are seen. You matter.
This one's for you.

Writing Playlist

WINGS OF DESTINY WRITING PLAYLIST

(Can also be found on Spotify under WOD Playlist 1 & WOD Playlist 2)
Morally Grey by April Jai
WITHOUT YOU by The Kid LAROI
Whatever It Takes by Stephen Stanley
Love Is Gone - Acoustic by SLANDER, Dylan Matthews
Love Is Gone by SLANDER, Dylan Matthews
Perfect by Boyce Avenue
Falling Slowly by Vwillz
Project by Chase McDaniel
Keep Riding Me by Ur Pretty
ALPHA by Mariah Counts
I miss you, I'm sorry by Gracie Adams
Beautiful Things by Benson Boone
Bruises by Lewis Capaldi
Like You Mean It by Steven Rodriguez
You Broke Me First by Lewis Capaldi
Hold Me While You Wait by Lewis Capaldi
Fire Up The Night by New Medicine

Overwhelmed by Ryan Mack
Be - Acoustic by Hozier
Almost (Sweet Music) by Hozier
Always Been You by Jessie Murph
If You Love Her by Forest Blakk
Better Off Without Me by Matt Hanson
Figure You Out by VOILA
Drinking With Cupid by VOILA
Half A Man by Dean Lewis
ALL I WANTED WAS YOU by Ex Habit, Omido
Lonely (with Benny Blanco) by Justin Beiber, Benny Blanco
Complicated by Olivia O'Brien
Hit My Spot by Ur Pretty
Half Life by Livingston
When I was Your Man by Bruno Mars
1 SIDED LOVE by Blackbear
That's Us by Anson Seabra
If By Chance by Ruth B.
Mean It by Gracie Adams
My Everything by Ariana Grande
Sad Beautiful Tragic (Taylor's Version) by Taylor Swift
Things I Could Never Say to You by Noni
Wish You Were Here by Avril Lavigne
Someone WIll Love You Better by Johnny Orlando
2 Soon by Keshi
I Luv Him by Catie Turner
If You Could See Me Cryin' In My Room by Arash Buana, Raissa Anggiani
Back To December by Taylor Swift
Meant 2 Be by Shakira Jasmine, Nuca
Losing Us by Raissa Anggiani

WRITING PLAYLIST

A Little Bit More by JP Saxe

Pony by Ginuwine

SAD FUCK by Ryan Mack

These were played in no particular order (besides A Little Bit More by JP Saxe which is for Chapters 40 and 41)

Chapter One

Erin

I ran as fear gripped my chest, making it increasingly harder to breathe. My throat was on fire and the air in my lungs constricted. I had to keep going. I didn't know what or who I was running from but instinct kept me rushing forward into the darkness that surrounded me.

My pace increased as I barreled through the pitch-black world. I sprinted forward until I slammed right into what felt like a wall. My balance failed me and I fell backward. Instead of my body colliding into the ground below my feet, I went into free fall. My lungs began to deplete of the oxygen within them; I was suffocating. As I used every bit of fight that remained within me to suck in my final staggered breath, I awoke.

It had been a week since that nightmare. It was on constant replay in the back of my mind, partnered with a sense of impending doom, which nagged at me night and day. My already wonky sleep schedule had taken a hit over the last week, tossing and turning as I revisited the same nightmare night after night.

"Miss Snow, are you with us?" The familiar boom of my college professor's voice pulled me from my sleep-deprived train of thought.

Shit.

I had gotten completely lost in my own world, and I'd been caught red-handed. I dragged my eyes from the top of my desk to meet Mister Jensin's aged, angry, amber glare as he waited for my response.

"Sorry, Professor, what was the question?"

"Miss Snow, it'll do you well to actually pay attention once in a while. The question was: who brought forward the realization that the empire was falling?"

Oh crap.

I racked my brain in search of the correct information. "Was it Lady Leonora?"

Mister Jensin heavily rolled his eyes as he tapped his pen on the sand-colored desk. "Correct. Now pay attention."

The end of class couldn't have come quick enough; I practically bolted when we were finally dismissed.

"Erin, wait the hell up!"

As I turned around, I saw Seth running toward me with a huge ass grin plastered on his face.

"So, what'd you do, fall asleep in Jensin's class? Guy looked like he was going to pop." Seth chuckled as he slapped a hand on my shoulder.

Of course, Seth thought it was funny. Usually, *he* was the one Jensin picked on. I couldn't even begin to count the amount of times Seth had fallen asleep or slacked off in his class.

And yet, jackass here is acing everything. Prick.

"Ugh, tell me about it! I space out one damn time." I huffed.

"Yeah, no kidding. So, what's got your panties in a twist, Snow?"

"I was thinking about that weird dream I had the other night, the one with the running and impending doom. It keeps popping up in my head and it's bugging me. I can't even get a solid night's sleep."

"Dunno, maybe you're just finally losing it"—I whacked him on the arm—"or may-be it's just a weird dream. People have weird dreams all the time. No biggie. And besides"—he flicked his brow-length, shaggy, midnight-black hair to the side and stuck his tongue out at me— "when do you ever 'get a solid night's sleep' anyway, Booknerd?"

I shoved my shoulder into his side. "You're a dick, you know that?" I let out a laugh. "But you're probably right."

He smirked. "Of course, I'm always right."

We walked down the hallway and made our way out of the main building on campus; Seth animatedly rattled on about his other classes, getting closer to finals, upcoming plans, his newest fling. That one kind of irritated me a bit, not that I had any right to the guy. Seth and I had been best friends since we were kids. We grew up right down the street from each other and never really crossed *that* line into the more-than-friends territory. Ever since girls stopped having cooties, he'd chase girl after girl and was always attached. Me, on the other hand? In college I'd only slept with one person, the first relationship I ever had and the guy was a total tool. Seth was more than happy to tell the douche to beat it after he called me a bitch for ending it. Until then, Seth had always been like a big brother to me, but in that moment, I felt a spark. A lick of something more attempting to burrow itself in my chest. I'd fought it and shoved it down every day until I'd been sure it was snuffed out once and for all.

"So, what do you think? Want to hit that new movie with Libby and me?"

Shit.

Apparently, my active listening skills were in the shitter.

"Uh, sure. Sounds good."

"Oh, and the best part, my buddy Derik, you remember him? He'll be tagging along, too. Maybe y'all will hit it off this time," he said with a wink.

I do not want to hang out with Derik. The guy is a freaking creep.

I nodded my head and kept my mouth shut. Derik was one of Seth's closer friends. Why? I had no idea, but I wasn't going to throw a fit about it. I'd been in a study hole again and, against my better judgment, I needed to get out and socialize with someone besides Seth.

I'd been in our little college town for several years. However, all I had to show for it was one bad relationship, a job at the campus library— that I loved—a tiny apartment, and college debt that had begun to near the several thousand dollar mark after burning through my scholarship.

If Derik tries anything, I'm kicking his frat boy ass.

My lip twitched at the thought.

"Great! We'll pick you up around seven tomorrow." Seth waved and walked out the metal doors at the building's entrance, sliding through the hoard of students as they headed home for the day.

I swung my backpack around and dug my keys out of the front pocket. I beeped my little, blue Civic open, got in, and turned on the radio. I let out a breath I'd been holding in. The onslaught of students and staff members at the end of the day had been nerve-wracking. Most days, I could handle the close quarters, people bumping into me, unintentionally shoving me as we each hurried toward the main lot, but with how little sleep I'd been getting, I was on edge. It was like there was static in the air, a snake of electricity, awaiting the perfect moment to strike.

At least my favorite alternative rock band, Roach, is playing.

I'd listened to them for years. My dad got me into them when I was a kid, before everything went to shit. Back then, we had a whole collection of CDs ranging from classic rock to heavy metal that lined the main hallway in my childhood home.

I briefly closed my eyes and felt a sudden shift. The air thickened, a weight fell onto my chest.

BAM!

What the hell!?

BAM BAM!

My eyes shot open as I whipped my head from side to side frantically searching for where the noise had came from. I was no longer in my car. And it was pitch black.

I swallowed the bile that rose in my throat. As my eyesight adjusted, it dawned on me that I was in some type of open field in the middle of what seemed like a mountainscape. I looked around and caught a glimpse of a treeline in the distance but no lights or buildings. The clearing was a field of scorched grass and debris. My ass was sitting right in the center of it. A wave of nausea hit me and my stomach turned as spots began to dance in the corners of my vision.

Where the hell am I?

I could've sworn I had been in my car in the parking lot on campus. I shook my head and closed my eyes once more as I rubbed the palms of my hands over my lids.

I must be more exhausted than I thought.

"You've arrived, it seems."

I dropped my hands and snapped my head to my right and found someone standing there. Their piercing eyes trained on me and their body unmoving. The hair on the back of my neck rose.

They reached their hand out. "May I assist?"

I kept looking up at them, a total deer-in-the-headlights. "Uh… "

They grabbed my hand and yanked me up to my feet. Once I was standing, I was able to get a better look at the man in front of me. He was tall with a slender face which contrasted with his broad shoulders. His muscles were clearly visible through his sheer robe, his chest practically bare. Snow-white hair sat just above his shoulders and his eyes were the deepest amber I'd ever seen. I was absolutely starstruck.

Dazed, the words tumbled from my lips. "Where am I?" *I flicked my gaze around the clearing again.* "Am I dreaming?" *My brows furrowed.*

"In a way, I suppose. We have been waiting for you." *His gaze bore into me as if he could read my every thought.*

Waiting for me?

A shiver ran up my spine. "I'm sorry, I don't know what you mean?"

"It is almost time. We must prepare." *His voice eerily low, echoed around us.*

What is this whack job talking about?

I narrowed my eyes.

I smell bullshit.

"Time for what? Look here, man, I don't know what you're talking about and quite frankly, I don't give a rat's ass but I'm about ready to wake up now."

This dream is getting weirder by the minute.

If looks could kill…

His eyes glinted in the moonlight as he stared down at me, a burning fury lit behind his frozen expression. "Be prepared, Erin Snow. The time has come, and payment must be made." *He pressed a long, willowy finger to my chest and pushed. The world around me turned black and I fell backwards into an abyss.*

My eyes shot open as I sucked in cold air. I was back in my car.
What the actual fuck!?

Chapter Two

Erin

The drive home went by in a blur. Too focused on the latest sweat-inducing nightmare, my pulse continued to race.

This is fucking ridiculous. It was just a weird ass dream.

I took a steadying breath; I needed to calm down.

I might need to dial it back on the coffee-fueled late-night study sessions.

That had to be it. The lack of sleep and running on fumes had to have been the cause of the nightmares.

As I pulled up to my apartment, a couple of my neighbors crowded on the front stoop of the building. Wisps of smoke swirled around them as they puffed on their cigarettes, the scent wafting as it drifted across the blacktop. I forced a smile back as they waved when I passed them on my way inside. I was glad to be home but I was not in the mood for conversation. My neighbors were great; quiet, friendly, and mostly kept to themselves.

I shoved my key into the lock of my apartment door and shuffled into my open living area. It led into my barely used kitchen, with the bedroom and bath off to the right side. My apartment wasn't huge but it worked for me. I made a beeline for my espresso machine, the only appliance I bothered buying after I moved in.

"Okay, so I'm not cutting back on the coffee, but hey, it was a thought at least," I mumbled to myself.

Coffee was my comfort and I would take all the comfort I could at that moment. While the coffee brewed, I grabbed my small laptop and scrolled through a few news articles. I typically would check them twice a week to keep up with the latest local news.

'We must prepare.' Prepare for what?

I shook my head to clear it. It might've just been a dream but something about it nagged at me. I scrolled further down the news article on my screen.

> "Mass Power Outage Overtakes Riverside, Thirteen Disappearances Follow"

That was weird.

> *Thursday, January twenty-ninth, around ten p.m., the main power plant caught fire, leaving the town of Riverside without power. The cause of the fire is unknown and is currently being investigated. No casualties were reported. However, thirteen residents in the surrounding area were discovered missing after the event.*

Woah. I guess it was a rough night over there.

Riverside was a quick twenty-to-thirty-minute drive north from my apartment, so not too far away.

I wonder why we didn't lose power?

I shrugged. It was probably a different power grid. I continued to read through the article but there wasn't anything else that stuck out to me. I closed out of the browser, shut my laptop, and grabbed my piping hot coffee from the machine.

It was so warm. Just what I needed.

After chugging it, I placed my mug in the sink and headed toward my room to grab some clean pajamas and hop in the shower before another night of studying. I could *not* wait for finals to be over. My brain was about fried at that point. In addition to the nightly dream terrors, I'd been up late almost every night to cram as much studying material into my brain as possible. We were over a month away from finals but with it being my final semester, I needed to ace each one.

When I got out of the shower, I wrapped my hair up in a towel to dry and got dressed in my go-to pajamas: my baggiest T-shirt and sweatpants that I stole from Seth. My phone beeped and I grabbed it off the bathroom counter.

> Hey, did you see what happened in Riverside?

It was Seth.

> Yeah, I can't believe they lost power last night, and the fire. It looks like they don't know what happened either.

He usually kept up with this stuff more than I did, especially since his uncle was a cop. Seth had really gotten into the crime shows around the time he graduated high school and it just escalated from there.

> Definitely weird. I'm thinking about heading over there, mind if I stop by?

> Sure!

There goes my study time.

I looked in the mirror then poked my head out and scanned my living room. Suddenly very aware of how messy the place looked and that, even though I'd just doused myself with all the sudsy things

I had stashed in my shower, I matched. I quickly pulled the towel off my hair, flicked it back a couple times, swiped on mascara, and darted out to the living room to clean it up before Seth got here. He might've been my best friend but that didn't mean I wanted him to see myself or my apartment completely disheveled.

I ran around the main area of my apartment, tossing clothes and blankets into the washer as I went.

Living room, check. Now for the damned kitchen.

I swooped my eyes over the counter that was in desperate need of being decluttered; several used coffee mugs were spread across the surface, followed by a couple of pans from when I actually remembered to cook over the last week, and empty plates. It was gross and a wave of disappointment in myself washed over me.

I need to clean this place more. I never let things get this bad, even after dad left.

I shook the thought from my mind and went to work. Setting the water faucet on my metallic, farmhouse style sink to scolding hot, I dunked each dish into the bath of soapy water and scrubbed away.

Seth knocked right as I placed my last freshly cleaned and dried mug in the cabinet. He had a spare key, so he let himself in and tossed his keys onto the small, fake-oak side table next to the door.

He walked over and arched his eyebrow as he eyed me. "Did you eat yet?"

"Does coffee count?"

He shook his head, chuckling. "You know you can't survive strictly off coffee, right? You'll melt away, and I'll be left to suffer Jensin's lectures all alone." A slight pang pricked my chest.

Dear lord, that grin.

"Good thing I grabbed some snackage on my way over." And by 'snackage' he apparently meant a whole ass meal big enough to feed a family of four. To be fair, Seth was built like a tank: tall and covered from head to toe in muscle. The amount of food he went through easily doubled, if not tripled, what I ate on a day to day basis.

"We're going to have to talk about the definition of 'snack,'" I said, grinning back.

"Let's add 'food' too, Miss 'Does Coffee Count.' I picked up your favorite, Chinese. Grab a box and dig in," he said as he dumped the overfilled, white plastic bag on my kitchen counter.

I grabbed a box of chow mein, padded to my living area, plopped down on my midnight-black sofa, and went to town. I realized if he hadn't brought food over I wouldn't have eaten anything the whole day. I was too caught up in the dream and mayhem this past week.

I guess, dream-s, since I'm up to two now.

I shoved a fork full of noodles into my mouth and moaned. "Oh my lord, Seth. This is fucking delicious." My eyes were on the verge of rolling back in my head from the onslaught of pure perfection until I heard Seth snort and caught sight of a rogue half-eaten noodle as it rocketed across my couch. I smacked him on the arm and nearly choked from how hard I laughed.

After we'd calmed down and got a hold of ourselves, we ate in a comfortable silence. I looked up every once in a while and caught Seth staring at me before his eyes quickly darted away. No idea why. We'd smile at each other every so often and I would steal an extra glance or two when he wasn't looking; watching his shaggy onyx hair barely hover above his eyes as he'd lean forward to shovel another bite of food into his mouth.

My mind drifted off, imagining myself brushing the hair from Seth's face as our eyes met. He would lean in as he wet his lips...

"Hey, you're planning on staying in tonight, right? No late-night escapades?" he asked. It sounded light but there was a slight edge to the way he was looking at me...

Oh fuck. Did I think that out loud?

I panicked. The little fantasies I had involving Seth were rare but sometimes it was difficult to keep my mind from drifting into the off-limits-and-entirely-impossible territory. I swallowed back the panicked embarrassment and prayed that I hadn't actually said anything.

Just react like you weren't fantasizing about his delicious lips being hungry for yours.

My eyes widened.

What the fuck is going on with me?

I plastered on a tight-lipped smile. "Considering we have finals coming up, yes. I was actually planning on getting some more studying done. My brain is absolute mush at this point but I need to ace this thing."

A glimpse of relief spread across his face. "Always the bookworm, Erin. I'll help you study, if you want. I'm barely passing right now, so it'll do me some good."

I'd much rather study something else.

My face felt like it was on fire.

What is going on with me? Where the hell did that come from?

Seth got up and took our empty takeout boxes with him to toss in the trash. Then he walked back over to the couch, grabbing my notes and textbook on the way.

I really need to reel it in.

He sat opposite of me and stretched his legs across the length of my sofa, propping his feet on my lap. He tossed my notes to me and we started flipping through them, quizzing each other along the way. About halfway through, I noticed he was dozing off so I smacked his arm.

"I'm awake! Jeez."

By the time we were done, both of us mentally exhausted from information overload, it was almost three in the morning.

"Weren't you heading to Riverside?" I yawned. I forgot he had planned on just stopping by.

"I'm just going to crash here tonight. I really don't feel like driving back to my place," he said lazily as he stretched, elongating his chiseled body, and exposing the tanned skin above the waistband of his fitted sweats as his shirt lifted.

Fine by me.

My face flushed at the intrusive thought. I wriggled my way out from under his legs and got up, needing to put some distance between my overly-tired brain and the heat of my best friend's weirdly attractive body.

There's something wrong with me. This is weird.

I felt better knowing he wasn't driving halfway across town barely awake. I went and grabbed an extra blanket and pillow from my room and handed them to him.

"Thanks for letting me come over, Erin." He yawned.

"I'm sorry I kept you here so late." Guilt welled in my stomach.

"Nah, it's fine. I'd rather hang out here. I'll head that way tomorrow." My heartbeat quickened.

Breathe. Chill. Not like that, he probably just didn't want to finish the drive.

"Alright, well, goodnight."

"Night," he mumbled.

I shut my door and turned on my bedside lamp. Processing the day and the dreams I've had.

I'll talk to Seth about it in the morning, see what he thinks.

The past few years he'd gotten really into that kind of stuff, dreams and their deeper meanings. Maybe he could help me figure out what they mean, give me an idea of how to get them to stop. Then maybe I could actually get a wink of sleep.

I woke up with a start. The smell of fresh coffee wafted in through my door. I inhaled as I stretched my arms above my head.

Yum!

I got up and headed toward the kitchen, my mouth salivating.

"Looks like someone slept hard. Nice hair." His voice teasing.

I stopped and sprinted to my bathroom.

Oh lord.

I had raccoon eyes and looked like I had a freaking rats nest on my head. I grabbed my brush and ran it through my hair as quickly as I could; splashed some water on my face and wiped what was left of the mascara on the—now blackened—hand towel. I walked back out to the kitchen to see Seth doubled over laughing.

Ass.

"Jerk. I'll have you know, my sleep schedule has been screwed up lately. Between school, work, and these freaking nightmares"—I paused as I caught him swiping a tear from his eye—"Gee, could you laugh any harder? Jerk." I stuck my tongue out at him.

"Alright, alright, sorry. Just the look on your face was priceless. Want some coffee?" He slid me a cup across the counter and I snatched it, needing the morning boost.

"Actually, I was wanting to run something by you. I had another dream yesterday, after class."

His brows furrowed, confused. "What do you mean?"

I explained what happened and his confused look morphed into one of concern. He was processing.

"Did this guy say anything else to you? Before he…Before you woke up?" The way he said it was like he almost knew something about it. I cocked my eyebrow at him.

"No, that was it. They just said 'be prepared,' pushed on my chest, and I woke up. I think."

Did I wake up? Thinking about it, it was almost like I didn't wake up and just ended up back in my car.

An uneasy feeling settled over me.

Seth was definitely worried about something. "Well. What do you think it means? Because honestly I'm confused as hell."

"Hmm." He was thinking. Minutes ticked by and it felt like we'd been standing there forever.

"Hello. Earth to Seth."

"I think I need to talk to one of my buddies. He might be able to help."

Why would Seth need to talk to a buddy about my dream? It was a dream, a weird one, but it can't be that serious that he'd need to consult someone about it.

He grabbed his keys and headed out the door. "I'll text you later."

My brows furrowed. I stood there confused and wondering what had him worried. I shook it off and chalked it up to overthinking then grabbed some cleaner and finished cleaning from the night before.

Once the apartment was spotless, I checked my phone.

Still no text from Seth.

I chewed my lip between my teeth for a moment before deciding there was no point in waiting around. I threw on a pair of running shorts with a black T-shirt, grabbed my keys, and headed out the door, locking up behind me. It was beautiful out; a comfortable heat from the sun with a light breeze and not a cloud in the clear blue sky.

Perfect weather for a jog.

I double checked my shoelaces and took off.

Three miles into my run, I felt my phone buzz. I stopped at a nearby bench using the opportunity to rest for a minute. It was a text from Seth saying we'd talk after the movies tonight. I took that as a good sign, if it was urgent or important, he'd want to meet up sooner. I texted him back and slid my phone back into my pocket. I still had a few hours before they picked me up and decided to run a bit further.

By the time I made it back to my apartment, I'd jogged almost eleven miles. Lost in thought, running further than I'd originally planned and drenched in sweat. I pulled out my sweat-slicked phone, suddenly very grateful that I had caved and gotten a case for it, and checked the time.

Still have about an hour to spare. Fastest run of my life apparently.

I walked into my apartment and made my way to the shower, stripping off my running gear as I went. I turned the water on high and scrubbed away, using my favorite peach scented shampoo.

Twenty minutes later, I was out of the shower and finishing my makeup: basic winged eyeliner with a light coat of mascara, smokey eyeshadow, and lip gloss. Once I was done, I threw my hair up in a loose ponytail, my go-to. I pulled a pair of jeans and a clean black T-shirt out of my closet along with my Converse. A reliable combo.

I checked my phone for the time. Seth, his newest girlfriend, and Derik would be there any minute. I ran through my mental checklist: keys, phone, wallet.

Check, check, and check.

As I peeked out my window, I saw Seth's gun-metal grey Honda Accord pull up. I locked up and headed downstairs.

"Hey there, Erin! Car's kinda packed, sorry 'bout that." Seth got out and opened the rear passenger door for me to get in. I slid in next to Derik and offered a tight-lipped hello. His eyes beamed as he took me in and slid his arm around the headrest.

Great. I did a mental eye-roll.

"You've got to show me how to do my makeup like that!" Libby exclaimed, overly excited about the premise, considering she was already gorgeous. Short blonde hair, pixie nose, big green doe eyes, body like a swimsuit model. Me, on the other hand, plain brown hair, grey-blue eyes, and average face; easy to blend in, very forgettable. I gave her a small smile and nodded. I appreciated the compliment and knew it came from a good place but...I never took compliments about myself well and didn't know how to really react toward them. They always felt forced or like they were said out of obligation rather than being genuine; I knew I wasn't much to look at or think about. And Libby was gorgeous with a bubbly, magnetic personality. I was just an awkward girl who usually had her nose shoved in a book.

Wow. Slow down on the pity-party there, Snow. It's been a whole five seconds.

I gave her a small smile. "I, uh, I watched a few videos online a while back. I can see if I could find them to send to you?" I added awkwardly, a pinch of heat flared on the apples of my cheeks.

Seth put his car in gear and we headed off. I snapped my attention to the side, grateful for the reprieve. I watched as the buildings and small cityscape passed by the window; I zoned out with the hope that Derik would ignore me. It seemed my thoughts had been answered; he didn't try to speak to me the entirety of the short drive and I got lost in the scenery that followed us. The warm weather from the day had followed into the evening leaving the sky clear with a picturesque sunset of coral, lavender, pale yellow, and the deepest blush. I sighed.

It's been awhile since I've gone to the movies.

We parked close to the theater entrance. Derik got out first and made his way around to my side of the vehicle and opened the car door; it threw me off a bit.

Wow. Playing the gentleman. Weird.

Usually he was kind of a dick and a creepy one at that. Politeness was not in his genetic make-up from what I'd seen. "Yo, Snow, you comin' or not?"

Ah, that was more of what I'd expected.

I got out and Derik shut the door behind me. Seth and Libby had already made their way to the entrance. Libby giggling at something he said as she looped her arm through his; I bit back the jealousy that rang in my heart.

Not yours.

Best friends, Erin. You have no claim and no right to the guy. Calm your tits.

I shook my head at myself, I was being ridiculous.

"I saw some reviews on this thing, sounds like it's pretty scary. Might need someone to hold your hand, Snow." I side eyed Derik and caught his creepy Cheshire grin as it spread ear to ear, a glint in his eye.

In your dreams.

"I'll be fine. Thanks though."

"Suit yourself." He shrugged and slipped his hands into the pockets of his jeans. We grabbed our tickets from the booth in front of the concession stand and gave them to the lobby attendant before our group walked lazily to our movie.

As we filed into the theater, the hair on the nape of my neck stood on end. My body tensed and the feeling of being watched washed over me. I whipped my head around and searched for the source of the eeriness that coursed through me and found nothing. The only people in sight were the staff at the snack counter which were preoccupied with bored chatter between them as they counted down until the end of their shifts.

"You good there, Erin?" Derik's concerned voice caught me off guard.

"Yeap, I'm fine. Just thought I saw someone I knew."

Derik cocked an eyebrow at me as I quickly stepped by him and led the way to our seats. Libby and Seth were already huddled together and giggled at the movie trailers on the massive theater screen.

The movie wasn't overly terrifying, just your average thriller. Libby curled up with Seth the whole time with her face hidden in his chest and boy did he lap it up. Derik on the other hand, to my delight, jumped up about halfway through saying he had to run to the bathroom and stayed there the remainder of the film. Prior to his abrupt exit from the movie, I caught him wanting to make a move a few times and I swatted his hand away repeatedly. Needless to say, I was rather relieved when he ran off.

When the three of us walked out to the lobby, Derik was over by the concession stand chatting up the cashier. Which meant his attention was drawn to someone besides myself.

Fine with me.

Derik saw us and waved, signaling to Seth he'd catch up later.

Libby waited at the main door with me while Seth went to grab his car. Unfortunately, the weather hadn't held out and it had begun to rain heavily outside.

"That was so scary! I can't believe you just sat there the whole time! I was shaking. It seemed so real!" Libby exclaimed, her emerald-green eyes round with the hit of adrenaline from the movie.

I gave her my best shrug. "I used to watch a lot of horror. It doesn't really phase me much." Not a lie. When your childhood mirrors some of the most intense horror films, the fake stuff doesn't really get to you much. Not when I had been abandoned and left to fend for myself at a young age.

It is what it is.

The only person who knew of what I had gone through was Seth and I planned on keeping it that way. Okay, maybe that was a little dramatic. Things easily could've been far worse. I was just glad it was me and not someone else.

Most young girls wouldn't have been able to defend themselves.

I shook myself out of it before the memories clawed their way through my brain and claimed me.

Not the place for a flashback, Erin. Breathe.

Seth pulled the car up just in time, before my minimal control over my train of thought could begin to derail and stumble down that path.

"Would you ladies, fancy a ride?" Seth waggled his eyebrows at us with a shit-eating grin plastered between the stubble that covered the lower part of his face. Both Libby and I laughed, hers a high-pitched musical tone. Mine on the other hand mimicked that of a hyena. Libby opened the passenger door and slid into the front seat while I climbed in the back and strapped myself in behind Seth.

The drive was quiet; he dropped Libby at her place first. She lived in a large apartment complex right outside of campus, a quick walk from the sorority she helped oversee and was once a part of. Seth had filled me in a bit on that a few months prior. She was one of the nice ones though. Libby so far hadn't really fallen into the sorority stereotype, besides being gorgeous and thin. I thought back to our brief conversation before the movie, my chin rested in the palm of my hand as I watched our small city drift by.

She did seem genuine.

"We're going to head back to my place to talk. If that's alright. It'll be easier," Seth stated, the throatiness of his voice caught me off guard. I nodded and snuck a quick sideways glance. His shoulders were relaxed and his eyes were trained on the road ahead of us. His body flush against the leather of his driver's seat with one arm laid against the center console while the other controlled the steering wheel: the picture of cool, calm, and collected. I quirked my brow.

Worked for me. I loved my apartment, but Seth's place felt like home. Part of it could very well have to do with the guy who owned it, but only a small part. His house was beautiful. Seth lived in an old schoolhouse he bought for almost nothing a few years ago. He completely renovated it and the place was massive. An open living room-dining room with a decked-out gym area off to the side; including lifting equipment and an array of cardio machines. There was only one treadmill but that worked out since neither of us enjoyed running indoors, typically. The walls were lined with floor to ceiling windows, which showered the main living space with sunlight during the day and provided a perfect view of the stars at night.

Seth unlocked his front door and we walked in. He switched on the lights as he went and flooded the space with light from the overhead lamps and fixtures that dotted the tall ceiling. The light danced off the pale-grey that painted the walls. I made my way into the living area and plopped down on his plush sectional and quickly made myself at home. I peaked over and saw Seth was in the process of making two mugs of coffee; three spoonfuls of sugar to his and a splash of milk with a measly five spoonfuls of sugar to mine.

He walked over and handed me the mug of coffee before he sat next to me. "So, I talked to my friend about the dreams you've been having, and we both think it's about time you and I talk about some things."

"Oh ho, sounds pretty serious there, Seth," I responded sarcastically as I blew on my coffee to cool it down. When I didn't get the lighthearted response I expected, I looked up to find his face was stone cold serious. "Did I miss something?"

He took a deep breath. "There's some things you don't know, Erin. About me and about yourself," I had a sinking feeling. "The dream you had yesterday, it wasn't *just* a dream."

What does he mean by that?

I felt the hairs on my neck stand up as panic welled within my chest, my pulse quickened and acid rose in my stomach. I swallowed the lump that began to form in the back of my throat.

Get it together, Erin.

I sat up, my back straightened.

I might be freaked about where this was going but I refused to show it. Calm the hell down.

Whatever it was that he was about to tell me, it was important. Important enough to have cool, calm, and collected Seth on edge. "Okay. I'm listening."

Seth took a slow breath to steady himself before he began. The words escaped his lips as if they scratched their way out, leaving him barely an octave above being hoarse, almost gravelly. "Remember when we were kids and we would go on all those adventures in the woods around our houses? We'd run through the trees, battling our made-up monsters with sticks we'd find, pretending they were swords?" I nodded him on, unsure of where he was going with the trip down memory lane. The deep blue of his eyes softened, an apology within them. I furrowed my brows as I waited for him to continue.

Why do I feel like I'm not going to enjoy where this little story-time is headed?

"That summer when I turned sixteen, when my mom died and I had to leave and move in with my Uncle...The last summer we ran through those woods and before..." He trailed off, the memory of what felt like the beginning of the end hung between us. Seth didn't have to say it. After that summer, things had changed. I had been in the midst of my transition into eighth grade and he was going into his second year of high school on the other side of the country. When Seth had left, things in my young life started to go south pretty quickly. My dad disappeared within days of Seth moving across the country and left me on my own. I was a few weeks shy of fourteen and had been left to fend on my own, utterly abandoned. My heart had shattered; I'd found an envelope under his mattress with enough money to last me the school year and a note that simply said: *I love you. Please forgive me -Dad.*

I felt the air in my lungs thicken as the memory of one of the worst times of my life shrouded me in darkness and plunged me right back to the day it truly hit me that it was just *me*. And no one was coming to save me.

I had cried for days. There was no one to tell, no one to confide in. It had always been just me and Dad. And then Seth and his mom. Everyone was gone. I was all alone, without anyone close to me.

Except...I do have Seth.

The thought had slivered in the recess of my mind as I numbly combed through my schoolbag the day before class began for the new school year.

I gathered myself and wiped the crusted tear trails from my cheeks.

I need to tell him.

I wrote him a letter and stamped it with as many postage stamps as I could find, saying I was okay but that Dad was gone and I was alone.

Seth wrote me back with the promise that it'd be okay. And I believed it, at first.

A week after my dad disappeared, I walked home from school and narrowly avoided tripping on the cracked sidewalk that led straight through my small neighborhood. As I drew nearer, I noticed there was a car parked outside my small ranch-style house. One I hadn't recognized. An eerie feeling settled in the pit of my stomach and I slowed my steps as I grabbed my keys from my pocket just in case. I peeked through the car windows and found that the car was empty so I made my way to the house. I shook the alarm in the back of my mind and walked up the pathway that led to my front door.

Probably one of the neighbors' or something. Maybe they got a new car.

I went to unlock the door, only to find it opened. "Erin, is that you?" A high-pitched male voice I didn't know. I stopped. Someone *was* in my house. Panic swelled and coursed through my veins. As I turned to high tail it out of there and down the street, a heavy thump rang in my ears as I was struck from behind. My vision blurred before it went black.

I woke up in my room, blind folded, and tied to my desk. I heard some shuffling around me. "You couldn't have waited until she walked in? This chick's neighbors could've seen us. Idiot." A deep grating masculine voice huffed. I felt my heart start to race.

There are people in my house.

I'm trapped.

Hell, I'm tied to my desk. What is happening? Dad, where are you? Why the hell did you leave me?

A presence shifted closer to me as I fought back the panicked tears that threatened to rain down my pale cheeks. Their hot breath brushed against my face. Their calloused fingers gripped my chin, squeezed my face between their fingers, and roughly tilted my head upwards, exposing my neck. "She sure is pretty. This might be more fun than we thought." It was the same grating voice that had spoken moments before.

Shit. Shit. No, no, no. Come on, Snow, think of something. Distract them. Reason with them, anything.

Bile rose from my stomach.

"Where's Mr. Snow, Princess?" Poison laced the guy's voice. My mouth was clamped shut, fear raked my body. I was frozen. "Not gonna tell us? That's not nice." His breath brushed against my skin again as if he was only mere inches from my face.

His hand went for me once more; I fell out of my frozen trance and spat in front of me, with the hope that I'd hit my target. That pissed the guy off. "You bitch." His buddy was laughing not far off. Suddenly, the blind fold was ripped off, taking some of my hair with it. I blinked rapidly as my eyes quickly adjusted to the sudden light. I bared my teeth and gave the men the best *leave me the hell alone* glare I could manage. "Awe look, Princess here is trying to scare us." This time they were both laughing, their shoulders shook with the movement. In my peripheral vision, I spotted the second guy as he inched closer, a sinister look in his molten eyes. I made the mistake of moving my head in his direction and left myself vulnerable to the man with a cheese grater embedded within his vocal chords.

The first guy, closest to me, grabbed my face in his burly, calloused hand and shoved it back toward him; his eyes locked with mine. A pointed smile crept across his face.

This isn't good.

Fear gripped me. I shoved it down as I tried to remember some of what Dad had taught me. He had been adamant about teaching me self-defense from a young age. I had always thought it was stupid. In that very moment with my back literally up against my wooden desk, not so much. Cheese Grater Man moved closer, and pushed, no, crushed his mouth on top of mine. He jabbed his tongue in and out of my mouth as I gagged and choked back the vomit that rose from the back of my throat. His hand reached under my uniform and slowly inched up my stomach.

I fought back tears. I had to find a way out of this. He grazed the small space below my chest when I had my opening. While he was distracted and intent on his attempt to steal what remained of my innocence from me, I shoved my knee straight up and right into his groin. It knocked the wind out of him and sent him to the floor withering in pain.

"Mother *Fucker*. You prissy-ass *bitch*!" The second guy lunged toward me.

I pushed myself to the side the best I could while my wrists remained restrained and he landed with his head smacking right into the corner of the desk. He slumped over, unconscious.

One down. One to go.

I had to move quickly, so I started yanking my hands out of the rope. I silently prayed that I could get myself free before either one got up. The first guy started to catch his breath. I was running out of time. He rolled over with death in his eyes, ready to finish what he started, or worse. He grunted as he pushed himself up from his spot on the floor and stalked toward me.

Now or never.

I yanked my hands free, grabbed a pen from my desk, and stabbed him as he pounced. The pointed tip impaled his eye, blood violently spurted from the wound. His burly hands shot to his eye socket as he fell to the floor, screaming profanities. I sucked in a breath and bolted straight out of my room, out the front door, and didn't look back. I kept running, the wind whipping through my tangled hair, until I reached Seth's old house.

I snuck around back and kept to the shadows as I tried the door. No one would've been home; it had been put on the market the day Seth had gone to live with his uncle after his mom had died. That was the only family he had left. Something we'd bonded over; I only had my dad, and it was just him and his mom, until she passed and discovered he had an uncle he'd never met. It was a quick move. So, part of me hoped that the landline was still up and running.

I sighed in relief as the handle clicked open; the door was unlocked. Nerves twisted and strangled my insides as I walked in. It was dark with no furniture in sight. I didn't try the lights for fear that the men who broke in at my house might see it. I felt around the empty space, my hands patting the textured walls as I made my way to the front room where I'd be able to see out the front bay window and hopefully find Seth's old landline. I was in luck.

I picked it up, hearing the dial tone.

Yes!

I punched in the number for the cops, my voice trembled. "I think there was a break in down the street. It sounded like there was a bunch of screaming and there's a car out front I don't think I've seen before." I rattled off the address and gave a fake name. I didn't want to risk anyone knowing I was alone, or that my dad abandoned me. A few minutes later I heard sirens as they barrelled through the neighborhood, stopping right in front of my lawn and blocking the intruders' car. I hunkered down and watched as several cops dragged the guys out of my house. The one I stabbed had a rag stuffed against his face, yelling. The officers shoved the two men in the back of one of the cruisers. One cop went back in, gun drawn, while two others stood guard.

Probably making sure no one else is in there.

Once the cop stepped back outside, they cleared the area and left. I waited with bated breath for what felt like hours. I searched the deserted street from the shadows of the abandoned room to make sure the coast was clear before I ran back over to my tainted childhood home.

I rummaged around, keeping the lights off in case any neighbors peeked outside to see what the commotion was. I made it back toward my room and shuddered at what had almost happened. I forced the foul memory of the man who stuck his tongue down my throat to the furthest edges of my thoughts. I needed to focus.

I crept to my bed, lifted my mattress, grabbed the cash my dad left me, and shoved it in my pocket. I snatched my now empty backpack off the floor. They'd clearly dumped it and gone through it but found nothing by the looks of it. I shoved a few days' worth of clothes, my ID, schoolwork, and some other necessities in my bag, including my notebook and the locket my dad gave me for my birthday the year prior. I gripped it to my chest as the tears began to fall.

Why?

Dad, why is this happening?

I shoved it in the inner pocket of my bag and zipped it up as I dragged myself out of my periwinkle colored bedroom, down the small narrow hallway lined with photos of my dad and I, and out the front door. I looked back at my house as I left, my shirt wet with salty tears.

My childhood home.

Home.

I have no home. Not anymore.

All the winters Dad and I would try and fail to build snowmen and forts flashed through my mind. We'd give up and turn to snowball fights instead. Seth would come over and he'd join in too. His mom would make her special hot chocolate afterwards, her own secret recipe she refused to share with any of us. The summers Seth and I would run around the woods from sunup to sundown, coming home covered in dirt and mud laughing like crazy; our parents shaking their heads at us as we'd trample through our houses and leave the muck in our wake.

A sad smile lifted the corners of my lips at the memories, the realization sinking in. A chip of my already broken heart fell.

That chapter of my life was over. The innocence was gone.

"Erin?" Seth's face was covered in concern.

"Sorry, I zoned out. Go on." I shook my head in an attempt to clear it and met Seth's saddened eyes. He looked at me with understanding as if he knew I replayed what had happened to me. He placed his hand over my shaking coffee mug and set it on the table. I squeezed my empty hands together in my lap to try and control the tremors.

The huskiness of Seth's voice cracked as he spoke. "I'm sorry. I know I wasn't there. I wished so many times that I was. I would've been able to stop..." He trailed off, regret and pity lurked within the oceanic depths of his irises.

Don't look at me like that. I can't take the pity.

I can take care of myself. I'm fine.

I'm always...fine.

When I had written to him months after the break-in, I finally told him about the attack, what had happened, and that I moved and wasn't going home. He'd offered to have me come out and live with him and his uncle. I promised that I'd be fine. I was old enough to get a job at that point, under the table at least. So that's what I did. And shortly after I found a job, I moved into a little apartment downtown. The owner didn't ask questions. She looked at me as if she knew I was running from something. I hadn't known how or why and decided that she had probably seen her fair share of trouble. Hints of mischief swirled within her eyes. It helped that I paid a whole month's rent upfront.

"Seth, it's okay. You didn't know, you couldn't have known."

He sighed. "It's not okay though, Erin. I didn't tell you the full reason why I moved, why I left," I looked at him, question in my eyes. "It wasn't just because of mom. There was more to it."

I waited.

He took a deep breath. "My mom, she didn't die the way we were originally told. She died protecting me. Us," my breath caught. "Way before I was born, she was a warrior. Her whole existence was focused around protecting people. Protecting them from what they couldn't see with their human eyes."

Seth paused.

"My mom was a Nephilim. And...so am I."

I stared blankly at Seth, my brows furrowed, unsure of what he meant.

"What is a Nephilim?" My thoughts churned.

What did this mean? Is this some joke?

"Nephilim are the result of Angel and human breeding," I was dumbfounded. Seth had to be pulling my leg. "I'm a second generation Nephilim. My mom was an Angel who fell in love with my very human father. And had me. I didn't know until years after she died. My uncle... he explained it to me when I turned eighteen."

A knot formed in my stomach.

This cannot be real.

"Okay, if she was this 'Nephilim' then what was she protecting people from?" I narrowed my eyes. I had my legs curled up and knees tucked under my chin. I wrapped my arms around my thighs and dug my fingernails into my skin in an attempt to give myself some semblance of control.

"Demons. They find their way through the gates of Hell and torment innocent humans on Earth. They cut loose and cause chaos by bringing back the dead, the damned, and all the things that go bump in the night. And Nephilim were created to protect and defend against them." Seth searched my eyes, trying to gauge my reaction, my understanding.

Tendrils of fear licked my insides, my pulse quickened.

"So, what does that have to do with me?" I did not like where our conversation was headed. "Wait, you said you were Nephilim. How come you didn't tell me? Why now?" My voice rose, the reddened flare of irritation began to bloom.

What the hell is going on?

Seth ran his fingers through his onyx hair as he cleared his throat. "I know. I know, it's a lot. But you have to trust me and understand that we were trying to protect you as long as possible. I discovered I was Nephilim a few years back. When my uncle took me in, I had no idea. I never even believed in any of that stuff. The whole Angel and Demon situation, I thought it was a whole lot of horse shit. But around the time I turned eighteen, things started happening to me. I'd get irritated, break things that I shouldn't have been able to. I started hearing conversations between two people at the opposite end of the hallway at school, the length of eight classrooms between us. At one point, I remember slamming my fist into one of the lockers and the whole wall came crashing down. As you can imagine, that didn't go too well. Then, my uncle sat me down and explained what was going on." To prove his point, Seth walked to his rec area and picked up one of the cardio machines like it was nothing and tossed it back down with a heavy thud, a dent forever embedded in his otherwise perfect floor.

Holy. Shit.

My jaw dropped, my heartbeat hammered in my chest.

There's no fucking way.

I tried to reason with myself and make sense of why Seth had been able to lift a piece of workout equipment that easily weighed several hundred pounds, if not more. My mind reeled, unable to come up with a reasonable explanation. I was lost for words.

"See? We workout and lift together, but I shouldn't be able to lift that thing like it's a bag of flour. And I shouldn't be able to hear my neighbor down the street practicing a lecture for her class on Monday. Or your heartbeat when my ear isn't against your chest and I'm on the far side of the couch." Okay, that spiked my already pounding heart. He flashed a teasing grin. My face flushed.

Dammit.

I squared my shoulders. "You're super strong and have stupidly good hearing, cool, I get it. But you're still dodging what my involvement in all of this is. I'm just a weak human," he raised his eyebrows, guilt tinged his cheeks and the tip of his nose. "I *am* human, right?"

For the love of all things sane. Seth Draven your ass better say yes.

His lips formed a thin line as he stared at me.

Nope. This is a dream. This has to be a freaking dream.

Demons? Angels? There's no freaking way.

I started hyperventilating and felt the blood drain from my face. "No."

I gulped, sand in my throat as my vision blurred.

No.

"Erin, you're Nephilim as well. Your mother was human but your dad...he was an Angel."

My dad was an Angel?

I'm...

I'm not...human?

My heart sank as the bandages that mended the cracks within it split in two.

Seth lunged forward, his arm extended, worry etched across his face. His lips moved but the words fell mute. A harrowing ring filled my ears and engulfed me. Its screech dug its claws into me and dragged me down as the room fell away. Everything disappeared. I was shrouded in darkness.

CHAPTER THREE

Erin

My head was spinning and someone was shaking me. *Where was I?* My eyes blinked open, slowly focusing. Seth was inches from my face, his mouth moving. I groaned as bright light hit my eyes. I peered around Seth and glared at the fixtures that hung from his ceiling.

Too bright.

"Erin? Erin! You okay?" He stopped shaking me. "You passed out." He cupped my cheek, checking to see if I was coherent.

"Yeah, yeah, I'm fine, sorry," I rasped as I swatted him away; the little story he dropped in my lap before I blacked out replayed in my mind. I gathered my thoughts and processed what I could, my brain still foggy. "Is that why I've been having these weird dreams? Is that what they mean?" I mumbled.

He nodded, his tensed jawline relaxing as I propped myself up on his couch. "We're not sure who spoke to you but it's not necessarily a dream. Typically when a Nephilim is getting close to transforming or 'coming of age,' there's more detail in it and typically happens at a younger age. Eighteen for most of us, some make it to nineteen or twenty. Never this late."

Me, a late bloomer?

That sounded about right considering more often than not, I was late for just about everything.

"Hitting Nephilim puberty at twenty-three, pretty on brand for you, huh?" Seth cracked a smile, practically reading my mind.

I reached over to the coffee table and grabbed my cup, my coffee now ice cold. Seth went further into detail, explaining our capabilities and histories of the battles between Nephilim and Demons. I slowly sipped while I listened, absorbing everything I could while I kept my growing irritation at bay. Apparently, I'd experience increased strength, hearing, vision, immortality— unless I ended up being killed by one of the Demons—and maybe even some type of additional power mumbo-jumbo. Which apparently was different for each Nephilim.

Seth said he had the added ability of memory manipulation, meaning he could manipulate the memories of others.

If I have added abilities, I'll be alone in it. Alone in figuring things out. Again.

Suck it up, Erin. Seth left you in the dark about all of this until now. You've been alone the entire time.

The strings in my chest tightened at the realization. I blinked back the wetness that threatened to spring free.

"With the memory thing, can you change any memory? How does it work?" I felt the panic well in my throat.

"Not really. I have to be near the person when a memory occurs to be able to manipulate and change it. It can make it kinda tricky depending on the situation."

Okay, well, that's good to know.

But he still kept this from me.

My best friend. The only family I have left. He kept me in the dark.

I inhaled through my nose to steady my runaway thoughts, my jaw clenched.

"Before you ask, no, I haven't done it around you." He looked at me, his eyes leveled with mine.

But how do I know that?

We sat in silence. Seth watched me while I mulled everything over and tried to make sense of it. If my dad was an Angel, why didn't I know? Why didn't he tell me before he left? And why didn't I get a heads-up on all of this? I wanted to call Seth on his crap, tell him to stop screwing with me but I knew deep down, what he told me was the truth. My mind screamed at me but my gut begged me to believe the guy.

I wanted to hurl.

"There's something else you need to know. Now that this is happening, it's safer if you aren't alone, at least not at first. These Demons, they can sense us out and find us. And until you're strong enough, it's safer for you to stay here."

My eyes bugged out of my head.

Stay at Seth's? As in, live here?

I hadn't lived with anyone since my dad disappeared. I've always been on my own. And it was *Seth*. Sure, we'd been best friends for years but living under the same roof with someone else is just a whole other level. An intimate level, one that I was in no position to partake in. I could feel the heat as it ran across my face.

Seth chuckled. "Erin, chill out. You practically live here anyway." He had a point. We would hang out at his place after class most days and get some form of lifting in. I snagged dinner a couple times a week before I would drive back out to my job at the library on campus. Not to mention, we'd help each other study for different classes throughout the year. Another thought popped into my head.

Crap.

"What about Libby? I mean, would she be cool with me staying here?" He arched his eyebrow. "She's your girlfriend. Shouldn't you run that by her?" Seth looked at me like I was an idiot, a twinkle in his eye.

Like the midnight sky's reflection in a clear blue ocean, the waves moving so that the stars appeared to dance.

"You do realize Libby is a friend, right? We hooked up once but that's all there was to it," I guess I missed that bit of info somewhere along the lines. "Don't get me wrong, she's hot and all but not my cup of tea"—he winked at me—"I prefer the hot nerdy chicks." I choked on what was left of my coffee.

"Oh, is that so?" I responded lazily.

Breath, Erin.

He was just screwing with me.

Seemed like 'your cup of tea' at the movies earlier.

Seth grinned, enjoying my reaction. "Strike a cord, did I?" He waggled his eyebrows at me. I smacked his arm as I fought the rising burn on my cheeks.

"Alright, well if she's not your girlfriend then what's the deal?"

Not that I should care.

"She's a part of the cool kids club."

"Meaning...?"

Seth chuckled, his voice husky. "Libby's a Nephilim, Erin. And so is Derik."

Great, so I really was just left in the dark.

"So, *everyone* is Nephilim and y'all didn't bother to tell me? Keep me in the loop? Did it for even a second cross your mind that ya know, *maybe* this is something I needed to know sooner?" I fumed, my voice rose with each word. "We're best friends, we're supposed to tell each other everything, especially a bombshell like this. What the hell, Seth?"

I was right.

My nostrils flared as I stared him down, my fists clenched in my lap.

"Erin, I couldn't tell you until it was time and you started showing signs. It's not exactly something to bring up randomly. It was for your own good. I swear."

For my own good?

"I don't need a babysitter, Seth! I can take care of myself, dammit. I could've done...something. Train, study. Be more prepared and not just have this stupid bomb dropped on me."

"I know, Rin," he said softly. "I wanted to tell you...but I couldn't. Not until the time was right."

Guilt washed over me.

Was Seth right? Maybe. But I was still irritated and hurt.

"Fine." I crossed my arms over my chest. It was a lot to take in and I had every right to have a tantrum about the whole thing. I glared at Seth for a solid ten minutes and thoroughly imagined all the ways I could get my revenge; replace his ground coffee with ground tea leaves, move the coffee mugs to a different spot in his kitchen? Flip the toilet paper roll in the bathroom the opposite direction?

Not that I'd ever act on it...but the thought is nice.

He finally stood up, making his way to one of his hallway closets. He grabbed one of the biggest and fluffiest blankets he could, along with a spare pillow, and tossed them to me. They covered me instantly, drowning me in a pile of down feathered, stuffed, slate-grey fabric. "Here. I'll grab some sweats for you to borrow tonight and we'll grab your stuff tomorrow. If you want a shower, you know where the towels are."

I sat under the blanket and chewed everything over. By the time I was done pouting and over analyzing the boatload of information, I realized Seth had already dumped the sweats and baggy

T-shirt—okay baggy on me but fit Seth like a glove—on the coffee table and had left me to wallow in my own thoughts.

I really can zone out with the best of them.

Silently, and a bit begrudgingly, I mentally thanked Seth and made my way to the bathroom. A shower sounded like a good idea.

As I stepped out of the shower, I got dressed, splashed some water on my face, and padded out to the hallway. I hesitated and swung a left towards Seth's room. As much as I hadn't wanted to admit it, I was kinda being an ass earlier when all he tried to do was explain things.

I knocked on his door to let him know I was coming in. I opened his door and found his back was to me. Shoulders slouched forward, head in his hands. "Seth?" I asked quietly. He stiffened. "Hey, you alright?" He slowly turned towards me. His eyes were heavy and revealed just how tired he really was. A small ball of light shone from where he sat on his bed and illuminated the dark circles under his eyes. The rest of his room was cast in shadow.

Has he not been sleeping lately either?

He popped on a slight smile. His fingers wove between his onyx hair as he gazed up at me sheepishly.

"Hey, sorry. You get that shower in?" I really felt like an ass at that point, I probably woke him up.

"Yeah. Thank you, by the way," I had one hand behind my back holding onto my other arm, uncomfortable as I stood in the doorway, as if I were invading his privacy. "I'm going to head to bed and wanted to stop in. Go ahead and get some sleep. I'll see you in the morning."

Seth looked at me, his eyes seemed to grow heavier by the second, suddenly looking like he was carrying the weight of the world on his shoulders. I turned to walk out to the couch.

"Wait, Erin?" I turned my head.

"Yeah?"

"You wanna sleep with me?" My eyes damn near shot out of my head and his usual grin spread across his face, a glint of mischief in his eyes.

"Excuse me?" I finally managed to cough out.

He laughed. "Get your mind out of the gutter, Snow. I meant, you wanna sleep in here with me. Not *do* me. Although, I could show you a thing or two." He winked at me.

I huffed. "You're ridiculous," he patted the bed. "Fine, but you better not try anything fishy, you jerk."

Seth threw up some type of finger salute. "Scouts honor."

I scoffed.

Honor my ass.

I caved and fumbled over to the empty side of his bed and climbed in. Not going to lie, it was probably the softest bedding I'd ever laid on. I pulled the covers up over myself and snuggled into them. I felt the blankets behind me rustle and Seth climbed under, facing away from me.

Thank God.

I stared straight ahead and tried to focus on his bedroom wall and not the irrational thrumming in my chest.

Breathe, Erin. Damn.

"Hey, Snow."

"Yeah?"

"I'm sorry."

"For what?"

"I'm sorry I didn't tell you sooner."

I sighed.

"I'm sorry too."

"Night."

"Night, Seth."

Chapter Four

Erin

I woke up to snoring. Loud, obnoxious snoring. I rolled over, pulling the blankets with me to cover my head and try to drown the thunderous noise out. The snores grew louder. Giving up, I threw the covers off and found Seth's open mouth about three inches from my face. Then it hit me, the foulest morning breath. Rotten eggs had nothing on him. I gagged as I fumbled my way out of bed, chucking a pillow at his head in the process.

Seth groaned. "What the hell, man?" He sat up, glaring at me. His hair tousled in what should've been a rats nest but for some reason it unfairly looked wildly untamed and sexy like he just walked out of a magazine.

"Your breath smells like ass, Seth." I pinched my nose for exaggeration.

He rolled his eyes. "Yeah, well yours ain't much better, short stuff."

"Short stuff? Dude, I'm *barely* shorter than you. Anyone would be short compared to your six foot four inch ass." I jabbed back.

Five foot seven isn't short, you jerk.

"Yeah, yeah. Whatever you say, small fry." He tossed the rest of the blankets off and onto the floor into a heap. Seth swung his legs over the side of the bed, stood up, and stretched. His back muscles flexed, causing my cheeks to flush. Again.

When did Seth get so...muscle-y?

And...hot.

Ew, Erin. Stop.

"I'll, uh, go make some food." I practically ran to the kitchen. Maybe all of these weird reactions to Seth are from the whole Nephilim thing. Hormones via puberty 2.0. Even when I had that small crush on him a few years back, I'd never been remotely *that* bad. I felt like some love-sick teenager.

I fumbled around Seth's kitchen in search of eggs, toast, or honestly anything to whip up some much needed food. I was about to give up when a pack of bagels shoved in the back of the pantry caught my eye.

Yes! Victory!

Setting the toaster to the least toasty level for mine and damn near burn status for Seth's, I popped the bagels in and waited.

Right about the time they popped out, Seth made his way to the kitchen and plopped down at the island. "So, what's for breakfast?"

"We're doing bagels, considering your pantry and fridge are both bare as hell," I replied as I slid his crisped breakfast across the island. "Once we're done, you and I are trucking up to the store. Then we'll hit my apartment once this place is restocked."

"Sounds like a plan, boss," he mumbled around bites of bagel, crumbs clinging to his thick stubble.

We finished our food in a comfortable silence, neither of us are morning people, so sliding past the awkward chit-chat worked perfectly for me.

Seth cleared the plates while I whipped up a couple of coffees to take with us. Between the temporary move-in-with-my-best-friend situation and shopping, we were both going to need it. Extra espresso in each, no questions asked.

Grabbing our liquid energy for the day, we headed out; Seth locked the door behind us. The great thing about his place? It's a huge lot right off a small paved road with only a handful of neighbors. Downside, the local grocery store is a two mile walk, which is unfortunately too short of a distance for Seth to justify a quick drive. Running is one thing, but walking two miles one way with bags of food. No thanks, I'd rather be stuck in Jensin's class for a whole ass evening.

Ugh.

I mentally groveled about the trek ahead of us when Seth took off in a sprint. My eyebrows shot up. "What are you doing?" I yelled after him.

He glanced over his shoulder, laughing. "Racing obviously." The jerk stopped and stuck his tongue out at me, clearly challenging me, so I sprinted after him.

You ass.

I caught up to him quickly. Just because he had a head start, I refused to lose to him. I ran past Seth, stuck my tongue out, and blew raspberries at him.

Ha! Suck it!

We ran, laughing. I glanced back at Seth to shit talk him but before I could get a word out, I tripped and tumbled head over ass. Landing flat on my back, the wind damn near knocked out of me.

Seth rushed up, checking to make sure I was okay. "Holy shit, Snow, you good?" Concern plastered across his face.

"Yeah, yeap. Peachy." I grunted, a blunt ache spread across my back. Seth must've decided I was fine because he busted out a full bellied laugh, the corners of his eyes crinkled.

"Oh my god, that was freaking great. It was like it was right out of a movie. Damn, Erin, you really know how to fall." He clutched his stomach as the laughter continued to spill out of his mouth. He looked absolutely ridiculous and I started cracking up too.

We sobered up and I got back on my feet. We apparently ran further than I thought because right around the corner was the store. As we walked through the entrance, I ran through everything we needed, pointing down the different aisles. I gave Seth a list of food to grab and made my way towards the produce.

I was sorting through a pile of apples, picking the least bruised, when I heard someone walk up behind me, startling me, and annoyingly caused me to drop the only non-bruised apple I could find. I turned around with the best RBF face I could manage, to find Derik smirking at me. And holding the damn apple like that vampire in the *Twilight* movies. Talk about cringy. They're great books but in real life, kinda cheesy. Especially when it's a guy you can barely stand.

"Fancy seeing you here, Snow." His smirk morphed into...a smolder?

"Buying food, obviously. What do you want, Rider?" He looked confused at the movie reference. "Rider, as in Flynn Rider? *Tangled*?" I arched my eyebrow at him and it seemed to click.

"The main guy?" His confusion turned into a big ass grin. "So, if I'm Flynn, that must mean I'm supposed to save the damsel in distress. How may I be of service, Ma'lady?"—he winked at me and bowed. I rolled my eyes—"Or maybe...a kiss?" I smacked his arm. He threw his hand across his forehead feigning offense.

"You're so dramatic, you know that? And you didn't answer my question." I shifted my weight to one side and crossed my arms over my chest.

Derik straightened, the corner of his mouth twitched. "Same as you. Just saw you and Seth walking in and thought I'd say hello." He gave me a look that said *you two came in together*, with an emphasis on the *together* part.

"Oh, uh, yeah. I'm crashing at Seth's for a bit. He's helping me…" I remembered Seth saying Derik was in on the whole Angel-human half-bred thing too. "With some things." My eyes met his, a bite of annoyance resurfaced.

He must've understood what I was really saying because he followed up with. "So, Seth gave you the rundown, then? Pretty cool, huh?" I nodded, a sigh fell from my lips.

There would've been no reason for Derik to have told me himself.

I don't know why I continued our conversation because I usually couldn't stand Derik. "I'm still trying to wrap my head around it. It's a lot to take in out of nowhere. They don't exactly teach you this stuff in school." I shrugged my shoulders.

"True."

We stood awkwardly for a few seconds and stared at one another, unsure of what to say. Derik turned to walk away and saw Seth stride towards us. "Hey, man, how's it goin'?"

"Just chatting with Snow, she said you two were on a mission." Derik laughed lightly.

"It's not my fault his place has no food," I snapped.

Seth shrugged in agreement. "What can I say, I've been busy. Got a lot on my hands lately." He glanced at me briefly before he turned to Derik.

"No kidding. Have you heard anything about what went down at Riverside?" Unease dotted Derik's chocolate eyes as he waited for

Seth's response. The article I'd skimmed about the disappearances popped in my mind.

The hair on my neck pricked up at the thought of it.

Seth let out an exasperated sigh. "Nothing new. I've got a few of the crew looking into it. I meant to check it out but haven't made my way out there yet."

I pressed my lips together, the guilt licked at me. He skipped his trip out there because of me.

Why did he need to go in the first place? Why would what happened at Riverside have anything to do with Seth?

Derik pondered that for a minute. "How about we head that way tonight? See if we can find some more intel," he looked at me, a mischievous grin played at the edges of his mouth. "You up for it?"

I furrowed my brows. "Up for what? Wouldn't Riverside be roped off and considered an off-limits crime scene with all of the people missing?"

He smirked at me. "Oh, Rin, Riverside was *so* much more than *just* a fire with missing bodies. This has Demons written all over it." A fire burned in Derik's piercing slate-blue eyes. His hatred for these things bled out into the air around us.

Seth's face darkened. "I don't think Erin should go. Not yet. She's just now going through the transition. She's not ready."

Excuse me?

I threw my hands on my hips, the grocery basket swung around my left arm. "The hell do you mean 'not ready'? I'm not just going to sit around and wait for this whole Angel-human hybrid bullshit to happen to me. If this is what I'm going to be looking forward to, then I damn well have every right to check this place out too." I glared Seth down.

"But you can't protect yourself yet. You just started changing into a Nephilim and you don't have any powers yet. It's not safe, Erin."

"Well too damn bad, Seth, because I'm coming." I growled and crossed my arms over my chest.

If your ass is going, so am I.

Derik decided to chime in. "Dude, she has a point. If she's a part of this mess now, she has a right to see for herself."

Well, what do you know? Ten points to Derik. Maybe he wasn't so annoying after all.

"Two against one, Seth. I'm going. We'll grab my stuff from my place then go," I cooed, the small flame of irritation extinguished.

"Fine, whatever. But you stay close to me. And don't do anything stupid," Seth grumbled.

Victory!

I did a mental fist pump.

I grinned. "Now let's get this grocery shopping done."

Three hours later, we had food back in stock at Seth's place and my necessities packed up in his car from my apartment. Makeup, clothes, mattress, and textbooks. Okay, my mattress was strapped down on top of his car but same difference.

I locked up my apartment and we headed to Seth's car, Derik in tow. "That didn't take nearly as long as I thought it would." I breathed out. I thought we would've spent half the day getting my belongings loaded into Seth's car. Benefits of being surrounded by Nephilims apparently.

"Yeah no kidding. You sure that's all you need, Erin? It ain't a lot," Derik said, turning around in his seat to look at me.

"Honestly, I don't need much. And considering Seth wouldn't let me take *my* car, I didn't see the need to overfill this thing with my stuff. I'm not planning on being there long so I just grabbed the necessities. If I get bored or need anything I'll just raid Seth's stuff." I grinned up at Seth in the rearview mirror.

Seth smirked as he rolled his eyes. "You raid my stuff half the time anyway." This was true. I couldn't count the amount of times I'd gone through his bookshelves for a new read or rummaged through his closet in his spare room to snag clean sweats after a gruesome workout. Not to mention the hell I've put his workout equipment through.

I watched out the window as we pulled up to Seth's place. The previous twenty-four hours were on repeat in my head.

None of this feels real.

Seth parked and we made our way inside; I carried a couple boxes of my belongings while the guys tag teamed my mattress with my bag of clothes and the rest of my boxes piled on top. I dropped the boxes on his front step and reached for the doorknob. Before I could twist the handle, the door swung open and practically scared the shit out of me.

"Hey girl!" squealed Libby. She threw her arms around me. Hugging me.

"Uh, hi? What are you doing here?" I stammered as I looked over my shoulder at Seth and Derik. Why the hell did Libby, someone I *barely* know, squeal at me? I appreciate the enthusiasm, but a warning would've been much appreciated.

"Derik texted me earlier to meet you guys here. Said we're paying Riverside a visit tonight." She grinned ear to ear and stepped aside to let us through to Seth's living room as I picked my boxes back up.

"Thought you'd want in, ya know, in case there's any action. Plus, Pretty Boy here doesn't think Erin can handle it. Figured if all of us went, he'd ease up," Derik had a glint in his eye as he stared directly at Seth. "Some extra protection for *his girl*." My eyes damn near bugged out of my head. I high tailed it to the kitchen, nearly dropping the boxes I was carrying.

His girl? The hell does Derik mean by that? Seth would be about as interested in me as a raccoon that found itself in a trash can doused in peppermint oil.

Seth smacked Derik on the back of his head. "Erin just started the whole process, dumbass. She doesn't know how to protect herself yet. We don't even know what she'll be able to do." I faced away from the three of them but I could feel Seth's eyes as they bore into my back.

"I'll watch her, Seth! She'll be okay with me," Libby said a bit too cheerily.

I whipped around and glared at them. "I don't need a damn babysitter. I'm not some child." I threw my fists on my hips as I glared them down. Derik sported a shit eating grin. Seth rolled his eyes and Libby pouted. Okay, that one I felt bad about. "Not meaning to be a bitch, Libby. I'm sorry."

Libby perked back up. "It's okay! I know Seth here can be overprotective. You should've seen how he was when I transitioned. The guy wouldn't leave me alone." She giggled and I felt a stab in my chest, like someone shoved a damn knife right through.

He said they weren't dating...but did they before? Did Seth have a thing for her? Does he still?

I shook my head to clear my runaway mind. Even if that were the case, it shouldn't bother me.

It's Seth, you're just friends, always have been.

Chapter Five

Erin

We pulled up to the power plant in Riverside a few hours later, Seth and Libby rode in his car while I hitched a ride with Derik in his oversized, metallic-grey Silverado. In part because I wanted to avoid being stuck in a small car with Seth and Libby after the little tease-the-new-Nephilim fiasco earlier.

I went to push the passenger door open when Derik hit the automatic button on his side and locked the doors. "What the hell, dude?" I huffed.

"Chill out, Snow. Just want to brief ya before we head in. I know I was messing with you earlier but Seth was right about needing to be careful," he leveled his eyes with mine. "We don't know exactly what we're heading into here. A couple of our guys have been looking around scoping the place out but you need to be careful. Don't run off and stick with one of us. I know you and I ain't buddies so I'm not going to be up your ass but...just stay close at least to Seth or Libby."

I'm not some lost puppy.

I bit the inside of my mouth and nodded my head. "Okay, got it. Don't run away from the superhumans. Anything else?"

He cracked a smile at that. "Try not to lose your shirt when you see what I can do." He winked at me and I rolled my eyes as I held back the gag that wanted to follow.

I wrinkled my nose. "You wish, perv. Now let me out of this damn truck."

Derik unlocked the door and I might've pushed a little too hard because I stumbled forward as it slammed open.

An arm jutted out and caught me before I face-planted on the cracked pavement. I grunted out a thank you and steadied myself, using the individual as leverage.

I'm blaming my lack of coordination today on this whole Nephilim bullshit.

Had I spent the entirety of my life clumsy? Maybe. But that was beside the point.

"Are you alright?" A gravelly male voice kissed a deep part of me, Holy hell. I slowly looked up at the person attached to the savior arm. Talk about hot. Oh my *lord*. He stood at least half a foot taller than me. His hair was a deep chestnut brown, cut short, and lightly spiked in the front. His jawline chiseled and kissed by one hell of a five o'clock shadow. His eyes, a piercing blue speckled with flakes of gold, like what you'd see looking out at a tropical hot spot. I was completely captivated.

"I...I...uh. Um. Yes! Yeah, I'm good. I'm fine. Thanks." I was a stuttering mess. And pretty sure a drop of drool hung onto my gaping mouth for dear life.

Chill out, Snow. Take a breather.

"Thanks for the save." I laughed nervously as I snatched my arm out of his warm grip, my blood hammering in my chest.

"My pleasure," chills shivered down my spine at the deep timbre of his voice. "I'm Josh."

"Erin. Erin Snow." I croaked.

We stood there staring at each other for what felt like forever.

Wow.

"Yo! Snow, Josh! You coming or not?" Derik yelled, snapping me and Josh out of our little trance. Derik was already across the pavement, jogging into what remained of Riverside.

We started toward the ghost of the building, following the path Derik had taken. "So, you must be the new blood then, Miss Snow. What are your thoughts so far?" Josh kept his voice low and even, as if strolling through a pyromaniac's abandoned funhouse was a daily thing for him.

I kept my eyes forward, doing my best to avoid tripping over the rubble surrounding the outside of the building. The power plant was in complete disarray; the concrete walls were blown out, the pavement cracked and broken beyond repair, and glass from what used to be narrow windows scattered around the grounds. Black ash surrounded the premises. It was utter devastation.

Were there really no deaths?

An ache pierced my pounding heart at the possibility of the missing people somehow being here when everything went down.

What if they...died?

A tear threatened to slip.

Not now. Not in front of someone you don't know.

I sucked in a steady breath. "Definitely overwhelming but Seth explained the basics and his whole memory manipulation thing. Not sure what superpowers Derik or Libby have going for them but that's what I've got so far."

Josh chuckled. "Superpowers? You mean our abilities?"

"Superpowers, abilities. Same thing. Either way, more than human," I said, waving my hand up and down to brush it off.

"Fair enough. So, Seth didn't fill you in on the rest of us, I take it."

"Nope, nothing," I glanced sideways at Josh. "But I am curious. What tricks do you have up your sleeve? And how many of 'us' are there?"

"Nothing too intimidating, Miss Snow, I assure you. There's but a handful of individuals you've yet to meet. As for myself, I'm simply capable of invoking illusions and causing someone to see things that aren't really there. My ability seems limited to Demons and humans, but it comes in handy during battle."

"Two out of three doesn't seem so bad. Why would you want to use that against another Nephilim anyway?" I glanced at Josh out of the corner of my eye once more.

Illusion against the bad guys and the people we're supposed to protect doesn't seem like a bad thing.

"To shield other Nephilim from the worst of the worst. Imagine seeing your closest friends, fellow warriors that you've fought side by side for decades, centuries, slaughtered right before your own painful death. There are some...that I wish I could've saved from experiencing that...in their last moments." Josh's face fell, shadowed with grief.

"I'm so sorry." It came out barely more than a whisper.

He nodded as we passed another massive pile of debris and reached the rest of our group. Seth, in the middle of giving a run down to Libby, Derik, and a few others, motioned to Josh.

Seth continued, the authority emanating from him as he spoke, catching me off guard. "From what Josh has found so far, it's definitely pointing toward the fire and disappearances being Demon handiwork. Black rings of smoke and ash were found around the entire premises in addition to three of the larger electrical panels on the main floor of the power plant, as well as the homes of the individuals who disappeared. Nothing from their homes was taken either," he paused, rubbing his thumb and pointer finger across his brow line, pinching the bridge of his nose. "Right now, we don't know what the tie between each person is or why they were targeted. Be on the lookout. Keep your eyes peeled. We'll split up into teams to cover some more ground"—Seth's eyes grazed over the group. His finger pointed in my direction—"Erin, you'll be with Libby. Derik, with me and Josh. Everyone else take the perimeter and be on the lookout." We all nodded in agreement and separated.

Libby led the way toward what would've been the east wing of the plant, if there was anything left of it. She stopped in the center of the ash-covered remnants of the wing. Kneeling, Libby placed her hands flat on the cracked cement floor, her arms spread away from her body. She breathed in, her eyes closed. A sudden breeze picked up, snaking its way toward Libby. It picked up speed and encased her in a whirlwind of debris, whipping her shoulder-length hair across her face and neck. Sparks flew from chunks of cement as they made contact with the ground at a mind blowing speed.

What the hell is happening?

My throat tightened as Libby's head snapped back. Her back arched, the wind stopped, and the rubble that had encircled her dropped, colliding with the broken concrete floor. The whole area stood still. And then, she crumpled to the ground.

Panic welled in my stomach and I launched forward barely catching her head before it slammed into the ground. "Libby? Libby! Hey!" I looked around frantically, trying to see if any of the guys were nearby. The blood rushed from my head and it was just the two of us.

And Libby was unconscious.

Fuck fuck fuck. What do I do? Think, Snow. Think!

Libby shifted in my grasp, turning her head slightly.

"Libby? Are you okay!?" The panic was evident in my voice.

Thank God, she's awake.

She blinked up at me, her emerald-green eyes clear. She wiggled out of my arms and sat up. Libby shook her arms out and gathered herself as a proud grin spread from ear to ear. She stood, dusting off her blue jeans and held out her hand to help me up. She rested one hand on her hip, as if she didn't just collapse in the midst of some miniaturized tornado. "Thanks for the catch, Erin!" I furrowed my brow.

"Are you ok? What was that? You collapse and now you're completely fine? How are you okay right now? What the hell happened?" The words rose frantically as they rushed off my tongue.

Libby shrugged. "Yeah, that happens. No biggie." She waved me off, her smile almost angelic.

"No biggie? Dude, you almost busted your head and looked like your ass was possessed."

My heart continued to race.

"It's just a part of my power. I have the power of retrocognition, meaning I can see the past. Events or situations that have happened," she must've noticed that it made *zero* sense to me. "Okay, think of a fortune teller"—I nodded my head, wanting to understand—"where a fortune teller can see the future and things to come, I can see the things that have been. Even if I wasn't present for it."

A reverse fortune teller?

But...aren't fortune tellers just a sham?

My brows pressed together, not fully believing it. "How does that work? Is it just random?"

"Nope, not at all. Thank goodness. I don't know how I'd be able to function if these visions and memories hit me out of nowhere all the time. I need to be in the space to be able to conjure the memories of it. And in instances like this, having physical contact and touching a significant part of the area intensifies the memory. And it's the same with people, too. Except I actually have to have physical contact with someone to dive into theirs." My mouth was hanging open.

Holy hell.

There's no way that can be real.

I wavered. "Can you show me?"

Libby blinked at me.

And then a giddiness enveloped her as she leaped in the air, her smile wide as she squealed, "Hell yeah, I can!"

Oh god. Maybe I shouldn't have asked. I should've just took her word and her crumpling to the ground like a wet tissue at face value.

Libby giggled and grabbed my hands, palms up. "You need to trust me, okay? I'm not going to be all creepy and try to learn all your deep dark secrets. I'll look for something recent."

I racked my brain, thinking of anything that could cause this to be a terrifying trip down memory lane, even if it's supposedly recent. My eyes widened.

Oh no.

"Ah...wait. What exactly are you going to be able to see?" Heat spread across my face.

Seth. What if she can see the way I've started panting over him the last few days?

Shit.

She giggled, a knowing twinkle in her emerald eyes. My stomach twisted. "Oh, don't you worry, Erin. It'll stay between us," my eyes widened. "I'm just messing with you, love. You're in college, right? I'll just search for a class memory." She flashed another killer smile before she squeezed the palms of my hands. Her head snapped backward once more, her mouth agape, and eyes closed. The wind lapped at the air around us, far less intense than before.

I closed my eyes in anticipation.

It's not going to be anything bad. Breathe.

I was half-right.

An image of Seth and me on campus fluttered behind my eyelids. We were eating lunch in between classes and he was droning on about our history finals that were quickly catching up to us. He'd thrown his tattered notebook on the grass and ended up spilling his coffee all over the contents. He cursed up a storm and I laughed my ass off before offering to share mine. He grumbled the rest of the day but it was a highlight for me. As that was the day after the first of my recent nightmares and for those few minutes of heavy laughing, I forgot about the darkness.

My eyes flew open in awe.

"Seth is the one who ruined his notebook? That goober. He told us that he lost it."

I laughed. "Lost it? Far from it. He burned that thing after it dried. The ink was completely smeared and unreadable. He was so mad! It was hilarious."

Libby winked. "I could see that. And I'm totally ratting on him to Derik. He had some details on the Demons written in that thing, too, so it was kind of important."

"No wonder he was so cranky about it."

"Yeap, he never stops, whether it's with us or the Demons. He's non-stop."

Tell me about it.

A soft smile lifted at the corners of my lips. "Thank you for showing me that, Libby."

She quirked a brow at me. "What do you mean?"

"For showing me that memory?"

Libby tilted her head to the side, studying me. "When I use my ability on someone...I'm the only one who can see the vision of their past."

Oh.

"Am I broken?"

She barked out a laugh. "Oh my gosh, Erin. No! That's just the first time that's happened to me! No one's been able to see what I'm pulling from them before."

"Well damn. It's official. You're way cooler than Seth." She cracked another killer smile.

"Oh, please, for the love of God, tell him that. I'd love to see the look on his face," Libby laughed. "Let's go ahead and catch up with the guys so we can fill them in on what we found."

Libby's contagious excitement dwindled within me.

What you found...I did nothing.

We walked toward the opposite end of the power plant in search of the guys and the other Nephilims. My mind began to wander. "Hey, I um, I don't know if Seth told you, but I'm staying at his place for a few, at least until this whole human-turning-into-a-Nephilim thing is over. I hope that's okay. I...I don't want to intrude or anything," I said, wringing my hands.

Libby smiled down at me. "Yeah, he filled me and Derik in before we picked you up last night. His place is super nice. I'm so jealous!" Guilt flashed across my face. "Not like that, Erin! *That* whole thing was a while ago. We ended it like *months* ago. There just wasn't any chemistry there. I mean, don't get me wrong, the guy is an animal in the sack but we just didn't work like that."

My checks burned with embarrassment. "I...uh, okay, cool. I...I didn't want to, you know, overstep or anything. Seth's been my best friend since forever but when a guy has a girlfriend, you know, it's...I don't want to cause any issues," I stammered.

Libby stopped abruptly, her determined gaze locked with my own dull, uncertain stare. "Sweetie, look at me. Me and Seth? We are not dating. He's my partner and leader in the whole us-against-the-demons business but nothing hitting the romance line. I got my eyes on a different piece of candy." Libby winked at me as we caught up and neared Derik, Josh, and Seth.

The three of them were huddled together, each focused intently on their conversation. Seth's eyebrows were knitted, his jaw clenched. We wedged ourselves into their superhuman huddle. Libby between Derik and Josh; me squished between Josh and Seth, our shoulders brushing.

Seth and Libby aren't together.

So what?

Josh peered over at me, flashing a grin. I returned my own as best as I could and turned my attention to Libby.

"We got 'em." She beamed.

Derik hooted, "Hell yeah, Blondie! That's what I'm talking about." He slapped Libby on the shoulder causing her to roll her eyes. A dusting of pink tinged her cheekbones.

"What did you find, Lib?" Seth asked.

"From what I was able to see, there were three of them who hit this place. Luckily, it was empty when they ransacked it and burned the place down. All following the typical big bad and scary look. From what I could tell, the leader was some dark-haired douche canoe with a scar covering his left eye. They left heading away from town, so they might've just been the decoys while the real party was going down with the snatching."

Seth nodded, his jaw loosened slightly. "Okay, did any of them say anything important or anything that stuck out to you?"

"Unfortunately, no. There was nothing that spilled the beans on the why behind it or where they were heading next."

"Damn." Seth closed his eyes, pinching the bridge of his nose again. That seemed to be his go-to that day. He was usually the most carefree, ain't-no-thang-but-a-chicken-wing type of guy. But at that moment, the Seth I knew was nowhere in sight. His eyes softened as he looked back at Libby. "Thanks for backtracking for us, Lib. Much appreciated." My chest tightened at the hint of affection in Seth's voice.

They might not be together...but there's something there between them.

I turned my head wanting to hide the sliver of jealousy plastered on my face only to find Josh staring at me. Concern briefly flashed across his features. Our little group spread across the lot, each walking in our own direction—except Josh. He tilted his head in question. I shook mine, shoving my hands in my jean pockets, praying he left it alone. Left *me* alone.

Erin, get a grip. You didn't have any of these feelings a few days ago. Slow your roll.

For some godforsaken reason, Josh took that as his cue to move closer to me. Could the guy not read body language?

"Hey."

I quickly glanced up at him. "Hey."

He gave me a small smile. "Was it just me or did you turn a shade of green for a moment, Miss Snow?"

I shrugged my shoulders, feigning ignorance. "No idea what you mean. Just distracted for a second. It happens a lot."

It's nothing.

I'm just being weird.

It's hormones.

A low chuckle drifted from Josh's lips, curling its way into my spine. "I'm sure, Miss Snow. So, tell me, what is it that distracted you *this* time?"

I glared at him, clenching my fists. "Nothing. It's none of your business, Josh." *So much for earlier. This guy was kind of an ass. Okay, maybe not but,* "Ugh!"

"Erin, you good over there?" Seth asked.

Shit.

That came out louder than I thought.

I nodded. "Yeah, sorry." He went back to addressing a person I'd yet to meet. They stood a couple of inches shorter than Seth but equally built with broad shoulders and waves of muscle easily seen with the tight jacket that morphed into his form.

Okay, are they all freaking gorgeous? Because this is nuts.

"For what it's worth, Miss Snow, he'd be crazy not to be attracted to you. You are quite beautiful," Josh whispered in my ear. Blood rushed to my face.

"I...I...what!?" He gave me that low chuckle again, a slight victory lit with his freckled eyes, sending another shiver through me.

I huffed, begging for the rosiness on my cheeks to vanish. I closed my eyes to settle myself and breathed in deeply. When I opened them again, I caught Libby watching me, her gaze flitting back and forth between Josh and me.

Chapter Six

Erin

We made our way back to our vehicles. Seth and Derik discussed a game plan for the following day as we walked. I zoned them out, thinking back to Libby and her ability, then Seth's and Josh's. I wondered what I'd be able to do when the time came. I felt so useless. Okay, not that we'd done much at that point beyond playing a quick game of supernatural CSI, but still.

I did nothing.

"You're gonna kill your last brain cell if you keep thinking that hard, Rin," Derik said as he slowed his pace and fell to the back of our little group next to me, lightly shoving my shoulder.

"Still more brain cells than you," I retorted, shoving him back.

"Yeah, you're probably right," he laughed. "What were you and Mister Dark and Mysterious nagging each other about earlier? It looked like he got you a little riled there, girlie."

"First of all, do *not* call me that. I'm not twelve. Second, nothing important. He was just getting on my nerves. You two seem to have that in common."

Derik busted out laughing. "Ha! I have something in common with Grey Impersonate over there. That's fucking hilarious!" Derik smacked me hard on the back, knocking the wind from my lungs.

"You're an ass, dude." I coughed.

He shrugged. "Makes sense since I get plenty of it."

I scrunched my nose. "Gross."

"That's not any way to speak in front of a lady, Derik."

Speak of the damned devil.

I internally groaned while assface plastered a dubious grin on his face.

"My bad. Didn't mean to offend ya, Erin." Derik held his hands up in a feign apology, sporting a toothy grin.

"Yeah, right," I scoffed and turned to Josh. "I appreciate you doing this whole courteous crap but there's no need. I know Derik is an ass." I shot Derik an irritated look.

"My, my. Quite a mouth you have there, Miss Snow." Derik practically choked on air, while I gaped at Josh. He flashed one hell of a smile. His teeth gleamed in the early evening sun, a dimple appearing on his right cheek.

"What are you? The damned language police? This is the twenty-first century. You realize that, right?" I deadpanned, crossing my arms over my chest.

Derik wiped a tear as it fell from his eye from laughing so hard.

Bastard.

I glared at Derik, my face hot from the not-so-subtle innuendo.

He choked back another bout of laughter. "Alright, alright, Snow, you ready to head out?" I narrowed my eyes at Josh and turned on my heel, reaching for the passenger door of Derik's Silverado.

Where does this guy get off? I can damn well talk however I please.

I yanked it open and hopped inside, slamming the door behind me. Derik swaggered toward the driver's side, Josh right on his heel.

"Would you mind if I rode with you all?"

No. Please no.

The most mischievous glint shined in Derik's slate-blue eyes. "After that? Hell yeah. I'd love a frontrow seat to see Erin squirm."

Asshole.

"You're disgusting."

"It's what I do best, baby." He shrugged and hauled his ass into the driver's seat, leaving me to squeeze in the center between him and Josh. The last place I wanted to be at that moment.

For how massive this behemoth of a truck is, you'd think he'd have extended cab seating.

I was hyper-aware of Josh's body next to mine. It was a tight fit in Derik's truck, with it only being a front seater. My shoulders were, unfortunately, firmly pressed against Josh's, okay and Derik's too, but let's be honest, I didn't pay much attention to Derik's burly shoulder. I caught a whiff of Josh's scent as he slung his arm over the back of the seat.

Cedar and...musk?

I breathed it in, relished it, and images danced in front of me.

His stubble sent tingles down my stomach as he grazed my neck, gently caressing the spot between my shoulders with his lips. He flicked his tongue, causing me to shiver, a slight pool forming at my center. A moan escaped my lips that snapped me out of my little fantasy.

Derik cleared his throat. "Uh, Erin, you good? You spaced out there for a sec." I shot straight up in my seat, my face beet-red. I slapped my hands down on my lap, facing forward.

Nervous laughter bubbled in my chest. "Yeap. Peachy. Must've dosed off. You know, with lack of sleep and everything lately."

Breathe. I'm just imagining things. I just met the guy today. There's no reason to get all hot and heavy just because he smells delicious. This isn't some romance novel.

"Oh yeah, Seth did mention something about you not sleeping. Said you've been having those dream run-ins with the Angels. Sounds like a fun time."

I sighed, nodding my head; grateful Derik didn't push it and make a spectacle of my spacing out.

So that must be what that guy was in the second nightmare. But what about the first one?

A blanket of darkness surrounded me and it was as if I couldn't escape. No one was in that one, at least not that I could see even though I felt hundreds of eyes on me. There was nothing but the fear of being chased and not being able to escape that encompassed my whole being.

"Have you had any others? Since the one after class?"

"No, there haven't been any more. I'm keeping my fingers crossed that it stays that way. If I'm going to be a part of this whole 'hunt the Demons' thing, I'm going to need as much rest as I can get. I get crabby."

"I can't imagine you crabby, Miss Snow," Josh said, his voice laced with a hint of playfulness, his dimple prominent.

Derik snorted. "You have no freaking idea, man. This chick can send wild animals running when she's in a mood. Should've seen when we met. She looked like she wanted to kill my ass."

"You were being an absolute ass and it was during finals my freshman year. Within five minutes of meeting me, you hit on me, gave me the up-down, and immediately moved to hit on the other chick that showed up with Seth's girlfriend at the time. Not to mention you were shit-faced. You were being a pig, a drunken pig. Of course I was pissy."

He shrugged. "Eh, it's alright. The other chick was hotter anyway," I slapped him on the shoulder. He tried dodging and failed, being behind the wheel and crammed together on the seat. "What!

It's not like you were interested in me anyway, Snow. You only tagged along because Seth dragged you out."

He wasn't wrong. I was in the trenches of studying and preparing for finals with absolutely no interest in leaving my apartment. I had been holed up in my living room for days when Seth dropped in—without warning—and gave me ten minutes to throw on something besides sweats or he threatened to do it himself. In hindsight, he wouldn't have actually stripped me down but I was so fried from my textbooks, that the threat was enough. I hated finals. We both did. They always stressed me out so much to the point where my ability to eat or even sleep became non-existent.

Finals. Shit.

I slapped my hand on my forehead, startling Derik and Josh. I glimpsed the confused looks on their faces through the rearview mirror in front of me. "I totally forgot we have finals coming up again. I need to get back and cram some work in. Ugh!"

I could picture Jensin's willowy figure barking at me, his frustration visible in the smallest crevice between the wrinkles of his skin. I shivered. He was an excellent professor and extremely knowledgeable. However, he was terrifying if you fell on his bad side.

"Well, good thing we're here," Derik said, parking his truck in front of Seth's place. I chastised myself for forgetting as I slid out of Derik's truck.

I need to figure this out.

Just because I was thrust into this whole immortal world, didn't mean I was about to chuck my education out of the window. I had plans. A quiet life I wanted to build for myself. And I refused to let some literal hell-bent Demon bullshit that I knew nothing about until a week ago ruin said plans.

I followed Derik and Josh into the house, mulling over potential scheduling conflicts.

Maybe if I get up earlier, I can get school work out of the way? Then the "saving the world" gig after class? I only have a handful of classes now, so that shouldn't be a problem.

Okay. I'll do that.

I don't have a choice but to make this work. No matter how much I don't want to be a part of it all.

I'm going to need to stock up on coffee if I'm going to make it through all of this.

"Woah there, girl. What's got you so worked up?" Seth slapped his hand on my shoulder, startling me.

I squeezed my lids close before responding, my mind in overdrive. "Derik was reminiscing on when we met and reminded me about finals coming up and all the school work, studying, and cramming I need to do. And how I'm going to work it all around this," I half groaned. "But I think I have an idea of how I'm going to keep it together."

A look of pure panic spread across Seth's face as his body tensed and eyes bugged out from his skull. "Dude, that didn't even cross my mind. Fucking finals, man," he ran his hand through his hair, dust that seeped its way into his shaggy strands perfused the air between us. He coughed. "You wanna take mine for me? I might actually pass for once. I don't want to sit through *another* year of the same classes."

"What, don't you want to bump it up to graduating college three years late instead of the two you're up to now?" That earned me a glare from him that had me laughing.

"Maybe I failed on purpose."

Yeah right.

Seth was smart, actually one of the brightest people I knew. Okay, that didn't say much, with how small my social circle was, but still. The guy's always been a bit of a genius. School just wasn't his thing.

Never has been. But with a monumental passion for reading, he'd acquired a whole library's worth of books in his home, displayed throughout the living room. It's one of the many things we have in common. If I could live in the various realms found within the pages of my favorite stories, I would. And so would Seth.

Derik used the lull between Seth and me to jump into our conversation. "I think you might've, Lover Boy." I swore, some of the most devious looks appeared on Derik's face. Libby seemed equally as giddy, her eyes bright.

"Wasn't there *another* reason you retook your classes this year?" He placed his pointer finger on his chin, tapping it. "It involved someone..." Seth's face turned a deep shade of red. "Erin? Don't you guys share a few?" Derik turned to face me. I nodded, not seeing what his point was. "Ah, yes. You wanted to land the same courses as Snow."

Derik officially lost it. Seth was devastated when he realized he failed most of his classes last year.

I furrowed my brow, questioningly glancing at Seth. "I...I figured if I was repeating, I might as well snag the same classes as her. I don't see what your point is, Derik. I don't do school, man. We all know this," he chattered, avoiding my gaze. Behind Seth, Libby shielded her mouth, fighting to hide her laugh. I felt my cheeks begin to flush.

Okay, but why is he stuttering and being awkward about it?
What does that mean!? There's no way.
Does Seth...is there more to it? Does he have a thing for me?
My heart leaped in my chest.

Libby regained control, clearing her throat. "Alright, lay off the poor guy, Derik. You know how he likes to play protector." Libby winked at me, and my heart fell.

Protector. That's right.
It's literally a part of who he is.

It wouldn't mean anything more than him wanting to make sure I'm okay, especially with the Nephilim and Demons. I internally kicked myself for even entertaining the idea of Seth caring for me as more than a friend. And for caring in the first place.

Stupid.

I let out a small laugh. "Yeah, always the big brother type, huh, Seth?" For a moment, I swore there was a glimpse of sadness and pain in his eyes.

He smiled, but it barely met his eyes. "Yeah, that's me."

I reached my hand out and my fingers brushed his toned, sun-kissed forearm. There was a jolt of electricity between us. Seth's breath hitched. His cerulean eyes skirted my pale skin, stopping where my hand rested on his arm. I felt the blush return to my cheeks and pulled away.

"I...sorry, Seth, I didn't mean to..."

Except that felt like more than just static.

When my hand touched Seth, it was like a jolt of electricity shot through me, right down to my bones. Goosebumps pebbled along my arms, my heart pounded, and a warmth spread throughout my body.

He slowly nodded. "No worries, Snow." He was still looking down; his gaze had followed my hand as I tucked it behind me. His brows threaded together and he reached around me to pull my hand back out. He held it up.

What...what is he doing?

I gasped and my eyes grew wide. There, bouncing along the tips of my fingers, were bouts of electricity, miniature lightning bolts. The flesh on the tips of my fingers tingled and a low hum echoed in my ears. Copper infiltrated my mouth as if I'd shoved a handful of pennies onto my tongue. My pulse slowed, my vision became blurry, and blood rushed from my head. Seth disappeared from view, my limbs heavy as I fell into a pit of nothingness, the world around me shrouded in black.

Chapter Seven

Seth

"Erin!?" I yelled, barely catching her head before she hit the hardwood floor. I scanned her face and her seemingly fragile body in search of any sign of damage or any effects that lingered from the electricity that pulsed from her hands.

Derik was on the ground with me at Erin's side, his palm pressed to her chest, sending his power inward in search of internal trauma. Derik's chocolate eyes met mine as he lifted his hand from her unconscious body. "She's okay. Just knocked out from her power suddenly deciding to make an appearance. She's not drained. It was more of a shock to her system."

Thank God.

I exhaled a sigh of relief, sending a silent prayer that Erin hadn't suffered any damage. More often than not, the first time our power awakes or comes to fruition, it could leave us worse for wear.

I sent a glance to Libby, our eyes locking. The memory of her initial onslaught of power played in my mind. When the retrocognition hit her, cuts raked across her skin, blood spurting out of each one. We'd been near a site where a Demon had massacred a group of college kids; Libby had rested her hand on top of one of the wooden crosses left by one of the victims' friends when the vision hit her.

Libby slowed and walked to where I remained on the ground with Erin still cradled in my lap. "She's okay, Seth. She's strong. You've got to see that," Libby cracked a smile. "Erin really is electrifying, huh?" She crouched next to us, patting my back.

I laughed. "She really is."

Erin began to shift in my arms, groaning as she unintentionally angled herself toward me, nuzzling herself into my chest. I smiled down at her, my heart thumping. Wisps of her chestnut brown hair had escaped her ponytail, caressing her face. The rest trailed across my lap and to the floor.

So beautiful.

Using the back of my hand, I lightly brushed away a few strands of her hair from her face, coaxing her awake. Her brows pushed together. "Erin?" I said, barely above a whisper.

Erin's eyes fluttered open, her sapphire blue eyes blinked up at me, surprise dawning on her face. A pink blush rose across her cheeks and spread down her delicate neck. A chuckle escaped my lips and she bolted upright, stuttering. My heart ached as her warmth left me.

"I...I'm so sorry! I...What happened?" Confusion spread across her face.

My smile widened. "Look down, Snow. Or maybe we should call you Zeus." She smacked my arm, embarrassed. Then, taking a breath, Erin switched her focus to her hands. They were pulsing. Bites of electricity and miniature lightning bolts skipped across her fingertips, illuminating her striking features. Her eyes sparkled as if they were the night sky on the brink of early morning.

She dragged her breathtakingly sapphire blue eyes back up to mine. They widened, practically bulging out of her skull. "I...Seth.

There's...why is there lightning coming out of my hands?" Erin's shoulders started shaking. Her lips began to quiver. Barely a whisper, "Did...Seth, did I hurt you?" A tear escaped.

A little spark is nothing in comparison to the things I've seen and done, Erin.

I pulled her back to me, my arms wrapping around her shoulders as they shook in an attempt to will her to stop shaking.

She blacks out on me and asks if I'm okay. Go figure.

"Erin, no, I'm fine. Look at me." I slid my finger under her chin, tilting it upwards so she would look at me. Another tear had escaped down her soft, yet angled cheekbones, matching the jagged outward, no-fucks given facade she puts out. While inside, after everything Erin had been through, her heart beat stronger than she would ever admit and larger than any soul I've met. And right now, that heart, its concern, was set on me.

At that moment, as selfish as it was, I wished it were just the two of us. So I could fully wrap my arms around her small—okay, small to me—frame. Hug her close and whisper all the promises I've silently made to her over the years since we were kids. Tell her before she learns everything. About Me. About herself, the past. The pain to come. I want to take her and hide away. Tell her...tell her...exactly how much I care for her, always have.

And how I have to do everything I can to keep her safe.

But we weren't alone. And the risk was too great. I had people, including my band of Nephilim, who relied on me. Who needed me to lead them. Protect them. And Erin, she needed it most. None of us knew what was to come. Between the Demons, the attack in Riverside...the disappearances...I had a feeling that it was only the beginning. And with that, I would do what was required of me; suck it up.

This is so much bigger than us. Than all of us.

I sucked in a breath, forced out a laugh, hiding the thoughts that trampled through my mind.

Erin kept her attention on me, her eyes grounding me. The thought of simply losing myself in the beauty of her gaze gripped me. I swallowed, my throat suddenly dry. My lips parted only to be interrupted as someone cleared their throat across the room.

"Miss Snow, I assure you that Seth is okay. We're all concerned about you at the moment considering the fact that *you* are the one who collapsed." She snapped her head in Josh's direction, her eyes wide once more.

"Oh," Erin blinked. "I think...I'm good. Just...frazzled." A reddened hue returned to her cheeks.

Josh took that moment to stroll over to where we were huddled on my hardwood floor. He reached his hand out to help Erin up. I bit my tongue.

Back the fuck off.

She placed her hand in his, her lips forming a smile so beautifully bright I swore I felt my heart scream.

"Thank you," Erin said, her voice an octave higher.

Josh met my glare, a glint in his freckled eyes. A wave of nausea rushed through me. I caught the faintest smirk before he returned his attention to Erin, both of her feet now firmly planted on the floor, her hand still in his.

I have no claim on her.

Years of firmly planting myself as her protector ensured that.

Josh consistently worked to get a rise out of me with his old *gentlemanly* ass bullshit. I get it. Josh was a few centuries older than the rest of us but he irked me. I was unsure what it was about him but it was as if he had this air circling him that screamed, 'I'm above you. Above this.' As if we were lesser. It made my blood boil.

Breathe. It's not worth it.

I reminded myself. I was worked up and without a valid reason. I rolled my shoulders to shake off the little green monster that lingered beneath the surface. Shifting my arm behind my back, I pushed my hand against the floor, propelling myself up to a standing position to match Josh's towering stance over Erin.

I dusted myself off, for no reason other than to keep my hands busy and resisting the urge to grab Erin from where she was standing with Josh, only a few inches between them. He pulled her closer to himself than I thought.

Too close.

The lick of jealousy crept its way into my chest again.

"So Zeus, any ideas on how you spurted those bolts out of yourself there? Ya know, for research purposes," Derik said, breaking the building tension between Josh and me.

Erin growled, the fire beneath her surface returning. "First of all, don't call me Zeus. I'm not some horny-ass Greek god," she yanked her hand out from Josh's and threw it on her hip, glaring at Derik. "Secondly—"

"Okay, so Bolty, got it." Derik smirked.

Atta girl.

My mouth twitched while Erin crackled.

"Ugh! Stop, dude! I don't want any weird nicknames!" She closed her eyes briefly, inhaling deeply to steady herself. "Secondly, I have no damn clue what I did. It just kind of happened, jackass," Erin's nostrils flared as she fixed her piercing eyes on me. "Any ideas? It didn't happen until I touched your arm." A faint blush graced her cheekbones.

"I'm not entirely sure either, Erin," I ran my thumb and pointer finger through the stubble on my chin, contemplating. Her eyes followed the movement. "More than likely, it was probably just random timing. I mean, you've been around us most of the day and

I don't think I was the first person you've had physical contact with, right?" I could feel Derik grinning beside me. Libby had a glint in her eye; Josh, a shadow of some sort, passed across his features, and Erin...the peach tint that caressed the angles of her face deepened and spread down her neck, stopping at the collar of her shirt.

She began fumbling over her words. "Yeah, you're probably right. Just weird timing. Josh helped me when I fell out of Derik's truck at the plant and...after Libby had her flashback. Then on the drive here I was stuck between Josh and Derik." Her eyes rapidly flickered between each of us. Mostly Josh and me. Erin bit her lip and her gaze finally landed on me.

My heart skipped.

"Don't sweat it. It's no big deal. For the time being"—I relaxed my shoulders as I smiled at Erin—"let's focus on how you're going to do it again."

Chapter Eight

Erin

Libby, Derik, and Josh worked with me for hours, pushing me in varying degrees to try and figure out how to trigger my little handheld lightning show. I was so exhausted and still felt like I made no progress. I flopped on Seth's sofa, throwing my arm across my face to shield the ceiling lights from further permeating the headache that pounded behind my eyelids. Seth played spectator, laughing every time I got frustrated. The traitor.

Libby's ideas ranged from replaying the whole situation out with her retro-what's-it. She latched her palms onto my shoulders to try and bring the cause out. No luck. Just a lot of sweaty hand prints and Libby being overly positive.

"You can do it, Erin! Just believe in yourself!" I appreciated the effort but dear lord, there was only so much the positive-no-matter-what hype thing could accomplish.

Derik decided to throw a solid right hook into my left eye *at full strength* and knocked me unconscious again, leading to a concussion. Which he just so happily healed. Freaking asshole. Hours later my entire body was still sore and I was ninety-nine percent sure that was the main cause of the killer migraine. Derik might've had the power to heal damn near anything, according to him and Libby, but apparently couldn't do jack-squat about a piercing headache that his ass caused. I called bullshit. Maybe not to his face but he landed his ass back on my shit list for the time being. The only upside was, after realizing I was actually unconscious, Seth whipped his ass.

Josh...was interesting, to say the least. He placed his hand over mine and nothing had happened. And that was entirely expected, given his ability wasn't effective on other Nephilim. However, moments after he released me, the room faded...I was suddenly surrounded by pitch black. A harrowing feeling surrounded me. Then there was screaming. Blood. Everywhere. I couldn't breathe. I felt as though I was suffocating. Then I was shaking, or rather, being shaken. The panic fell away and Seth, once again, shook me by the shoulders, pulling me out of it. When it fully fell away, I was pretty sure the look on my face matched Seth's: drained and pale. Their eyes hollowed, as if they'd witnessed a ghost cross their path. Fear gouged my core. Josh's face twisted and a shade of green tinged his skin, his jaw ticked.

Seth kicked everyone out after that. Derik and Libby complained, wanting to stay and keep 'helping.' Josh apologized, unsure of what the hell had happened, by pulling my hand to his mouth and placing a kiss right in the center. His eyes held mine, which had sent a shiver down my spine. Even thinking about it hours later, the way he looked at me, so devilishly handsome, sent another shiver down the length of my body. I sighed.

I have a panic rendering of the nightmare that started all of this and all I can think of is some ridiculously tall guy I just met.

What the hell is wrong with me?

I shook my head at myself, frustrated.

"I'm sorry about today, Snow. I didn't think they'd all gang up on you like that. Derik...I should've warned you about that...his favorite method of finding answers, ironically, usually involves some form of getting physical. His reason behind it is that he can just heal whatever the hell he ends up doing. Libby, she...she means well, but besides you, she's the newest to our little group so you're the first Nephilim newbie she's been around, besides herself, obviously."

No kidding. A heads-up on Derik would've been helpful.

Seth sat down on the sofa next to me, slinging my legs on top of his as he did so. He leaned over and placed a warm towel across my arm, covering my eyes. "This'll help."

I hope so. I get it. Derik was trying to help but this fucking hurts like hell.

I took it and laid it across my eyelids, where the headache throbbed the most. I groaned as the warm towel instantly eased more of the pain.

"God, Seth, this feels amazing," he chuckled as he traced circles on my knees. I felt myself relax a bit more, the aches from the day beginning to fade. "I could just lay here like this forever." I sighed, not realizing I had said it out loud until Seth stopped mid-loop.

Fuck. He's going to take it the wrong way.

I held my breath.

I can just picture it now. "Oh, you got the hots for me, Erin? Weird. Sorry bro, I'm just not that into you." And then I'd hide in his guest room until he forgot about me or until I simply died from embarrassment.

But it's fine. Everything's fine.

Oh my God, I'm fucking losing it. What is wrong with me?

Snap out of it!

"I know, right? Probably the best damned couch I could've bought."

I breathed out, lifting the towel slightly to catch a glimpse. Seth had his head down slightly, staring at the spot where my legs rested across his, the smile that sounded in his voice not present. There was a twinge in my heart like there was a pull, an urge, to move closer.

Weird.

I removed the warm compress from my head and set it on the coffee table, my gaze fixed on Seth. "Hey, you okay?" I cocked my head to the side.

He turned his head toward me, plastering the smile I heard on his face. "Yeah, of course. Just tired as hell. Long day, remember?" He moved to get up, lifting my legs off his lap, and laid them back along his couch. "We should probably get some rest. You care if I snag the shower first?" I propped myself up on my elbows and shook my head.

My brows furrowed as Seth hurried toward the bathroom. I stared after him.

What's going on? After today, does he not want me hanging out here?

I let out another sigh.

Or maybe it was *the stupid 'forever' remark?*

I sat up and ran my fingers through what was left of my ponytail. I held the end of it in my palm, rubbing it between my thumb and forefinger. It was caked in dust and grime from the day.

Maybe that's why he bolted for the shower. I look like a mess and a half.

I sniffed, scrunching my nose.

Ugh, I smell like ass too. Gross.

I stood and walked toward the guest room, passing the island in Seth's kitchen. I heard my phone beep. I picked it up and saw a message from...Libby.

As it turned out, I grabbed Seth's instead.

> Hey, you doing okay? I didn't mean to push Erin so far today. Would you want to grab a coffee tomorrow? We can go to our usual spot. LMK :)
>
> -Libby

I gripped Seth's phone. Tears trickled down my face.

Stupid.

My chest tightened, my throat closing. I couldn't breathe.

Stupid. Stupid. Stupid.

I heard the bathroom door click open and I dropped his phone on the counter. I sprinted to the guest room and slammed the door shut behind me.

"Erin?" He knocked. "You okay?" he asked, the words gravelly and laced with exhaustion.

I wiped the tears from my eyes and opened the door just enough to see his six-foot-four finely chiseled body standing outside the frame with a towel barely hanging across his hips, accentuating the deep V leading down. My cheeks flushed.

"Yeah, I'm fine. Just going to bed. Good night." I went to shut the door but he braced his arm on the frame, keeping it propped open.

"Erin...I can see the tear trail. What's wrong?" I balled my fists, squeezing my eyes shut.

Stupid.

"I'm fine. All the bullshit from today is just hitting me harder than I thought," I opened my eyes and looked up at him. "I just want to go to bed, Seth. Thanks for checking on me and for everything. But I'm *exhausted*. Night." I stared at him until he lifted himself from the door frame. I slammed the door shut.

"Goodnight," I heard him whisper.

I listened at the door until I heard his footsteps walk away toward his room down the hall. The click of his door as it opened then relatched behind him echoed throughout the silent hallway.

I let myself slump to the ground and wrapped my arms around my knees as I brought them to my chest. I began sobbing.

Why is this bothering me? Why?

I fell asleep like that as my body slowly slid to the floor, knees still close to my chest. Streams of tears caressed my cheeks as I dreamt of Seth. And Libby. And...me. Left all alone. Again.

Chapter Nine

Erin

I woke the next morning sprawled on the floor, shivering, my back aching, and head pounding.

That's what I get for sleeping on the ground. And bawling my eyes out for no reason other than being dramatic.

I groaned as I sat up and arched my back, aiming to stretch out the kinks, then rotated my head from side to side to crack my neck.

Crossing my legs, I brought my elbow to rest on my knee, leaning my chin into the base of my palm. I stared at my bare mattress across the room, my eyes unfocused, my dream from the night front and center:

He was there again, the man from the first dream. His back faced me with his hands clasped behind himself, looking out over the surrounding mountain scape.

We stood atop a mountain range, seemingly at the highest point. The sun was setting, casting various shades of pinks, purples, and reds across the sky. A single beam of yellow shot through the middle, piercing its way through the horizon. It was breathtaking.

"It's beautiful," I said.

Out of the corner of my eye, I saw him nod.

"Who are you?" I asked, the curiosity getting to me.

"That is not of importance," he responded flatly.

"Okay...then where are we? And why? Why are you here, again?"

The man turned to me, his expression blank. "I am here...to assess how you are progressing and...your abilities...What you have uncovered thus far...," his eyes trailed the length of my body, as if searching for something. "As well as a message." His amber eyes shot up, a fire blazed within them, burning a hole through me.

"You must be careful. There are things coming. Trust the light that finds you in the dark. But. Be wary of the darkness that appears as part of the light."

I huffed. Cryptic much? "Okay, message received, mystery man. Can you tell me how I get my power, the electricity, lighting, or whatever, to work? Because, I got to be honest, I tried and it left me worse for wear."

The slightest smirk played at the edges of his lips. "For that, you must dive inward. Look to the mirror and you will see, for there is so much more beyond the shallow depths at the entrance to your soul."

And then he was gone.

As much as I didn't want to go out and face Seth after having an emotional breakdown, I needed coffee in my system to get my ass in gear.

Upset over a text.

What am I, twelve?

And as I thought it through, especially if I took into consideration what Libby had said about them *not* dating, I was more than likely just reading into it way too much. Coffee didn't automatically mean a *date*.

I shook my head.

I'm getting worked up again. Just mention it and ask about it. Don't make a big deal out of it.

I stood up and made my way over to my unpacked bag of clothes. I grabbed a T-shirt with one of my favorite bands plastered on the front of it, a pair of black leggings, my front-zip sports bra, and a pair of panties that had seen better days. With my clean clothes balled together under my arm, I padded across the hall to the bathroom to hop in the shower.

Erin, there are so many things going on that are far more important than suddenly having a little crush on Seth.

Things like, you know, figuring out the whole lightning power situation and why thirteen people are missing.

Seth came grumbling out of his room at the same time. His hair tousled, midnight blue eyes bleary, his stubble along his jawline slightly thicker than the night before. "Morning," he mumbled, his voice gravelly.

Talk about hot.

For fucks sake, stop it.

I swatted the thought away. "Morning," I grumbled as I shifted my weight. "Hey, can we talk later? I want to explain about last night...and apologize." I pulled my bottom lip between my teeth, nervously waiting for his response.

He blinked, attempting to clear his still drooping eyes. "Uh, yeah. Yeah that's fine. But I'm gonna head up to the coffee shop to meet up with Libby first. You want anything?"

At least he's not hiding it.

I nodded. "Sure, just the usual. Maybe throw in one of their blueberry muffins too, please?"

Don't say it, don't say it.

"Tell Libby I said hi." I gave Seth a tight-lipped smile, hoping he didn't catch the bitchiness in my voice.

You dumbass. He's going to realize you're being weird.

Libby is a sweetheart. Slow your roll.

He nodded and trudged his way toward his pristine kitchen, grabbing his keys. My gaze trailed behind him as he went through his living room, slipped on his black and white sneakers, and lazily stepped out his front door. I stood in the bathroom entry, staring after him even when the door closed behind him.

"This is stupid." I huffed and turned back toward Seth's marble-covered bathroom. I slammed the powdery-white door shut behind me and stripped off my clothes from the day prior. I tossed them on the Carrara marble tiled floor and turned the water on in the shower to scorching hot. I wanted to feel the burn from it. Melt away these god-awful pangs of jealousy and bitchiness winding their way through my veins.

This isn't me.

I grabbed the bottle of shampoo Seth had along the wall and squirted half the contents into my hand, then slathered it into my hair. I might've wanted to scrub away my mood, but I would still be petty and use more of his expensive shower products than necessary. The downside? I smelled like him—pine mixed with a hint of bourbon.

Home.

I jolted. "Home? Where the fucknuts did that come from?" I scrubbed my arms red in hopes of chasing that thought from my mind.

Giving up, I shut off the water and grabbed the towel off the hook outside the shower. I wrapped my hair on top of my head and walked over to the double vanity. I pulled out my toothbrush and scrubbed my teeth until my gums bled, spat, and stared myself down in the mirror.

"Erin. Calm your tits," I steadied myself. "You're acting like a lovesick puppy and throwing a hissy fit." I pinched the bridge of my nose. I met my reflection once again. This time analyzing.

Average chest, I've been a whopping C-cup since middle school. Still perky-ish.

Thank you, weight-training.

Since I hit my twenties, my hips have widened ever so slightly. In addition to all the workout routines, running, hiking, and just overall muscle tone I gained, I had developed curves over the years. I had a crescent moon tattoo resting on my left hip with stars mirroring on my right. A scar from when I had it pierced was showcased at my belly button. Below that, I had various tattoos covering both of my thighs, following the theme between my favorite television shows and movies with a pop of book characters. I was nerdy and obsessed with books. And still a mess and a half, even after spending a good fifteen-to-twenty minutes in a scalding hot shower.

Everything about me screamed average. And Seth was not. He was built like a freaking Greek God, that even dark and mysterious Josh couldn't compare to. Seth was a genius, even though he hid it; under his carefree, borderline frat boy demeanor, he had a heart of gold. Long story short, he was out of my league. I never stood a chance. I scrunched my nose at myself displayed in the mirror—at the disappointment in how I looked and that I allowed it to bother me.

"Suck it up, Buttercup."

I know what I look like and how I appear. I long ago accepted where I stood in society's attractive scale. Why is it suddenly bothering me so much?

I unwrapped my hair and finished toweling off. I grabbed my bundle of clean clothes off the counter and threw them on. Scrounging around the under-sink cabinet, I found a dusty Onyx blow-dryer. I plugged it in and flipped it on high. The blasting air helped to drown out the thoughts running through my head—it was too loud to think.

After my hair was dried, I took one more long, disappointing look at myself in the mirror, then padded out into the hallway. I glanced down the hallway to Seth's room, my shoulders slumping forward.

I tossed my dirty clothes into the guest room. Then, against my better judgment, headed toward Seth's bedroom. Not entirely sure what drew me to it beyond pure curiosity and nosiness. Even though we shared his bed the other night, I hadn't gotten a good look around his room. I'd only been in there twice the whole time he'd been in this place, both occasions having been in his room *with* him in it. Bedrooms are like a sacred spot...and there I was, snooping and invading that privacy.

No going back now, I guess.

I stepped over the threshold, taking in the full space. The fourteen-foot ceilings were reoccurring throughout the old-school-building-turned-residential home. Exposed light oak beams ran the full length of the room, angling upward, and meeting at a point in the center. The walls were painted a light cream. Three large bookcases stood flush against the far wall, finished to perfectly match the exposed beams overhead. Above them, an arched window spanned the width of the room.

His bed was positioned at the halfway point leading from where I stood in the entrance to his bedroom with one slate-grey side table nestled on either side. The oversized, shiplap headboard was painted in the same shade of grey. Seth's almost-bleach white down-comforter, along with his favorite navy-blue throw, was rumpled in the center of his king-sized mattress. Pillows, naked and not a pillowcase in sight, were tossed randomly around the room. One barely hanging on his bed and two others sprawled on top of the blue-grey shaggy rug that took up a majority of the hardwood floor. It stopped just short of the lounge chairs and reading table that were positioned a few feet in front of the bookcase furthest to the left.

I padded over to his book collection, not having seen these ones before. Since he showcased a whole library out in the living room, I assumed that was all the books he owned. Boy, was my ass wrong. Going by the looks of it, there were at least another several hundred in here. I stared in awe. It was like a freaking dream. The only books I personally owned were a handful of signed special editions that Seth had gotten me a few years ago as a high school graduation present.

I scanned the shelves, memorizing the individual authors, titles, and the different spines. There were framed artworks scattered along the various shelves, each no bigger than a small sheet of paper. Some were fantasy scenes, others were animals or abstract pieces. Each one I had a feeling he had painted himself. One in particular caught my eye. I had to reach a few shelves above me, pushing up onto the tips of my toes. I leaned against the bookcase to keep my balance.

It was within my grasp when I heard the front door open. I lost my balance and fell backward, bringing half of the bookshelf down with me.

"Oof!"

Footsteps started toward Seth's room.

No point in hiding the fact I was in here. He probably heard me.

I sighed and pushed myself up. I heard his footsteps stop at his bedroom entryway and turned to send him an apologetic smile.

Only...

It wasn't Seth.

CHAPTER TEN

Seth

I spat out my coffee, spraying it all over the barista on the other side of the coffee bar Libby and I sat at. That earned me a death glare from the pink-haired pixie behind the counter. And bellowing bat of laughter from Libby leaving her snorting and clutching her stomach.

"Why? Why would you think I'd need to know that, Lib?" I held back a gag. I loved my friends but...I did not need to know their sex lives. Libby, on the other hand, as innocent as she seemed, often had zero filter and laid it all out on the table. It was not something I wanted to picture. Her and Derik.

"Oh my God, Seth. Take a chill pill," she laughed. "Me and Derik haven't actually done anything. He won't make a move and I can't take it. He's just so scrumptious and I could climb him like a freaking tree. The pure muscle on that man. Partnered with that dirty blonde hair of his? Gah!" She started fanning herself with her hand. "He's like right out of a damn dream."

I pinched the bridge of my nose. "Is this really what you wanted to talk about? Don't you have any girlfriends you can talk about guys with? Ya know, ramble on about your sexual frustration to them?"

Hearing about another guy's dick size or the hots you have for him is the last thing I want to hear right now. Let alone, the guy who's like a brother to me.

She pushed her bottom lip out, pouting. "Seth," Libby whined. "You know I have like zero friends outside of you guys. I don't have the time for it, and they wouldn't understand. Especially with the gag order and not being able to tell people what we are, remember?" She sighed and hunched forward in her stool.

True. If we told humans about the dangers that were truly around them, they would flip and the world would fall into pure chaos.

I rolled my eyes. "Yeah, you have a point but I'm sure you could make it work." Libby was always a magnet for women and men alike. Partially because of her looks but also because she was a beaming ray of sunshine. To the point where it could become overbearing. I tried to be positive, but she was on a whole other level. I sipped what remained of my coffee. "But what did you really drag me out here for?"

Libby fidgeted with her coffee cup, either trying to gather her thoughts or avoiding what she wanted to bring up. Which only meant it was probably another subject I wanted to avoid thinking about.

I grumbled, "Just spit it out, Lib."

She sucked in a breath. "I..."—she shot a glance at me before looking away—"I'm worried. About the increase in Demon activity, especially with the fire at Riverside and the disappearances. We still haven't found anything and it's been a few days since it all went down. We're usually quicker on these things...but I'm worried about you too." Libby's eyes met mine, searching.

I feigned ignorance. "I don't know what you mean. Josh, Derik, and the others are working on it, and I'm picking up the loose ends."

Or trying to, at least.

"You do realize I know you better than that. And so does Derik. What's really going on, Seth? Let us in." Libby rested her hand on my shoulder.

"Lib, I don't know." I shrugged her off and crossed my arms, leaning against the coffee bar. She waited. Her wide-eyed stare bore into my flesh. I caved. "I just...I'm scared. She's new to this world. And...I couldn't protect her last time. What if it happens again? I...I can't lose her, Lib. We don't even know what she's capable of. I haven't had any inclination from any of the guides, not even Nicolai." I buried my face in my hands.

"So does this mean you're finally being honest with yourself? About her?"

I didn't respond. My lips pressed together.

"I'll take that as a 'yes' then," Libby said. "Seth, she's going to be okay. She just started experiencing all of this. Give it time. Have some faith in the girl. She's got some serious fire. And as for the guides, you know they always have a stick up their buttcheeks. The only one with any heart or fraction of giving an honest damn about being blunt and to the point, is Nicolai. So if he hasn't visited you or said anything then either he doesn't know or he's been gag-ordered about it."

"You're probably right."

"Excuse me, I'm always right. Thank you very much," Libby retorted, back to her typical bubbly tone. "So, until we hear anything, stop being such a party pooper. *Maybe* take that chill pill I mentioned and let some things play out." She winked.

"I'm always chill, Lib. And on the other subject, she's never so much as glanced at me in that way. I don't see anything happening there and I don't plan on ruining anything or putting her in danger. You know how these things go: Demons discover who's important to us and they become targets. She's already got one on her back with being Nephilim. I don't want to make it bigger."

"I get that, but you don't have to play savior all the time, Seth. You deserve to be happy, too," her eyes softened. "Take a chance. It just might be worth it."

Maybe Libby's right. But even beyond the risks...she deserves better than me...better than what I could offer her. She deserves the world. She—

A tingle raced up my spine, sending chills down my arms and the blood in my veins turned to ice. A panic began eating its way through me.

Something's wrong.

"Libby. Libby. Something's not right." I frantically looked around the coffee shop, searching for the cause. And found nothing. I focused on my heightened hearing and sense of smell to see if I could pick anything up. Nothing.

It's just the two of us. I can't pick up any Demons.

A cold sweat dripped down my face, my hands suddenly clammy. I stood up, sending the stool I was just in crashing to the floor.

"We need to go. *Now.*" I yanked Libby's arm, and we ran out of the coffee shop.

We ran at a faster-than-should-be-humanly-possible speed. There was no time to be concerned with passersby seeing us. My breathing grew shallow. Shades of black and cream blurred images darted in and out of my peripheral vision.

Shit.

I felt a tug. It was as if a string were attached to the muscle that pounded within my chest.

"The house." Realization dawned on me.

Erin.

A growl ripped from my throat.

Libby must have reached the same conclusion. We were both sprinted at full force, the lactic acid building.

Erin, please. No. No. No.

They couldn't have found her. Not this soon.

We turned the corner onto my deserted street. The panic welled through my entire being. We bounded up the stairs to my front door. It was flung open. The living room was trashed. Streaks of black scorched the walls, fractals spread in every direction. Libby took to searching the living room, weight area, kitchen, and guest room. I followed the black marks, leading me back to my bedroom. I stood frozen in the door frame.

In front of me, the room that had once been was gone. Fractals covered the floors and walls. Scorch marks, singed fabrics, pillows that continued to burn, and books were scattered throughout the room. Blood splattered along the walls.

No.

I fell to my knees.

Libby gasped behind me.

My worst fear had come to life.

"She's gone."

This is all my fault.

Chapter Eleven

Seth

She was *gone*.

And it was my fault. If I had been there, they wouldn't have taken her. I could've protected her. Fought them off. Destroyed the Demon or Demons that no doubt had her and were probably going to torture her if she wasn't already dead.

"Seth, I know what you're thinking but she's not dead. Not yet, at least," Libby said, crouched in front of one of the destroyed bookshelves. "It looks like they snuck up on her. There's a painting over here with a few bloody fingerprints on it."

Libby brought it over to where I sat on my knees, dumbfounded, on the floor. She shoved it into my hand, my gaze dragging to the painting. Erin. Or rather, a painting I had made of her. I made it after she moved out here for college. She had the biggest smile on her face. Feeling especially accomplished after our first successful run together. The image was etched into my brain: Erin was covered in sweat. Her hair had fallen out of its ponytail, sticking to her forehead and neck. The black leggings that she gravitated toward had been hiked halfway up her legs, bunching behind her knees, and her sweat-soaked T-shirt had been thrown off and wrapped around her wrist. Her eyeliner smudged and the biggest, brightest smile covered her face. Grinning ear to ear.

That was Erin.

It had been one of the rare moments where she had been most herself since her dad disappeared. Not the watered-down, put on a brave face, shadow of herself she had been. My heart swelled back then, with admiration. The memory, the painting of it, caused my heart to tightened.

"Lib, we have to find her," I said, eyes glued to the painting in my hand. I felt her body grow still next to me. The bloodied books, wrecked pillows, and shredded paintings began to hum. I dragged my eyes away from the painting in my hand, forcing my focus to where Libby sat beside me. The hum became louder as the objects began to swirl around the room, forming a crimson-soaked funnel, encasing us within it. Libby's fingers clawed the floor beneath us, her mouth forced open as a scream ripped from her. Her back arched, throwing her head back. If she were solely human, her spine would've broken. Her scream filled the room, the ground shook, the windows above what remained of my bookshelves shattered. She collapsed, and the last of her screams left her body. My stomach churned.

The more violent her reaction...the more violent the encounter.
Erin, where did the Demons take you?

Libby's eyes shot open and darkened with fear. "I found it," she inhaled sharply. "I know who has her."

Derik bolted through my front door. A roaring flame blazed within the depths of his eyes. Pure anger encapsulated his features. The blonde strands that staggered at the edges of his face were disheveled as if his anger had embodied itself even to the tips of his hair.

"What the *fuck happened?* Who the *fuck* took her?" His nostrils flared as his body shook.

The searing cold that ensnared me the moment Libby discovered who had taken Erin, met the fire in Derik's eyes. Encouraging the need for bloodshed building within myself. Although Erin had a disdain for Derik, he cared for her and cared for his fellow Nephilim. We were the only family either of us had. We were brothers. That meant we would protect each other...as well as those we held close, no matter how *not* close they may be. I would burn the world to find Erin. And he would be right by my side, both of us taking down anyone who stood in our way.

Ice filled my veins as Libby said the name neither of us wanted to hear, "Erebus."

Derik paled, his pupils dilated with fear. I was willing to bet the same memories that plagued my mind went through his as well. It was the day we met. A group of Demons had stampeded through a large city, destroying homes, burning them to the ground, murdering tens of innocent humans, and kidnapping others.

It was the day Derik had lost everything.

We raced between each house. Nothing but embers remained. Nicholas, my right-hand man, followed behind me. No one was left alive. We were too late. All the humans were dead. Shredded and burned beyond recognition. Traces of the Demons who had caused this chaos covered the block.

"Keep searching. There has to be some sign—some sign of where they took the ones they didn't kill." Nicholas growled before he darted out to the buildings we hadn't yet searched, unsheathing his dagger he'd nicknamed Lucky Blade. He never went anywhere without it.

We'd been hunting in our territory when we caught word of the slaughter and had made it out as fast as we could. We were too late.

All these innocents. Dead. Because I couldn't get here in time.

A fire built within me.

There has to be someone. At least one had to have survived. Please. God.

For the love of humanity. We need to find survivors.

I neared the final lot, not even the frame of the home remained. Shattered glass covered the blackened yard. The large oak near the front was scorched, leaves still aflame. Bile climbed its way up my throat. A single rope still dangled from the lowest branch, the swing that had been attached now gone. I slowed, carefully stepping around the bits of leaves and debris scattered around me.

Coming to a stop on the pebbled walkway that would've taken me right up to the entrance, I gulped. A hollowness enveloped me, drowning me. Crackling thundered in my ears, followed by the echoing of the people who had been slaughtered. Their lives taken from them far too soon. Screaming.

I failed.

I failed these innocent people.

Screaming. Someone was screaming. I snapped my head in the direction it was coming from. I bolted through the ashes toward the back of the lot. Another tree had caught fire and collapsed. There were legs sticking out from underneath it, soaked in blood.

"Help! Someone help! Please!" It was a male voice. Strained, muffled. I catapulted myself over the three-foot thick bark and landed beside two humans. The screams turned into sobs. Continuing to beg for help.

"I'm going to try and move the trunk off of you. You need to trust me. We'll get you out of here." I braced my hands against the brunt of the tree and urged as much strength as I could to push it forward. If they hadn't been so close to the base, I would have been able to lift the tree off of them instead of risking crushing their legs further.

Come on.

Please.

Nicholas came running as I made my final push, releasing both humans from its weight. "Holy shit."

I followed his line of sight, landing on the person next to the male who sobbed. His cries echoed, filling the destroyed town. The growing puddle of blood that I'd seen soaking their legs hadn't been coming from him. Next to the male...was a human body that had been completely flattened. Skull caved in, dark curls sprawled behind it. Crimson stained the ground around them. Pieces of flesh splattered. Bones poked out and then shattered, completely crushed. The only thing that tore me away was the male whose sobbing had morphed into a howl. Mourning his loss. I turned my head, meeting the males muddled brown eyes that screamed *it should've been me.*

Nicholas picked the male up. His legs were broken and he had a few scrapes here and there, but the rest of him seemingly intact. None of the blood had come from him.

No human would have survived that.

"What's your name?" Nicholas asked.

"I..."—the male choked back painful sobs as he tried to explain—"my name's Derik. And...That was my sister. We ran...I tried to save her but...they dropped it on us. Those people. Things dropped that tree on us...I couldn't save her. I couldn't save them."

The air in my lungs constricted, a lump forming in my throat.

A laugh cackled behind us. Nicholas and I swung around to find a Demon. Onyx black, hell-spiked wings jutted from his back. Flame orange hair fell down his back and his hollow white eyes sized up his prey. Us.

"I see you managed to find this one," the Demon settled his hollow gaze on Derik. "Pity really." He flashed a pointed smile. "She was such a pretty one." Hunger flickered across the narrowed irises of his eyes.

I stepped in front of Nicholas and Derik. "Who the fuck are you?"

"Ah, who am I?" The Demon waved his hand in the air, sending a wind slicing through the air and onto our exposed skin along our arms and faces. "I am the one whom you should fear most. I am the darkness. I am the embodiment of your worst fears, dear boy"—he paused, lifting his chin—"I am Erebus. The Son of Chaos." A chill scraped down my spine. Erebus smirked, as if he knew exactly the effect he had. "Not that my explanation will be of much use to the three of you. As you'll soon be dead."

Within a split second, Erebus lunged forward, fingers tipped with claws, mere inches from me. The next thing I knew, I had been pushed to the side. My shoulder slammed into the ground as Nicholas took my place, lodging Lucky Blade into Erebus's chest right as his claws raked Nicholas's throat. Erebus hissed, clutching at his gushing chest and disappeared, a promise of our death in his eyes. Nicholas collapsed to the ground with his hand clutching the deep wounds across his throat.

"Told you, Lucky Blade," he gurgled, blood spewed from his neck. I pulled him into me.

Tears streamed down my face. "Damn right, you ballsy asshole." He smiled up at me. The blood coated his teeth.

"Always got your back, Seth," he sucked in a ragged breath. "Take care of this kid. You saved 'em, Seth. You did good. You got one. One less person died today because of your ass"—he placed his hand on my arm—"Now stop that crying, so it isn't the last damned thing I see." I half laughed, forcing the tears to hold for just a moment. "Atta boy." Nicholas closed his eyes and released the last bit of air from his lungs.

It should've been me.

I shook my head, urging the memory away. My mouth formed a tight line as I closed my eyes and pushed a breath out through my nose. The news channels later reported it as a manslaughter by a group of bandits. It had been a close call on the existence of Nephilim and Demons alike being exposed to the otherwise ignorance of the human race.

I channeled the ice-cold fury, the fear, the pain that bubbled to the surface. "We need a plan," my eyes opened slowly, locking them once again with Derik's. "Erebus signed his death wish. The second I find his sorry ass, he's done for." Derik's jaw clenched.

Josh took that as his queue to stroll in. "Well, well, gentlemen"—he nodded to Libby—"and Miss Libby, let's get this hunt started. You might need a location for where we're to find Miss Snow." He smirked and slapped a scrap of paper onto the kitchen counter. A single word scribbled on it.

Riverside.

Chapter Twelve

Seth

My breath caught.

Riverside.

Erebus took her to Riverside.

I smashed my fist into the counter, sending the damned scrap of paper careening through the air and pieces of granite crumbling to the floor. "Son of a fucking bitch."

Josh tsked. The fucker. "I would save that rage for when we find exactly where in Riverside they are keeping her, Seth. There's no point in wasting our energy on outbursts. You need to use that thick head of yours if we're to retrieve Miss Snow unharmed, I imagine."

I glared at him. Although what he said was true, Josh's pretentious tone did nothing but deepen the burning rage coursing through me. My body trembled, searching for an outlet.

The corner of Josh's mouth tipped slightly upward. He knew he got under my skin.

Derik squeezed my shoulder, probably to distract me from clocking Josh upside the head. "He has a point, Seth. We need to be level-headed about this. We don't know what their plans are or why they took Erin," his dark eyes pierced mine, knowingly. "And...they might have the people who went missing."

The color that had returned to my complexion in my fury paled once again. My jaw tensed, the vein in my neck straining against my skin.

Fuck.

I shook Derik's hand off of me as I swiveled my head back toward Josh. "How do we know that's where they took her?"

"After Miss Libby called, I took it upon myself to hunt down my informant," his cold eyes gleamed with satisfaction. "Took a bit longer than it should have to retrieve the information out of him, but he was able to scratch it onto...that paper for me. After some...negotiating, of course."

Meaning you blinded them and tortured them until you got what you wanted out of them.

I crossed my arms over my chest. "Are you sure that it's accurate?" I shifted my stance, squaring my shoulders. Josh returned my glare, clearly agitated that I doubted his talents. For a good reason, too. There had been several instances where lesser Demons, the lackeys, had binds placed on them that would keep them from spilling information, no matter how much power Josh threw at them.

Far too many lives were lost because of it.

And I wasn't about to allow that to happen again with so many of them on the line. Including Erin's.

Josh slipped his hands into his front pants pockets, rolling his shoulders back, suddenly the perfect picture of nonchalance. "Well, of course, Seth. I wouldn't dare risk taking a chance with Miss Snow's safety." The look he gave me read loud and clear, *unlike you.*

I nodded, as if I hadn't registered the jab. "Fine," I turned to Libby. "We need a plan. Can you and Josh run back through what he gathered?" Libby glanced sideways at Josh, forming a smile, not quite reaching her eyes.

"Of course!" She chirped and moved to stand with him. She lifted her hands, palms up. Josh placed his hands in hers. As her head snapped backward, her eyes glazed over, fading from their usual emerald green to a ghostly white. Libby's gift was far more tame when she replayed a person's memories through them versus what an affected environment had taken in, but watching Libby use her ability was always intense.

She gasped, bringing herself out of the vision of the past. Her eyelids fluttered, returning her irises to their normal shade of green. She stared at Josh a moment, then faced Derik and me. "What Josh gathered was as helpful as it was going to get. They have Erin at Riverside, in one of the abandoned factories up in the mountains. There's no telling if the others that went missing are there, but Erin is. At least...last the Demon was aware," she glanced over her shoulder at Josh and he nodded, his face vaguely grim. "It might...be their headquarters. Josh gathered from his intel that it's pretty guarded and...that she'll be dead before we would even find it." It was like a knife was plunged through my heart and wrenched downward right into my gut. Libby shot me a pained look.

They're going to kill her.

I swallowed the budding suffocation. Ice-cold hatred saturating my very core, injecting itself into my tongue. "Then we make it before she's dead." My footsteps thundered as I stormed toward the locked closet beside my kitchen pantry. I aggressively plunged my lock pin into the tiny hole in the center of the iron door handle and wrenched the door open. Reaching in, I pushed down on the top shelf, causing the closet's back wall to shift backward and slide to the right, revealing my weapon room. Various swords, knives, daggers, and switchblades lined the walls. Even a few claw-shaped blades. In the center of the room stood a long island of sorts, stocked with fighting gear, all lined with blade-resistant fabric.

It had been passed down to me from Nicholas. He'd been the only family I knew after my mom had passed. He took me in, trained me, taught me everything I knew. He was the closest thing to a father figure I ever had. Nicholas had taken me in when I was a teenager, claiming he was my long-lost uncle on my mom's side. Turned out...he was so much more. As my strength flourished, he gave me the reigns and I became the leader around here, he was my second in command. And then...Erebus took him from me, ripped the only person in my life I didn't have to hide myself from, away from me. The only thing I had left of him was the vast weaponry collection he attained over his long three centuries fighting Demons. A collection I refused to allow them to get their grubby, murderous hands on.

Libby and Derik followed me through the threshold and beelined for the daggers. They each had their own weapons at home in case of an emergency, but they both had a few they favored here. Derik leaned toward an elongated silver dagger with an onyx hilt, engraved with serpents along the edges and a single jade gemstone embedded in the center. Libby gravitated toward a pair of twin blades, handles coated in gold, the daggers themselves silver.

I reached for my harness, shrugging it over my shirt. Turning, I walked to the far corner and pulled a sword from the wall. The blade was made of high-carbon steel, handcrafted by one of Nicholas's old friends about a century before he was murdered. The blade was black as night and sharp enough to slice clean through the neck of a Demon. I sheathed it into the harness on my back then grabbed a couple of fighting knives, fastening one to each of my hips.

We each pulled black leather arm guards from the island. Libby and Derik slipped on their blade-resistant long sleeve jackets, designed to be form-fitting to keep our torsos and arms protected while also being able to move freely during battle. Josh came up and grabbed one as well. We fastened the arm guards and rechecked each of our weapons, making sure they were secured and ready to be drawn at a moment's notice. I looked at Libby, then Josh, and finally, Derik. We nodded to one another.

"Let's go."

We're coming, Erin.

We raced to Riverside. Once we reached the outskirts of the town, we began trekking up into the forested mountains on foot, avoiding the extra attention driving any of our vehicles would draw. We kept to the shadows, listening; our senses on high alert.

The sun dipped below the horizon by the time we spotted what I hoped was the abandoned factory we were searching for, nestled atop the mountain ridge ahead of us, the roof barely visible from where we stood. The light provided by the moon was our only guiding light. Even with heightened vision, it was damned difficult to see through the dense forest.

Derik threw his arm out, stopping us in our tracks. I scanned the trees around us, searching for whatever set him off. I heard a branch snap then a thud behind me. I whipped around, coming face to face with a Demon.

Its face wasn't visible except for a bloody grin spanning the full width of its head. Razor sharp teeth glinted in the moonlight as its yellow eyes shot open, pupils absent. The Demon stepped closer and his full frame became visible. Jagged crimson wings spread from his hunched back, hands spread wide as they transformed into claws ready for the kill, each one extending several inches beyond the tips of his fingers. The Demon menacingly licked his lips and howled, lunging forward and aiming for whoever was closest. And right then, that was Libby.

She stepped back, luring the Demon in before she launched her daggers upward, landing them right through the Demon's neck. Black blood spurted erratically from the lacerations. She yanked the blades out, the Demon began choking on the tar pouring from its wound. He grabbed for his throat, trying to stop the blood. And in its panic, it must've forgotten about its claws as they dug into the gashes, opening them further. The Demon shot his ochre sockets in Libby's direction and lunged again, catching Libby in the stomach with one of his claws.

I hurled my body into the Demon's side, sending him flying into the trunk of a tree. I pulled one of the blades from my hip and rammed it into his chest, right through to his black heart. Tendrils of fear seeped into the yellow of the Demon's eyes as the reality of its death became apparent. I pulled it back out, the blade scraping against his chest cavity, and shoved it back through his neck. For good measure, I withdrew the blade once more, the corner of my mouth twitching, and sliced it clean through what remained of its throat, sending the head falling to the ground. I resheathed my blade, my chest heaving with adrenaline. There was coughing behind me.

Libby.

I jogged back to where Derik held Libby up by her elbow. She was crouched on the ground, clutching her stomach as blood coated her fingers. Derik's eyes met mine, jaw tight, concern rippled across his face. I knelt down in front of Libby. "How bad is it?"

"He got her pretty good. Went right through her gear and into her stomach. I got most of it closed and she should be good by the time we make it up to the factory." Derik pressed his lips into a thin line, helping Libby stand with his grip tight around her arm.

"Are you sure you're good enough to keep going?"

She shouldn't be bleeding this much. Not between Derik's ability and the rapid recovery time from being Nephilim.

"I'll be fine. We need to go." Libby grunted as Derik slipped his arm around her waist, offering her support. She slung her arm around his neck, leaning into him. I gave everyone a quick once-over before we continued our trek upwards through the dense woods and toward the flattened peak of the mountain.

We neared the top, evading any additional Demon run-ins the remainder of the hike. The abandoned building finally in sight. Parts of the roof were caved in, piles of rubble scattered the leveled plot of land, broken windows lined what remained of the outer walls. A massive security fence outlined the perimeter, the only thing not run down or wrecked. In the center of the metal coils, was a single gap, wide enough for us to sneak through.

As we drew nearer, I pulled my sword from my back, bringing it to my side slightly angled as we stalked toward the abandoned building. The others followed suit. Derik clutched his onyx-handled dagger, and Libby drew her gold-plated twin daggers. Josh played lookout, searching for any Demons who may have been lurking on the hunt for their next victims.

I slipped through the opening first, sword at the ready, and scanned the inner perimeter. Libby and Derik followed quickly behind; Josh pulled up the rear. I crouched down as I inched forward until I came to a stop behind several large piles of rubble. I signaled for the group to follow me.

A slight breeze snaked its way across the nape of my neck, chilling the sweat slicked against my skin. A shiver shot down my spine. I swung my arm out, stopping Libby and Derik in their tracks. "Something's not right. There should be Demons out here patrolling. They never leave their shit unguarded."

Libby stiffened next to me.

"Move!" Josh shouted, pushing us out of the way. A massive burst of fire erupted into the ground where we'd been hiding, shrouding us in a blanket of dirt and cement debris. Josh had landed on Libby and Derik, taking the brunt of the forceful blast. I, on the other hand, had pricks of pain along the backs of my legs. I rolled onto my back and pushed myself onto my elbows, taking in the fit of flame still licking the ground. "Holy shit."

I heard Josh grumble, his voice muffled by Derik's shoulder. Libby took that moment to wiggle herself out from under the two of them. She pulled herself into a sitting position and dusted some of the dirt off her fighting gear. Derik grunted and knocked Josh off his back. "Fuck me, dude. What the hell just happened?" He shook his head, utterly pissed.

"They know we're here. That's what happened," Libby said, her voice on edge and expression grim.

"That's why we only ran into one Demon hiking up here," I whispered as I mentally chastised myself for not suspecting the mostly quiet hike to their territory. There should've been more out there. My eyes widened, and a sudden realization hit me. "It's a trap."

Leaves crunched behind me. "Well, well, well. Look who we have here." A macabre sneer sent chills down my spine.

I whipped my head around and launched myself upward onto my feet, arm shooting for my sword. Derik and Libby scrambled to their feet on my left. Josh readied to my right.

"You seem to have finally arrived. Your friend has been waiting for you. Well, she was." They cackled.

I felt my face pale and then a throbbing pain encapsulated my skull, snaking its way through my body. And everything went black. The last visible thing as my vision disappeared was the Demon who stood before us. Smiling.

Erebus.

CHAPTER THIRTEEN

Seth

My head was pounding like I had the worst hangover of my life. I blinked my eyes open and squinted as my vision cleared. Confusion hit. "Leave them the hell alone," a woman growled. The sound ransacking the frozen pain that had a vice grip on my chest.

Erin.

My eyes frantically darted around what looked like a medieval throne room. A whip sounded, catching my attention and bringing it directly to where Erin half hung-half stood at the front of the room. Her wrists bound in rope, spread above her head. Her ankles chained to the stone floor. The shirt she wore was shredded, exposing her stomach, shoulders, and chest, with barely a scrap of fabric covering her breasts. The black leggings she had worn were in pieces on the ground next to her. There were lacerations up and down her arms, whip marks across her abdomen and thighs. A single large gash sliced above her breasts. Her steel blue eyes were lit with fire, determined. The Demon, one of Erebus's lackeys, pulled their whip back once more. It cracked, biting her in her side. She bit down, clenching her jaw shut, her eyes locked with mine. I attempted to catapult myself toward her, only to be yanked back by chains anchoring me to where I knelt. Sweat coated her forehead, mingling with the dried blood stuck to her skin. Fury filled my body.

What did he do to you?

The Demon looped the whip around itself, resting it under his arm, and stepped back. Allowing Erebus to make his appearance. He sauntered into the throne room, arms resting behind his back, chest puffed, flaming hair swept back, and wings tucked in. He swept his yellow gaze between myself and Erin. Erebus chuckled, moving in and positioning himself behind where Erin hung. My gut twisted.

"Get the *fuck* away from her, you piece of shit," I growled.

An eerie smile spread across his face, flashing his pointed teeth. His tongue jutted out, he slowly leaned forward sliding it up and down the side of her neck. Then, the son of a bitch snaked his way upward and along her jaw to the opposite side, caressing her chin with the ashen purple-hued organ, his pupils laughing as he taunted me.

"Lovely, isn't she?" Erebus flicked his tongue. "And she tastes just as delicious as she looks." His tongue began to slip lower and fire erupted, engulfing Erin's body. Erebus jolted back, hissing as one of his wings caught fire. I peered closer. Her eyes turned a burning red, matching the flames...emanating from her body.

"How. Dare. You." Erebus snarled as he gathered himself, snatched the whip from the other Demon and struck Erin smack dab in the center of her throat, the whip wrapping itself around it. He yanked the handle back, snapping Erin's head to the side and her flames extinguished. Her eyes glazed over, returning to their slate blue before closing as her head flopped forward. Her body went limp.

My chest heaved.

No.

My lungs burned as her name fell from my lips.

"Rin."

Chapter Fourteen

Erin

I turned around and a hulking beast of a man stood in the doorway to Seth's bedroom. Darkness and all things that should send me screaming in the opposite direction—besides the fact that my stunned ass was currently propped on the floor, legs tucked under myself in the least intimidating position possible—shrouded the guy. Was that what people meant when they mentioned an 'aura' about someone? If so, I never wanted to see one again because the shit is fucking intimidating.

"Uh, hi. Can I help you?" Annoyance laced my voice.

Be polite, Erin. Play this right.

I cleared my throat. "Are you one of Seth's friends? He's out right now. I didn't realize anyone was coming over."

Shut up shut up shut up. Be polite, not give the guy a run down of the fact that you're here all alone, dumbass.

The man smirked, revealing pointed teeth.

Shit. Well, that can't be normal.

"Oh, he was not expecting a visit from me, dear, I assure you." A chill snaked its way down my spine.

"Who are you?" My voice surprisingly steady. I moved to a crouched position and edged myself backward, reaching for anything sharp, heavy. I backed into one of the loungers in front of Seth's bookcases and my fingers graced the spine of a book tucked underneath it. It was thick. And therefore—praying to whoever listened—heavy.

He inched closer, seeming to glide along the floor, hands shoved in the pockets of his jeans. "I'm an old friend of sorts. I've come to collect something important. Or rather, someone." He chuckled, and a pair of onyx black wings tipped with spikes sprouted from behind him. My jaw fell open. He cocked his head to the side, his smirk widening. Spindles of his flame kissed hair fell over his shoulder. Yellow eyes now stared me down. As if he were a predator and I was his prey. "You may call me Erebus, Erin Snow."

I chucked the hardbound book, landing it flat against his chest, then thudding to the ground. Irritation rippled through him and he lunged. He drew his arm back, claws ripping from his jeans. Aiming directly for my throat. He landed his mark, my neck clenched within his grasp. I struggled for breath, sucking in what I could as his grip tightened. He laughed, the sound reverberated along his arm and to where he held me in midair. My breath left me. I shut my eyes, scratching at his hand around my throat. I kicked outward, knocking him in the center of his chest. Nothing. No effect.

To all hell, what the fuck was the point of getting stronger with this whole Nephilim thing if kicking this dickwad in the chest isn't going to do shit?

"Open your eyes for me, dearest. I want you to see me as you slowly fade." I squeezed my eyes together harder.

I need to do something. Anything.

I thought back to the day before, when electricity jumped from my fingertips, then the dream I had.

There has to be a way for me to conjure it.

I dove deep. I sucked in what breath I could, then searched inward. Smoke flickered behind my lids.

There.

I imagined myself reaching for it. Grabbed it and tucked it into myself. My eyes snapped open, and I released it. But instead of my lightning, there were flames. I flicked my eyes to Erebus, cracking a strained cocky smirk of my own. I shot the flame outward, nailing him in the face. He yanked his claws back, dropping me to the ground. I landed square on my ass and scrambled back to my feet, slightly crouching into a defensive position. My flames danced in the palms of my hands, begging to be used. I shot them out again, hitting Erebus in one of his wings, then the other. He roared, shaking his head side to side, trying to dissipate the fire that engulfed his head, matching the hair that slowly burned. I took the distraction as my opportunity to dodge around him and sprint toward the living room and out the door.

I bolted out of the bedroom, throwing a look over my shoulder to see if my newfound flame still held, as well as another ball of fire, aimed directly for his ass for good measure. And ran right into solid rock. I stumbled back, my gaze trailed upward. Standing above me was another not-human-but-not-sure-what-the-hell-he-was seven-foot or more brute. Black hair shaved short on the sides, a raised, red, welted scar through his left eye, the corners of his mouth turned downward, in a scowl. He jutted his arm out toward me. I called my flame up and braced myself to fight. He stopped. Flexed his hand open, his claws extended.

A black smoke floated away from his hand. His mouth formed a loose 'o' and blew the thick vapor at me. My mind became foggy as a wave of confusion fell over me.

"Sleep."

I'd woken up chained and dangling from some stone-clad ceiling. I took in the room around me. The walls followed the same theme as the ceiling, built entirely out of stone. Decorated with iron shields along the stone, marigold-stained fabric draped in between. Hues of purple accented each piece. Flails, morning stars, and a variety of other weapons dotted the spots in between. Out of the corner of my eye, I caught a glimpse of a throne—a literal fucking throne—all decked out in the same yellows and purples that decorated the rest of the room. I huffed and rolled my eyes. Clearly someone spent too much time at the renaissance fair.

Where the hell am I? The thirteenth century?

Someone snapped their fingers, gaining my attention.

"Ah, Erin Snow, you're finally awake. Here I began to worry that you might need some rousing. Well, maybe *worried* isn't the right word." The rimy statement dug its claws into my flesh. My narrowed gaze found the man attached to the vomit-inducing voice. He ran a grayish-purple tongue along his thin lips. I racked my brain trying to recall where I recognized the spawn-from-hell looking guy. My memory felt hazed. "You're probably still feeling the effects of Asier's *talents.*" He spread his mouth into a bone chilling grin. Dread pooled in my stomach.

Oh no.

"Erebus," I whispered.

Erebus threw his head back and laughed. "Not so slow after all!" He clapped. "A gold star for the little Nephilim."

I shot him a glare and flicked my wrist as best as I could in the shackles that bound my wrists. I dove inward until I found what I was searching for. I pulled on the tethers of my lightning and shot a couple bolts at his feet, missing by a few inches.

Erebus scowled. "Now, that wasn't very polite, Erin Snow. You should mind your manners."

"Oh, bite me, you hell-spawned dick with wings." I spat at him and sent another spark flying toward him.

He growled, managing to catch it in his hand like he was Zeus for fucks sake. It dissipated. Vanished.

What the actual fuck?

"What the hell are you? And what do you want with me?" I demanded, gritting my teeth.

He glided forward, stopping inches from the tips of my breasts. His yellow eyes licked their way up to my face, causing me to squirm in my shackles, a cold sweat broke out along the nape of my neck. Erebus lifted a single clawed finger to my chin, lifting it slightly, assessing my pale, exposed skin.

I gulped.

His pupils dialed in on the movement. "I, little Nephilim, am your worst nightmare," the pointed smile returned, spreading across his face. "For I am Erebus. One of the mightiest Demons from Hell." He swooped his wings outward in emphasis, a cloud of orange and red puffed around us. Erebus pulled my chin downward, his eyes pierced mine, holding me. "And you"—he closed his eyes and took a deep breath as if he were inhaling the fear that no doubt emanated from my body—"are The Key."

I furrowed my brows. "Key? Key to what, dude? Do I look like a small chunk of brass you could shove into a door? Have you lost your marbles?"

He licked his lips again. As his tongue neared the corner of his mouth, he flicked it, tapping my lower lip.

Pure anger filled me.

Son of a bitch.

A quick flash back to the break-in from my teenage years danced around the edges of my vision. His mouth widened in satisfaction. He lapped at me again. This time when his grey-slug of an appendage brushed my lips, attempting to slither its way into my mouth, I loosened my lips, to allow entry. Then bit down as hard as I could, drawing what I assumed was the Demon's equivalent of blood and spat black sludge in his face.

Erebus hissed, lurching back. His fist barreled toward me.

I shut my eyes, expecting the hit to land in the dead center of my face. Instead, his claws extended and lashed straight through my T-shirt, slashing it open, and tearing bits of my bra. I felt the gooey warmth of blood as it pooled at the top of my breast. The pain was scorching. Tears threatened to fall. I clamped my mouth shut, forcing them back.

Not today, you fucking creep.

Erebus brought his crimson coated claws to his nostrils. Inhaling, his pupils rolled back. His snake of a tongue slipped out and lapped my blood off the tips, a guttural moan echoed off the stone walls. "Absolutely decadent."

I braced myself for him to creep closer again. Instead, he waved his fingers, claws retracted, and the brute from Seth's house, Asier, stepped forward with what looked like a bull whip in his hand. My eyes narrowed.

Motherfucker.

I squirmed in my restraints trying to worm myself free, yanking at my wrists and ankles. Only managing to further mangle myself in the process. The cuffs etched into my wrists, blood slowly seeped down my arms from the skin being rubbed raw. Asier readied his whip, bound in leather. Erebus stood to the side, bulging arms crossed over one another to rest on his puffed-out chest, shoulders rolled back. Devilish wings splayed behind him.

This fucker is going to enjoy this.

Asier jerked his arm back then snapped it forward, cracking the whip against my thigh, tearing away at my black gunk-covered leggings.

I clenched my jaw, forcing the scream building in my throat back down.

Do not give them the satisfaction.

Asier yanked the whip back again, cracking it against my other thigh, another strip of fabric snatched away with it. Twin gashes ignited with a burning pain where the whip had made contact with my bare flesh. Erebus grew smug, his fangs glinting in the light of the stoned room. The whip cracked again, lashing against my stomach. I gritted my teeth.

The next one landed on my arm, leading the whip to fully wrap itself around before it was yanked back, tearing my skin. Asier went for my legs again. And again. And again. Each time, I braced myself for the impact. Slowly pushing down the pain. Forcing myself to go numb, extracting my self mentally from the torture. I could feel the wind from the constant cracking of the whip prickling up and down my thighs, my torso. Hardly anything was left of my clothing.

Do not give them the satisfaction of seeing the pain.

I chanted over and over.

Do not cry. Do. Not. Cry.

The whipping eventually stopped; my mouth still clamped shut. I dragged my glossy eyes upward from my focus point on the blood-stained stone floor beneath me.

How is there any left inside me?

The thought drifted lazily, a fog nipped at the outer rim of my consciousness.

Erebus had drifted closer, once again stopping mere inches from me. His voice, sinister, crept along my skin, leaving goose bumps. "You seemed to have left us there for a moment, Little Nephilim.

Maybe we must ensure your punishment for biting me and misbehaving...another way."

My stomach dropped. A whimper escaped my lips. The corners of his mouth lifted, excitement lighting his eyes. I squeezed mine closed, begging.

Seth, Libby...Somebody please help me.

Flame danced behind my eyelids, forming itself into a ball. My brows furrowed together. Energy surged from it. It was searching.

An idea formed. And I imagined it hurtling through the air.

Please. Please.

A tear rolled down my cheek as I prayed that somehow, the flame I pictured was real and not my mind playing tricks on me. I had no idea why or what pushed me to do so but I imagined the flame finding them, warning them.

A gust of wind nipped at my bare flesh and I was suddenly alone.

Run.

But it dawned on me.

If...if they come...Erebus will torture them too.

He'll torture Derik...and Libby.

Seth.

And it would all be because of me.

A sob fell from my lips.

I choked as the air thickened, my watery eyes shot open. Erebus stood before me, his tongue flicked against my exposed stomach. Bile rose in my throat. He snickered and snaked his way downward. My pulse quickened. A wave of nausea coursed through my body.

No. No. No. No. No.

He stopped at the hem of my panties. I stifled a cry. His pupils narrowed. He brought one of his talons near my center, stroking it up and down my inner thigh. My body convulsed, drained from the lashings, the fear broke through to the surface. He snagged his claw along the edge of my panties and traced the hem. His tongue jutted out and flicked my center before plunging into my folds. I cried out, tears streaked my face, as he pumped it in and out of me.

No.

I felt something inside me break and screamed as Erebus delved deeper with each thrust of his tongue.

"Erebus." He stopped. Slowly pulling his tongue out of me. He turned to another Demon, who was panting, hands clutching his knees. "They're here."

Another bone chilling laugh echoed throughout the room. "Excellent. Bring them in," Erebus returned his attention back to me. "It seems...the others have arrived." I shook, my eyes widened in fear.

There's more of them coming.

They're going to rape me and kill me when they're finished with me.

I choked back another sob.

A wrought iron door groaned open on the opposite end of the room. A Demon, their skin matching various shades of blue, walked in, dragging three bodies behind them.

I squinted my already strained eyes to catch a glimpse of who was being dragged into this hell hole. I gasped. Seth, Libby, and Derik were all knocked out and chained together. A bead of hope flickered in my chest.

They came.

Immediately it extinguished. They were unconscious and now damned with me, stuck in this medieval torture chamber. And I could do nothing to help them.

The others have arrived.

Erebus's overly-excited voice replayed in my mind. He was expecting them.

I was his bait.

It was as if a knife had been thrust directly into my stomach.

This is all my fault.

The Demon that had dragged them in, yanked Libby and Derik toward the wall adjacent to where I was suspended and lumped them together. Libby had a patch of blood that stained her shirt around her middle. Derik seemed unscathed beyond being unconscious. Seth was dragged directly across from me. The Demon adjusted his shackles, linking the cuffs around his wrists to the chain encompassing his ankles, bolting him to the floor. He was slumped over on his side, a gash on his forehead steadily bled onto the stone floor, his shaggy onyx hair became matted with it. From where I hung, he didn't seem to be harmed anywhere else.

Okay, so nothing too serious. Yet.

I breathed. Until I caught sight of Erebus sauntering his way to Seth, another smaller Demon trailing behind him. It was about the height of a large dog. Short, maroon wings jutted out from its back, twitching as they neared Seth's unconscious body. The little Demon snapped its fingers and a small blade appeared in its hand. A lump lodged in my throat.

They're going to hurt him.

I have to do something.

Anything.

I swallowed the lump down and yelled with all the venom I could manage, attempting to keep my voice from shaking, knowing full well what I might be subjecting myself to again. "Hey shit brains!" I took a quick breath.

Better me than him.

"Was that all you got? Here I thought you were supposed to be some big bad Demon," I forced a cocky grin. "Clearly, you're all talk, asswipe." Erebus snapped his attention back to me. But not before kicking Seth in the stomach.

The Demon nearest Libby and Derik followed suit, nailing each of them in their middles, Libby in her unconscious state coughed up blood. I lurched forward in my suspended restraints. "Leave them the hell alone." I spat in Erebus's direction. He growled and motioned for Asier, before vanishing into thin air.

What the?

Asier stepped toward me, his whip cracked. Landing directly on my thigh once again.

I focused my line of sight on Seth. He began to stir. I gritted my teeth as another lash came barreling down on my flesh. The little Demon pushed Seth upward, so he was kneeling. Head tilted upward.

These sick fucks.

He blinked, his ocean blue eyes blurry and unfocused. They widened as he seemed to register where he was. I kept my eyes steady with his, the distraction a lifeline as I heard the whip crack again, biting me in my side. Seth thrashed in his chains, only to be yanked back. I could feel sweat as it coated my forehead. Seth panted heavily, eyes darting around the room.

Erebus took that moment to saunter back into the room. His hands clasped behind him as he strode in. He looked between me and Seth. He chuckled as he moved to stand behind me.

Seth growled, "Get the *fuck* away from her, you piece of shit." Fire rumbled in my veins.

I felt Erebus's slimy tongue jut out, tasting my neck. I held back the shivering that threatened to overtake my body and forced the images of moments prior to the back of my mind. Erebus snaked his tongue along my jaw, gripping my chin. "Lovely, isn't she?" His tongue flicked my jaw, a demonic purr rumbled with the movement. "And she tastes just as delicious as she looks."

His tongue began to slip lower, flames charged forward, enveloping me. I sent them racing outward toward Erebus, unleashing them onto his deviled wings.

Burn you son of a bitch.

Erebus jolted back, hissing. "How. Dare. You," he ground out. He snatched the whip from Asier, raised it, and landed a blow directly on my throat. The air left my lungs. My flame disappeared.

And everything went black.

Chapter Fifteen

Josh

I swore under my breath. "Move!" The flame that came barreling out of nowhere threw me off. I jumped out of the way, taking Derik and Miss Libby onto the dirt and demolished concrete with me. I narrowly avoided touching Miss Libby. My face pressed into Derik's shoulder. "Idiots, inconsolable idiots," I mumbled.

Miss Libby wriggled herself out from under us and sat upright, then proceeded to dust herself off. I rolled my eyes internally.

The child is nearly caught in a fireball and the first thing she focuses on is the muck dusting her clothing.

They were all children in comparison to my three hundred years. Derik moved beneath me, shoving upward, knocking me backward. "Fuck me, dude. What the hell just happened?" Derik groaned as he shook his thick skull.

"They know we're here. That's what happened," Libby said, her tone clipped.

I kept my facial expression neutral.

Bravo, what, dear Miss Libby, tipped you off?

I drowned out their brief and ever-enlightening conversation recapping and stating the undeniable. Seth finished off with the oh so obvious, "It's a trap." My ears peaked at the sound of leaves crunching beneath footfalls. I shielded myself from the group ahead of us, an illusion falling in place around my person. I was nothing and that would be what the others saw.

The Demon, Erebus, and a pack of his Demon lackeys swaggered forward and out of the shadows. "Well, well, well. Look who we have here." His teeth shone in the light coming off the flame continuing to burn behind us. I braced myself.

The Demons cackled. Out of the corner of my eye, Seth paled. I skirted backward as he collapsed. Derik and Miss Libby followed suit, each slumping atop one another.

The Demons who answered to Erebus, proceeded to wrap each of their wrists in shackles before doing the same to their ankles. Derik and Miss Libby were chained together while Seth was left to be chained alone. One with a greenish hue to its flesh flicked its tongue along the side of Miss Libby's face, leaving Erebus to claw at the Demon.

"Not the time. We'll have our fun later." The greenish hued Imp hissed, lifting Miss Libby and Derik over its shoulders. Another Demon threw Seth over its shoulder as well. The pack stalked back to the shadows from which they came. Erebus waited until they were into the darkness before turning in my direction. His pupils took in the flame. His reptilian tongue flicked outward, tasting the air. Then turned on his heel, following his Demons into the darkness.

I paused a moment, allowing a gap to form before trailing them, keeping myself hidden under the illusion of nothing. The Demons strode through heaps of rubble and after half a mile, had bypassed the abandoned factory. They entered a tunnel that had been hollowed into the mountain side. An obsidian archway marked the entrance. As the Demons made their way inside, torches mounted to the walls began to flicker, illuminating the tunnel.

I shortened the gap between us in fear of the flames dwindling out, for this was not a place I wanted to be without a sight line. I wound my way through the tunnels, seemingly never-ending, stealthily keeping pace with a few feet between myself, Erebus, and his lackeys.

The Demon, whose skin matched the sickening shade of vomit green, spoke, its voice reverberating off of the tunnel walls, "Sir, we're coming up to your palace."

"I will leave you to it then. I must tend to our other...guest." Erebus's voice oozed into the air flowing through the tunnel before he vanished with it.

The dirt walls expanded, clusters of pendant lights hung from the ceiling, taking the place of the torches that had lined the tunnel further behind. Grey-speckled white sandstone replaced the dirt walls. Marble slabs appeared underfoot. The Demons stopped in front of a wooden door that spanned the height of the sandstone walls. Iron arched atop the stained maple and down the center. The doors held shut by a single iron bar the length of a human man. Two of the Demons went forward, one to the end of the bar and began lifting it upward. The second, unlatched another smaller bolt that had been hidden behind the iron bar. The metal hinge groaned as the heavy wood slowly swung inward. The Demons filed into the room on the other side.

I stepped forward, narrowly avoiding being flattened between the behemoth-sized double doors. The theme from the tunnel's edge continued, marble slabs covering the floor. Sandstone decorating the walls. Not a speck of the dirt nor grime visible. The muck that had speckled the flesh of the Demons had disappeared. The sandstone was naked, lacking décor. No furniture in sight. I swept my gaze across the large hall. Floor to ceiling pillars erected at each corner, carved of a marble equivalent to the slabbed flooring. A single Persian rug ran the length of the room, beginning at the door through which we entered and leading to a smaller door, made entirely of iron steel. My attention shifted back to the group of Demons.

The one that had been carrying Seth, tossed his limp body to the floor. The Demon who'd been tasked with carrying Derik and Miss Libby tossed them as well. The three of them once again piled atop one another. Their breathing deep, in the midst of a Demon induced slumber. I folded my hands behind my back, further assessing them, watching. Derik and Seth didn't budge beyond the rise and fall of their chests. Miss Libby twitched incessantly, from the tips of her fingers to one of her slender legs that stuck out from beneath Derik. If it weren't for her Nephilim strength and resilience, the imbecile might've even crushed her with the amount of muscle weighing his body down.

An absurd amount of muscle, truthfully.

I shifted my focus to Miss Libby as her body jerked beneath Derik's. Her face scrunched together, a bead of sweat trickling down her face.

I wonder if she's having any visions of the things that have conspired between these walls. Or possibly some of the horrors that haunt the two Nephilim she's caught between. Maybe even reliving her own.

The corner of my mouth twitched.

That would be interesting, a shopping spree gone bad. Or one of her few, and far between, bad hair days.

I pondered that thought as I recollected the information I had gathered on her history. Perfect childhood, wealthy Angel mother, inconspicuous mortal father. Outside of their wealth, there hadn't been anything notable about her family. Nor her. No dramatic backstory, or traumatic experience leading up to her transformation. Her parents explained her impending development to her rather easily as she had shown signs of becoming a Nephilim with a promise of abilities of some sort. As not all offspring between the Angels and humans gained power or any of the abilities—benefits as some would describe them—that came with being of the heritage. Instead, they lived out their days as simple mortals, their memories often wiped by the Angels themselves. Miss Libby had expected the information without question. Her Angel mother took her under her wing, teaching her what she could before Miss Libby ventured out here, finding Seth. Or rather, Seth finding her. Derik, as always, followed behind him, incapable of thinking for himself.

The Demons' movement shook me from my runaway train of thought. Erebus had reappeared and his lackeys were arguing with him.

"Sir, why do we need them? Can't we just gut them and have it over with? We've earned some fun around here," the Demon closest to Derik kicked Miss Libby's foot. "Especially with this one here. We could use a good fuck."

"As entertaining as that would be, Cerberus, we must think of the bigger picture," a grin curled upon his lips. "Once we've achieved everything that we've been charged with, we shall be rewarded pleasantly. Then, you may entertain yourselves in any which way you please. With whatever you please."

His ochre slits slid to Miss Libby's form.

"And you may start with this one," Erebus licked his thin lips. "But first, we play the game." He turned on his heel and side stepped, lifting his arm to motion for his pack of Demons to head toward the steel door.

They tugged Miss Libby and Derik, chaining them together, binding their ankles and wrists. They switched to Seth and followed suit, however, he remained unattached to the others. The Demons tugged on the chains, dragging each of them. Then trudged across the rug beneath their feet and through the steel doors. I slid in behind them.

The room in front of me was drastically different from the porcelain, clean-cut hall we had been in. Its walls consisted of mortar and stone. Weapons dotted the walls, ribbon strewn between them. A single gaudy throne sat in the center of the far wall. On an elevated platform, nonetheless.

Always with the theatrics.

The clanging of chains caught my attention. I scanned the monstrosity of a medieval impersonation, my eyes pausing upon Miss Erin Snow. She dangled from the ceiling, chained, fruitlessly attempting to yank herself free. As if she were able to break her restraints and run to Seth or the others. The look of pain and panic covered her face, possibly one of the worst things to allow oneself to do in the presence of any Demon. They thrived off of fear.

Worst of all, they lived for the hunt.

Erebus sauntered to where Seth lay in a heap. A little lesser Demon, an inconspicuous Imp, followed him. His minion snapped his fingers, calling forth a small blade. Miss Snow's mouth moved and a growl erupted from her, making a threat to the two Demons.

Silly girl. They have you backed into a corner. Your words do nothing to them.

Erebus snapped his attention back to the girl. His foot made contact with Seth's middle before prowling his way to where Miss Snow hung, still restrained.

Perhaps I was wrong. Interesting.

Miss Snow muttered a bout of profanity at Erebus. Then spat at him. I scowled.

You've done it now, Miss Snow.

A whip cracked, lashing her thigh.

I heard Seth rouse. He began to wake. Erebus unfortunately noticed as well, taking that moment to make himself scarce.

Odd.

The Imp moved to prop Seth into a kneeling position. His head tilted upward groggily. A moment passed before he registered where he was and what was happening. Another crack sounded, the whip cutting into Miss Snow's side.

They were waiting.

Seth thrashed in his restraints. The perfect entrance for Erebus. He sauntered into the room once more, his scrutinizing gaze flicked between the two. Soaking in their reactions to one another. Seth rattled off mute threats in Erebus's direction, giving him the exact reaction Erebus wanted.

Seth had played right into Erebus's hands. He took his time, further building the fury between them. Using his tongue to make a ghastly point. I wasn't interested in hearing his taunts. I crept over to where Miss Libby and Derik were lumped together. I released my power, lulling them from their Demon induced slumber, the one power of mine that could be of use to them in this moment.

I pulled an illusion around them, so as to not alert Erebus or his lackeys. Derik shot up. Eyes looking around wildly. Miss Libby, less animalistic, batted her eyelids open.

Derik was first to speak, after attempting to yank himself free, "What the hell happened. What's going on?" His wild eyes landed on where Miss Snow dangled unconsciously near Erebus's throne. He froze. Libby surveyed her surroundings, her back to Erin. She glanced over her shoulder, following Derik's line of sight and let out a gasp.

I made quick work of their shackles. "We need to get out of here. I'm going to unchain you both. Then I need you to get to Seth and free him. I'll hold the illusion. Once the three of you are up and ready to run, I'll grab Miss Snow. Erebus should grow bored now that she's unconscious," Derik's anger sizzled to the surface. "Follow my instructions. I will get us out of here alive. I had to wait for the opportunity to reveal itself in order for us to get her out of here," Miss Libby gave me a wary look. "If the opportunity to wake you all and stop this madness sooner presented itself, I assure you, I would've taken it."

Derik nodded, icily. He pulled Miss Libby behind him, crawling to where Seth knelt, awake, but paralyzed. His jaw slack and in utter shock. They began unshackling him, Derik thwacked the crown of his skull, gaining Seth's attention and relayed the plan. Seth's head turned in my direction, nodding, a plea in his moist eyes. I returned the movement and crept toward Miss Snow.

Erebus sauntered to his throne and flung himself into the cushioned seat. He swung his legs over the side, crossing them, feigning boredom. Seth remained sheathed under my illusion, as were Derik and Miss Libby. Erebus, none the wiser. "My, my. Now, look what I've had to do, Seth Draven. I've lost my entertainment for the night," Erebus let out a heady laugh. "It was going to be quite the show, as I'm sure you could imagine." The timbre of his implied threat boomed, his jagged teeth bared as he swept the tip of his tongue across them.

I illusioned for Seth to appear still chained to the floor, thrashing and devoured by rage. While truthfully, his face was fully encompassing his fury and bloodlust. He was now free of his restraints and moving swiftly toward where I was working furtively on the rope and chains from which Miss Snow had been bound. We worked simultaneously, unlatching the chains around her ankles first. Once they were cleared, Seth strained over head to free her from the other restraints. Her body twitched and began convulsing, the shackles stuck.

"Shit," Seth swore under his breath.

"You must hurry, Draven. I'm unable to hold much longer. And we must get her out of here quickly before whatever power she's attained unleashes on the two of us and deems this whole rescue completely futile and an absolute waste of our time." As the last bit of what I had uttered reached his brain, Seth, brashly, curled his fist into my shirt, bringing his face less than an inch from my own.

"You get something fucking straight here, *Josh*," he sneered, "I get that you think you're better than the rest of us and honestly I don't give a flying fuck. But you are under *my* command. And if you so much as even fucking *think* that saving Erin is a waste of time, consider yourself dead. That goes for *any* of our people. Say that again, and I will end your sorry pretentious ass. Do I make myself clear?" Seth snarled. His chest heaving, blue flame permeating from his eyes.

A true flame.

How interesting.

I held my hands up in surrender from his version of a verbal lashing and an absolute waste of time. "My apologies. However, we truly are running out of time." He glared at me, and then moved to free Miss Snow.

My arms extended as she fell, catching her. Her head rolled back, hanging from my arm. The added blood from the final lashings she'd received and Erebus's Demon's hands, still seeped from her side. Her clothing had been utterly destroyed, torn to nothing more than scraps. Her breasts were fully exposed, what material that had been left to cover having fallen away as she fell from the restraints. Deep gashes covered her body, lesions from her thighs to her small waist, breasts, arms; there was no skin left unharmed. I shook my head.

Idiotic, woman. You shouldn't fight battles you cannot win.

Seth reached for her and I maneuvered her into his awaiting arms. Miss Snow immediately curled into him, her battered hand subconsciously reached for the front of his fighting gear, grasping it. Her head leaned against his chest, no longer lopped to the side. Her twitching and convulsing eased.

I snapped our attention back to the task at hand. "Seth, we must go. Now." I pulled him forward, pushing him and Miss Snow toward the exit. Derik and Miss Libby were already waiting by the iron door. The heads of three different Demons at their feet. I held the Illusion until we made it through the wrought iron door, my connection with the throne room broken. We bolted, our enhanced speed kicked in. Chaos erupted behind us. Derik led the group, following the carpeted pathway toward the behemoth sized wooden doors they'd been dragged through not even hours before. He burst through them, the oak splintered from his sheer strength.

"Into the tunnel. Straight ahead! That's our only way in or out. Move!" I shouted. Miss Libby ran behind Derik, Seth followed, Miss Snow still tucked in close to his chest and unconscious. As we navigated through the tunnels at top speed, I left illusion after illusion behind us in order to distract the Demons that were rampaging through the tunnels after us.

They should hold for the time being. I sense no trace of iron within the earth. If we came across any now, although it would render my illusions pointless, I've bought them some time.

We were nearing the edge of the tunnels. Derik shouted for Miss Libby to keep going as he fell behind her. Seth followed suit, slowing to my side. I shuttered as the power that held the illusions left in our wake were shattered.

They broke through.

"Josh, take her. Derik and I will hold them off a bit longer. Take Erin and Libby, hide yourselves and get them to safety," that flame shone once again. "Keep her safe." And with that, he placed Miss Snow in my arms, his thumb traced her cheek before he braced for the Demons nearly on top of us all. Her body recoiled from mine. I gripped her close to keep from dropping her as Miss Libby and I continued to make an escape. Growling and screaming broke out behind us. Miss Snow shifted in my arms, her head rolling. Her eyelids shot open, her pupils a blood-red pit. Her head snapped in the direction of the chaos behind us, a hand shooting upward.

She's merely weeks into her transformation.
How is this possible?

A ball of flame erupted out of her palm. And barreled directly into the brunt of the fighting, taking out nearly half of the Demons that Seth and Derik faced. I stopped in my tracks, Miss Libby as well, her mouth agape.

Miss Snow, who are *you?*

A second flame erupted from Miss Snow's hand. Careening to the other half still standing. As it collided with its targets, a bolt of lightning stamped from the sky above. Shooting down a Demon that had been but a second away from beheading Seth.

Seth swiveled his head in our direction, eyes widening at the realization of where the elements had came from. He and Derik checked the small battlefield around them, astonished. No opponents remained. The two of them sprinted, giddy triumph dawned across their gore coated faces.

As they neared us, Miss Snow's body collapsed into mine, her eyelids closing shut, her body limp.

Seth pulled her from my grasp, pushing the hair from her face as he held her. Surprise and utter pride rippled across his face. Until he truly took in the shape she was in, having been even worse for wear than when he'd woken in the throne room. Seth gripped her close as Derik and Miss Libby both pulled off their outer fighting gear, draping it across Miss Snow.

Seth's voice broke, his cry muffled as he nestled his face into her blood soaked hair. "She's alive."

Chapter Sixteen

Erin

"Lovely, isn't she?"

"She tastes as delicious as she looks."

Flames.

Everywhere.

The sickening voice. Echoed.

Thundered louder and louder. Lightening. So many of them. So many creatures. Raced toward me. Toward all of us. They closed in. A man faced the creatures, giving us a few spared moments to try and escape. They didn't see how many were closing in on us. There were almost a hundred. I could feel it in my bones, ice clawing its way through me. We were going to die.

He *was going to die. The man, who's silhouette glimmered like the ocean on a clear blue day. He was going to die. To save us.*

A ball of flame barreled toward the creatures. Destroying them, the scent of burnt flesh encompassing us, death sliding down our throats. Lightning shot down from the sky, feasting on the creatures that remained.

The most beautiful eyes reached into my soul, caressing it. A sigh of relief brushed my skin.

He was alive. The ocean was alive.

My entire body hurt, as if I had the shit beat out of me. My legs ached, my stomach burned, and it was as if a lighter had been taken to my boobs. My arms and wrists weren't much better. I groaned. I attempted to pry my heavy eyelids open, only to slam them shut again as light flooded my vision.

"Mother of fuck. Turn the damn lights out." I grunted out.

There was a bunch of shuffling around me, a door opened and slammed shut. The air around me became stuffy. Voices excitedly mumbled. I had to strain my ears to focus on what they were saying.

"She's waking up. She's finally waking up. Go get Derik. And call Seth while you're at it! He'll want to know asap!" A high-pitched squeal escaped from somewhere close to my ear, piercing, and causing me to slap my hands over both ears.

What the hell is going on?

Someone please. Make it stop.

"Shit. Keep it down. Please. Holy fuck." A hand slapped skin, probably covering the squealer's mouth. I squinted, slowly, to test out the light of the room. It wasn't as bad the second time. I blinked, opening my eyes fully. Well, more than they were. I slowly pushed myself onto my elbows and took in the room around me.

I was in the guest room at Seth's. The curtains draped across the two arched windows at the front of the room were drawn closed, thankfully keeping any light from outside hitting me in the face. The overhead ceiling lights that hung in the center of the room had been dimmed. A pile of blankets, several actually, laid along the floor. There were three separate piles, the one closest to my bed dawned Seth's navy-blue throw and a scrunched-up pillow. Directly next to it lay a pile topped with a pink blanket. I scowled. And closest to the door was some light green sleeping bag dotted with pictures of what looked like red solo cups and monster trucks.

That one had to be Derik's.

Wait. Why is their stuff in here?

I caught Libby's big, beautiful, emerald-green doe-eyes staring me down. Her brows furrowed together and lips pouting. She bit her lip. Then attacked me by wrapping her dainty, toned arms around me and pulling me to her chest, as she squeezed the ever-loving-shit out of me. I flailed my aching arms, in an attempt to free myself from the death gripped hug.

"Libby! Libby, space, please. Personal space. I can't breathe,"—I could, somehow, but—"No touchy."

Her lip wobbled. "I'm sorry, Erin! I'm just so glad you're finally awake. We were so worried. And we've all been keeping guard since we got back and I just…I'm glad you're awake." A few tears slid down her face. She sniffled as she wiped them away.

She's drop dead gorgeous even when she cries. Woah.

But why is she crying?

"I'm sorry, I'm babbling. How are you feeling? Can I get you anything? Derik and Seth should be back any minute. They went to run a patrol and check on a few things."

My eyebrows knitted together in confusion. "Why would you guys be keeping guard? What hap—" I stopped as it all came flooding back to me. The Demons. The stone room. The whipping. The burning pain. Seth, unconscious. Libby and Derik piled on top of each other, out cold. Blood. Demons. So many Demons. *Erebus.*

Another memory flashed before my eyes. Erebus. Shredding my clothes. Touching me. His tongue, worming its way inside me. Pumping in and out of me. Violating me.

The air went cold around me, my vision glazed over. Tremors climbed their way up my spine and spread, my entire body trembling. A wave of nausea swept through me, the memory played again. And again. The room around me faded away. I was back in the stone room. With Erebus.

"Lovely, isn't she?"

Screaming.

I was screaming.

Claws raked their way down my face. Blood merging with my tears. *Stop. Stop. Stop.* There was burning. My skin was on fire. I was burning from the outside in. My chest heaved as my heart was on the cusp of exploding. I couldn't breathe. Everything was closing in on me. Erebus was killing me. His tongue tore me from the middle.

Snap out of it. Stop. Please, make it stop.

I flinched, thrashing my fists outward.

Erin.

I kept thrusting my fists in front of me.

Erin. Listen to me.

I was trembling, still fighting the Demon in front of me.

"Erin! Listen to me! It's me!" The voice didn't match the Demon in front of me, thrusting his disgusting tongue into me. "Erin."

Erebus began to disappear, his towering figure diluting.

"Come back to me, Rin. You're home."

The fog started to lift.

"You're safe."

I blinked.

And met Seth's eyes, deeper than the ocean, and filled with concern. I let out a strained breath, my chest still heaving. The nausea hit me again. Seth must have realized it because he grabbed the trash bin next to my bed just in time for me to barf into it. He pushed my hair back, holding it out of the way, his fingers brushing my neck.

I heaved and nothing but bile rampaged its way out of my body. I choked as the last of it spewed out. Seth's hand rubbed in circles along my back, my body relaxed into his touch. I slumped forward, my head resting on the rim of the trash can, my breathing shaky.

The smell from the puked-doused trash can hit me once I came up for air. "Oh dear lord," I squeezed my nose between my fingers, gagging. "Seth, I am so freaking sorry."

He shook next to me. The bastard was laughing. "It's all good, Snow. I mean, most chicks don't spew their guts when they wake up at my place, but I'll try not to be too offended." I shot him a sideways glare.

I'm puking my guts out.
Having some type of episode and he's laughing at me.
Ass.

"But seriously, you okay?" His arm wrapped around my shoulders, hugging my frame to his. He paused. "Is this okay? Me touching you? Do you need space?" I shook my head, my lips pressed together, forming a thin line as I fought back the silver that lined my eyes. Seth began pulling away and I curled my fingers into the fabric of his T-shirt. I leaned into him, resting my head on his broad shoulder.

Don't go. Not right now.

Seth pulled me in closer, twisting so he had both arms wrapped around me as my face pressed into his chest. I burrowed my nose into his T-shirt, inhaling his signature pine and bourbon scent. I wrapped my arms around his waist and he gripped me tighter, as if he knew how much I needed him right in that moment, holding me together. His chin rested on the top of my head, nestled in my hair. My heart wrenched. Tears began to fall, soaking the front of his shirt.

He broke me.

I let that damned Demon break me.
And they...they could've died because of me.

"I'm here, Rin. I'm here," Seth squeezed me. "You're home. You're safe." He repeated what he said as he pulled me out of the flashback.

Home.

Was this home?

I felt something crack inside me.

No. It's not.

They say 'home is where the heart is,' and mine...is gone.

"It's about damn time your ass woke up, Snow," Derik barged into the room, startling me, a huge grin plastered on his face. "Some pretty bad ass stuff you did back there, Short Stuff."

Libby came barreling in after him, smacking Derik on the arm. "I told you to give her some space, Derik! Leave them alone," she scolded him, her eyes wide, cheeks flushed, her short blonde ponytail bobbing behind her. "She's been through a lot the last few days. She doesn't need you bullying her."

Libby meant the best but said the worst. I stiffened in Seth's arms.

"She's been through a lot."

You're broken. And they all know it.

I pushed myself out of Seth's grip, immediately reaching behind myself, for something, anything to hide the fact that I was wiping the trail of tears from my cheeks. I didn't need the pity.

Stop it. Stop crying.

I swallowed the embarrassment and turned around, keeping my expression neutral.

"Yeah. And nice beer pong bag by the way, Asshat." I crossed my arms over my chest, straightening my back, as I changed the subject as quickly as possible.

Seth busted out laughing at Derik's diminishing grin being replaced by a blushing scowl. I arched my eyebrow, challenging him.

"Hey man, I've had that thing since freshman year. It was a special send off gift."

I laughed. "Oh yeah, from who, yourself?"

Derik stuck his tongue out at me. And I mirrored him by doing the same.

Josh came up behind them, taking up position in the doorway. "Derik, Miss Snow, will you two stop behaving like children?" Josh stared me down, his eyes shimmering.

Dick.

Hot.

But a dick.

"He started it," I mumbled, as Seth held back another bout of laughter next to me, our bodies no longer touching. I huffed, realizing how full the guest room was becoming.

Does everyone have to be here?

I passed out escaping a bunch of shitty ass Demons. Big whoop.

I'm alive. Let me suffer in silence.

I breathed.

Be nice.

"Look, I appreciate y'all running in here and for whatever reason camping out in here like it's a damn slumber party. But since I just woke up and probably look like a swarm of bats attacked me in my sleep, with what little sleep I've had, I need a shower and to change." I cringed, realizing how much of a mess I probably was. Then I remembered. My clothes. The Demons shredded them to pieces. I fought back the rest of the memory as I glanced down.

I was in Seth's sweats and one of his shirts. My face flushed as I looked up at Seth. Panic racing through me.

Seth held his hands up in defense. "It wasn't me. Libby got you changed and cleaned up when we made it back a few days ago." Relief flooded my panic state.

For a split second.

My spine stiffened. "Days?" Seth and Derik both nodded, Libby's brows furrowing as she spoke up.

"We made it back here to Seth's about four and a half days ago. You've been asleep since we escaped from Ere—" I tensed, her eyes softened. "Since we escaped from the mountains on the outskirts of Riverside. We were starting to worry."

I stole a quick glance in Seth's direction. "Why didn't you guys try waking me up?"

Josh chimed in, "We attempted, and you almost electrocuted Derik and Miss Libby. Although, to be fair, Derik's idea of rousing you awake involved sticking your hand in a basin of warm water, then dumping said water on you. Amongst other childish schemes. Miss Libby attempted a more friendly approach by shaking your shoulders and even kicking your feet. I came running in to find them both on the floor arguing with one another while the hair on their heads stood straight up. Truly a sight." The son of a bitch almost smiled.

"You tried to make me piss myself?" I rolled my head toward Derik. "What are you? Twelve?"

He shrugged. "They do it in the movies. And I've always wanted to try. The opportunity presented itself and I couldn't pass it up."

I directed my attention to the not-so-innocent Libby. "You kicked me?"

Libby squirmed, wringing her wrists. "It worked on Derik a few times in the past and we've had to do it to Seth to wake him up before too. So, I thought it might work. You wouldn't have been hurt by it. I don't think so at least. They gave me hell about it when they woke up, but no bruising. And I thought with you being a Nephilim now and your powers coming in, it'd be okay." I shook my head before dropping it into my hand, a migraine etching its way through my skull.

"You guys are ridiculous, you know that?" I raised my head back up to see Libby on the border of crying.

Dammit.

"Libby, I'm not mad. There's no reason to be upset. I'm fine," I sighed. "Obviously, I just sleep like a rock. And I'm not a morning person. Word of advice: do not try waking me up again."

"Already noted, Snow," Derik said.

"Glad we're on the same page," I turned to Seth. "Did I miss anything while I was down for the count?" I braced myself.

Seth shook his head, frustrated. "No, Derik and I have been trying to gather more information on those disappearances and what they wanted with you. Why they took you, and nothing so far. No ties."

"Right now, there's thirteen people that are missing and we can't figure out why they were taken either. I hate to ask, Snow, but did you hear anything while...while you were there?" added Derik uncomfortably.

I looked down at my lap, forcing myself to think of anything that might've stood out. Struggling to keep the panic and fear from creeping back through me.

Breath. Focus. Push back the fear.

His voice played clearly in my mind as if it were a recording. Claws hooked into the image.

"You are The Key."

My eyes remained clamped shut as I dragged myself from the memory. "They said...I was The Key." I removed myself from the memory and replayed it as if it were in third person, and I was observing from the outside—as if it were a movie.

It's not real.
It's not real.
You're at Seth's.
In his guest room.
It's not real.

I blinked my eyes. They were all staring at me. "What? Do I have drool on my face?" I wiped my arm across my mouth, not that it'd do any good at that point.

Seth gulped. "The Key." He looked toward Derik and Libby.

I stuck my neck out. "Hello? Guys? If you know something, do you care to elaborate for those of us—me—who don't know?" I waved my hands in the air for emphasis.

Seth tore his eyes from Derik and Libby, and he completely ignored Josh.

Weird.

"If you're The Key, then we're in for a whole lot of shit that's going to hit the fan around here, Rin."

"Well. Fuck."

Chapter Seventeen

Erin

"Okay, so explain this whole 'Key' bullshit to me again?" Seth and Derik had been talking their heads off, trying to explain it to me for hours at that point. Libby intervened a few times but just left me more confused. Josh preferred to play watchman, standing against the wall with his arms crossed looking all angsty like he had a stick up his ass. What made him even more annoying was how hot he looked doing it.

Prick.

Okay. He was the one who saved my ass and got me out of that stuck-in-the-dark-ages hell hole.

If Josh hadn't figured out where the Demons had me...

I shivered, the memory threatening to take over.

Josh hasn't done anything wrong.

I need to stop being so snippy.

I huffed, pushing my eyebrows together. I chewed on my lip, slumping into Seth's sofa as I crossed my legs applesauce style.

Focus, Dummy.

Derik looked at me like I was an idiot, while Seth practiced breathing and pinching the bridge of his nose. Letting out a final sigh, Seth started again. "Okay, Erin, focus. I know it's a lot to take in but please for the love of all things holy, pay attention."

"Dammit, Seth, I'm freaking trying. Don't be an ass. It's a lot." I stuck my tongue out at him.

So much for not being snippy.

Ass.

"Alright. I'll start over," he shook his head, eyes closed as he took in another deep breath before continuing. "Nephilim, Angels, and Demons have been at it damn well since the beginning. Angels and their Nephilim children protecting themselves and humans from the Demons who spawned from the pits of Hell. But it wasn't always that way."

"Demons, at one point, were able to roam free. Before the Hell pits were created. They wreaked havoc on the Angels and the humans. And their offspring, Nephilim. The Demons destroyed hundreds of civilizations. They craved power, destruction. They captured humans and enslaved them, tortured them. Once they were bored, the people would be massacred."

"The Angels finally had enough. One specifically, Raphael. He was one of—if not the strongest—Angels to ever exist. He led a civilization of humans, Angels, and their Nephilim children alike to success. Bustling cityscapes, abundance of wealth and health. His people were living long, happy, peaceful lives, spanning an entire continent. His people called their sanctuary Evanyia."

"With a population that large—as you can imagine—it caught the attention of the horde of Demons parading themselves around the world, thirsting for more and more power."

"Unfortunately, Raphael's paradise caught the eye of a Demon by the name of Kerebos," Derik gulped as Seth paused. "He was the embodiment of death, pain, and destruction."

"He led his Demons to Evanyia. Murdering any humans, Nephilim, or Angels who stood in his way. The women were taken and thrown into slavery. They were raped," I flinched. "Tortured and broken. Kerebos relished in the massacres."

I felt myself slipping again, the images of my own experience with the Demons threatening to take me, digging their talons into the edge of my mind. A hand squeezed my shoulder, knowingly. I shrugged it off, although a part of me was grateful for the brief distraction.

"Raphael caught wind of what was being done to the innocents in his kingdom and gathered his strongest Angels."

"They built an army to fight against Kerebos and his Demons. Raphael searched for the strongest warriors. Including the human-Angel offspring, Nephilim."

"Previously, Raphael cherished the Nephilim of his continent and trained them to defend themselves. However, he wasn't truly aware of their full potential, even while fighting alongside them in the centuries prior. As Kerebos and his Demonic army closed in, Raphael started taking note of the Nephilim within his kingdom. Noticing the strength that they wielded. Some were more powerful than the Angels themselves." I shifted in my seat, the fine hair on the nape of my neck raised.

Just how powerful were these Angels?

Seth swept his gaze over the room. "The Angels and their children trained as one. Raphael sent the strongest of his army to fend off the onslaught of Demons as they prepared themselves."

"Their numbers dwindled. The Demons kept coming. More and more of them, as they didn't need the same amount of time to breed as Angels and humans did, being created and developed enough to fight within months, sometimes weeks. The Angels didn't stand a chance."

"Raphael rallied the remaining Angels, called forth their Nephilim children, and forged their power together to form a pit. A place to trap them within the Earth and send them away from their world. Hell."

Yeah, and a unicorn really traveled to a candy-covered mountain.

"It was their last stand against Kerebos. Raphael's power was waning. His disciples were weakened from the constant battle, vast numbers of Nephilim being destroyed. He used his final burst of power to send Kerebos and his army into the pit. Closing the Demons off from the world. Or so they thought..."

"Destruction had been brought to Evanyia, thousands of humans murdered. Nephilim and Angels slain. Raphael had succeeded in freeing his people who survived the Demons, however, the guilt and the pain of seeing all who had suffered—who had been taken—weighed on him. His human wife was amongst the humans who were killed, having risked her own life to save the innocent beings ravaged by Kerebos's Demons."

"Kerebos finally fell at Raphael's hand and was thrust into the pit. Once the pit was sealed, the Demons became trapped within. Raphael plummeted, grief and sorrow enveloped him, sucking the life from him. His power rang out as he took his final breath. Lightning blanketed the sky and fire erupted across the mountains surrounding the continent. The rivers flooded, washing away the dead bodies of the fallen. The wind thrashed through the homes of his people who were taken. It was all destroyed."

"Before his death, his Nephilim offspring and closest Angel warriors, surrounded him. He warned them how determined the Demons could be. How bloodthirsty they would be after having been trapped. They say his pupils turned to white, seeing what had yet to come."

"Raphael warned his people who remained, those closest to him in those final moments, to be watchful. To be at the ready and prepare, for there would be those who escaped the pit. And one day, war would come. A war like no other. And the only thing standing between the Demons and destroying the world, would be a key. The Key. To end the Demons. Locking them away forever. But, if it fell into the wrong hands, it would be the end of humanity. The end of the Angels and Nephilim, as the Demons would once again wreak havoc on us all. And with them, bringing the end to the world as we knew it."

The tension in the room was palpable. Everyone was on edge.

Josh leaned against one of the massive windows in Seth's living room, his jaw ticking. Libby uncrossed and recrossed her ankles several times, her eyes fluttering between each of us. The tendons in Seth's forearms flexed along with Derik's. Both of them held death in their eyes.

I pinched the bridge of my nose.

"Okay, so let me get this right. Some ancient Angel, Raphael, kicked a bunch of Demons' asses. And said Demons want revenge. But beyond the whole kicking Nephilim and Angel ass thing. They straight up want to slice and dice us all until we're all gonzo?" I said, adding a touch of annoyance to my voice.

Derik chuckled, the fear on his face twisted into a smart-assed smile, chipping at the tension in the room. "That's one way to put it, Princess."

"That's freaking stupid. And what the hell does that have to do with me? Why would the shithead call me 'The Key'? I'm barely gaining this freaking Nephilim mojo. My dad wasn't anything special, besides, as you"—I glared at Seth— "informed me of being an Angel. My mom was human and as far as I can tell besides spitting fire and lightning there's nothing different between me and you guys. So. Why me?" One of my legs fell asleep, so I pulled it out from under my other one, tapping my foot against the hardwood, anger threatening to boil over.

I am nothing.

Why the actual fuck would I be this 'Key'?

The biggest thing I have going for me is lighting someone's ass on fire.

And technically, that can be done by throwing gasoline and a match at someone.

My pulse thundered in my ears.

Seth matched his gaze to mine. "I don't know. But we're going to find out. Because as of right now, we have nothing to go on," he shot Josh an accusatory look before turning his gaze back on me. "And there was no intel or tip off prior to the Demons taking you."

I wanted to scream.

Keep a lid on it.

I can panic and lose it later.

I glanced at Derik, then Josh. "Then what do we do?"

Derik chimed in; a crooked grin plastered on his face. "We get your ass trained up, Snow. Then Seth and Tight-Ass over there, get cracking on the books and interrogation tactics to get us some answers."

Seth and I both rolled our eyes. Derik winked at me.

And at that, even with all the doom, destruction, and dread that filled the room, a laugh escaped my lips. "Well, Beer Pong Man, show me how to kick some Demon dick-headed ass."

"I thought you had defense training when you were a kid?" Derik gave me the up-down. "What you're doing right now is trash."

I swung my fist directly for Derik's cheek and he made his point by catching it mid-swing. He followed up by kicking my legs out from under me. I landed clean on my back, knocking the air right out of my lungs. "Get it together, Erin. You're all over the place with zero aim or control. The strength is there but that's about all you got."

I huffed. "Excuse the hell out of me for being a human and assuming being able to kick a guy in the nuts and the defense moves I learned when I was *ten*, would hold up."

He cocked his head and clicked his tongue. "Well, do better. Demons don't give a shit; they just want you dead. So, suck it up, Pipsqueak. On your feet. I'm going to run you through some basic movements. Again." He bent down to reach his hand out and help me up.

Dick.

I flipped him off and rolled myself onto my stomach before pushing up and onto my feet. "You know, the whole serious asshole thing doesn't look good on you, Derik. I liked you better when you were just an annoying asshole."

Someone snorted at that. My eyes swept the room and found Libby holding her hand over her mouth, shoulders shaking; Seth standing next to her with a coffee mug in hand, busting out laughing.

"Hell must've frozen over. Erin, did you admit to liking me? I'm honored." Derik flung a hand over his chest.

I rolled my eyes, straining to keep a smile from creeping onto my lips. "You're so dramatic. And if anything, you being obnoxious is just far more tolerable," I widened my stance, bending my knees slightly. "Although, this gives me a reason to punch your face in without feeling guilty about it."

That's a lie. You'll sit there, overthink, and feel horrible about it if you ever actually land a blow on the guy.

Seth's eyes twinkled as they met mine across the room, knowing damn well that I'd guilt trip the shit out of myself. He flashed a smile at me and my cheeks flushed.

"Then let's see it, Sweetheart," Seth rang out. Heat washed over me, and his smile grew into a full-on Cheshire. Libby, giddy as her laughter spilled out from her.

Sweetheart?

What in the hell is that about?

I flipped him and Libby off.

Prick.

I lined myself up and sized up Derik's relaxed stance; arms resting at his side, legs slightly parted, boredom etched across his features even as his pupils tracked my every breath. The moment I waited for came, his attention briefly darting to where Libby and Seth were still chatting. I swung my arm out, Derik without hesitation, reached for it, opening up his stance while doing so. I took my other arm and swung upward, directly into his chin, his teeth clang together.

Ha! Victory!

Derik's eyes lit up. He snaked his foot behind my ankle and pulled it out from under me. Causing me to lose my balance and sending my ass back to the floor. My small victory evaporated.

"Son of a bitch."

Derik shrugged, turning on his heel and striding to the kitchen to grab his own mug of coffee. "What can I say, Snow, I got skills."

Libby snickered. "Yeah, right, you're just butthurt Erin actually landed a hit on you."

He sipped his coffee. "She got lucky. I was getting bored handing her ass to her all day; thought I'd throw her one."

"Yeah right," she snorted. "She caught you off guard. Or are you too afraid to admit to a moment of defeat, Oh Mighty One?"

"Pssh, whatever."

Is that a hint of pink I see?

"So," I said as I wiped non-existent dust from my sweats. "Now that I successfully wounded Derik's fragile ego, is it break time?"

A laugh escaped Seth. "From sparring, yeah. But we gotta try shaking out some of your mojo." I frowned at him.

"We gotta figure out how to control it and run some practice with it. Ya know, outside of when the shitheads are actively trying to gut us. Might be a little handy."

"Fine, but I'm stealing your coffee first."

"You've had half the pot already." His brow arched.

"Exactly. Only half."

"Have you even eaten anything?"

"No."

"You need to eat, Pipsqueak."

I threw my hands on my hips, staring Seth down. "Make me."

"Maybe I will, hangry-ass." Seth smirked, crossing his arms over his chest, sun-kissed—no sun-*worshiped*—biceps bulging, and tight-ass muscle shirt perfectly accentuating his pecs. I salivated.

I licked my lips, my gaze lingered before dragging it upward. "You know, I think I changed my mind," my eyelashes fluttered, giving my best impression of being sultry. "I think I am hungry."

I flashed Seth a smile. His eyes darkened, my pulse quickened.

That might've backfired.

"Oh, really now?"

Derik gagged. "Gross. Come on guys, we're right here. Get a damn room." Libby smacked him on the arm. Seth mirrored the color of a tomato. And I was pretty sure I matched.

Oh God.

Play dumb. Play dumb. Play dumb.

"No idea what you're talking about, Derik. I was actually going to say I was hungry for some tacos. What about you, Seth?"

"Uh, yeah," he ran his fingers through his midnight black hair. "Tacos sound great."

"Great!" I forced an exaggerated smile, the gesture leaving my face to ache.

"Great."

I twirled around and damn near sprinted to the guest room. Oh so casually slamming the door shut behind me.

What the actual hell was that? What is wrong *with me?*

My heart nearly beat out of my chest.

Did I imagine his eyes darkening? I thought that shit only happened in books and the movies. What is happening?

A knock sounded at the door.

"Hey, Erin, you okay?"

Seth.

I squeaked.

Shit.

"Ah, yeah. Yeap! I'm fine! I'm just going to get changed out of my sweats." I laughed nervously, my fingers crossed that he didn't notice.

"Oh, alright," he paused. "So, tacos...does hitting up The Taco House sound good?"

You sound better.

Oh my god. Erin.

No! Bad. Stop that.

I yelled through the door, "Yeah, we can do that! I'll finish getting changed then I'll be out and we can go."

"Cool. Do you need anything or need me to grab anything for you?"

An odd fantasy suddenly flashed through my head.

Seth opened the door, his eyes trailed down my body from head to toe. Hunger lit his eyes. He licked his lips and closed the distance between us.

His arms circled my waist, bringing my body flush against his, fitting together perfectly as if our bodies were made for each other. My eyes fluttered behind my lashes, looking up to his. He brought his face closer to mine. "I'd much rather eat you." His pupils dilated, closing the gap. Seth's mouth crashed into mine, tongue jutting in and out, dancing around mine. I wrapped my arms around his back, gripping the toned muscle beneath his shirt, digging my nails in. He growled, his grip around my waist tightening. He lifted me, his hands having traveled down to my ass, firmly grasping it. I swung my legs around his middle.

Seth released my mouth and began trailing kisses along my jaw and my neck, nipping as he went, before licking his way along my collarbone. I panted, needing more.

I raked my nails down his back slowly as I began rocking my hips against the large bulge forming in his grey sweatpants. His grip on my ass tightened as a moan escaped his lips against my skin, sending electricity down my spine. I arched my back, forcing my chest upward, his face now shoved between my heaving breasts.

Seth spun us around, pressing my back against the wall as he began thrusting his hips upward in motion with mine. I let out a moan. "Seth, I need you."

He moved one hand from my ass, reaching for his waistband and pulling out his rock-hard cock. He adjusted so that his length was between our hips and against my center, teasing me through my sweats. He began rubbing his length along my crevice. "If you need it so bad, Princess, then take it."

I wiggled, moving my hands to pull my pants away, fumbling being held against the wall. Seth let out a low, throaty laugh before carrying *me to the bed, tossing me on the comforter. He climbed on the bed, wedging himself between my legs before dragging my sweats down over my hips, tossing them to the side. He bent down, biting his way up the inside of my thigh, sending chills through me.* "Please, Seth."

He smirked, leaning forward. He rested his length against my entrance and began rubbing himself along my folds, teasing me. "What did I say, Sweetheart? You want it," *he thrusted against my clit, my hips bucked.* "Then take it."

"Erin?"

I blinked my eyes. "Huh?"

Seth strained. "Do...you need anything?"

My face heated, and I thanked the freaking Angels that he was on the other side of the door. "Uh, no! I'm fine. Thanks though, like I said, be out in a few!"

"Okay, just yell if you need me." His voice faded slightly as he stepped away.

"Then take it."

"Get it together, Snow." I chastised myself.

Holy fuck.

I took a few breaths to collect myself and calm the heat pooling at my center, then maneuvered over the bundles of blankets still scattered across the floor. I reached my clothes that were still huddled together in a pile on the floor, rummaging through them to find something to wear.

I spotted a pair of black denim shorts that I rarely wore, in part because of how short they were. They did make my butt look above average though. An idea popped in my head. I snatched my only low-cut black T-shirt and my only push-up bra. A rush of lust-fueled adrenaline danced through my veins, a devious smile playing across my face.

"Oh, what the hell. Why not?"

Chapter Eighteen

Erin

After I threw on my shorts and T-shirt combo, I plastered on some mascara and chapstick before tossing my hair up into a ponytail. There was no point in adding lip gloss when we were about to devour some much needed tacos. Not to mention that, although I'd already donned the out-of-character booty shorts, I didn't want to make it overly obvious what *exactly* went through my head after the heated little food stand off between Seth and I earlier.

I slipped on my Converse before heading out to Seth's massive living room. Libby and Seth were huddled together on the couch looking over a bunch of papers. Derik perched on one of the bar stools at the island in the kitchen scrolling on my laptop.

Everyone is so...engrossed.

My slim surge of confidence dwindled at seeing Seth and Libby so close. I shoved it down and redirected my attention to Derik.

Not important.

A few moments of delusion and weirdly fantasizing about my best friend, means nothing.

I strode to where Derik squinted at my screen, clearing my throat.

"Hey Derik, you know, you're supposed to ask someone before hacking into their laptop."

"It wouldn't be hacking if I asked, now would it, Pipsqueak?" He clipped.

"Smartass," I slid into the seat next to him. "What do you need it for anyway? You could've just asked, you know."

I peered unsuccessfully at my laptop, the screen unreadable with the protector I had covering it. After I'd dropped the damn thing for the third time within a week of owning it, I caved and chucked out way too much money on a heavy duty laptop case equipped with an attached screen cover.

"Yeah, but pissing you off is more fun."

I rolled my eyes. "It takes more than that to piss me off. You're just annoying. And you didn't answer the second part of my question."

"Technically, you asked two separate questions, Snow"—he sent me a sideways glance— "but if you really want to know, I'm trying to find out more about those disappearances from Riverside. It took me a minute to find your browser on here though," I panicked. Derik must've sensed it because he added, "Don't worry, I didn't check out your porn history, Short Stuff."

I smacked him on the shoulder. "I don't watch porn, you dick!"

Seth shouted from across the room, "I call bullshit, Rin. I see some of those novels you read. And the ones you've stolen off my bookshelves out here. Nice try."

"I do not!" My ears were burning. I whipped my head around and stuck my tongue out at Seth. "And even if I did, they're your books in the first place, you hypocrite."

His eyes sparkled. "Which is why I know *exactly* what's in-between those pages, Rin."

I snapped my head back to Derik and my laptop, grumbling. "Whatever." Sending all three of them into a fit of laughter.

I waved my hand at the screen. "What did you find out, Dickwad?"

"Captain Dickwad to you, missy."

I looked at him confused as all hell, eyebrow arched, and my mouth hanging half opened. "Captain? Captain of what? S.S. Ass Hat?"

"Nope, Captain just makes me sound even more like a badass than I already am," he claimed.

"You're an idiot."

"True, but the ladies love it." Derik waggled his eyebrows.

"I'm sure. Now, for the love of God, Dick-for-Brains, what did you find?"

Derik sighed, propping his elbow on the counter, his chin seated in his palm. "Nothing good. They weren't just isolated to the area around the plant like we originally thought. It seems the disappearances were scattered across the whole city. Over half of them were women. All single and living alone. The men that were taken follow the same profile. But that's what we already knew from the police reports and our own."

He scrolled down the page. "What we didn't know was that all the disappearances were tipped off anonymously. The first and last call placed within fifteen minutes of each other. And after some more digging, the phone numbers that were used to call in, were all local landlines from around here. Not Riverside."

"So what does that mean then?" I leaned forward, glancing, unsuccessfully, at the screen.

Freaking screen cover.

"It means that either the Demons have one hell of a phone number generator pinpointed here in town. Or they have some of their lackeys stationed out here. Watching and waiting for their orders."

A shiver ran down my spine. My body tensed, my voice a whisper, "Which would explain why they found me here." I gulped. If I'd been at my apartment, who knew how long it would've been before Seth and the others found me or what else would've happened.

"She tastes just as delicious as she looks."

I snapped myself out of the downward spiral before it dragged me under.

Derik responded vacantly, "Yeah, but if that was the case, we still don't know why they think you're this damn 'Key' or why exactly they wanted *you*. No offense, Erin."

"None was taken til' you added the 'no offense' part." I deadpanned.

"Gotta cover my bases." Derik shrugged.

"Uh huh."

"But anyway, the connection there is still in the air." He leaned back in the stool. He flipped a stray blonde curl that fell in front of his face and crossed his arms before swinging around to face Libby and Seth. "You guys got any ideas?"

Libby held up a finger, as she stuck her nose further into the papers her and Seth were digging through. We both cocked an eyebrow.

She shot up from the sofa and raced over to us. "Actually, yes!"

Seth strolled behind her, stopping next to my stool with his hands shoved into his jeans pockets. I stole a sideways glance; the fantasy I had earlier replayed in my mind. My eyes roamed, taking in the way his jeans sat perfectly on his hips, the material molded to his muscled thighs, waist band slightly dipping down from where his hands were pulling on the fabric, giving me a glimpse of the top of his boxers and the smallest patch of beautifully toned stomach.

Reel it in, Erin.

I sat a little straighter in my seat, placing my hands in my lap, folded over each other. "Let's hear it." I plastered on a smile, crossing my fingers it didn't give away the dirty thoughts floating through my head.

My eyes darted to Seth again, and I caught him staring down at me. I sent him a small smile as well. His eyes darted away, settling on Libby. My smile fell, the corners of my lips turned downward. I returned my attention to Libby and where she stood between me and Seth.

"The articles we were reading through—" Libby started.

"Wait articles? There are articles on this stuff? Like just out there on the web for anyone to see?" I blurted.

"No, they're articles from one of the larger libraries that specifically house hundreds of years of information on our kind, Angels and even Demons. The books and histories are housed in various libraries across the globe. These ones specifically, are from the Nephilim Library here in town. The Library of Cherin. It's actually underneath the library you work at."

"What?" I was racking my brain for any mention of a hidden library in the year I've worked there.

There's entire fucking libraries on this stuff? How is it that we are not common knowledge if there's all of this history and info out there? Am I just that out of the loop?

Irritation pricked my skin.

Seth jumped in, "You wouldn't have known about it. It's hidden from humans and Nephilim who haven't gone through the change yet. And Cherin, specifically, is warded from the Demons too. By some ancient Angel barriers, put in place before Raphael fell."

"Oh."

Well isn't that fucking convenient.

What else don't I know about that's going to be dropped in my lap like some damp towel?

I'm about at my limit of this crap.

Libby started again, "Yes. Anyway, the articles didn't have much more to go on about the 'Key' and the specifics of it. But what they did mention were instructions, or rather warnings of sorts." She gulped.

"The Key will bring the end.

Evanyia will rise once more.

Destruction will befall the kingdom.

The men and women, cower.

Hidden away.

Eight to bare, five to power.

The Key, the answer all seek.

The Key bares all.

The power, undiscovered.

Child of The One. Daliyis.

Child of The Queen."

Libby's eyes darted between the three of us, to see if we understood. I, for one, remained clueless and absolutely lost.

Uhm. So...we're fucked?

Derik spoke first, "What the hell does that mean? I heard zero instructions in there, Lib."

"What I'm gathering from this, 'The Key' is what will bring Hell upon the world, essentially. But we already knew that. So, the part further down," Libby flipped the paper around, pointing to the bit she'd recited. "Eight to bare, five to power. Add those together and we have thirteen. There were thirteen individuals reported missing. Eight women and five men. And they're now 'hidden away'. And more, considering how they disappeared, they're probably terrified. Hence the 'cower' portion."

"What would 'bare' mean then? Or 'power'?" Seth mumbled, his brows furrowing.

Libby met my stare, pity peaked out before turning back to Seth. "I have a feeling that means what the Demons seem to enjoy the most, when it comes to human women. Forcing themselves on them. And...potentially baring children."

I felt my eyes glaze over, my vision unfocused. An image of Erebus flashed before me, the evil glint in his amber eyes as his tongue flicked out, tracing my jaw—

A hand bumped against my side, sparks of electricity singed my hip, bringing me back. I took a deep breath, steadying my heartbeat that hammered in my chest. Seth moved in close to me so that his arm was resting against me. Libby shifted to stand on my other side between Derik and I. I leaned into Seth, silently thanking him.

"But as for how Erin is tied into any of this, I'm lost. We don't know what or who Daliyis would be or the Queen. I'll have to do more digging," Libby pinched the bridge of her nose. "Erin, by any chance, does the name Daliyis sound familiar in any way, shape or form?"

I shook my head. "No idea. Even if we're looking at the literal sense of 'Child of The One', my dad's name was Ben. Ben A. Snow. When I was little he would always joke about it." A memory danced in the far corners of my mind from before he hightailed it out of my life.

"Erin, have I ever told you where my name came from?" He grinned, his salt and pepper hair falling in his face as he bent down to kneel in front of me. His whiskey-colored eyes sparkled against the pure white fluff piled on the ground behind him, the beginnings of our snow-fort.

I rolled my eyes at him, laughing. "Ugh, yes, Dad! Like a thousand times."

His deep laugh reverberated, my heart warmed as it always did back then. "Well, let me tell you again. Can't have my little snow angel forgetting now." I chucked a snowball at him, smacking him right in the face. He shucked one right back at me.

"It had been snowing for days and your grandma had enough of it. Then I came along. She saw the snow outside and settled on Ben. Ben A. Snow, because it had Ben-a-Snow-ing. It'd been snowing. Get it?"

I gathered another handful of snow and threw it at him before he slung another snowball right back. We laughed for hours. Flinging snowball after snowball at each other.

We were happy. The two of us.

That was the winter before he left me alone.

A sadness filled my chest. "So name wise, no match. And as far as the Angel thing," I shot Seth a glare and cleared my throat. "I have no idea about the whole 'The One' business. You have any input on that, Seth?"

"Unfortunately, not really. My uncle didn't give me specifics on your dad or what Angel he was or anything before he passed, just that he was one."

"Well, that's no help."

Wait a damn minute.

"You're uncle passed? When did that happen? I thought your Uncle Nicholas was still alive."

Fuck. I totally missed that. Oh my god. Seth...

"Nick...he passed a while ago."

My heart tightened at the pain that flashed across Seth's features. "I'm so sorry, Seth. I had no idea."

He shrugged, his voice thick. "I didn't tell you. It happens. Especially with what we are. It's a part of the job, unfortunately."

"But—"

Seth placed his hand on my shoulder and squeezed. "It's alright. But about your dad, I only know what I know, Rin. Sorry, Sweetheart." He flashed an evil grin my way, chasing the mournful atmosphere away.

He's always been so good at that. Just flipping the switch on the drop of a dime.

Heat swarmed its way through my skin, my cheeks turned red. Another flash of my daydream spread through. It was as if he *knew* what he'd been doing to me.

For the last couple of weeks actually.

"Coolio," Derik slid in, saving me from more embarrassment. "Well, now that we have some of the death, doom, and destruction covered, how 'bout we head down to The Taco House and grab those tacos? My ass is starving."

I never thought I'd say this, but thank you Derik!

"Me too!" Libby perked up, pulling myself and Derik out of our seats and to our feet. "Let's go!"

"Alright, I just need to grab my keys to lock up and we can go." Seth circled around the island and grabbed his keys off the holder on the wall as the rest of us ushered ourselves out his front door.

The Taco House was a ten minute drive from Seth's place and after some nagging from Libby and me, Seth caved and agreed on driving instead of an agonizingly long walk. I rode with him while Libby hitched a ride with Derik in his truck.

I sat ramrod straight in the front passenger seat of Seth's little car. He had the bass turned up, the thumping from one of the Indie rock bands he liked vibrated the car. I stuck my hands under my legs to keep them from freezing, as the warmth from earlier in the day had diminished into a frigid, sunless breeze and left me shivering.

Shorts might not have been the best idea.

Seth turned the volume down on his car's dashboard. "We're going to figure this all out, you know." He rested his hand on the center console while gripping the steering wheel with the other. I fought the urge to reach out and grab it.

Stop it, Erin.

Friends. No touchy.

You're just hot and heavy because of this whole supernatural transformation bullshit.

Seth is off limits, you ding dong.

I let out a sigh. "If you say so."

His hand twitched. "And for all we know, this whole 'Key' bullshit is just that. Bullshit. We'll focus on the connection there and how to find the missing victims and that might lead to more answers."

"Maybe." I watched out the window, the outskirts of our small town slowly paced by. It felt like the weight of the world had lumped itself right onto my chest, squishing me from the inside out. The fully-leafed trees flew by, couples laughing ignorant to the reality of the world as they knew it.

There's so much that they don't know.

Ignorance is bliss. I get it now.

Seth's finger lightly brushed against my thigh. I held my breath. He squeezed my knee, reminding me of how my dad would when I was little.

"It'll all work out, kiddo. Just take a breath."

My chest tightened further. It'd been almost a decade since he left, and it still left a hole in me. I hoped, even though I lived hundreds of miles away from the home I grew up in, that one day he'd just walk back in my life. That I'd have my dad back.

That's never going to happen though.

He left me. I was nothing.

I am nothing.

Seth squeezed my knee again, bringing me back to the present. "Hey, Erin?" He rasped.

"Yeah?"

"I don't know what exactly happened...when you were gone. When *they* took you. And I'm not going to ask," he paused, his breath hitching. "But I recognize that look in your eye you've had since you came out of it this morning. I promise you, even if I have to burn the world to do it, I will end him. He won't hurt you again.

But if you try...you could die.

He could kill you.

And you'd be gone. The only family I have left.

And it would be my fault.

A tear slid down my cheek, I kept my sight trained on the townscape outside his car window.

"I'll kill him myself, Erin. He won't hurt you again. Not under my watch."

My vision unfocused, as I fought the sob building in my throat. I pulled a hand from underneath me and slid it in Seth's. He curled his fingers around mine and gave them a squeeze. A promise.

I choked out a whispered thank you and thought back to my dad again.

Then I realized that my mind and hormones had played me. Seth saw me as someone to protect. Like we were blood. The feelings that had surfaced, they were one sided.

Another tear slipped down my cheek, as my heart broke a little further. I was a burden. Not that he'd ever admit it. And if roles were reversed, I would never think that of him. But he always felt responsible for my safety. When he had no reason to. I couldn't risk him like that.

I'll kill Erebus first. I'll do what I need to and you...save those people.

I won't be a burden to bare any longer.
I promise.

I blinked back the tears and squeezed his hand back. I turned to look at him, flashing the most convincing smile I could muster, fingers crossed he didn't see the truth. I swept a stray strand of hair behind my ear.

I released a breathy laugh. "Well. How about those tacos, huh?"

He gave me a curious look, confused. We'd parked and were sitting in The Taco House parking lot. Derik and Libby were already standing at the curb, waving at us to hurry up.

"Yeah."

Chapter Nineteen

Erin

We waited outside on the curb. The line to get in the restaurant was out the door. Libby dressed in a pair of light-washed jeans and a cream long-sleeve blouse. Derik was in a pair of ripped skinny jeans that were bedazzled on his ass pockets and a hoodie plastered with the town's university logo on the front. Even Seth, who was a damn furnace, had a Henley on, and his jeans, which unfortunately for my one-sided ogling, cupped his ass as perfectly as they did his thighs.

I stood in line behind Seth and Derik, Libby in front of them. The three of them chatted, towering over me. I tried to keep up but kept stealing glimpses of Seth's rear end. I finally gave up and sighed.

There's no point. It's hopeless.

I can't focus long enough to catch the tail end of their conversation.

I wrapped my arms around myself, shivering. I was freezing my ass off and it was taking damn near forever to get inside. I bounced on the balls of my feet to warm myself up and get blood flowing.

These shorts really were a horrible idea.

This is what I get for leaning into my day-dreaming escapade.

Someone moved in close behind me and I shoved my elbow straight back before spinning around. My nostrils flared, and I threw my now clenched fists in front of me, blocking whatever was coming at me.

"Now, Miss Snow, is that how you greet friends?" It was Josh. He rubbed his ribcage where my elbow had knocked into him. "My apologies, though. I hadn't meant to sneak up on you. Seth had messaged me and invited me out to dinner with you all after I'd left."

I dropped my hands to my hips, digging in my fingers. I glared up at him. "Most people would say something instead of just moving in behind a woman, you pretentious jerk."

"You're correct, Miss Snow. Again, my apologies," he shrugged off his jacket, handing it to me and I shoved it back. "However, I'd noticed you were shivering and thought some additional body heat might've been helpful." He looked me up and down, judgment flitting through his blue eyes. I mirrored his grazing look. "Or maybe I was wrong in that assumption, as it seems you thought it an excellent idea to wander outside in shorts in this weather."

I was reeling. Seth and Derik finally realized someone else had shown up and turned around, Seth moving to stand a bit closer to me. I stepped further away, only to do so right into Josh.

I glared up at him. "At least I showed up dressed like a normal person, not some secret psych-millionaire crime boss. Who wears a suit to The Taco House?"

"This suit, if you must know Miss Snow, is what I wear for my day job. I drove here once I completed my work and a few meetings at the office."

"Uh huh."

Seth chimed in, "Nice to see you were able to make it out, Josh."

"My pleasure, Seth. I regret having to leave once Miss Snow awoke this morning. I had a few urgent matters to deal with at the office."

Seth nodded. "Can't help it, I figure. But Libby was there anyway, so no worries."

I stole a glance at Libby, having appeared on the other side of Seth. She smiled, but it didn't quite reach her eyes.

I wonder what that's about.

I faced forward, my back to Josh and his judgey-ness. The line moved forward until we were finally inside. I was still shivering. A heavy fabric slid onto my shoulders. I peaked over my shoulder to see that Snooty Ass had taken off his suit jacket, draping it across my shoulders. It was warm, really warm, actually. I mumbled a thanks and he nodded in response.

Doesn't mean you're off the hook for creeping up on me, jerk.

I rotated a bit to send Josh a quick sideways glance. He was looking at his phone. But he looked...hot. The sleeves of his white button-up shirt were rolled halfway up his arms, exposing his toned forearms, one hand tucked into the pocket of his black suit pants. The top three buttons on his button-up were undone, exposing wisps of chestnut chest hair, a shade lighter than his slicked-back, dark chestnut hair on his head. His jawline flexed in concentration while he typed away on his screen. His shirt was sculpted onto him, accentuating his shoulders, stretching at the seams around his biceps.

Any thoughts of Seth from earlier completely disappeared as I was sucked into thoughts of Josh and what *exactly* he might be able to do with that muscle hidden under his clothes. I licked my lips.

Well, that was a quick recovery there, Snow. Want to take it down a notch? You're practically panting after the guy.

I shook my head.

I've got to slow down on the books. Dunk myself in an ice bath. Something.

I'm out of control.

I hardly even know the guy.

"Hey guys, table's ready," Seth said to Josh and me, his thumb pointed over his shoulder to where Libby and Derik followed a young waitress, her fiery-blue ponytail bobbing behind her.

"Coming, coming," I hitched as I trailed behind Seth, gnawing on my bottom lip. Josh followed behind us. The waitress led us to a booth in the back of the restaurant and handed each of us a drink menu before sprinting off to her next table. Derik and Libby slid into one side of the booth and Seth slid into the other. I sighed and moved to sit next to Seth, Josh scooting in right behind me.

Too close. They're both too close.

My cheeks flushed and I forced down my rampant imagination.

I need space.

How the hell am I going to make it through this meal being sandwiched between these guys?

Fuck me, dude.

Not literally though, please.

OH MY GOD. Calm the fuck down, Erin. What is happening?

I'm losing my freaking mind.

"I think I'm going to get one of their bottomless margaritas. Anyone want to split it with me?" Libby asked, her bubbliness in full swing. I took her in, pulling back the jealousy goggles once again. I really didn't know Libby that well. At all actually, outside of her power and what little snippets of information I'd heard from Seth and Derik.

Oh what the hell.

"I'll split it with you, Libby. I used to get them here all the time when I first moved out here," I cracked a smile. "Although I had to sneak them back then."

She whooped, "Yay!" She lit up, flagging down another waitress. "How did you end up moving out here, anyway? Seth never told us."

That was surprising, as they all seemed to know about my dad and him having been an Angel, when I had zero inclination on that bit of information until recently. "I figured you guys knew," I shot Seth a glare, further pushing down thoughts from the ride over. "You didn't seem surprised about my dad being an Angel." My voice surprisingly even.

"I mean one of our parents has to be for us to be Nephilim, so process of elimination, Short Stuff," Derik said, sliding his arm around the back of the booth, fingers lightly resting on Libby's shoulder.

Wait...does Derik...?

"Fair enough." I wiggled my ass in the booth and scooted backwards so I was flush against the apricot-quilted booth-back. I angled myself so I was leaning a bit, loosely crossing my arms over my chest. I crossed my ankles as well, channeling the essence of being entirely nonchalant. I might've been mentally praying that they all bought the level of ease I was fully orchestrating.

The Angels, God or whoever, must've been listening because our waitress brought out the margarita for Libby and me. The damn thing was the size of a fishbowl with a few of those mini shot bottles scattered throughout. I hoped the guys would join in because I wasn't sure about Libby, but my ass was a total lightweight when it came to drinking. I didn't do much of it and never had. I've always preferred being alert and keeping my eyes on what was around me. But Seth was there. Derik, given recent events, I had a feeling that although he got under my skin, I would be safe around him. Josh, I still wasn't sure due to the whole emotional whiplash and seemingly patriarch response to my choice of clothing and personality.

Libby swung one of the straws my way before wrapping her lips around hers and sucking down gulps of the sugary alcohol. I leaned forward, drawing my straw to my lips as well, taking a deep pull. The alcohol burned on the way down.

"Holy shit they made this strong." A bright toothy smile split Libby's face. I couldn't help but smile too. A little relaxation was needed. Even if I'd only been awake less than a full day after being out of commission. We giggled at each other before each slurping down more of the party-sized drink.

A buzz kissed its way through my body, my cheeks heated and my lips freely curving upward. I twisted in the booth, grinning up at Seth. "I actually moved out here and applied to the university because of this guy."

To hell with it, he might only see me as Project-Protection, but I'm going to enjoy myself tonight.

I gave him an overly dramatic wink and I turned back to the rest of the table. "We'd written to each other after he moved away. A couple times a week for the entirety of my four years of high school. Once I was nearing the end of my senior year, and decided to give the college thing a try, I applied to a bunch of different colleges," I brushed a strand of hair over my ear. "None of them really fit what I was looking for. Then Seth wrote to me, suggesting I should come out here. So, I packed a bag, drove out here to visit the campus and do a few tours then decided this was where I wanted to be. And the rest is pretty much history."

Libby's eyes were huge and all doe-eyed. "Wait, how long have you guys known each other?"

I shrugged. "Since we were in diapers pretty much. Our parents knew each other," I twisted my head in Seth's direction. "Actually, you said your mom was an Angel. Is that how they actually met?"

Seth nodded. "Yeah. They were partners, I found out later." I wave of nausea hit me.

Oh no.

"When you say partners..." I felt like I was going to puke.

Seth apparently thought it was hilarious. "Oh, God no, Erin. Gross. I mean like on the front lines and in this whole external fight for the innocent thing. Most Angels work in pairs, as do we. They were a compliment to each others' powers and fought together so long, they were like siblings from what I was told."

Relief washed over me. "Oh okay, that's pretty cool. Way less gross."

Libby snorted. "No kidding."

I took another swig, the buzz ramped up. I looked around the restaurant, seeing if I could find our waitress because I needed food in me or I was going to be more of a mess than usual by the time we left. In my determination to find our waitress and flag her down, I managed to subconsciously pull one of my knees onto the booth seat. I propped myself up, leaning forward once I spotted her. I waved one of my hands in the air to get her attention. I lost my balance and fell forward. Directly into Josh's lap, knocking his beer out of the way in the process. My stomach landed right on top of his crotch. The rest of me halfway out of the booth, and my ass essentially on full view for Seth. Shorts—specifically the ones I stupidly decided on—were most definitely a horrible idea.

I scrambled, trying to fumble my way into a sitting position and off of Josh's crotch. He reached his hand out under my arm to help me back up, pulling me toward his chest while doing so. I used my other arm to push myself up. My hand gripped Josh's thigh in the process, making sure I didn't lose my balance. Josh grunted and I looked down to realize that it wasn't his thigh that I had my hand firmly grasping.

Oh no.

Fuck.

Fucking fuck.

I shot upward apologizing profusely, offering to cover his beer and the replacement. I grabbed a handful of napkins off the table, dabbing profusely at the wet spot now covering his pant leg. Libby and Derik were in hysterics, laughing their asses off. I could feel the heat that radiated off of Seth from where he sat half behind-half next to me since I was now sitting with my legs tucked under me.

Josh coughed out, "Ahem, Miss Snow, although I understand that was an accident and greatly appreciate your attempt to dry me off," Josh shifted in his seat, bringing his voice down to a husky whisper. "You're not exactly improving the matter." He gently grabbed the napkins from me, and I glanced down.

The blush that stampeded its way over every inch of my skin deepened. In my panic trying to dry the guy off, I ended up rubbing him down and he was sporting one hell of a tent. I looked back up to see that Josh's eyes held a glimmer of amusement in them.

Someone. Something. Shoot me. Now. Please.

Our waitress showed up at that moment, saving me from saying anything that would dig me further into the pit of embarrassment I'd landed myself in. "Are you all ready to order?" she asked, a fake smile and pitched.

I'm never going to live this one down.

We placed our orders, each of us getting a plate of tacos. I ordered a large thing of nachos, offering to split it with Josh as an apology. I could feel my ears burning and glanced at Seth out of the corner of my eye.

He seethed. Clenching and unclenching his fist on top of the table. He slid his other arm along the back of the booth after I sat back and tried to ignore the fiasco that I just caused.

Why are you the one seething?

You didn't just embarrass the hell out of yourself by unintentionally groping someone.

I took the straw for the margarita and slurped a good bit of it down. I was going to need it if I was going to make it through the rest of the evening.

"So, uh Libby, what about you?" I asked, needing to change the subject and shift any attention off of me.

"Bad breakup with a girlfriend. I wanted to move as far away from her as possible and ended up here," she waved her hand in the air, brushing it off. "And then a few months later I ran into these buffoons when my abilities started coming in and I've been stuck around them ever since." After I chugged the rest of our margarita, she called another waitress over, ordering a Sex on the Beach, dubbing it her go-to.

I laughed at that. "You've put up with Derik the whole time you've known Seth? That's rough."

Derik shot me a wicked grin. "Only 'cause Blondie here wants my body."

Libby damn near choked on her drink. Reddish orange shot out of her nose; a shade darker than the pink that flooded her cheeks. Derik and Seth were laughing their asses off.

Libby smacked Derik's chest, a loud *thwack*. "You, jerk!" She laughed. "I put up with you because underneath that jerk-exterior, you're a big softie," she ran her emerald eyes down his torso before looking Derik directly in the eye. An evil grin playing on her lips. "But maybe I was wrong."

"Okay, first of all, there is nothing *soft* about me, Blondie," Derik winked at Libby. "Secondly, I am an absolute delight to be around." He jutted his chin upward, crossing his arms and added a "hmph" for emphasis.

They'd make a cute couple.

I glanced at Seth out of the corner of my eye, his laughing fit reduced to a toothy grin as he looked back and forth between Libby and Derik as they continued to bicker.

The low light from The Taco House illuminated the deep blues of his eyes. The depths of the ocean danced within them, twinkling. His shaggy, midnight hair swooped across his forehead, bangs dangled at his brow. He was beautiful. My heart shuddered in my chest.

I sighed.

No chance in hell.

The condom of your livelihood, remember?

Captain Protector.

The Protectormator.

A breath of air tickled my neck. "They always bicker like this by the way," Josh muttered, his voice low.

I dragged my hungry gaze from Seth. "Oh really? How long does it usually last?"

Amusement laced his response. "Typically all night. But we'll see."

The corners of my mouth lifted. "They're like an old married couple." I felt Josh chuckle next to me.

"I would be inclined to agree"—he took a swig of his beer—"if they were genuinely interested in one another."

I mulled that over, hoping I wasn't reading too much into it as my mind immediately switched to how close Libby and Seth were with each other. He'd be crazy not to want her and vice versa.

Our waitress brought out our food. I pushed my apology nachos in between Josh and me, not taking no for an answer. Before she sprinted to her next table, I stopped our waitress to order another drink, asking her to surprise me as long as it was strong and sugary.

I snatched a nacho off the plate in front of me, dipping it in the bowl of melted queso before shoving it into my mouth. My eyelids slid shut, moaning as the salt and spice hit my tongue. One of the guys choked on their tacos.

"Oh my God, these are the best freaking things in town," I muffled, dancing in my seat.

Seth reached for the nachos, his arm brushing against my boob in the process, jolting me.

Excuse me, Sir.

I smacked his hand away. "Mine," I hissed, pushing the plate of deliciousness closer to Josh. "I didn't accidentally grope *you*, so get your own, Muscles. These are for me and Josh." I stuck my tongue out. Heat flashed in Seth eyes darting between the two of us, my side nearly squished into Josh's with how small our booth was.

Seth reached for the nachos again, snatching one before I could smack his arm again. He bit into it, eyes trained on me, darkening. My heart rate quickened as he slowly ran his tongue over his lips, the corners of his mouth twitched.

My mouth hung open.

"You're going to catch flies, Miss Snow. Might want to close your mouth. Or eat your nachos." Josh's husky tone sounded in my ear.

I clamped my mouth shut and went back to my food. I was fighting not to picture what *exactly* Seth could potentially do with his tongue.

If he was actually interested, Dumbass.

I huffed.

During our little standoff, one of the waitresses had dropped off my drink. It was baby-doll pink with some sour worm shaped gummies sticking out the top. And glitter. Lots of freaking glitter. I grabbed it and sucked it down. It was freaking heaven. Pure sugar, I couldn't even taste the alcohol.

"I take it your sugar-drink was up to par, Miss Snow?" Josh asked, amusement laced his tone.

I shook my head. "Mhm," I bit into one of the sour candies. "Really sweet. I kinda want another one." I giggled, as warmth spread through me.

I offered Josh a gummy worm as I took another bite of mine. "Going back to earlier, what's your story, Mr. Tall, Dark, and Mysterious?"

Ballsy, aren't we?

He let out a throaty chuckle. "Tall, Dark, and Mysterious? Aren't you original, Miss Snow?" He sipped from his beer again, really milking the thing. "I've been around for quite a long time, dear. Three centuries to be exact. Seen a few wars. Traveled our world to every known edge. Have bed numerous lovers. It's a long time but nothing more than what you'd expect, Miss Snow. I assure you my *story* isn't nearly as interesting as you think."

I pouted. "There goes that fantasy then. Bummer," my words began to slur. "So then, Josh-ua, how'd ya end up in this little ol' college town?"

He shrugged. "I was on a mission out here. And the scenery drew me in." Short and simple.

For someone so full of themselves, he sure is short in talking about himself.

Lame.

"No girl involved? No tragic backstory?"

His eyes flickered. "No, Miss Snow. I'm sorry to disappoint you."

I cocked my head to the side, really taking him in. Deep chestnut-brown hair, perfectly slicked back. Even the stray stand when he first arrived at The Taco House had been swept back into place. His jawline sharp, stubble now gone. His eyes the color of a clear summer sky, speckled with shades of a light, almost amber shade throughout. He was handsome, beautiful, even.

A grin crept across his lips.

Shit, did I say that out loud?

"I can stay here with Miss Snow to ensure she finishes her meal, if you'd like. I'm sure training could wait until tomorrow." Josh flicked his gaze behind me.

I must've zoned out again.

I swept my eyes over our table; everyone had finished their food but me.

"Are you sure? She can be a handful when she drinks."

I whipped around, shooting daggers at Seth. In the process, I knocked over an empty beer bottle. "I am not! I'm perfectly capable of taking care of myself, thank you."

Jackass.

Seth's eyebrows shot up, flicking his line-of-sight to the toppled over beer bottle. "Uh huh. I guess it knocked itself over then?"

He's enjoying this.

"I'm not a child, you jerk. You guys go, I'll finish my food then head out. I'll hail a cab or something." I shot back.

"Nope, not happening."

I whimpered. "Seeettthhh. Come on."

"Short Stuff, he's got a point. It'd be safer if one of us stayed with you." I glared at Derik, wishing at that moment I could catch his blonde mop on fire.

"Traitor."

Josh cooed, "Miss Snow, if you believe it to be that miserable sitting here with me alone, then I shall make it as if I'm not even here, if you'd like. But I'll be escorting you home."

Home.

The simple mention of it left an ache in my chest. Reminding myself.

"Fine. But you keep your mouth shut and let me eat in peace and quiet. And don't even pull some Seth shit and try to cover my meal. It's on me. Including those nachos." I growled.

Josh nodded before we both scooted out of the booth to let Seth out. I slid back into my seat and Josh gracefully slid into Derik and Libby's spot. They all said their goodbyes, Seth lingering for a brief moment. His eyes shifted between Josh and me. His brows pushed together before letting out a sigh and letting me know he'd see me at his place.

Weird.

I started eating once they left. Taking my time, mulling over the night and my wavering buzz. "You can leave now that Seths gone. I'll hitch a ride home."

"What happened to wanting me to keep my mouth shut?"

"You can still do that while you leave. Like I said, I'm fine," I shoved another street taco in my mouth, mumbling as I chewed. "He just wants to play protector. He's done it since we were kids. I was always the clumsy, reckless, frail friend, who he decided he had to take care of and protect," I threw a crumb from the tortilla on my plate, slumping into the back of the booth. "I know Seth means well, but I'm not helpless. I don't want to be a project. I can take care of myself."

I've done it long enough.

"Miss Snow, as I'm sure you very well could handle yourself, you are still new to this world. You aren't even a fully fledged Nephilim. Your powers are just beginning to expose themselves. And you have zero battle training. Although Mr. Draven and I don't always see eye to eye with one another, you have been through a great deal over the last week and it would be best that someone stays nearby for the time being. It goes beyond 'playing protector.' It's our job. By all means, be absolutely irate with Seth, but please for the sanity of the group, please don't make it more difficult than it must be."

I just stared at Josh.

Way to guilt trip me.

I'll play along but I'm not some lost kitten that needs to be coddled or nursed back to health.

"Whatever. You guys are like helicopter parents. Maybe worse." My buzz was totally gone, this conversation drained the last of it.

"Explain, Miss Snow. What exactly is a helicopter parent?"

"Seriously? It's someone who's overbearing. To an obnoxious level."

"Ah, I see. If it helps, I don't find any more joy in being your babysitter than you do," he leaned forward, clasping his hands together in front of his face. A darkness flooded his pupils. "Although, I will say, you are rather entertaining. I don't typically get groped in group settings."

I fumed. "Prick."

CHAPTER TWENTY

Erin

Josh dropped me off at Seth's place an hour later. My stomach was beyond full, and I was extraordinarily grateful that Josh hadn't said a word since we left the restaurant. He tried grilling me a few more times and I just shut it down, shoving food in my mouth and another drink to avoid the need to answer. The only time I opened my lips to respond, a bite of food remained on my tongue. It caused Josh's lip to curl. He was prompted to keep his thoughts and twenty-questions to himself after that.

We pulled up and the only vehicle in sight was Seth's. I groaned, not wanting to deal with him alone after his little decision about the need for me to be assigned a babysitter. I sighed and let myself out of Josh's car before I headed up the stairs to Seth's porch and through the front door.

Seth spread himself along the couch, feet propped up on the arm rest, one arm behind the pillow situated under his head.

Well, isn't someone comfy?

The door shut behind me, catching Seth's attention and he waved me over. I dragged myself over and plopped down in the small space next to Seth's head. I flung my head back and closed my eyes. If he was going to lecture me about anything or talk doom and gloom, I was at least going to be comfortable.

"You good?"

"Yeap. Just getting comfortable before you smother me," I grumbled. Seth shifted next to me but I kept my eyes shut.

"Smother you? What are you talking about?" His voice hitched.

I ignored him. "Do you have any beer or anything?" I hated the taste of it but beggars can't be choosers. And right then, some additional liquid courage sounded like the way to go, since what was in my system from The Taco House was pretty much depleted.

A few minutes passed as we sat in silence. I peaked one eye open to see Seth staring at me. "Can I help you?" I snapped at him.

"Ah, sorry. No beer but we have that wine you like." His mouth formed a thin line as he stood up and made his way to the kitchen.

"Rather have that anyway," I mumbled.

Glasses clinked as he grabbed the only two wine glasses he owned out of his cabinet. The wine splashed as he poured, the bottle's glugging filled the silence.

Seth set the glasses on his coffee table before he sat down again. I lifted my arm and made a grabbing gesture in the air. He huffed out a strained laugh before he placed the glass in my hand.

"You're ridiculous, you know that?"

"Maybe. But I have every right to be. I've been up for less than a day since y'all rescued my ass, risking yourselves"—I squinted both eyes open, sending him a sideways glare—"and it feels like a whole ass week has gone by."

"I mean, technically, it has been a week, Erin. And we would've done the same for Derik or Libby. You might be new to all of this, but we're a team. And we have each others' backs."

"That's different though."

"How?"

I gulped down my wine, noticing he'd filled mine to the rim.
Good.

I smacked my lips together. "Because you don't have some big-brother complex about either of them and they don't know me that well."

I'm just here. Being a burden.

Seth scoffed. "I'm sorry, but a big-brother complex? Did you hit your head on a rock or the doorway on your way in?"

I rolled my head to the side and stared at him. "You act like I'm this frail fragile girl who can't take care of herself. When I clearly can and have since middle school," I took another heavy gulp from my glass. "Even when we've been lifting or running together over the last few years it's the same thing. I know I'm clumsy but I'm not helpless. I would've figured a way out." I chugged the rest of my wine. I stood up and headed for the kitchen to grab more when my foot caught on the coffee table. I whipped my arm out, catching myself before I face planted and proved exactly the opposite.

Go figure.

I grabbed the bottle, now half empty, near the edge of the kitchen island and slung it back. I eyed the unopened bottle perched across the island and reached for it as well before I sauntered back toward the couch. I sloppily set the unopened wine on the coffee table before taking another pull from the one still in my hand and hitting Seth with a dead stare.

Give me your worst, Seth.

"You could've been killed, Erin. And until we have this whole 'Key' bullshit sorted out and you have a hold on your powers, I'd rather make sure you're safe than risk your clearly drunk ass getting swiped or worse. If you don't like it, too damn bad." He boomed, his jaw twitching.

"Well, fuck you then, Seth." I quickly drank the rest of the wine and moved to open the second bottle.

"Tell me when and where, Snow. When. And. Where," Seth rumbled. My cheeks flushed.

I scoffed and flipped him off. "Ha. Yeah, right. I'm just a damn protection project for you. I'm not *your* type. And you wouldn't dare."

He'd leaned forward, his nose mere inches from mine causing me to jump, my breath hitched. Erebus's face flashed before me and I screamed.

Amber eyes stared at me, hunger flashed.

Seth jumped back, apologizing profusely. "Erin, are you okay? I'm sorry, I didn't mean to scare you. Shit," he ran to grab some water and a blanket. My body shook. I fought back the living nightmare trying to take over. "Erin, listen to me. I'm just going to put this blanket over your shoulders, is that okay?" I absently nodded my head. The clank of another glass sounded from the coffee table. "I'm here, Erin. Whatever just happened, wasn't real. It's me, Seth." He paused. "We're in my living room. It's you and me. You're safe," his voice was unwavering. "You're safe." Seth repeated until the shaking stopped.

I came back to myself. The living room came back into view. I blinked a few times, pushing the final scraps of fear into the far recess of my mind. I pulled the corners of the blanket further around myself and kept my half-dazed line of sight focused on my lap.

"I'm sorry," we said simultaneously.

"Erin, do you want to talk about it?"

I shook my head. "I don't know. No. Not really, I guess. I don't know what's wrong with me. I've freaked out, what, twice since I woke up this morning now?"

I'm a broken mess.

He reached his hand out, stopped, and waited for me to reach my own out to his. I slid mine out from behind the blanket and rested it in the palm of his hand.

Don't cry.

You cry, he'll know.

"Rin, you went through a lot. I'm not going to say it's fine. Or that it'll be okay and get better because I can't promise that. But I got you. And not just because of some 'big brother' complex you're accusing me of," he let out a soft chuckle. "You couldn't be further from the truth actually."

"What do you mean?" My confused eyes lifted and met his. Deep as the ocean, a twinkle of light escaped from their furthest depths.

"I..."

The front door burst open, Libby and Derik barreled in, laughing their asses off. Reeking of tequila. Seth and I yanked our hands apart and pushed ourselves to the far edges of the couch, putting as much space between us as possible.

Seth's face was beet red, a sight I've rarely ever seen. My eyes widened in response.

What was he going to say?

I shot the drunk assholes a glare before busting out laughing as I took in their states. Derik was full on shitfaced and grinning so hard he'd damn near end up with his face stuck that way. His clothes were covered in leaves and grass. Libby wasn't much better off as her makeup was smeared halfway down her face.

"What the hell happened to you two?" I laughed.

Libby giggled, her sing-song voice slightly higher. "After we left The Taco House, we went out for more drinks at the dive bar a few shops down. Did some crappy karaoke and a group of girls talked Derik into a few shots and I joined in," she hiccuped. "On our way back, I tripped and took Derik down with me. We landed in a ditch down the street," she hiccuped again. "He had dirt all over him, it was hilarious."

"Yeah well, Blondie, you weren't much better off. You had a whole ass tree in your hair," Derik said as he stuck his tongue out at Libby.

Seth and I snickered at them.

I held up the new wine bottle, waving it at them. "Y'all up for anymore?" My head swiveled in Seth's direction. "You got anymore?"

"There's one more bottle. But I can make a run to the liquor store real quick. Or the gas station," he glanced over at Libby and Derik fumbling their way to the guest room. "Gas station it is."

"Wait, should you be driving?" I asked, my brow furrowing.

"Yeah, I'm fine. I didn't even finish my beer when we grabbed food earlier." I peaked at his wine glass, barely touched.

He swiftly grabbed his keys and left.

I sipped my wine; I decided to go ahead and claim the bottle for myself when I heard giggling as it echoed from the guest room. Where all my stuff was. And currently both of Derik and Libby's things were as well. Including blankets and a beer pong cup covered sleeping bag of a notable player.

Gross.

I held back a gag as I stumbled through the living room and toward the bedroom, closing my eyes and hoping they weren't naked. I knocked before peeking around the door.

They were both sprawled on the floor bellies down, fully clothed, thank god. Their heads were close together and drunken eyes glued onto one of their phones.

"What are you guys doin?" I slurred.

"Funny cat videos. Derik pulled them up. They're *so* cute, Erin! There was even one with a kitten waddling like a little duck." Libby squealed over her shoulder as she kicked her feet.

"This woman loves her cat videos, Snow. She can watch 'em for hours," Derik added. A hint of admiration in his voice.

I padded into the room and sat down next to them, leaning forward to see which one of the thousands of feline viral videos they had playing. It was a compilation with snippets of the animals mewling, some sounding as if they were human. Others involved some of the cats jumping and bolting through homes, knocking over bowls, landing on their human's head or directly on their crotch, sending their human right to the ground. That last one sent Libby and me into hysterics and Derik covered his groin, scrunching his face.

We sat huddled together giggling and pointing at Derik's phone until Seth came back bearing more booze. He'd brought back all the fixings sure to cause some trouble. Vodka, tequila, wine coolers, and a few packs of pre-made jello-shots.

He'd walked in, two plastic bags dangling from his arms on the borderline of ripping open. "Who's ready for some fun?" He winked at me then turned on his heel and headed to the living room. We heard him rustle around, bottles hitting the coffee table, bags being dug through, so we drunkenly pushed ourselves to our feet and out to Seth.

Derik slung his arm around Libby's shoulders, then pulled me under his other arm. "Alright ladies, looks like Seth's ready to party." He slurred. Libby giggled. And I threw a fist in the air, whooping.

Seth handed each of us a jello-shot; Libby's was pink, Derik's green, and mine blue. Seth took a yellow one. Derik and Libby slurped theirs down like champs. I, on the other hand, did not. Half the shot landed on my chest.

Dammit.

"Okay, I suck at these. How do these go again?" I half smirked, embarrassed, at Seth.

"Oh, come on, Rin. It's easy as hell, let me show you." He popped the top off and brought it up to his mouth. His eyes burned a hole in me as he darted his tongue into the little plastic cup, slowly twisting it around, running his tongue along the inside, agonizingly slow. Heat pooled in my stomach as he pulled the cup away, licking his lips, hunger seemed to fill his eyes. Blood rushed to my cheeks and spread across my chest. The corners of his mouth lifted. "Need another demonstration?"

For the love of...

"Nuh...no. I think I got it," I stuttered. I snatched another one, going for round two. And I in fact, did *not* have it. The whole thing ended up all over my mouth and chin. To further push my embarrassment as Seth laughed at me, he reached out and wiped the red jell-o off my chin with his thumb before proceeding to stick said thumb into his mouth, sucking it off.

Holy hell.
Suck me, would ya?
Oh my God.
Erin. Calm yourself.
Oh dear lord.
What is going on with me?

I diverted my attention to the rest of his haul, grabbed a few green plastic cups, along with the bottle of vodka, and began pouring. I topped each cup off with a splash of lemonade and passed two to Libby and Derik then pounded my own back before handing one to Seth. They all sloshed theirs back. I poured a second round while Seth slipped into the guest room. He came out dragging all of our blankets, pillows, Derik's sleeping bag, and tossed them in a pile on the hardwood.

"The hell man, we just started drinking." Derik whined.

"You three have been drinking all night, asshole. We ain't crashing yet. Thought we'd play some good ol' fashioned drinking games before hitting the hay and sleeping out here." Seth drawled.

"Are you from the country now, Seth?" I laughed.

"Nope, want me to be?" He waggled his eyebrows.

"Freaking weirdo." I smacked his arm as I bent down to grab my blanket from the pile. I laid it out on the floor, closest to the front door on this side of his couch. Seth came up behind me, throwing his on the floor next to mine, leaving zero gaps between our makeshift sleeping spots. "Uh, personal space, much?"

Seth said, his voice low and rumbling, "Thought I'd help keep you warm with how cold it can get out here," I spun around, my eyes wide. He chuckled. "I'm kidding, Rin. I know what you're doing, putting yourself closest to the door. On the off chance something *were* to happen, I'm not leaving you as our first line of defense."

I stuck my tongue out at him. "Jerk."

"Yeap, that's me. Now how about we break out another round and get sloshed?" he said, his cheeky smile spread across his face.

I tried fighting it, but it was contagious. The corners of my lips lifted, matching his. "Let's fucking do it."

Chapter Twenty-One

Erin

"Quite an evening. Did you enjoy yourself?" The familiar booming voice echoed through the air. Once again, the man from my dreams stood with me atop a clearing surrounded by mountains upon mountains. Not a cloud in the purple sky, on the cusp of a sunset. Stars twinkled in the distance.

"It was needed." I replayed the groping mishap at the restaurant, arguing with Seth, and the overwhelming embarrassment. The kidnapping prowled the edges of my memory, waiting to pounce. I shook my head, chasing away the thoughts.

He pondered that for a moment. "I see you've discovered your flames. But have yet to control them through practice?"

I narrowed my eyes. "Not like I've had the opportunity to. Considering I was unconscious until this morning"—I threw my hands on my hips—"and thanks for leaving that little detail out by the way, could've been helpful to know beforehand that I could do that," I shot him a glare. "There's only so much one person can do in a twenty-four-hour period, you holier-than-thou prick."

The wind caressed my shoulders, as if in agreement.

"And you chose to spend that time flirting, watching others attempt to solve the situation at hand without lifting a finger, and becoming intoxicated beyond common sense. You very well could have focused your time on more important tasks at hand." He lectured.

I bristled. *"Excuse the hell out of me for wanting to let loose. It's not like I suddenly had all this bullshit unloaded on me recently that I had no say or choice in."*

"This isn't the first time that this has happened, Erin Snow. You have been through many trials before. You shall persevere again."

"Lay off, dude. It was one day."

"One day could be the difference between life and death." Clouds rolled in from the distance. Lightning lit the sky as they raced forward. Darkness began closing in. The air suddenly thin, grasping my neck, suffocating me.

I snapped my head sideways, only to find that the man had disappeared.

Screams echoed along the horizon, growing in volume as the thundering storm raged in toward me. The sky wept, flooding the clearing. The mountains oddly morphing.

Against my struggling breath, I squinted, forcing my eyes to tap into their enhanced vision. Gone was the beautiful green scape. In its place were mountains, no longer formed by eons of the land moving and colliding, but by bodies. Millions. Their mouths hung open, eyes hollowed out, streams of tears the color of oxblood trailing from their sockets. Rivers of blood flowed down the landscape. The clearing flooded, becoming the deepest shade of red. The thick liquid rose above my ankles, over my calves, and knees. Rising higher and higher, quickly enveloping me. It reached my chin, and I sucked in as much strangled air as I could. The blood began to fill my mouth, seeping in through my nose, choking me. Drowning me.

A voice from within the depths of the Earth rang softly through my head as the darkness enveloped me.

"Save me."

I jolted awake gasping for air. Sweat slicked down my back, loose strands of hair clung to my forehead. My heart thundered in my chest as I tried to calm my breathing. I frantically searched the room; Libby and Derik were still huddled together asleep, her body turned sideways with her head resting on Derik's chest. Seth snored next to me, his arm loosely wrapped across my lap, as he laid on his stomach. His thick, black hair messy and covering the upper half of his face—peaceful. I let out a breath, calming myself.

Everyone is here.

They are all safe.

It was just another weird nightmare with the silver haired weirdo.

My eyes began to roam over Seth's form as he slept. Taking in the toned muscle down his bare back from the years of weight training and apparent fighting. I did a double take. Bare back.

Seth was shirtless.

And had his arm around my lap.

I panicked and threw my blanket off my legs.

I let out another breath, relief. I was still fully clothed, not a scrap missing.

Holy hell.

I racked my brain through the fog of the night before. The Taco House, a giant ass margarita, accidentally squeezing Josh's junk, Seth going over-protective on me, again, coming back here, getting sloshed, and playing drinking games.

Oh no.

I slapped my hands over my face, dragged them down as the rest of the night replayed.

It started with two additional rounds of heavy poured Vodka Lemonades, racing to see who could slurp theirs down the quickest. Seth and Derik tied. While Libby and I choked ours back.

Derik grabbed the emptied bottle of vodka and had us all sit cross-legged in a loose circle, a mischievous grin played on his face. "Who's sup fora game of Truth er Dare? Each turns a-nother shot," he slurred.

I shot him my best devilish smirk and reached for the bottle, spinning it. "I'll go first."

"Ballsy. I like that on ya, Short Stuff," Derik said, an octave lower.

"Get in line, Derik." Libby giggled, pointedly glancing to my right. Where Seth was lounging propped up on his elbows.

I scoffed. "Ha, yeah right," the bottle landed on Libby. "Not his type. And nobody is in line for this mess fest." I waved my hands up and down, emphasizing my lack of allure. Libby rolled her eyes at me.

"Ssoo, Lib, Truth oor dare?" Derik asked.

She hiccuped. "I think Erin's supposed to ask me that."

My grin held. "Well, which is it, Libby?"

A glint danced in the corner of her emerald eyes. "Dare."

"I dare you to..." I racked my brain. I didn't know her well enough to think of anything. "Take another shot."

Seth laughed beside me. "Oh come on, Rin. That's the best you got? Lame."

I narrowed my eyes at him, my tongue heavy in my mouth. "Like you have anything better."

"Watch me." Seth leaned forward, his arm brushing my thigh as he spun the bottle. This time it landed on Derik.

"Hit me man, show the Princess how it's done." Derik gleamed. Challenge danced across his features.

Princess my ass.

Seth clicked his tongue. "I dare you to give us a little show by dancing on the coffee table. Dancing and clucking like a chicken."

"Done." Derik hopped onto Seth's coffee table; how that thing held, I had no idea. Libby pulled her phone out and played some throwback-cheesy-as-hell dance music. Derik threw his shirt off, swinging it in circles above his head before tossing it at Seth. He bent forward, sticking his hands under his arms and flapping his bent elbows in the air, clucking as he went. His sculpted stomach shook with the movement.

We busted out laughing. Seth was barely able to contain his laughing fit while he recorded the entire thing on his phone. Tequila spurted out of my nose, burning as it came out, which only caused us all to laugh harder to the point where my ribs ached.

"Alright alright! Point taken! Someone else go!" I half laughed-half shouted.

Derik hopped off the table and sauntered back to his green beer pong themed sleeping bag, pointedly taking the vodka bottle, and spinning it as he plopped back down next to Libby; the forest green of her eyes lapped at his shirtless body. Derik winked and her cheeks instantly turned crimson.

Okay, well that's adorable.

I smiled at the two of them.

And it was short-lived because the following turn, unfortunately, landed on me. I threw back another shot, the tequila burning as it rushed down my throat. "Alright, hit me with it."

"Truth or dare, Snowgirl?" Derik sang.

"Snowgirl?" I deadpanned, rolling my eyes. "I'll take a dare, Beer Boy."

He cracked another smile at that. "Dare ya to show off that lil fire trick."

I shoved down the nausea that stabbed my insides at the thought of attempting to conjure my flames. "You're on," I said, flashing him a toothy grin essentially saying *be ready to eat shit.*

I closed my eyes, diving deep into myself, which was a bit hard considering how intoxicated I was.

To be fair, it would've felt impossible regardless.

I staggered my way through a world of pitch black; bumping into and stumbling over nothingness until I reached a tiny orange orb. I squatted down, cupping my hands around it as it began to morph into a singular rolling flame. I crossed my fingers that it worked as I pulled myself back from the pit and opened my eyes. Lo and behold, in the palms of my hands stood the same flame I envisioned.

It's so tiny though.

Fuck it. I still did it.

Score one for drunk me!

I rolled my shoulders back and sat up a little taller. My grin widened, and I winked at Derik. "Easy peasy." Seth, still next to me, seemed to beam with pride.

He leaned over, nudging me. "Nice job, Rin."

"Gotta put playboy here in his place." I motioned at Derik, giggling.

"Oh I know my place, Snowgirl. It's right in the heart of all the ladies." Derik waggled his eyebrows at me, sending us into another laughing fit. Libby grabbed the bottle—her turn to spin. It landed on Seth, and he picked the first truth of the night. I nibbled on my bottom lip, waiting.

I'm going to puke.

There was a twinkle in Libby's eye as she asked, "So Seth, playboy over here has his eyes on all the ladies, as per usual," she paused, letting the suspense build apparently. "Is there a lady who's caught your eye?" I froze. There had to be. Of course there was. Nausea rolled through me.

I mean look at the guy.

Seth stiffened beside me before loosening up once more. I waited with bated breath. "Lib, what are we, teenagers? You can ask a better question than that."

"Hmph! You can either answer that or you're getting a dare instead," Libby retorted. Her playful expression soured.

"Guess I'm taking a dare then," Seth clipped.

Libby's expression morphed into an evil grin and on her delicate, beautiful pixie-like features, it was utterly terrifying. "Then Seth, it's your turn to give some of us a show," her eyes flicked to me. "Throw that shirt off. Derik, you pick the music."

Oh my God.

Please no.

Libby. Don't do this to me.

I need a boulder or a building, anything to hide under.

Derik hit play on his phone, another throwback song came on. I threw back another shot and nearly choked as the music that came out of Derik's phone was directly from a very specific movie that had came out a few years ago that revolved around male strippers. I'd snuck into a theater to see it when it first came out, having dragged Seth with me. It was right after I moved out here and I didn't want to go alone.

That's it. I'm going to die. Right here.
My best friend is about to strip his shirt off.
And I can't keep my newly dirty thoughts to myself.
I'm done for.
Fucking fuck.

And Seth must've remembered too because he threw me a wink. Then proceeded to take his time gliding his shirt up over his tanned, sculpted-by-the-gods abs. Black wisps of hair trailed from his chest down to the hem of his pants, perfectly accentuating the deep V leading directly to what was hidden underneath. My eyes trailed up and down, soaking in the view. I'd seen him shirtless countless times during lifting sessions, running, and just lounging around his massive house during the summer. But this was wholly different. Seth tugged his shirt over his head and swung it in circles above his head, his hips rotating in time with each whirl. My mouth hung open, practically panting. My heart did a somersault.

Holy shit.

Libby and Derik whooped and hollered for him to drop his pants. I snatched another shot off the floor and gulped it down. Seth took that opportunity to toss his shirt at me and winked. He lowered his pants down, stopping right at his hips, his boxers peeking out.

My eyes widened; cheeks fully flushed. He jumped off the table, landing lightly on his feet, swaggering back to his blanket pile next to me.

I...I...

He whispered, "Enjoy the show, Erin?" He chuckled huskily.

Yes. A thousand times yes.

Wait no.

This isn't me.

I blinked at him, shock and heat coursing through my entire body.

It has to be all the alcohol.

Libby dared him. You're all drunk as hell.

And he knows how easy it is to embarrass you.

Chill the hell out. That's all that was.

No tension. None from him anyway.

Reel it in, Snow. No jumping the guy's bones.

Libby threw an empty jell-o shot cup at me, dragging me out of my runaway thoughts. I yelped.

Libby snickered. "Now the real fun's started, why don't you take another spin, Erin?" She rolled the vodka bottle over to me. I spun again, this time landing on no-man's land. We all took a round of shots. The night continued on until we passed out. Libby and Derik were the first; Seth not long after.

As I sat there, pondering and regretting the night before, it hit me.

Even with all the liquor that had coursed through my system, I didn't remember falling asleep.

Chapter Twenty-Two

Erin

I shook the thought from my mind as I stood, being careful to not disturb Seth. I stretched, working out the kinks in my joints; my back ached from the hardwood floor. I quietly padded across the living room and down the hallway to the guest room, softly pushing the door open. I stepped inside, holding my breath as I clicked the door shut.

I scanned the room. Clothes, presumably Derik and Libby's, were strewn around the floor and on top of the birch wood dresser Seth kept in the room. I tossed my hair into a poor excuse of a messy bun and began picking up different shirts, skirts, pants; folding and separating them into their own piles. The clothes that looked like Libby's I sat on the bed, and Derik's I placed on top of the dresser, organizing them by type of clothing. Once their clothes were neatly folded and arranged, I picked through my own pile, grabbing out some joggers and a baggy T-shirt before going to town organizing mine as well.

Once it all was put away, I clapped my hands together. Satisfied with my temporary room and deemed it livable. I threw on a pair of running shoes and a hoodie then quietly made my way back out to the main area. Libby and Derik were still in the same spot asleep. Seth had rolled onto his back, mouth hanging open, snoring loudly, surprisingly not waking the others

What a dork.

I snickered as I grabbed a water bottle from the fridge and headed out the front door, locking it behind me. I twisted the cap off and gulped down half of the bottle, then stuck my keys and cellphone in the zipper pocket of my joggers, galloped down the steps, and started on a run. The upside of not getting hungover, I could go for a run first thing in the morning.

Point: me.

I ran the opposite direction of town, keeping a steady pace. Sweat beaded on my forehead and neck, loose hair stuck to my skin. Birds chirped, leaves rustled, and a light mist cloaked the sidewalk. I inhaled the morning air, a calmness settled over me.

Perfect.

A truly perfect way to shake off another nightmare.

Trees grew closer together and the sidewalk widened as I neared one of the larger parks that bordered the woods on the outskirts of town. I slowed to a walk, taking it all in. Maple trees lined the walkway, various shades of reds, yellows, and oranges painted on their leaves. Fresh dew rested atop the recently trimmed grass. Little sprouts of wildflowers slowly danced in the morning breeze. It was peaceful, quiet.

I stopped at a bench half a mile into the park. I sat down, pulled my knees to my chest, and stretched the fabric of my hoodie over them; folding my arms over the top of my hoodie. I rested my chin on them, closed my eyes, and breathed in the world around me.

I needed this.

It could've been mere minutes but felt like an eternity—in the best way possible. Being out in nature always had that effect on me. It centered me.

My mind drifted to the past few weeks. I allowed myself to feel all the emotions: the draining stress, lack of sleep, Seth dropping the 'I'm this supernatural being called a Nephilim' thing on me; Demons, Angels, and that my life—at least part of it—had been a lie.

Nothing will ever be the same.
Everything I had worked so hard for...taken from me.
And now...all I can do...is control the controllable.
This isn't how things were supposed to go.
I had a rough childhood. That was supposed to stop.
I'm an adult now. Things are supposed to be easier. Better.
Less life-threatening.
Less surviving and more thriving. Or at least managing.

I let the image of the Demons play in my mind. I attempted to picture Erebus and what he did to me, and there was a mental barrier. Nothing but a memory fog.

Huh. That didn't seem to be a problem when I had that flashback yesterday.
Imagine that.
How convenient.
And there goes my whole 'control the controllable' spiel.

Those last words that had rang in my ears before I'd gone unconscious pranced at the edge of my memory, Erebus's bone-chilling voice echoed but nothing more. I grew frustrated and moved onto the nightmare from the night before. Processing the mountains of bodies.

What did it mean?

A chill ran down my spine. I missed something. I repeated the dream over and over, picking at every minute detail.

My phone rang, my eyes popped open. I wrangled around in my hoodie to slip my hand in and unzip my jogger pocket. By the time I pulled it out it'd stopped ringing, so I checked the call log and saw it was from an unknown number.

My phone beeped, a text floated onto the screen.

> Running alone this early in the day, Madam?

> Would you be open to some company?

I swiveled my head in search of whoever could've been out there watching me. Panic welled in my stomach. I shoved it down and stood up, speed-walking back the way I'd come. I scanned the park for any signs of movement. My phone rang again, and I picked it up, hissing.

"Alright, creep. Who the hell are you and why the fuck are you following me?"

"Miss Snow, is that anyway to say good morning?" Josh.

Son of a fucking bitch.

"Considering I don't have your number and you're apparently stalking me, I'd say I can speak to you how I very well please, *Josh*." Venom laced my words, making my point clear.

Fuck dude. I know I clumsily felt you up last night but it was an accident.

That'd be obvious even to me.

"My apologies, Miss Snow. I should've prefaced my message with informing you that it was me reaching out."

"You can shove your 'apologies' right up your ass. You didn't answer my question as to why you're following me."

A slick black car pulled up next to me, the tinted windows slid down. Josh bent forward in the driver's seat and flashed a tight smile. "Why don't you get in? I have a few errands I need to run."

"Didn't your parents ever tell you not to get into a car with strangers?" I huffed, staring him down.

"For starters, Miss Snow, we are not strangers. Secondly, I arrived in this life far before motor vehicles came into existence."

"You sound ancient when you speak, you realize that? No one calls cars 'motor vehicles' anymore."

"Call it a habit, then," he reached over the middle console and pushed the door open. "Given the weather calls for rain, humor me, Miss Snow. I won't bite." I looked up, planning on calling bullshit. Unfortunately, the sky had indeed darkened since I'd ran out there.

I rolled my eyes. "Fine, whatever," I stepped into the front seat and made a show of slamming the door closed. "Only because I don't want to run back to Seth's place completely drenched."

Asshole.

"Of course, Miss Snow." Josh put the car in gear and drove off. Out of the corner of my eye I scanned the dashboard and interior of his car—black suede. The dashboard was some type of cherry-red leather and the windows were borderline dangerously tinted.

"Okay, seriously what do you do outside of this superhero stuff?" I snapped.

Josh let out a low chuckle, the sound sent a jolt down my spine. "I'm a businessman. And a good one at that."

Explains the car...man I really did not get a good look at this thing when he dropped me off last night.

Even I know a luxury car when I see one.

"How do you have time for it? I don't even know how I'm supposed to balance the Nephilim stuff and school. Let alone my job." A headache pressed at the front of my skull.

The husked tone of his voice slivered across my skin, goosebumps left in its wake. "Years of practice, Miss Snow," Josh flipped his turn signal on and turned left down one of the main intersections in town. "You work at the library, correct?"

I stiffened, venom spat from me. "Yes. How did you know that?" I tracked his every move as he drove.

Did Seth tell him?

"Miss Snow, as I mentioned, I am a businessman. With my position, I keep tabs on each individual that myself or any colleagues associate with. And given that we are now colleagues, in addition to the familial relationship you had with Seth, I began keeping tabs on you the moment you two reunited a few years back."

A punch in the gut, my lips pressed together.

Familial Relationship.

Ouch.

Not wrong.

But ouch.

"Got it, so you're Captain Creepy?" I jabbed, slightly unnerved by his admission.

What else does he know about me?

As if reading my mind Josh responded, "No need to worry, Miss Snow. Unless a criminal record is found, I do not delve into my colleagues' pasts. That is none of my concern."

I looked him over. His button-up a solid black with the sleeves rolled neatly to the elbow; a suit jacket hung on the headrest of his seat. His suit pants matched, held together by a slim black-leather belt. The tendons in his forearms were relaxed but defined. Not a hair out of place.

He's so... immaculate.

I... I don't know if I trust that.

We drove in silence as Josh weaved through the road map of streets as we neared campus, then to the outskirts, leaving the city.

"Where are we going?" I finally asked.

This is like the start of a slasher film.

"As I mentioned, I have a business matter to attend to. Thought it would be beneficial for you to accompany me."

"You said errands. Not business," I clipped.

"Miss Snow, any errand of mine falls under that category."

"That sounds awfully boring and mundane," I said, watching as the trees flew by. I stole a quick glance at the dash, eyeing the speedometer as it slowly crept into the triple digits. "You, uh, want to slow down?" Don't get me wrong, I enjoyed speeding as much as the next person but given the fact that we barely knew each other—well I barely knew him, at least—it made me uneasy. Butterflies jostled around in my stomach, threatening to crawl their way up my throat.

Josh let his foot off the gas, bringing the speed to a saner pace. Barely. "When you're near immortal, the little nuances of human frailties, such as the fear of perishing in a motor vehicle, are of no concern or consequence."

Well isn't someone cocky.

"Okay, I get that to an extent, but I'm new to all of this so if you could maybe *not* drive like a maniac that would be absolutely fantastic. And you know, take into consideration that it might be drastically more difficult for you to get killed or injured, but the humans who share the road are very mortal and not indestructible."

"Careful, Miss Snow. Wearing your heart on one's sleeve is quite dangerous in the world. If you allow your enemy to see what you hold dear, that may be the very thing they use to break you."

I rolled my eyes. "Yeah, yeah. Whatever you say, Captain Creepy. Just a damn ray of sunshine."

"I prefer to consider myself realistic," Josh retorted, the corner of his lip twitched

"I prefer to consider you annoying," I mumbled.

"Two different perspectives. Although mine is the correct one."

I rolled my head in his direction, shooting him a dirty look, and flipped him off.

"You may deem me annoying, Miss Snow, but you've entered into a whole new realm that you know very little about. Which is particularly why I sought you out this morning."

So, you were following me then. Creep.

I ignored him as he pulled into a vast parking garage attached to one of the largest buildings along the cityscape. We'd been in his car for well over an hour and the closest city to my little college town was Charshire. I pulled up the GPS on my phone to verify if that's where we were, lo and behold the little blue dot in the center of my screen pinpointed us in the heart of downtown. With no way to hightail it back to Seth's on my own, I was stuck following Prissy Pants around until he either got bored of me or finished his 'errands.'

Josh parked in the spot closest to the walkway that led into the building. I peered at the sign through the windshield, *Reserved* barely visible. I leaned forward in an attempt to make out the text below.

The passenger door swung open, and I jumped. I grumbled a thanks, grabbing Josh's hand as he helped me out of the car. He shut the door, considerably more graceful than when I'd slammed it earlier.

"Wouldn't want you to break the door off of its hinges, Miss Snow, with your developing and untrained strength."

"Wouldn't want to hurt your ego," I clipped. Twirling on my heel, I rolled my shoulders back, stuck my chest out, and lifted my chin, sashaying in the direction of the walkway. My messy bun thumping against the nap of my neck, loose hairs fanning out to the side of my head. I thanked the gods that the toe of my running shoes hadn't caught on the curb leading up and sent me face planting right into the concrete.

Looks like someone might be on my side, for the moment.

Josh followed silently behind me. Until I remembered I had no clue where we were going. I forced myself to fall back so that I was in step with Josh.

The heel of his Oxfords clacked against the porcelain-tiled floor as we strode through the lobby and into the elevator encased in frosted glass on the side opposite from where we entered. The ride up remained silent as well, to the seventy-eighth floor. The elevator dinged and the doors slid open.

I followed Josh out. We were greeted by double-wide glass doors, windows on either side of them spanned the entirety of the floor. I kept my expression neutral as I took in the white floors, polished so intensely that I could see our reflections. The walls and ceiling matched, both beautiful and sterile. Through the glass doors stood a single large reception desk; the sides an equally blinding pearl with a slab of grey granite rested on top.

We passed by the empty reception area and down a hallway lined with abstract paintings of various shades of blues and reds, greens and yellows, morphed wing-like shapes.

I halted. A piece near the end of the hall caught my attention. The background had been painted a deep purple that faded into a charcoal on the outer edges of the canvas. Merlot splattered in the center outlining a body, wings spread from its back. Each feather meticulously painted. I peered closer. Within the body, was the shadow of a long sword slit through its center, a black pit puddling at its knees.

"Haunting, isn't it?" Josh said, his breath tickling my ear, causing me to jump.

"That's uh, one way to put it." I shivered. A thought crossed my mind, curious if it were based on reality.

I wonder where it came from, who the artist is.

Josh led me to the end of the hall, framed by two mahogany doors spanning the entirety of the wall. It stood wildly out of place from the remaining parts of the office. He pulled a wrought iron key the size of his hand from his pants pocket, inserting it into the lock and twisting it.

How in the hell did he hide that thing in there?

It's massive.

I quirked my eyebrow as the door creaked open. The room was covered in shadow. A single overhead light illuminated the center of the room, casting a spotlight. A lonely metal chair stood within it.

And in that chair, sat a Demon.

Chapter Twenty-Three

Seth

I held her face in my hands, beautiful eyes staring into mine. My heart thrummed in my chest. This was it. Her eyelids fluttered closed as I leaned in. Her lips met mine, softer than I could've ever imagined. So lush, tasting of honey. Her lips parted, allowing me access. My tongue darted inward, dancing with hers.

"I love you," I rushed out, breathlessly.

Silence.

I pulled back, searching her depths to find they'd gone pitch black. Her mouth widened, forming a smile that sent chills down my spine.

A figure appeared behind her, circling its arm around her waist and pulling her in close. It formed into the shadow of a man. He bent forward, twisting a strand of her hair between his fingers, inhaling. Then kissed down her neck.

She sighed. "Oh, silly, silly boy. If only I loved you."

A blade shot through my chest, piercing my heart. The last thing I heard was her laughter, ringing, as a tear trickled down my cheek.

"Why?" I choked, the metallic tang of blood flooded my mouth. My vision blurred until all that remained was her hate-filled pitted eyes.

High-pitched laughter echoed in the darkness. "You abandoned us, Seth Draven. And now, we'll get our revenge on you."

I groaned as the sunlight blinded me. I threw my arm over my eyelids, attempting to shield myself from the brightness.

"Why the fuck is it so bright?" I grunted out, rolling over right onto another blanket. Squinting one eye back open, Erin's spot came into view. Empty.

I shot up and barreled to her room. She wasn't there either. I slammed open the bathroom door. It was empty too. "Fuck!"

I ran to my bedroom, grabbing sweats and a shirt, tossing them on and ignoring the still disheveled state of the room. I'd been far too focused on making sure we were all guarding Erin after we escaped that bastard Erebus and his lackeys to even care about the appearance. Keeping my people safe was more important than cleaning the place up.

The harrowing voice from my dream dug into me.

"You abandoned us."

As I went to reach for the door handle to the front door, Derik yelled behind me.

"Bro, where the hell are you rampaging off to?"

"Erin's gone. I need to find her. They could've—"

Libby cut me off, "Calm down there, Seth. She's fine. Erin left a note saying she was going for a run."

My shoulder slumped forward in relief. Then stiffened again. "She went running alone?" Panic laced my voice, even I could hear it. Libby thought it was hilarious. "What? Why is that so funny, Lib? She could get hurt. That shit head could be waiting to strike again."

What if Erebus takes her?

"Seth, sweetie, as much as I'm sure you want to follow her like a lost puppy, she's okay. We both know Erebus wouldn't be stupid enough to attack this quickly. And she probably needs to clear her head. Think about how much she's been through this last week alone. If you're worried, text her. Or you know, check her location on your phone. There's this amazing thing called technology." I shot her a glare. She flashed me an overly bright smile in return.

"Lib, you can be as much of a pain in my ass as Derik sometimes, you know that?" I grumbled as I dragged myself into the kitchen.

Erin could've woken me up.

Why didn't she?

"True, but you adore me for it," she laughed. "Anyway, Josh messaged you not too long ago saying he'd keep an eye on her today."

"Of course he will," I sighed. "I'll shoot him a text back. Can you toss me my phone?" It'd been sitting on the counter, how it made it there last night, I had no idea. The last thing I remembered was falling asleep listening to Erin animatedly give me a deep dive of her latest read. Something about one of the why-choose romances she loved so much with vampires and werewolves. Her voice sang as I drifted off, a smile plastered on my face. It felt like things were normal again. The haunted look that had plagued her eyes when she had finally awoken yesterday morning had been—for however briefly—replaced with pure book-obsessed Erin.

How often am I going to be able to see that now?

That light? Will it disappear if Erebus gets his claws into her again?

Or is she…is she already disappearing?

I texted Josh.

Hey, thanks for keeping an eye on her.

I stared at my screen, awaiting a response. A few minutes passed, nothing came through. I checked Erin's location out of curiosity. It had her pinned in Charshire. I let out a breath. They were at Josh's building. As a businessman with one of the biggest wigs on this side of the country, Josh owned one of the largest buildings in Charshire. Far grander than any structure we had here in our town aside from the college campus.

Wonder what they're doing there.

The only other person in our group who had ever been inside was Libby. She said she hated the drive so she'd only gone with him once and never told me or Derik what it was like beyond being massive.

My hands were too full to entertain the idea and to be entirely honest, I wasn't too keen on voluntarily sticking myself with the Prick for an unnecessary amount of time alone. My temper would undoubtedly get the best of me and I worked too hard to keep myself in check to allow that to happen.

I checked my messages once more, then shoved my phone into my pocket.

"Looks like they're in Charshire." I sighed. Derik rustled around in the pantry, more than likely clearing out my food stash that Erin and I'd bought last week. "Hey, before your ass eats all my food, wanna toss me a bagel?" A bag of the 'bread circles' came barreling across the kitchen at me. I caught it right before they nailed me in the nose.

A little memory popped into my mind.

A few months prior, Erin had been over and crashed on the couch after a long day of classes and then work and I'd been figuring out what to make the next morning. She had said 'bread circles' because she forgot the actual name of the cinnamon bagels I kept on hand.

My mouth twitched, a half smile peaked out.

"Is she going to be okay?" Libby asked, shaking me from my thoughts. Libby had the cream cheese out of the fridge and slid it over.

I belted out a laugh. "If anything, you should be asking if *Josh's* ass will be okay. The amount of sass in that woman is inspirational."

Derik nodded in agreement as he emerged from the pantry, arms full of protein bars, coffee, and bread. "You got any jam in the fridge?" Derik asked, the words muffled around the toaster pastry he had dangling from his mouth.

I shook my head at him. "Top shelf, man. Leave some for the rest of us."

The corners of Libby's eyes lifted in amusement. "You're going to need to make another trip to the store, asap. You guys only bought enough food to feed two people, not four."

I rolled my eyes in response.

"Yeah well, I wasn't exactly expecting you two to be mooching off me for the foreseeable future. You can buy your own shit, you know. Save me some cash."

I might have money from mom when mom passed...and also Nicholas, but it's not endless.

Derik huffed. "Why can Snow mooch off you, but it's a problem if we do it? We're bros, Seth, come on man."

Libby snickered. "Oh I know why." I shot her a glare. She snapped her mouth closed, the edges of her mouth twitching.

Traitor.

Derik eyebrows arched, eyes traveling between Libby and I. "Spill it, Lib. I gots to know." He begged. I stared her down, praying that she kept it to herself.

Don't you do it, Lib.

A Cheshire grin spread across her face. "Nah, I think I'll leave that for you to figure out, Pretty Boy." Libby batted her lashes at Derik, feigning innocence.

His gaze stuck on Libby and she winked at him. He shook his head, gave up, and chomped down on his toast.

Thank fuck.

If Derik had even an inkling of what Erin meant to me, he'd never let me live it down. Teasing to a whole other level. And with Erin convinced that I'm 'playing protector,' I'd rather leave it at that to avoid the embarrassment of potentially being turned down—at the moment.

Libby cranked up the coffee machine, tossing in the grounds Derik had stolen from the pantry. Fresh coffee quickly filled the air, a trace of French toast filtered with it. Libby poured each of us a mug. She offered to add cream and sugar to mine, and I declined, allotting to do it myself. I wasn't wanting to choke on enough sugar to take down a horse.

Something Libby and Erin have in common...their sugar addiction.

We chatted for a bit after scarfing down breakfast. Libby and Derik offered to dive into hunting down any new information or potential sightings for the humans who disappeared. I opted to stay back, backtrack our notes and findings, hoping maybe we'd missed something. I shot Erin a quick text, then dove in.

I logged onto Erin's laptop and the first thing to pop on the screen was an excerpt from some fan-fiction site. I stifled a laugh as I read through the page.

> His hand grazed my nipple. I shuddered. My knees shaking as he...

I scanned the rest of the page, imagining Erin kicking her feet as she read it, her face flushed; the giggling and little sounds she would make when she got really into her reading material.

She might be embarrassed about it but it's kinda cute.

I clicked a new tab open and typed in the name of the first woman on the list: Cassandra Eldren. I scrolled through her information;

work history, social media, most recent residence. I wasn't finding anything that stuck out. I pulled up the next woman, Aevalyne Eltroit's, information. Then the next. Nothing.

Fuck. I'm not getting anything helpful on these people.

There's no tie between them.

I raked a hand through my hair, frustration seeped into me.

I'm going to go nuts if I stare at this thing any longer.

I'm getting fucking nowhere.

And every fucking day we take to figure this shit out and where Erebus is hiding them…the less likely it is we'll find them alive and in one piece.

I shut the laptop and went over to the training area. The need to move, throw, or smash something gripped me.

I can't help anyone if I lose my shit.

They're all depending on me.

Starting with dumbbells to get my blood pumping and muscles warmed, weight low at hundred and fifteen pounds in each hand, forcing my anger into the movements. I rotated through five drop sets of overhead press, bicep curls, and lateral raises. Once those were completed, I moved to my dead lift pad, lining up the fifty-five-pound Olympic bar. I slid on four forty-five-pound plates on each side for my warm-up. Every set brought me further from the edge. If only a mere inch at a time.

On my next set, I secured two additional plates to each side and continued with drop sets. Increasing the weight after each set and finishing on the final thrust upward with twelve plates on each side. Sweat glistened on my skin in the mirror across from me. My shirt was soaked and glued to my skin. I lifted it up over my head and tossed it to the side before moving to the squat rack.

I set the bar to my height and stepped under the bar. Erin was the last one to use it so it had been nearly a foot too low for my shoulder height—irritation still floated in my veins—I loaded plate after plate onto the bar until it equated to just over twelve hundred pounds. I got into position under the bar and unracked, dipping into my first squat. I kept going, ending at thirty-five repetitions, then added two more plates, beginning the next drop set. Three sets later, my quads, hamstrings, and glutes pulsed. Sweat slicked down my abdomen, my core highlighted. I grabbed a towel off the rack by my cardio equipment and wiped it across my face, drying the sweat that had accumulated.

Hopping on the treadmill, I set the incline to seven and cranked the speed up to an eight-minute mile, going for distance rather than speed. My head cleared around mile six, the frustration finally worked itself out of my system. I ran through the information in my mind, comparing it to what we'd discovered from Erin's lead about The Key. I stopped, nearly slipping face first onto the treadmill belt. I regained my footing and hit the stop button on the center of the dashboard and ran for my phone, shooting texts off to Libby and Derik, then Josh. Telling them to get their asses back to my place as soon as possible.

Chapter Twenty-Four

Erin

There was a Demon. A fucking *Demon* in the hollowed out room—if I could even call it that—of the office Josh had brought me to. The entire space was shrouded in darkness aside from a single special-agent-interrogation-room-spotlight that illuminated the hellish creature in the center of the claustrophobic quarters. I whirled on Josh.

"What the actual fuck is going on?"

"Right in this moment, you have your back to a Demon, albeit it is unconscious and chained to an obsidian and salt coated iron chair, in addition to wards and being under my illusion. However, that does not excuse the fact that you have yourself exposed to an enemy. I would suggest refraining from doing so in the future."

You son of a bitch.

I threw my hands on my hips and dished out a flat glare in Josh's direction before I faced the Demon, begrudgingly.

"You're still not answering my question. What is going on and why the hell do you have a Demon in here? And the fuck does obsidian and salt have to do with anything?"

Josh stepped further into the room, shutting and latching the door behind us. His body pressed to mine. The hair on my neck stood at attention. I adjusted my stance and leaped to the side, giving myself a better defensive position. Josh and the Demon in my line of sight.

"Miss Snow, I can assure you, I did not bring you here to harm you. Simply to request your assistance," I narrowed my eyes. "He is here for questioning. You wish to find those humans, yes?"

This reeks of bullshit.

"What assistance am I to you?" I kept my stance and bared my teeth.

He glanced at my hands then flicked his eyes to meet mine.

"Oh."

So, I'm a scare tactic.

Great. I don't even know what I'm doing.

Nice planning, Josh. Not.

He moved to the shadows, rummaging through what sounded like metal cabinets and drawers, then emerged with a forearm length dagger, thick at the base, thinning to a sharp point at the tip. In the low light of the office-turned-interrogation room, the blade glinted a green hue, almost that of jade.

Josh's Oxfords barely sounded on the marbled floor as he strode towards the Demon. He snapped his fingers and the creature awoke, head whipping left and right, snarling.

"Release me! I cannot be contained, I am Artremias," he foamed at the mouth, a crazed look within its unseeing eyes. "I will devour you. Your soul. Release me, you scum. Or face my wrath." The Demon howled.

Josh squatted in front of Artremias, twirling the dagger in his hands. "Now, you know I can't do that, Artremias. You're *far* too valuable," Josh's voice dropped, power emanating from him, pure threat lined each word. "I do have a proposition for you, however." Josh leaned forward on his knees, skating his dagger along the Demon's thighs. "My acquaintance"—he pointed his dagger in my direction—"has quite an array of talents. Talents which can make you pray for death." The Demon's milky eyes widened in fear and flicked in my direction. He trembled. "Now, now, Artremias, no need to fret. Cooperate and I'll have my acquaintance here rein in her skills and leave you in one piece. Understood?" The corners of Josh's mouth tilted upward and spread the width of his face. He stood, turned on his heel, and backed towards the shadows.

The Demon spat on Josh as he stepped away.

Josh whirled around, dagger in hand, and slit the Demon's throat. It gushed black ink, soaking its front in the dark sludge. A stench of dead fish filled the room and sent me silently gagging. I covered my nose and mouth with my hands and caught a glimpse of Josh. He slid the blade across his tongue, licking it clean of the black blood. My stomach turned.

Oh my god. What is wrong with him?

He moved in, nearly nose to nose with the Demon. "Did you forget what happens when you choose to play with fire, Artremias?" He then snapped his fingers and the Demon screamed. My blood curdled in my veins. The dim room began to spin. I felt the floor rush towards me. An arm slid underneath me, catching me before I crashed to the ground. My vision blurred, black spots flitted in and out of my peripheral vision. My mouth watered and I heaved. A hand stroked my back.

I blinked back the spots and blurriness, taking in several panting breaths before looking up to find Josh was holding me, being the one to have caught me.

No shit Snooty Pants caught you. There's only three of you in this psycho's office of torture and one is almost completely incapacitated.

I pushed out of his embrace. "What the actual *fuck*, Josh?" I hissed. "Was knifing the guy necessary? *Licking* his blood? What kind of psycho are you?" I panted, my body convulsing.

"I needn't scare you, Miss Snow. But this is how I attain the information that is needed in vital situations, such as the one we've stumbled upon." The gold flecks nestled within the blue hues of his eyes reflected in the low light, the shadows danced in the edges of his pupils, as if in invitation. The rasp that fell from his lips caught me off guard. "As your safety is of the utmost importance."

Hot.

He's a hot psychopath.

Fucking hell.

My mouth hung open. I clamped it shut. Anger rose within me, suffocating my shock. "Does Seth know about this? Does he actually condone what you're doing?" They were Demons and absolutely terrifying but...they were still living creatures.

There has to be a less murdery way of getting the truth from them.

"No, I keep my...tactics to myself. It's simpler that way. And we're going to keep it that way, Miss Snow." He stared me down, the threat weighing.

Oh gee wiz. I feel so much better.

No one knows how bat-shit crazy this guy is.

Great.

Just great.

The Demon screamed louder, my head began pounding from the sound. I pressed my hands over my ears to keep them from bleeding and shouted, "What does this have to do with my safety? I get the humans. We need to find them quickly—yesterday, actually—but why factor my safety into it?"

Why do I matter in any of this?

Josh looked at me as if I was an idiot. "Do you not remember yesterday? The potential of you being 'The Key'? If what the Demons suspect is true, then you are in grave danger. And whatever you experienced in your time with the Demon Erebus, is nothing compared to what they will put you through."

My vision unfocused, as the images threatened to play and drag me down into the murky blood-soaked depths of the memory.

He flicked my nose and it vanished. "Out of it, girl. You continue to zone out like that, it will be the end of you. Your enemies will notice and take advantage."

My voice shook, "I'm fine. I'm fine."

He flicked my nose. Snooty Pants actually flicked my nose.

His eyes flicked between mine, searching. "Good. Now, Miss Snow, I need you to work with me on this. You do not need to conjure your powers unless I specifically request you to. I'll illusion what is needed to keep the Demon in line as I did before. I need you to cooperate if this is to work. Do you understand?"

He's right. The asshole is right.
I need to keep it together.
Or it won't just be my *ass on the line.*

I nodded in agreement, irritating curiosity nagged at me. "What did you show him earlier?"

Josh smirked. "I had him seeing you as you were during our escape, but more. Covered in flame and lightning. Truly a Goddess of the flame and skies; the two elements bending at your will."

I scoffed at him. "Exaggerate a bit much?"

He shrugged. "The dramatic tends to benefit more often than not in interrogations."

"Whatever, just give me some type of heads up if you're going to go all slasher on me, please. I don't feel like puking, again."

I really have no choice in any of this anymore.

He gave me his hand and pulled me to my feet. "I'll do my best, Miss Snow."

He sauntered towards the Demon, the dagger once again moving between his fingers as if it were a snake, caressing each finger as it flitted across. He ran the blade along the shoulders of the Demon and Artremias halted his screaming. His mouth clamped shut and milky eyes darted around the room as if he faced countless terrors before him. With nowhere to run and without a means of protecting himself.

"Now, let's try this once more, Artremias," Josh paused, his dagger caressing the Demon's neck as if it were a lover. "Where are the humans?"

The Demon's voice trembled. "I...I don't know." He shook.

Josh removed the blade and stuck it into the Demon's side, down to the hilt. The Demon yelped in pain as its black blood seeped from around the blade. I went to turn away but Josh caught my eyes and held me in place; urging me to continue watching. I gulped down the bile building in the pit of my stomach and refocused my attention on the Demon in front of me.

Josh pulled the dagger from the Demon's side, painstakingly slow. He reinserted it into the Demon's thigh, driving it through to the metal seat, a slight clang vibrated in the thick air. The Demon screamed.

"Okay! Goddammit. Okay!" He panted. "The others. They took the humans. They're being held in the mountains. I wasn't present for the exact drop off location," the Demon snarled as Josh wriggled the blade in its thigh, causing blood to further pool. "That's all I know! I was with the others as we burned down that building. I was not a part of the extraction itself." His face scrunched in pain, sweat slicked his forehead, tears trailed down his face. "Please. That's all I know. Please, let me go." A whimper escaped its thin lips.

Josh twisted the blade once again then slowly pulled it out, scraping against bone. The Demon panted in relief. "Who led your operation?"

The Demon shook his head, unsure. Repeating that was all he knew; he wasn't told who was leading the whole thing.

Josh turned his back to the Demon. "Very well." He whipped around, driving the dagger straight through the Demon's neck. Its head bounced on the floor, inked blood spraying from its headless body. The fleshy cranium landed, rolling to a stop at my feet. The milky eyes cleared and a bright, white, borderline-iridescent shine took their place before fading to onyx pits. Black blood seeped from the corners of its eyes, coating them. The dead fish stench hit my nose, and I fought the urge to double over.

"What the hell, Josh?!"

He pulled a handkerchief from his pants pocket and began wiping down his blade.

At least he didn't lick the thing clean this time.

"If I allowed him freedom, he would have ran back to his pack of Demons and dispelled everything. My building, location, whereabouts, and the intel that's been gathered. Which would have enlarged the target on your back, as well as mine, Miss Snow. They would've come for us before we were ready. The only feasible option was to dismember the Demon and be done with it."

I pinched my nose between my fingers, attempting to keep the stench from gagging me. "You could've warned me at least, asshole."

"Very true, my apologies, Miss Snow."

I looked down. My sneakers and bottom of my joggers, as well as my sweatshirt, were now covered in Demon blood. I shivered. No amount of showering was going to wipe this little experience from my skin. I fought the nausea as it threatened to make another appearance. "I'm going to need thirty showers, at least, to get this gunk off of me."

"You may use the shower I have here, if you wish. There are spare clothes as well, although they may be a bit large on your frame, Miss Snow."

I went to open my mouth when our phones dinged. Josh pulled his phone out of his pocket before I could get to mine.

He scanned his screen, his expression shut down. "We must go. It seems Mr. Draven has discovered something that could be of use to the situation."

He sheathed his cell phone into his pocket and the dagger into the waistband of his belt. Then hastily made his way to the door; he had the bolt unlocked within seconds.

I looked back as I followed Josh out of the office, the Demon's empty eyes sent chills down my spine. As if it were alive...and watching me.

Chapter Twenty-Five

Erin

Seth was pacing when we walked in. Josh sped here and nearly gave me a heart attack with the speedometer ticking one-eighty. My pulse was out of control from the adrenaline.

I am never getting in the car with his ass behind the wheel again.

I shut the door behind me as we walked into the house. Seth's head snapped up, his calculating gaze meeting my confused one. He quickly glanced between Josh and me, his jaw tensed.

Libby and Derik sat at the kitchen island, snacking on a bag of cheese crackers, chatting, tones hushed. Libby turned and sent us a little finger wave. Josh ignored her. I waved back, a small smile formed on my lips, still attempting to process Josh's little interrogation tactics. Libby seemed to give me a knowing look before turning back to her conversation with Derik.

Am I reading that correctly?

Does she know how Josh does his info grabbing?

I nibbled on the inside of my cheek, the thought nagged at me.

Josh said that Seth didn't know, but did Derik or Libby?

Fingers snapped inches from me. I jolted. Josh eyed me, urging me to keep quiet. Seth grumbled a slew of words under his breath and picked up his fidgeting once more.

"Dude, you're going to burn a hole into your floor pacing like that. Everyone's here. Out with it." Derik huffed at Seth.

"I found another connection between the humans that disappeared," he paused in front of Josh and me. Under his gaze, a slight pang of guilt shot through me, as if I'd done something wrong. I sidestepped, putting a few inches between us. Seth continued, his eyes refusing to leave mine. "The eight women and five men that disappeared. They all worked for the same company before it went bankrupt and was forced to close down."

"Okay, there's only a few large offices around here, Seth. That's not really all that surprising." I arched my brow, feigning off the knot that formed in my stomach.

"Yes. But there's only two warehouses between here and Riverside. And even Charshire." He twitched.

Bile rose. "Seth. What do you mean, warehouses?"

"The missing humans...all were on staff up in the mountains in these warehouses. Before the buildings were shut down and abandoned," Seth's eyes rapidly searched mine. "The exact buildings which once stood above the stronghold Erebus had you hidden within."

I froze. Libby cursed under her breath.

Derik scoffed. "Well, isn't that convenient." His stool scraped against the hardwood as he pushed back from the island, striding towards where I stood. It took everything in me to keep the flashes of Erebus from overriding my vision. An arm flopped across my shoulders, the weight pressed down on me, distracting me. "You ready for some payback, Princess?"

I tore my unfocused eyes from the ground and took in the guy who was using me as an armrest. Derik had a goofy grin plastered on his face but a fury danced in the depth of his irises. He'd pulled me out. As did Seth. And Josh. And even Libby. They saved me.

A pang of guilt ran through me. They'd pulled me out but had put themselves in danger doing so. The four of them watched me. A flash skirted through my mind. The four of them. Dead. Defending me. And the missing humans, in pieces.

I couldn't let them put themselves in harm's way. Not again. I couldn't risk the humans either. They were innocent in this Demonic conquest.

I had to find a way to save them first.

All of them.

I swallowed down the fear. A flame lit within me; lightning cracked outside the windows.

"Hell. Fucking. Yes."

Chapter Twenty-Six

Seth

We had another connection but the fact remained that we were without a definite location for where Erebus hid away his human captives. If he kept them at the abandoned warehouse where he trapped Erin, that'd be too obvious, too easy. He was far too calculating.

It was infuriating.

Derik sat crossed legged on a pile of pillows with Erin's laptop propped open on his lap. He let out a frustrated groan as he waded through the factory's history.

His jaw twitched. "Where else could they be keeping them? Those tunnels we ran through used to be mine shafts from what I'm finding. Way back when Riverside was first founded. Then when it was bought out, they were declared maintenance tunnels. Apparently, they were pretty shitty if they were still pure dirt. Can you imagine having to worm through those as a maintenance guy? Fuck that. No wonder the factories went out of business."

Erin and Libby were on opposite sides of my couch researching on their phones, adamantly ignoring us while we groveled.

We're at another standstill. One ah-ha moment and now we're stuck again.

"You do realize, you can use my laptop instead of Erin's right?" I cocked my brow.

"I could, but then I couldn't snoop on these fanfic sites. Aren't you a frisky chick, Snow?"

Erin dropped her phone and dove for Derik from the couch, tackling him and knocking her laptop out of his lap. "Stop it, you asshole!" She squealed. Her cheeks were pink as she scrambled for her computer. Derik grabbed her, tickling her. Erin laughed, begging him to stop. She rolled onto her stomach, attempting to escape and he sat on top of her. Pinning her down. Erin let out an, "Oof."

I smirked.

Well. She won't be moving for a hot minute.

Libby snorted from the couch while Josh briefly looked up from his own screen. His expression devoid of emotion beyond a slight twitch of his lip; a faint light glinted in his eyes as they swept across the squabble.

Erin grunted. "Fine! I give up, just get off of me, you brute!" Derik wiggled on Erin's back and she groaned, giving up.

"Oh man, Seth, I'm really digging your new chair. Pretty comfortable. I could chill here all day."

"Fuck off," Erin grumbled. "Can you at least budge so I can use my arms to scroll through my phone? You're a pain in the ass." Derik lifted his ass, barely giving her space to yank her arms out, before plopping back down, causing her to let out another huff of air. Libby kicked Erin's phone across the floor to her, stifling another chuckle.

I cracked a smile as mine and Libby's eyes met; green and speckled like the blades of grass caressed by dew droplets in the morning sun.

My eyebrows furrowed, confused by the thought. I looked to Erin, begrudgingly scrolling through the browser on her phone, stuck under Derik's frame. A warmth cradled me seeing her goofing around and slowly opening up around them, even if that meant she was pinned under Derik at the moment.

I shook my head and went back to my laptop, searching for any information on other buildings that had been left to ruin in the area, as that seemed a prime base of operations for the Demons. Somewhere in which humans wouldn't go snooping around.

Avoid any suspicion. Not that it really mattered.
Most of them hid themselves unless they were hunting for prey.
Whether they were hungry, bored, or in need of...release.

I growled at the thought.

The next few hours were quiet as we threw ourselves into our browsers and newspapers. Searching for anything to find a potential lead on where Erebus could be hiding the humans. Every minute we spent searching, and not finding them, made my skin crawl.

Erin tapped away on her phone. Libby switched to various newspaper articles she'd printed, spanning the last decade, long before the factories shut down. Josh stepped out onto the front stoop and made a few calls. Derik had slumped down, moving to where he was then using Erin as a pillow instead of a seat, his head resting on the middle of her back. A slight pang of jealousy ran a clawed finger through the inside of my stomach at the sight of the two of them.

It would never happen.
Enemies to lovers, my ass.

My leg bounced as I swallowed the sour tang of the little green monster. I scrolled through the search engine on my screen, clicking page after page, for any tip-off. Nothing. I rolled my shoulders, neck and arms tingling. Setting my laptop onto the coffee table, I stood and reached for Libby, pulling her from her phone and off of the couch.

"I don't know about you guys, but I need a damn break. Who's up for some sparring?"

Libby bounced, delicately landing on the tips of her toes before padding the small distance to Derik and yanking him up from the floor. She twirled, her hand still cupping his as she led him to the sparring mat next to the lifting equipment.

I bent down, elbows propped on my knees. "Need some help, Snow?" She groaned, pushing herself onto her knees.

She slid her hand in mine, and I pulled her up with me as I stood. Erin arched her back, stretching her arms above her head before swooping them back down to her ankles, getting the kinks out of her back. Erin may have been in sweats, but her physique was still noticeably beautiful. Her arms toned, her legs strong and defined by all the strength training we've done together. Her curves peaked through the fabric of her clothes; sweatpants hugged her hips while her sweatshirt dipped inward at her waist. Even covered in dried Demon gunk, she was breath-taking.

Wait.

Has she been covered in it this whole ass time?

I glared at Josh.

What the hell happened when she was with him?

She righted herself, standing up. I quickly averted my eyes to Derik and Libby dancing around each other, waiting to see who would strike first. Libby flinched. Derik shot his arm out, anticipating catching and locking her arm. She smirked and took in his movement, swinging her leg behind his and pulling it out from under him. Derik realized his mistake and reached to grab her. Libby dodged and spun around him, her fist slammed into his shoulder blades, sending Derik sprawling on the floor, face first. She pranced backwards a step and blew nonexistent dust from her nails. "Awe, Ricky, you went easy on me. How sweet."

I stifled a laugh. The prickling irritation towards Josh eased.

I'll find out soon enough. Erin will tell me.

Erin snorted, looking to me for an explanation. "Ricky?"

I quirked a smile. "He hates that nickname. It's a sure-fire thing to get under his skin and get him riled up when his head isn't fully in the game. Or when he's going easy during sparring." Erin's eyes twinkled, filled with mischief.

She batted her lashes up at me. "So, who do *I* get to spar with?" Blood rushed south and I imagined the two of us going head to head. Her landing underneath me, chest heaving, sweat glistening on her forehead. Her cheeks flushed; lips formed into a perfect pout as I bend down to kiss her, her chest pressed against mine.

I shifted, thankful as all hell for the invention of compression boxers. And that I had a long enough T-shirt on. I cleared my throat, realizing Erin was still waiting on a response.

"You get either me or Josh. Take your pick," I rasped.

Erin clicked her tongue, briefly mulling it over. "I think I'll take you on. I've had enough of working with Josh for the day."

I raised an eyebrow at her. "What work did the two of you do together today? I thought he was just tagging along, playing chauffeur."

Erin side eyed me, locking her jaw before saying, "Nothing too important."

"And just so you know, Rin, I didn't put him up to it. I swear." I searched for any hints of what conspired between the two of them. She gave nothing away.

What's she hiding?

No. She'll probably tell me later, when it's just the two of us.

"Okay." Her lips pursed. She strode to the mat, watching Derik take Libby down with a final blow. I had a feeling she'd let him win that round.

Derik held his hand out to Libby and yanked her off her back. They both wore a thick coat of sweat. "Nice effort, Lib," he flashed a grin that most of the ladies went wild for. "But next time, don't spare my ego." She blushed and feigned innocence. They walked off the mat, aiming for the fridge to grab a few water bottles.

"After you, Rin." I made a show of swooping my arm towards the mat, causing Erin to roll her eyes and her smile returned, even if it didn't fully reach her eyes. Instead they lit with a flame, determined to do everything in her power to hand my muscular ass right to me. I kicked off my shoes. "Ladies first." The fire within her ignited further.

Erin darted forward, aiming for my abdomen. I clasped my hand around her wrist, stopping her in her tracks and spun her around. I pinned her against my chest before sliding my hand to her neck. "Fatality." Her chest heaved and she drove her heel backward into my shin, I cursed under my breath but held her firm. She needed to learn how to get out of it.

You need to be able to keep yourself safe, Rin.

Erin wiggled under my strength, attempting to drive the top of her head into my chin—failing. She shoved her elbows back, pointing to my ribs. I swiped her legs from beneath her and she fell. The wind knocked out of her.

She glared up at me. "Again."

We got into position and fought. Over and over again. Her frustration increased with each lost round. An hour later, Erin plopped down onto the mat, waving her discarded sweatshirt in the air in defeat. We were both slicked in sweat. She'd stripped down to her sports bra and sweatpants and I'd tossed my shirt to the floor. Libby and Derik watched onward from the island while Josh played spectator from the couch. Each analyzed her every move.

"Okay. I give up. Holy fuck." Erin gasped in between labored breaths.

Libby brought us a couple of waters and I tossed one down to Erin, splayed across the mat with one arm sticking out to the side and legs sprawled. Wisps of her hair curled at her neck before fanning out around her. Her loose bun had fallen halfway through the sparring session.

I sat down next to her, arm resting on my knees. "You have the strength. And the drive. But your movements are trash, Snow."

"Yeah, well you try fighting a super-powered half-human for the second time ever. Eat shit," she said between breaths, her eyes squeezed shut.

I chuckled and took a sip from my water bottle. "Suck it up, Snowgirl. You got a lot to learn."

Chapter Twenty-Seven

Seth

The entirety of the two weeks that followed were spent sorting through sites and news articles, hunting down whatever resources we could find to point us into the right direction. Any direction to where Erebus could be keeping the humans. We kept coming up short. We even hiked up to the same spot Erin had been trapped in and searched every bush, cement pile, and tunnel. The place was utterly abandoned, as if the Demons were never even there. I had Derik and Libby scour the woods on the edge of town. They crashed at my place most nights, deeming it easier than traveling halfway across town every morning to check-in beforehand.

While they stalked the treelines, Josh hunted in the mountains. Nothing.

The Demons were nowhere to be found.

Erin picked up a few shifts at the library on campus, stating she'd see if she could stumble upon any theories or potential mythology on the Demons and The Key. Although, I had an inkling that it was her subtle way of escaping out of the house for a few hours. Classes had been canceled due to several students' bodies being found shredded to pieces across campus, so that left both of us with a few extra hours during the day. And extra motivation to find the creatures responsible. All the signs pointed to the Demons but the officials chalked it up to wild animals.

Humans had no idea the danger they were all in.

And we were running out of time. With no trace of where the hell-spawns were hiding and how the fuck they had snuck into campus, right under our noses.

It all went by in a blur. The tension was palpable; each of us on edge, day by day. I'd catch Erin eyeing the time on her phone, groaning each time. She'd twitch more and more as she scrolled through her laptop, or flipped from article to article.

By the second Sunday, she'd had it.

Erin stormed in, smoke bellowed from her ears. The front door slammed shut behind her, barely hanging on by its hinges. I let out a whistle.

"What's got you all pissed off, Snow? Rough day at work?" I stifled a laugh; she reminded me of an angry rabbit on the rare occasion where her temper *truly* made itself known.

Someone is feeling feisty.

She flipped me off as she beelined to the fridge. Erin yanked it open and pulled out a milk jug and strawberries. She thumped her hip against the door, pushing it shut before she rummaged through the pantry, reappearing with a tin of cookies under her arm, one already dangling from her mouth.

"This is fucking stupid. It shouldn't be so damned hard to find where a bunch of supernatural assholes are keeping a bunch of helpless humans. They should stick out like a sore thumb. Some type of blip. Hell on earth, anything," Erin chomped down on her cookies, dipping them in a glass of milk. "I mean for fucks sake, they slaughtered a bunch of college kids on campus!"

"Rin, believe it or not, they aren't going to have a big-ass neon sign pointing at their hideout saying 'Look! Here we are! Demons inside!' It's a pain in the ass, I get it."

She stared me down, nostrils flaring. "No shit."

I shrugged. "You said they should stick out."

Erin huffed and stomped off towards the guest room. Libby stopped her before Erin reached the hallway, her slim fingers loosely wrapped around Erin's wrist. I couldn't make out what Lib said, her whisper was too low even for me to hear, but her fingers twitched and pulled Erin in closer, wrapping her arms around her. Her eyes locked with mine, glazing slightly then snapping back.

What did she see?

Libby released Erin, patting her shoulder and flashing a warm smile. Erin's shoulders tightened as she stepped away from her and down the hall. Erin locked the bedroom door behind her.

I stepped towards her, the curiosity nagged at me. Lib turned on her heel, ignoring me, her short blonde hair whipped the air. Then pranced to the couch, scooting in next to Derik as she slipped her phone from the front pocket of her jean shorts.

"Did I miss something?" I directed at Derik, Libby scrolled on her phone not even giving me a glance.

"Who the hell knows, man."

I sat on the edge of the coffee table across from Libby, urging her to look up at me as I stared at her.

She popped her head up only to acknowledge Josh as he walked through the doorway with his phone pressed to his ear, decked out in a light grey suit, and chewing someone out by the sound of it.

"I do not care if we are short staffed at the moment. I need as many eyes and ears on this as possible. Hire additional staff, if necessary, as long as they meet the requirements."

"You sure you wanna snap that thing so hard? You could crack the screen, then you'd be out a few grand," I said.

The vein in his forehead throbbed. "Seth, you know as well as I that a few thousand dollars in the scheme of things, is but a drop in the ocean."

"Maybe to you. But if I buy something, I'm taking care of it, not blowing through and destroying it."

Unappreciative prick.

"For those of us who don't have our pockets loaded, one of you is paying for dinner tonight. I'm starved," Derik chimed in.

"I second that," Libby added. Her phone dinged. "So does Erin. She said she wants something greasy."

Derik's mouth salivated. "Man, I like her. My type of woman." He winked at Libby, and she smacked him on the arm. A flare of heat punched my gut.

"Pizza, it is then." I shook it off, reminding myself that Derik didn't fit the bill on Erin's type. Although, neither did I.

Derik and Libby whooped, while Josh nodded in agreement.

I gave Josh a sideways glance, and jealousy reared its ugly head.

But he does.

Chapter Twenty-Eight

Seth

Erin padded into the living room when the pizzas arrived half an hour later. I tipped the driver a couple twenties, impressed he got all five grease-covered pies out here in record time.

Lib sat on the floor, huddled next to Erin on a pile of pillows they'd dragged out from the guest room. Josh rolled up the sleeves of his button down and lifted the pizzas from my arms then placed them in the center of the coffee table. Derik was the first to dive in, tossing open the lid of the box on top, double fisting two slices spanning the length of his head. Libby and Josh followed suit, each grabbing two slices of pizza. Erin sat, leaning back on her hands, legs spread out in front of her, the corners of her mouth lifting as she watched Derik attack his pizza; sauce covered his chin, cheese oozed onto his shirt. She looked up, her grey-blue eyes meeting mine and the rigid pang of jealousy from earlier melted away as her lips spread, her tongue darted out, and she giggled. The sound wrapping itself around me.

Erin flicked her gaze to the diminishing pizzas. *Grab some, and I'll get a slice too* she seemed to say, her eyes meeting mine once again.

I grabbed a piece of meat lovers and plopped down on the hardwood floor, flanking Erin's side. She reached for a slice of cheese pizza, a long string roped between her and the almost empty box. She pulled it above her head, the string of melted heaven finally breaking. Erin opened her mouth, dropped the melted gooeyness onto her tongue, and slurped it down. Her cheeks were stuffed, resembling a squirrel harvesting nuts for the winter; eyes closed, hips wiggling as she did her little food dance. Libby and I chuckled. Josh smirked. Derik was too focused on polishing off the last of the food.

Erin's eyes popped open. "Mwhat?" She muffled, cheeks still stuffed.

"You're adorable."

Pink rose to her cheeks as she gulped down the remainder of her slice. Libby took that as her opportunity to loop Josh into a conversation, her back to Erin and I.

Erin cleared her throat. "Yeah, well...You're ridiculous." She brought her knees to her chest and wrapped her arms around them.

I bit down on my pizza slice as I felt Erin scoot closer. I met her movement, resting my hip against hers so she was still on top of her pillow pile. She leaned into me. A sigh escaped her lips as she rested her head on my shoulder.

"I'm sorry, Seth," she whispered. "For storming off."

Ah. So, she's guilting herself for earlier.

"No need to apologize, Rin. It's frustrating, I get it." I polished off my slice and pulled her in, hugging her tight. I buried my chin into the hair on top of her head, the scent of her peach shampoo intoxicating.

"Does any of this get any easier?" she asked meekly, my chest tightened.

"I wish it did, Rin. I really wish it did."

The remainder of the night, we all sat around the coffee table. Erin had grabbed a box of cards from the hall closet and set about dealing them out, declaring a giant game of War. How in the hell that was going to work between five people, I had no idea. But dammit, she made it happen.

Erin and Libby took turns kicking everyone's asses, Josh got close once. Derik and I, our asses were handed to us each round. I threw my cards on the table. "I give up. This is freaking rigged."

The girls swapped looks as they giggled. Across the table Josh smirked. Derik gave up and took up polishing off the last bit of alcohol in the fridge. "Gotta learn when to quit, man." He laughed.

"Poor Seth, getting beat by a couple of girls," Erin teased. "This is payback for when you wiped the floor with me during training these last couple of weeks." She high-fived Libby, triumphant.

"Yeah, yeah. Whatever. At least I don't cheat."

Erin scoffed, grinning ear to ear. "Oh, don't be a sore loser. You lost. Fair and square. Not my fault you suck at cards."

"I'm still saying it was rigged," I grumbled.

Erin stuck her tongue out at me and swiped our cards, reforming them into a full deck and slipped them back into their case.

A bag of chips thumped in the middle of the table. "I don't know about you guys, but my ass is starving." Derik said as he flopped back onto the couch.

"Yeah, losing really works up an appetite, huh?" Erin quipped.

Derik shoved a handful of chips in his mouth. "Hell yeah it does. It took real effort letting you two win."

"It truly does. You ladies put up quite the formidable front in the game of War," Josh chimed in, winking at Erin.

"Wow. Did you actually just use sarcasm? Who knew Snooty-Booty had a sense of humor." She deadpanned.

I choked. "What?" Libby was clutching her stomach laughing. Josh actually looked shocked.

Erin shrugged her shoulders as she reached for the bag of chips. "What? He's snooty and kind of an ass about it. Fits him perfectly."

"Snow's got a point." Derik nodded, hiding a grin as he sipped from his empty beer bottle.

Josh leaned into the couch; arm slung along the back. "I do take pride in my appearance and how I conduct myself and business," the corner of his mouth twitched. "And I believe the portion about my rear, is more pertained to the way my pants fit in that area, wouldn't you agree, Miss Snow?" He winked at her. Again.

Erin stuttered, her skin flushed pink. "I...I don't know what you're talking about."

Josh chuckled, a gruffness infiltrated his tone. "I'm sure, Miss Snow."

Erin averted her eyes, looking anywhere but at Josh. Her flustered gaze landed on me. Guilt flashed across her face as jealousy gripped my throat.

Does she have a thing for Josh?

"I dunno, Josh. Your pants might be too tight, seems like you might be cutting off circulation to your brain if you think anyone's looking," I snipped.

Amusement flashed in the furthest edge of his narrowed pupils. I forced a neutral expression.

Libby stopped laughing long enough to throw in an, "Oooh buurrnn." Which provided a brief moment for Erin to recover.

She slapped her hands on her thighs and clicked her tongue. "Alrighty well, I'm going to hit the hay," she turned to Libby. "You want to bunk in the guest room with me?"

"Yeah, we can let the stinky men have a little slumber party out here." Libby giggled.

Derik let out a laugh. "Nah, I'm good. I'm not down for sharing a bed with dudes. Nothing wrong with it, but I don't wanna wake up with hardware against my back."

I scoffed. "Here I thought we were bros, man," he threw a pillow at my head. Catching it, I blew Derik a kiss and flipped him off. "Josh, what about you? You're more than welcome to crash here. There's an inflatable mattress around here somewhere."

Derik's mouth hung open. "You have a freaking air mattress? Since when?"

"A while, actually. I just don't remember where the hell I put it."

"Well, that would've been useful to know, instead of you know, us sleeping on the couch and floor half the time."

"Oh, whatever. You pass out on the floor half the time anyway, man."

Derik threw his hand over his face in exasperation. "How could you? My own friend, forcing me to sleep on his couch. I shall become an old, aging man before my time from the nights I've suffered, scrunched up on these cushions."

Erin rolled her eyes as her and Libby headed to the guest room. She yelled from the hall, "Coming from a guy who can't sit up straight to save his life. And has decades, if not centuries, before he shows signs of aging," she waved her fingers behind her before closing their door. "Have fun whining!"

"You heard her, Old Man," I turned toward Josh. "So, what're you thinking? Here or heading home?"

Josh thought it over and checked his watch. "I'll remain here for the evening. Do you mind if I use your shower or borrow a change of clothes, Seth?"

"No problem, go for it. Clothes are in my room in the back and towels are in the hall closet." I pointed my thumb over my shoulder.

Josh nodded and padded down the hall towards my room then the bathroom a few minutes later.

"Looks like it's just the two of us now," Derik said, sprawled out on the couch, hand tucked behind his head.

"Yeap." Silence drew between us. I laid back on the floor, using Erin's pillow pile and folded my hands on my stomach as I crossed my ankles. My thoughts lingered to her. My eyes drifted shut as I imagined it was just the two of us, the others having gone to their own homes.

We laid on the floor, shoulders touching with her hair fanned out underneath us. Erin's hands moved frantically through the air as she spoke about her day; the fantasy book she'd finished reading, the crazy incidents that only seemed to happen to her at work, such as embarrassing herself in front of a patron as she tripped over the foot of one of the book carts. Or when she'd gone on and let the type of fantasy novels she read slip and couldn't look the person she was talking to in the eye afterwards.

The fear and worries of the disappearances, gone. The safety of so many, not on our shoulders. Just us. Her laughing. Me soaking in each word that floats in the air around us. Our own little bubble of happiness.

"What do you think?" Derik asked, tearing me from my daydream.

Damn it all to hell.

"About what?" My eyes slowly opened.

"Were you even listening?"

"Would you believe me if I said yes?"

He blew out a breath. "Nope. But as long as you weren't off in some dreamland getting a hard on, I don't give a damn."

"You wish."

"No, I really don't," the couch groaned as he flipped onto his side. "While you were fantasizing, I was talking about the humans we've been searching for and some potential leads. I might've found something, or somewhere we could search for some more answers on where they could be."

"What've you got?"

"Everything seems to be pointing to the mountains. Well, at least the small bit of info I dug up today," he stifled a yawn. "I went on patrol and ran into a couple of Demons. Finished them off but was able to get a bit out of them first."

Huh.

"Is that where you went off too after Erin left?" I eyed Derik.

"Yeah. I initially left to keep tabs and follow her from a distance. Her fighting's been getting stronger, but I figured why take the chance. A caught them trailing her about a block away from the campus library." He bristled.

"They got that close? And you didn't sense them?" My mind began whirling.

"They caught me off guard. I was pissed."

My jaw tightened. "What did they say?"

"Beyond the usual, 'We will destroy the Nephilim Scum' spiel, I was able to beat the direction of where the humans might be out of the Demons."

If they are in the mountains...where?
How do we keep missing them?
How are they sneaking down here without us sensing them?

"Anything else? Why were they following her?"

"Why do you think? The Demons think she's this 'Key'. They saw the opportunity and tried to take it. They were weaker ones, weirdly enough. They probably thought if they captured her, that piece of shit Erebus would grant them some sort of reprieve or praise or some shit."

If they were weak, Erebus probably sent them after her as a warning.

"You're probably right. But if that were the case, how did they get past you?" Something didn't sit right, my stomach turned.

The weight of the world sat on both our shoulders. Air whooshed from Derik's lungs. "I don't know, Seth, but we need to figure that out asap. And in case Erin really is this 'Key' they're looking for, we might want to up the ante on her training. Fighting and her powers."

And keeping her as far away from Erebus's grimy hands as possible.

Josh walked in at that moment, towel slung over his shoulders. "I can help with that."

Of course.

Chapter Twenty-Nine

Erin

"Erin. You are beginning to run out of time."

"I'm trying here. What more do you want from me?" I reigned in the defensiveness in my voice.

The man from my nightmares appeared in front of me. His hair flowed behind him, cascading down his back. Shimmering outlines sprouted from behind him. Black nothingness encapsulated us. No skies or valleys to be seen. Everything had been striped away, only the two of us remained.

"You must try harder. Look closer at the things around you. Your powers, they must be strengthened. There are beings coming. Things you are not yet prepared for. I'd thought our previous encounter would've given you more incentive."

I blew out a breath. "Okay, mystery man. What exactly do I need to do? I'm training daily. I run to work, I'm sparring and fighting with Seth and Derik. I've mastered the fire and sparks. What more do I need to do?"

"You must train harder. The information you've been gathering on the Demons, you must dive deeper."

"What am I missing?"

"That is not for me to disclose, Erin. You must discover it on your own, as you did with your fire. Look within."

"You've got to give me more than that."

"Dive deeper, Miss Snow."

And then he was gone.

I awoke to a light thumping on the bedroom door. I groaned as I rolled over, attempting to drown it out. Libby was still asleep next to me, her breathing heavy, indicating that she remained in a deep sleep.

Lucky.

The rasping continued and I hissed under my breath as I dragged myself out of the warmth of my blanket. I peaked in the mirror on the dresser, wrinkling my nose at the mop of tangled hair, strands poked out every which way, mascara smudged under my eyes, baggy shirt doused in pizza grease stains and chip dust from the night before.

Talk about a mess and a half.

I sighed as I silently opened the door and stepped out. It clicked behind me, and I looked up to find myself nearly face-to-chest with Josh.

Jeez, warn a girl, could ya?

"Good morning, Miss Erin. Did you sleep well?" Josh asked, his voice husky.

I hissed under my breath. Then poked him in the chest. "Okay, first of all, personal space please," I half-whispered. "Second of all, it's rude to wake someone up before dawn. Borderline criminal offense in my opinion."

He let out a low laugh as he took a *small* step backwards. "My apologies, Miss Snow. I didn't have the intention of offending you," he smirked and lifted a to-go cup from behind his back. "Would a hot cup of coffee ease my retribution?"

I eyed the cup in his grip, quickly glanced up, squinted, and snatched the cup from his hand. "There better be sugar in this," I grumbled.

"Well of course, Miss Snow. I even added milk," he winked. "Now, shall we begin the day?"

I'd rather not.

My lips pursed as I followed him out to the kitchen and sat at the island. "What exactly are we beginning?"

"Training." My mind flashed to the dream visit I'd had from the mystery man.

"Oh? And we're starting in the middle of the night because?" I asked as I sipped my coffee.

"Miss Snow, five in the morning is not middle of the night. I'm typically awake and already sweating." His face was neutral but there was a brief glint in his eye. I fought the blush that attempted to grace my face. He hooked his thumbs in the pockets of dark-blue fitted joggers he wore.

Those look familiar...wait a minute.

Is he wearing Seth's sweats?

Josh continued, his gaze hardened. "If we are to achieve the goal of finding these humans and rescuing them alive, we cannot have any loose ends. And that involves making sure that *you*, my dear, are equipped with the skills truly needed to defend oneself and others from Demons. You have barely begun your defense training," I went to correct him; he stuck his hand up. "The defense courses you partook in as a child are not relevant in this situation. We are discussing Demons. Powerful creatures. Not mere mortals."

"Look, Mister I-wake-up-when-normal-people-are-still-sleeping, I understand Demons are stronger, but there has to be some correlation between the two, right? I mean I kicked one of them in the nards, and that was a decent distraction. So...I'm just saying." I shrugged.

He quirked his brow then grabbed a granola bar and apple from the pantry. As he tossed them to me, he responded, "That is merely the basics, Miss Snow. The opening to kick a Demon in their genitals is slim, rarely does it take them down like it would a human being. I applaud your luck in that situation but do not count on it. You must learn to fight with a weapon. Swords, daggers, knives, whatever you chose. Even a gun, if need be, although not recommended."

That caught my attention. "Why not a gun? That would seem like the easier, obvious route?" I gulped down the remainder of my coffee and Josh pulled another from the counter behind him.

Someone planned ahead.

"A few reasons. First, beginning with the amount of time it would take for a bullet to unload and reach a Demon to inflict a fatal wound. They would already be on you. Secondly, they heal far too quickly for a bullet to do much damage."

"But a blade wound wouldn't heal too quickly?" I pursed my lips. "That sounds like a whole lot of bologna. And incredibly inconsistent."

"I assure you, Miss Snow, it is not 'bologna'. Demons are weak to few things. One being iron and weapons that are forged from it. That and pure silver."

"What? Are they werewolves or something?" I rolled my eyes. Josh didn't find that funny. "Wait. Are there werewolves?"

His face grim. "No, Miss Snow. However, there are Demons who have the ability to transform themselves into terrible creatures. Many of which have led to curating the nightmares and terrors that haunt humanities dreams."

"Oh, well. Isn't that comforting." I snorted.

Josh shook his head. "This is serious, Miss Snow. And needs to be taken so."

"My dude. I am taking this seriously. I just might not be too keen on learning that Demons can turn themselves into other creatures."

Have you heard of a sense of humor?

He sighed. "Miss Snow, would you rather not know and be caught entirely off guard by an animal, such as a puppy, who shows itself to you, wanders into your home here, and then ambushes you when it transforms into its true Demonic form?"

"They can turn into puppies!? What? What am I supposed to do then? Just ignore every sweet, innocent furbaby that I see? Because I can tell you right now, I'm not doing that. I'll take my chances." I slammed my cup on the island and crossed my arms across my chest.

If a dog or a cat comes up to me...I'm risking it.

Josh just stared at me, like I was an idiot. "Well then. Lucky for you, that was an extreme example. They often turn into fearsome creatures. Only if a Demon were desperate enough, would they turn into such a feeble, harmless house pet. They deem actual creatures or 'fur babies' as you called them, weak, useless."

"Well clearly, they had their dicks shoved up their asses. Because puppies are adorable. And far from useless."

He pinched his brows together and ran his hand down his face. "Miss Snow. These are literal Demons we're discussing. They have no need for simple creatures or to take into consideration their target's concerns for wildlife. Will you focus, please."

"Fine. But I'm not fighting any puppies."

"Oh my God, Miss Snow. Drop it. No puppies. Dear Lord," he took a breath. "Okay. Demons. Iron is what ultimately causes them the most harm from our weapons. Therefore, always keep a dagger, sword of some form, or knife on your person. Today we will begin training with weapons."

"Do I need to use any specific weapon, or can I take my pick? Where do I get one? Because as far as I know there's not a swordsmith anywhere around here considering we're, you know, in the twenty-first century."

He let out another sigh, once again shaking his head. "Miss Snow. This might be the twenty-first century but there are still swordsmiths out there," he stepped to the pantry. "That being said, take your pick." He blocked the inside of the pantry. There was a click.

I blinked and the wall moved. Exposing a whole other room filled to the brim with weapons. I got up from the island and tiptoed in behind Josh. My eyes widened, taking in the scene in front of me. Swords, daggers, guns. Weapons of anything one could imagine lined the walls. My mouth gaped. "Holy shit."

Well, doesn't this look all...stabby?

I peered at Josh out of the corner of my eye. "By the way, I don't know if you realize this. But you sigh and shake your head like a disappointed parent. Like a lot."

He mumbled, "It comes with the territory."

I scoffed. "Of course it does." I was astonished at the different blades that donned the walls. In the middle of the room was—what I assumed to be—anti-weaponry/bullet and fighting gear. Any lethal equipment you could think of was all held within the room. "What the hell is this place and why didn't Seth tell me about it?"

I swear to all hell. If he keeps one more damn thing from me, I'm going to blow my top.

"I would assume that would be a better question to ask Seth. Rather than myself, who would only assume he withheld this information in an attempt to protect you. And if that were the case, as you can assume, I believe that you being aware is far more beneficial to your survival. As well as the humans at stake."

Although I knew realistically that it would do nothing and Seth was more than likely passed out in his bed, I shot a glare in Seth's direction at the likely implication of him doing exactly what Snooty Pants hinted at. I wouldn't have put it past him.

"Okay, well. Assuming that you're correct and Seth was attempting to shield me from this—for whatever idiotic, big brother complex reason he has—why are *you* showing me this room?"

Josh faced me. Assessing. "Truthfully, Miss Snow. I believe you have potential. That you very well may be 'The Key' to attaining these humans and have the power behind you to do what needs to be done."

"Josh, I am flattered. That may be the nicest thing you've ever said to me," I slapped my hand over my chest. "I'm *truly* honored, oh all-knowing-mighty leader."

He shot me a glare and I smirked in return. "I am not your leader, Miss Snow. That position falls to your beloved, Seth."

I stammered, "He's not my beloved. This isn't the sixteen hundreds, old man."

Josh turned his back to me once more, unfazed. "My apologies, once again, Miss Snow," he waved me over. "Take a look at the blades available and choose what calls to you."

I side eyed him. "What *calls* to me? What is this? Some magical bullshit?"

"No, Miss Snow. The blades have a hum. Each unique, calling to different powers and auras. They have souls of sorts. Therefore, listen for the one that calls to you. You may use others, as Miss Libby or Derik have, but the weapon that fits you most, will call to you."

I mumbled under my breath, "Sounds like a whole lot of magic mumbo-jumbo to me."

I ran my fingers over the different swords and daggers that were laid along the shelves and walls in front of me, feeling each one out, attempting to listen for one that 'called' to me, as Snooty Booty described. I grew frustrated.

How the fuck is this supposed to work?

Do one of these things just jump up and start rattling off some musical number?

"Ugh. I'm getting nothing, Josh."

"Try closing your eyes, Miss Snow. And truly focus. Remove everything else from your mind and focus. Listen."

I closed my eyes and evened out my breath. I let go of the thoughts of Seth, the weapons surrounding us, the Demons.

I reached further in. The little voice I had avoided in the back of my head, laughed at me. Taunted me with the fact that if I don't get it together and get stronger then everyone will end up dead or worse.

If they die. It's my fault.

I suffocated the thought.

Not the time.

A hum began to vibrate within me. It grew, expanding to the top of my head and down to the pit of my stomach. It pulled me across the room and I followed. My arms lifted, searching for the source. Everything fell away. A bright orange hue appeared behind the lids of my eyes.

"You've come." *A melodic voice floated within my mind.*

I squinted my closed lids. "Who are you?"

"*I am yours.*"

"Does that mean you are my weapon? The one that calls to my power?"

A flame appeared, forming from the orange aura in front of me. "Yes. We are one in the same."

"What does that mean?"

"*We are the flames. The flames that ignite in the realm surrounding us. Whether chaos or savior, the decision is up to us.*"

"Oh."

A warmth caressed me, as if in a comforting embrace. "Now, we must find my sisters."

"Sisters? Blades have sisters?"

"In our case, yes. And you must find them. There are two within this room. Take me into your warmth. Then listen. We will call to them together."

I grabbed for the flame in front of me, vaguely feeling a sharp blade in my grasp.

"Concentrate. You must concentrate. Beyond my hum. And you will find them." The voice hurried.

The hum emanating from within me thickened. The air around me closed in. I gripped the flame closer to my body.

"Keep going," it whispered.

I honed in on the humming. Following it, my body moved forward. The energy pulled me towards itself, growing louder the closer I became.

"Here. We're here. Sisters, it is us!" I heard twin voices ring between my eyes. I reached my hand forward, the other grasping the blade I'd gathered close to my chest. My fingers slid along two small blades. I pulled them into myself and the humming stopped as I drew them in. "Sister." Echoed behind my lids.

My eyes fluttered open to find Josh staring at me, dumbfounded.

"What? Did I get coffee on me or chocolate chips from the granola bar somewhere?" I frantically began taking in my grease covered shirt from the night before, reminding myself how much of a mess I was.

And then I saw the blades. A long sword and two daggers, all cradled in my arms.

"Ah, well. Um. I guess I found my weapons?" I said to Josh, my voice pitched.

"Indeed, Miss Snow. It seems you have."

Chapter Thirty

Erin

Josh sent me to the bathroom to swap out my pajamas for a pile of black-on-black clothes he'd handed me, perfectly folded. I shook them out and found lined black leggings, a plain, black long sleeve, a zip up with padding in the chest area and stomach, sown in arm guards, and a strapping holster. Once I had the clothing ensemble on, I attempted to set the holster in place around my thigh and failed. I gave up after three tries and walked out to Josh.

"Okay, I think you gave me a holster made for the hulk or something because this thing is way too big for my thigh." I waved it in the air.

Josh chuckled. "Miss Snow, that is not for your thigh. The holster I provided you rests on your back. You'll sheath your long sword within it."

"Well. Would've been nice to know that," I pressed my lips together and worked to slide it on. "This still doesn't feel right."

"That's because you put it on backwards, Miss Snow," he motioned toward it. "May I be of assistance?"

I huffed. "Fine."

Josh moved behind me and slid the straps up my arms, his fingers brushed against my arm as he did so. I was grateful for the long sleeve and jacket, as goosebumps formed along my skin at his touch.

I cleared my throat as he finished strapping me in. "Thanks."

He nodded in response.

"Now what?"

He smirked. "Now, Miss Snow, we train." Josh headed to the front door; I followed a few steps behind, grabbing my sword from where I'd placed it on the counter along the way. We trailed to the clearing behind Seth's house, another bonus of being on such a large plot of land on the edge of town. The clearing was hidden by a line of evergreens on all sides, full and thick, shielding us perfectly from the rare passerby.

Josh stopped in the center and drew a wooden dagger from his waistband. I lifted the sword from my side, testing the weight of it in my grip.

This feels great. Should be easy enough.

Not sure if I'm holding it right but we're going for it.

As I held it steady in front of me, Josh shot forward, knocking it out of my hand and nearly landing me on my ass.

"What the hell, dude?" I yelled, dusting myself off. I went to pick my sword off the ground and jumped when one of my daggers came flying at me causing me to yelp as it narrowly missed me, landing right at my feet. "Josh!'

He sauntered over, twirling his wooden dagger between his fingers. He bent down and reached his hand out. I swatted it away.

"What the actual fuck was that? What is wrong with you?"

He shrugged. "Never let your guard down, Miss Snow. You never know who your enemies may be."

I glared at him. "So, your solution was to send a dagger. A fucking dagger. Right at me? Versus talking and explaining 'hey be on the ready in case someone tries to kill you.' Please tell me how that makes more sense."

"Miss Snow, given your attitude, if I'd simply stated that, you would've brushed it off, huffed at me, and went about another one of your begrudging staredowns in an attempt to come off far more intimidating than you actually are."

My mouth hung open.

"Hm. Interesting. Silence, that's a first," he drew his wooden dagger and eyed my iron one on the grass. "Now, let's begin. Pick up your weapon, Miss Snow."

I grumbled but followed his instruction and reached for my sword. Josh swatted my hand with the wooden dagger.

"Not that one."

"Well, why the hell not? Bigger is always better right? More damage and all that jazz."

Josh's expression fell neutral. "In certain instances, absolutely, Miss Snow. But not in this case. You have yet to truly train whilst holding a weapon, and beginning with an elongated sword would not be wise if either of us wish to retain *all* parts of our bodies attached."

"That's assuming of you, *Joshua*. I can handle it." To prove my point, I gripped my sword and stood. I lifted my arms and swung it above my head. And to my horror, the sudden weight distribution had my arms continuing backwards. Suddenly pulled downward by the weight of the sword, the rest of my body followed, and I ended up flinging myself backward. My feet hit the air as my back landed flat on the grass with a loud 'oof' escaping my lips.

Josh cleared his throat. "As I was saying, Miss Snow..."

I huffed between breaths, and flipped him off. "Fuck. Right. The. Fuck. Off."

"Alright, let's get you to your feet then," Josh bent down and grabbed my wrists, hauling my bruised ass up. "And just so that you are aware, it is strictly Josh, not Joshua."

I mimicked him as I stuck my tongue out.

"Now, Miss Snow, if you are finished screwing around, we may begin your lesson." He stood with his hands behind his back, staring at me.

Excuse me...you mean we haven't started yet?

I let my sword drop to the ground and winced as a hiss scratched the edges of my mind.

What the heck?

I filed that away to deal with later, picked up one of my daggers, and stepped toward Josh.

"First, getting into a fighting stance. Loosen your body and spread your feet slightly, allow your body to have the option to move at a moment's notice," he directed. "Dominant leg forward, so when the moment comes for you to thrust your weapon forward, you have that capability on more stable footing."

I righted my stance, hobbling in the process. "Okay, now what?" Josh stepped in close, his hand light on my waist then thigh guiding my body into a more precise position. Heat rushed to my cheeks at the touch.

Okay. Head out of the gutter.

Come on, now.

He stepped back. "Bring your dagger upward, elbow pointing outward, pinky faced outward, and following the direction of your blade. Shoulders back." Josh once again adjusted my body, moving my arm, weighted by my dagger, into a prime position that he approved of.

"Okay. Thrust your arm downward. Your dagger should make contact with your opponent, if not stabbing them straight through.

The blade will slide down their front, causing serious damage and blood loss, buying you a few extra moments," his eyes dropped to mine and whispered, "you will not harm me, Miss Snow."

I averted my eyes from his, closed them, and thrust my arm out and downward as I braced myself for the twang of the impact. Nothing. I squinted one eye open. Josh hadn't moved an inch. I wholly missed my target. I gaped while Josh wore the same neutral expression, unsurprised by my failed attempt.

"As I stated, you will not harm me."

My jaw dropped. "You knew I'd miss?"

"Even the most revered soldiers begin with the weakest combat skills. If you'd made contact with myself, it would've been deliberate on my part," he added as he nonchalantly dusted off a feather that floated onto his shoulder.

My eye twitched in time with my upper lip. "Freaking Prick."

"Call me what you wish, Miss Snow. However, it is best to see this as a learning experience. As well as an excellent gauge for where you've begun and exactly how far you have to go," his lips formed a thin line. "Go again. This time, eyes open."

Josh guided me through various basic fighting movements, rather what he considered basic movements, I considered them forms of torture. The training continued well into the morning, the sun rose above us as it broke on the tree line. There were several times where I fell, misplaced my feet, being 'too ambitious' with my blade as Josh had said.

Too ambitious my ass.

I finally collapsed onto the grass, panting, and cussing up a storm. The grass behind us rustled. "If someone's going to kill me, just do it now. Please. I don't know how much more of this I can take."

"Where is the fun in that, Princess? I kinda like seeing you all sweaty."

I groaned and closed my eyes as I threw my arms out to the side. Sweat dripped down my face, coated my armpits, and soaked my thighs. "It's too early, Derik. Please go flirt with someone else. Someone more willing."

"You wound me, Erin. Truly."

"Yeah, right."

Liquid sloshed from where Derik stood near the house. "Would coffee help?"

I shot my hand straight up, flexing and waving in his direction. "Yes. Please. For the love of all things holy. That and water if you got any." My throat was on fire.

Footsteps neared my head; I kept my arm extended, fingers splayed, awaited the roasted deliciousness. A thump sounded next to my ear, chilling it. Then a cup was placed delicately into the palm of my hand. I blinked to find Derik bent over me, staring down with a shit eating grin plastered on his face. His blonde untamed locks fell forward, his chocolate-brown eyes lit with amusement. His white shirt wrinkled from sleep.

"I aim to please, Princess." Derik winked. I restrained myself from rolling my eyes as I sat up and gulped the entirety of the coffee down.

I choked as the last of it hit my tongue. "Ugh, this is disgusting. What did you do to it?"

He shrugged. "Nothing, actually. That's straight coffee with a triple shot of espresso. Thought the added sugar and milk might slow ya down, Snow."

"Gross. Thanks, but next time, I'll take the damn risk." I washed the bitter taste down with the water that he'd dropped next to my head.

"Unfortunately, I must agree with Miss Snow. Based solely off of her training session this morning, the added sugar and dairy wouldn't have slowed her down by much."

I flipped Josh off and gulped down the remainder of my water. I tossed the empty bottle to Derik and pushed myself to my feet, dagger dangling from my hand. I padded to where my sword and second dagger lay in the grass and picked them up. Humming filled my ears.

"You mustn't simply toss me on the ground again. That was obscurely rude."

"What?"

"Surely you must realize how rude it is to simply toss us to the ground, as if we are nothing more than trash. Honestly, given your heritage, one would think you would know better."

"Heritage? What do you mean? My dad, from what I very recently learned, was an Angel. How was I supposed to know any of that?" I crossed my arms, glaring at my sword. It rang, a slight orange hue surrounded it.

"It is your responsibility to learn," the orange hue flared. *"Now, look alive and not as if you are speaking with your weapons. Sheath myself and hold on to my sisters tightly. Do not allow us to leave your sight. Do you understand?"*

I held back my glare, as the sword had a point. I didn't need Derik or Josh thinking I was a nutcase, or that the training and Nephilim shit was getting to me. *"Understood."*

I held my weapons close, snapping my attention back to Josh and Derik, the two of them conversing. Josh seemingly busting my chops once again on my fighting techniques.

"Oh, up yours, Josh. I'm new to this whole fighting with a weapon thing. Cut me some slack."

"Cutting you *slack* is what could get you and everyone else here killed. So, no. I will not be 'cutting you slack,' Miss Snow," he looked at Derik. "I believe we shall need to continue this at minimum twice a day for the foreseeable future. Derik will reassess over the next couple of weeks. As will Mr. Draven as his schedule deems fit."

"And what exactly do you mean by that? Mine and Seth's schedules are damn near identical with the exception of my job at the library." I narrowed my eyes on the two of them.

Derik ran his hand through his tousled hair. "Actually, Erin, he has a point. Seth needs to really focus on finding the humans with this whole 'Key' business. We were talking last night and he's not going to be in classes for a while once they resume."

"What!?" I gripped my daggers and sword closer to my chest and stomped around to the front of the house. I kicked open the door to see Seth and Libby sitting at the kitchen island, nonchalantly chatting over coffee, no doubt with actual sugar in it.

I stomped inside, practically growling. "Seth Draven. What the actual *fuck*? Why are Derik and Josh saying that you're leaving me to suffer alone through classes while your ass is off hunting down this Demon and missing human bullshit?" I went to toss my sword and daggers on the couch when the humming and weird vision-slash-inner-monologue replayed. Instead, I carefully set them down on the couch, patting my sword for good measure. I stomped to where Seth and Libby sat, flames building in my stomach.

Seth shot his hands up in front of himself in defense. "Woah, woah, Rin. Easy there, girl."

Fire erupted at my fingertips.

Nifty.

"You want to try that again, Seth? Do I *look* like a damn horse to you?"

His eyes flicked down to my hands, flames still ignited. "No. Shit. I'm sorry, Rin, I didn't mean it like that. I just...I'm taking off a bit to focus on getting this shit figured out so we can find those humans. Who the hell knows what they're going through right now.

And The Key...I want to find out more on that and I can't do that wasting time at school," he rushed. "Besides, they're just repeater classes for me anyway." He stopped. His eyes widened. "Shit. Erin I didn't mean—"

"If they're just 'repeater classes' then *why the fuck* are you taking them? Are you wasting damn money on classes you don't even need!?" I paused. A conversation from a few weeks ago popped into my head. "Oh, my actual fuck. Are you only taking those classes to keep a fucking eye on me? What the hell is wrong with you? Do you think I'm that incompetent?" Ice lined my voice. My chest vibrated, the hurt rampaged through me. I wanted to scream until my heart burst into the flames that filled me.

Stop keeping shit from me.

I can't fucking take this anymore.

Seth stammered. Libby swooped in. "Erin. That's not what Seth is saying, I know it's hard to believe, but trust me on this. Please. There's just a lot going on right now, as you know," she shot me a pointed look. "And if you both miss class it might raise some suspicions if anyone looks too closely."

"Lib, I get that. I really do. But who the hell would be suspicious of that?"

Sounds like an excuse to me.

I snipped, "If any humans were to get 'suspicious' of anything it would be along the lines of two individuals who've been absurdly close since practically birth, suddenly not showing up. I don't know about you, but in my world that screams knocked up or giving up on their dreams. And considering Seth and I aren't even on that first plane, I'm not about to have our professors think for a minute that he's a drop out." I sucked in a steadying breath.

"He's a great student and highly intelligent. A huge pain in my ass but a great person with a future. Beyond just our jobs as Nephilim." I panted, fire dwindling as I caught a glimpse of pain in Seth's eyes.

I drew in a long breath before continuing. "If you're going to take off and avoid actual in person class, can you at least, please, look through my notes and try to keep up? Go over the material with me. Check in with our pain-in-the-ass professor about switching to online self-guided courses. Something?" I pleaded.

An idea popped in my head. "If you promise me that you'll do that, then I'll promise to stay out of the way. I'll stick to school books, work, and training. And away from the action. I'll let you do all the protector-of-the-masses crap."

I know it's selfish. Just please say yes.

Seth stared at me, minutes passed by.

"Okay."

"Thank you."

I offered him a faint smile.

Little did he know, my fingers were crossed.

I don't know what else you're keeping from me.
But I need to find out. I need my own answers.
Please forgive me after all of this, Seth.

Chapter Thirty-One

Erin

Seth, all but admitting he was in school and not moving forward because he felt the need to be overly baring, continued to taunt me as I changed out of most of my training gear and into black skinny jeans and a hoodie; I left the long sleeve on.

If he doesn't graduate, it'll be my fault.
Or if he gets killed. Or Libby. Or Derik. Even Josh.
It would all be my fault.

A stabbing pain flooded my chest, my heart and lungs squeezed. I gasped for breath, pushing the thoughts into a little black box. I panted as I clamped it shut and blinked away the salty tears that were on the verge of erupting.

I flopped onto my bed and stared at the ceiling until my eyelids fluttered shut.

"I see you're finally taking things more seriously."

I kept my eyes closed, my hands resting behind my head. "I see you're still interrupting my sleep. Screw off. Can't you let me be?"

He disregarded the question. "The swords have found you. I wonder, do they approve?"

I scoffed. "Don't you mean I found them? Josh had me go into that not-so-little hidden room Seth just so happened to have in his house, another secret he refrained from informing me of."

"Ah, but you see, the long sword and daggers were not there until recently, Erin." The mystery man rumbled.

I peaked one eye open in his direction, taking in the dreamscape. We were once again in the mountains. Mist covered the mountain ridges, a hint of rain in the air. "What do you mean?"

"Nephilim blades are specially designed, created. And those made in particular for the strongest of Nephilim, those who may be extraordinary, are not created, rather, they appear. They come to fruition when their wielders come into their power. It is a rarity to which that is already so rare. Not only had yours appeared, but more than one attached itself to you."

"Great. So, I'm extra special. I can spit fire and lightning out of my fingers, and I get three weapons of the stabbing realm which can talk to me."

"You can hear them?" His brow furrowed.

"Yes." I pressed my lips together.

"Hm. Interesting."

"Tell me about it. I feel like a freaking psycho. At first there was just a hum and then I heard their voices. Well, once voice, from the sword. And it called the daggers its 'sisters'. Mind cluing me in on that one?"

"The humming, that is rather unusual."

I huffed and sat up. "Is any of this 'usual'? Because this whole thing still feels like I'm on some prank show. Josh said there should be a hum. And there was. So, if it's not usual then why did he say something about it?"

He pondered that for a moment. "I am not sure. However, power attracts power, Miss Snow."

"That answers absolutely nothing." My eyes rolled.

"My apologies, Erin." He faced away. His back to me, hands clasped behind him.

I sighed. "It's whatever." I stared at him, the mysterious man who continued to appear in my dreams.

I pulled my legs to my chest and wrapped my arms around them as I rested my chin on top of my knees. "Am I doing the right thing?" I asked, my voice carried on the breeze that flowed through the mountain ridge.

"I know what you are asking, Erin. And unfortunately, that is not for me to decide, nor to disclose, the path which would be most beneficial. That ultimately would be your decision. Whichever path you chose, you must be willing to fight your fears, for that which haunts you may very well be not only your undoing, but the world as you know it."

My fingers pressed into my skin, my laugh lifeless. "Nothing like some good ole' 'world rests on my shoulders' pressure, huh?"

He nodded and slowly faced me once again. "You are much stronger than you realize, Erin."

The dream faded away and my eyes fluttered open, a weight sat heavily on my chest. "It sure doesn't feel like it," I whispered to myself.

My phone beeped. I groaned as I snatched it off of the nightstand and plugged in my passcode. A text from Seth popped up.

> Hey, I'm sorry for not telling you about me skipping out...and that you had to hear it from the guys. Not very bff behavior.

> It's fine.

> Want to grab some grub later? On me?

> I have a shift at the library.

It wasn't a total lie.

> What about afterwards? I'll pick you up. Just the two of us.

> What about Libby and Derik? Or Josh?

The little typing bubble appeared on the screen.

> Nah, Lib and Derik are heading back to their places tonight and Josh said he needed to get some work done. So just us.

My heart pulled a bit.

> Alright. But I'm paying.

> Uh. How about no, it's on me.

> Let me take care of it please. You've been letting me live here and it's the least I can do.

> Take it as an apology for my overreacting earlier.

> Rin, you weren't overreacting, you're fine.

> I'm stealing the check so you can't pay.

> Bet. I'm faster than you Snow, and you know it.

> Psh, yeah right.

> And what was your time on our last run?

> Excuse me, Seth, I was half asleep.

> Smh, lol

> What does that even mean?

A knock sounded at the door. I slowly sat up, not wanting to leave the comfort of my bed and opened it to find a smirking Seth.

"Do you really not know what 'smh' means?"

"No? What is it? Smh?" I crossed my arms over my chest, my hip leaned against the door frame.

He belted out a laugh. "Shaking my head."

"Well, why not just say that? So much easier." The corner of my mouth lifted.

"It's texting, Erin. Not a novel," he chuckled, the ocean blue of his eyes sparkled. "You're ridiculous."

"Okay, look. I am not the brightest crayon in the crayon box, Seth. We know this."

He rolled his eyes. "So, dinner. What time am I picking you up?" He braced himself against the side of the doorway, his forearms supporting his body against the top of the frame. My breath hitched at the close proximity. His plain grey V-neck clung to his chest, accentuating the muscle beneath, wisps of his dark chest hair peeking out.

My eyes nearly bugged out of my skull.

I'm salivating. I'm fucking salivating.
Someone throw a bucket of ice water at me please.
This is getting out of hand.

"I, uh. I'm off at seven. But I can meet you somewhere. You don't need to drive all the way to campus to pick me up," I stammered.

"Rin, it's not a big deal. I'll pick you up then," he gave me a quick up down, corners of his mouth twitching. "All black? The classic Erin vibe. Nice choice." He turned on his heel and headed down the hall towards his room.

I yelled after him, "What does that even mean!?"

He threw his hand in the air, waving back at me. "I'll see ya later, Erin. Better hurry up before you're late."

I stared after him, a thousand questions running through my head.

The main one being: *What the hell was that?*

I smiled to myself. "Weirdo."

I checked the time on my phone, it was a quarter after three; Seth was right. If I didn't leave now, I'd be late. I grabbed my backpack from the closet, ran to the living room, and out the front door, barely taking the time to lock it behind me. I hopped in my car, stuck my key in the ignition, and drove off.

Let this be a quick shift.

Chapter Thirty-Two

Erin

My shift went by agonizingly slow. I returned cart after cart of books to the stacks, our shelves overflowing. A steady stream of students and professors returned hoards of books throughout the day. Unfortunately for me, among the professors who decided to grace the campus library that day was Mr. Jensin.

"Miss Snow." His greeting was coarse and oozed annoyance.

So much for being a favorite student of his.

"Good afternoon, Mr. Jensin." I forced a tight-lipped smile.

"It seems you and Mister Draven have missed a class or two of mine recently. Care to share?"

We missed one *prior to those students being mauled by 'animals.'*

And that was when my ass was unconscious.

Bite me.

I fought to keep the fake smile plastered on. "Some personal things have come up. It's not for me to say, as I've been assisting Seth with a few things. I'll be back in class once they resume next week."

"And Mister Draven?"

"He should be reaching out to you shortly, Mr. Jensin."

He clicked his tongue. "You know, Miss Snow, I do see quite the potential in you and would hate to see you throw that away for a mere boy. Man-child if you will." His mud-colored eyes flicked to my stomach before returning to my face.

I cleared my throat. "I appreciate your concern, Mr. Jensin. I'll be in class next week. Have a nice day." I twirled on my heel with his returned books and headed to the staff room.

His voice followed me. "Be sure to have your paper on Lady Leonora submitted by this coming weekend, as it counts for a majority of your final. I'll see you next week."

Shit.

"He's kinda a dick, huh?" I whipped my head to the side, to find my boss, Ashlin. She was short and petite, barely five foot two. Her brown hair was styled into a pixie cut, bangs and all. Her pink-rimmed glasses sat on the bridge of her nose as she peaked over them, her amber eyes looking up at me.

"Little bit. But his class is a bit of a necessity. The semester is almost over, then I'll be rid of him." I closed my eyes, praying the next couple of weeks went by as quickly as possible.

Ashlin twirled a pen over her fingers. "Is it though? Last time I checked, we have several history professors here that could get you the credits you need for your degree," she arched her brow. "What is this Lady Leonora business he has you writing about?"

"Honestly, Ashlin. I don't even know. We went over it and began studying it almost a month ago and my sleep schedule—among other things—had been a mess so my memory and attention span were trash lately." I dropped the books on the desk with a thud. Two months ago, I would've been winded, even with all the lifting. Now, with the strength of me being Nephilim, the stack of books felt as light as a feather.

"Sounds like you might need to get cracking on that then. Unless...this is really a knight in shining armor issue?" She smirked, and her eyes glinted in the lowlights of the library.

"There is no knight in shining armor, Ash. I'm permanently single." I deadpanned.

She scoffed at me. "Oh please. That friend of yours, Seth? He follows you around like a lost puppy. I see the way you look at him."

My cheeks flushed. "He's not into me like that. He has some big-brother complex towards me," I waved her off. "He's nice to look at lately, but that'd never go anywhere.

Ashlin chuckled. "But are *you* into him?"

I stuttered, "I...I don't know. I mean we've been friends since we were in diapers."

"And?" She craned her neck.

"And that would be utterly ridiculous."

"Would it though? From what I've seen, you are smitten with one another," her grin spread. "And speaking of tall, muscular, and handsome, it seems as though someone is here to pick you up, Erin." Ashlin vibrated with excitement.

Please no.

I tensed, quickly spinning around to see Seth striding towards the front desk, his fingers brushed through his hair, the midnight strands glistening. The dark-washed denim jeans he wore hung low on his hips, the waistband barely covered by the same grey V-neck he wore earlier in the day. His favorite zip up hoodie hung open, the underside of his jacket a light-grey contrasting the charcoal of the outer shell. The heat on my face heightened.

He stopped and his cologne drifted through the air—pine. "Hey, Rin. You ready to go?"

Ashlin, the meddling fiend she was, elbowed in. "Yes, she just finished up, actually."

"But, I—" I stuttered, Ashlin cutting me off.

"I'll finish up here, Erin. You two have fun. I'll see you in a few days." She shot me an innocent grin. Seth turned his attention to his phone briefly and she mouthed '*text me.*' I rolled my eyes.

Seth threw his arm over my shoulder. "So, you ready for dinner, Snow?" Ashlin snorted and I looked around Seth, glaring at her. He followed the sight line of my death-glare. "What? What'd I miss?"

I yanked him forward, nearly causing him to fall, which would've knocked us both down. "Nothing, nothing at all," I forced a nervous laugh. "Let's go. I'm hungry as hell."

My phone buzzed in my pocket. It was a text from Ashlin.

> Don't do anything I wouldn't do! ;)

"Who is it?" Seth asked.

"Uh, no one. Just Ashlin, reminding me...about that paper for Jensin's class. I need to get it done by next week," I shot her a text back, telling her to shove it. "And speaking of, that means you need to get it done too."

Seth pulled his arm from around my shoulders, leaving me slightly chilled, even with my hoodie. His thumbs looped in his jeans. "Actually, Jensin let me off the hook for that assignment. I emailed him before I got here, and he responded almost immediately."

"Huh. That's awfully convenient. He was in the library not too long ago returning a bunch of books and giving me a hard time."

"Snow, you're one of his prized students. He's going to be harder on you." He shrugged.

"And you should be too. You're a hell of a lot smarter than I am."

"You say this, Rin, but your brain's pretty solid too. Even with how thick your skull is."

"Like yours is any better, you ass," I quipped.

"True. Now what's the paper on?" He cleared his throat.

I smacked his chest. "Did you really not pay any attention? Like at all?"

Seth shrugged, not a care in the world. "Honestly, not really."

I sighed, shaking my head. "It's about someone called Lady Leonora. She was some type of ruler or something, I think. We started covering it almost a month ago. And given everything, I'm behind. Really behind."

Seth deflated. "Do you want to head back to my place to get started on it?"

I quirked my eyebrow. "Uh, hell no. My ass is starving, and I owe you dinner."

Seth perked back up. "I'm not letting you pay for dinner. I out eat you. As a guy, that's not cool."

"And as your best friend, that changes the whole men-pay-for-dinner spiel, Seth," I swore I saw the light of his eyes dwindle slightly. "You can get the next one. Deal?"

He grinned down at me. "We'll see about that," the devilish glint returned. "I'll race you to the car for it. First one there, pays." He bolted, speeding off towards his car at the edge of the parking lot.

"You cheater!" I yelled, giggling as I raced after him. I caught up with Seth, to see—to my disappointment—he already reached the car and won, a triumphant grin slapped across his goofy face. As I took another step forward, my shoe caught on the pavement and I went barreling toward the ground.

Seth caught me, his arms reaching under me before I hit the ground. I peered up at him, the light from the sunset casting beautiful shadows across the planes of his face, accentuating his jawline, and the ever-present five o'clock shadow that ran the full length of it. The blue dusk in his eyes twinkled, softening as they stared into my ordinary grey-blue ones. "You okay?" he asked, a hint of huskiness in his voice.

My mouth was dry, unable to form actual words, so I nodded. Seth helped me to my feet and propped open the passenger door so I could slide in.

When did he become so...beautiful?

Okay. I might need my head checked or something.

I gathered myself, shaking off the way he'd looked at me and added as much umph into my voice as I could and whooped as Seth started the engine. "Ready to rock-and-roll?"

Chapter Thirty-Three

Erin

"I told you. I eat twice, if not three times, what you do, Rin. You should know this by now." Seth leaned back in the booth, his arm hanging over the edge. Triumph laced his voice, the corner of his mouth tilted upward.

"I eat like a horse though. It's not my fault you can take down three," I flicked a speck of chicken parm off my fork, landing it on his nose. "Ha! Got ya!"

"You want to play that game, huh?" He grabbed his unwrapped straw, tore off the top, and blew through it, shooting the wrapper at me and hitting me right in the center of my forehead.

We'd landed on a local Italian place. I was craving pasta and breadsticks, and he had a hankering for anything Italian. Seth ordered two plates of Chicken Alfredo and I went with one of my favorites, Chicken Parmigiana; he alone choked down two breadbaskets, the third was all me. I felt like I was going to pop.

"Rude." I scrunched it up, tossed it back at him, and missed. I blamed my poor aim on the overload of delicious food in my system.

"Psh, you shot first, Rin."

"Only because you provoked me. I feign innocence."

He snorted. "Yeah right. You're as innocent as Derik."

"Excuse me, how dare you." My gaze narrowed.

Seth shrugged. "I dare because it's fun," he shot me a wink and I rolled my eyes. "Do you want dessert or anything? We have all night. The crew went to their places for the night," he grabbed the small pocket menu off the table, scanning it. "I might get a beer or a Peach Bellini. You want one?"

I wiggled in the booth, testing my stomach to see if I could handle anything else without needing to shove tums down my throat. "Sure, I'll take one. Since when do you like Peach Bellinis? You usually stick to the hard stuff or beer when we've gone out." All the years we'd known each other, Seth would pick on me about my fruity drinks, switching between peach and strawberry—most of the time—with an occasional wild card.

"Actually, I'll have you know they're one of my favorites. I just don't get them that often because I'll wake up with a major hangover most of the time," he waved our waitress over and put in an order for our drinks. "But I'll make an exception." He winked at me again.

"Of all the drinks out there though, why that one? I mean I absolutely love it, but I'd expect you to be more of a 'on the rocks' type of guy."

Seth set his elbows on the table and leaned forward. "Rin, we might've been friends since we were toddlers, but there's a decent amount you *don't* know about me," I narrowed my eyes at him, and his darkened. "Nothing you'd consider important, I promise. One of them being that peaches are not only one of my favorite fruits, but also a favorite scent, and flavoring of mine."

His eyes held mine as I gulped. "Oh really? Since when?" I had to be reading too much into it.

There's no way in hell, Snow. Calm yourself.

These ever-growing feelings towards your best friend? One-sided, remember? Always have been, always will be.

He caught my eye once more as our waitress brought our drinks to the table, setting one in front of each of us on a pale, cream napkin embossed with the restaurant's name. He thanked her before turning his attention back to our conversation.

"So, how'd training go this morning? Heard you got a knife thrown at you."

I blinked at the abrupt subject change. "What?"

"Your training? With the almighty Josh? How'd it go? Did you land any hits on the guy?" His eyes had returned to their typical glimmer and expression remained neutral, although he continued to lean forward.

"Are...Are you going to ignore the whole peachy thing? I want answers, Seth."

"Eh, there's not much to tell, Rin," he pointed a finger at me. "Training. Speak."

I harrumphed. "I'm not a damn dog"—I crossed my arms over my chest—"but it was fine. Josh wore me out and I was about ready to collapse afterward. My little nap I tried to take got interrupted by another dream. Apparently, according to whoever the dude is that continues to show up, my whole picking a weapon experience was a bit of an anomaly. So. Yay." I added a flare of jazz, my hands waving in the air.

He quirked his brow. "What do you mean? What happened in the dream?"

I relayed the whole story, his brows furrowed. I finished with the whole sword and dagger trio situation as he waved the waitress down for another round.

We sat there staring at one another as we waited for our refills. His hands were clasped in front of his face, hiding his lips, his eyes trained on me. I stared back, gathering his reaction.

He thinks I'm some kind of nutcase. There has to be something wrong with me.

"Interesting."

I craned my neck. "That's it? 'Interesting?' You're not high tailing it? Running to Derik or Libby to see what's wrong with me?"

He gave me a dead stare. "Are you trying to be funny?"

"No. I'm serious."

He shook his head, the light-heartedness dissolving. "Erin. You should know me better than that. Yeah, it's unusual. Especially how much this guide has been popping in on you, and the weapons. But why in the hell would you think I'd high tail it out of here? When have I *ever* done that to you? Not talking about when we were younger. That was different, we were both minors and had no idea." Seth's eyes flared.

"I should but they seem to know you better than I do. Even though we're *supposed* to be the best of friends." I tore my gaze from his. Avoiding the sudden turn we took.

Seth sighed, the flare of anger softened. "Erin, I'm sorry. I'm just...I'm just concerned. And confused. You don't deserve for me to act that way."

Oh but I do. I deserve the worst. And you deserve the best.

I swatted the thought away. "It's fine," I faced Seth, searching his eyes, finding hints of pain. "Can you tell me a bit more about these 'guides'? Is that what, or I guess who, has been visiting me?"

Seth smirked. "Do you not remember when I explained all of our Nephilim stuff to you?"

"Honestly, it was information overload. So. No." I grimaced.

Seth shook his head. "The figure who's been visiting you in your dreams, yes. That's a guide. They're typically Angels, either those who have been slain or who never made it to Earth and instead chose to stay behind in their realm."

"Heaven?"

"Not necessarily. If it's easier, sure. But it's another realm that the Angels originally come from. And that's where the guides are. Hence why they only visit in dreamscapes. Usually."

I sipped the refreshed Bellini our waitress brought. "Define, 'usually.'"

He studied me before speaking. "There are various realms. Ours, Hell, the ones the Angels' dwell in before they come to Earth, the afterlife, and the inter-realm. Which honestly is what it sounds like: the in between. Purgatory, if you will."

"Well. That's fun. Great. Fantastic. Ten out of ten."

Seth blinked. "What?"

"That sounds like a lot of work. Keeping all these different realms separate. And keeping tabs on them."

Seth looked at me like I was an idiot. "What. Erin. No. We focus on the Angels and Demons. The others are simply other levels or interconnected. Angels do the dirty with humans and we're born. Demons want to destroy and rule the human realm. The others are extra. Okay, not really, but that's not our concern."

I slugged back the rest of the peachy deliciousness. "Yeah, yeah. Okay. Got it. Demons bad, Angels, including the ones who haunt my dreams, good."

He just stared at me.

"What?"

"Are...Are you drunk? Or processing?"

"Yes."

He blinked and shook his head; his smirk returning. "You're fucking ridiculous, Snow."

"Tell me something I don't know, *Draven*."

"Okay. Fine," he sat back in the booth, tossing his arms over one another. Challenge lining his features. "You're *adorably* ridiculous."

I choked. "Well. Excuse me, Sir. Adorable? That's a bit much. Ridiculous, absolutely. Adorable? Did you hit your head when you took a leak earlier?"

Seth busted out laughing. "Jeez, Erin," he snickered once more as I shot him a half-hearted glare. "You ready to head out?"

I dramatically whipped my head back then towards him once again. "Are you? Sir, Knight?"

"What. What does that even mean? You've had two. *Two*. Peach infused drinks. How are you this tipsy?"

"It's called forgetting to eat most of the day due to stress." I shot him some finger guns and he waved for the check.

"Dear God," Seth shook his head, shoulders bounced as he laughed. "I'm going to have my hands full."

"Hell yeah, you are." I shot him a tipsy wink. His cheeks flushed. Then he rolled his eyes.

"So, handsome, childhood friend of mine. What are our plans for the remainder of the evening?" I slurred.

Shit. These Bellini's really are hitting me hard.

His eyes darkened. I felt my nether regions sob in response.

Nether regions? Really? What is this the seventeenth century?

He ignored me. Slipping his card into the card pocket of the bill holder. I scoffed.

"What?"

"You ignored me."

"You're drunk. Off of two drinks, nonetheless."

"So? You could still respond."

His smirk returned. "Well, Erin. What did *you* have in mind?"

I clicked my tongue. "A competition. Who can drink who under the table while maintaining their control?"

He eyed me suspiciously. "What do you mean by control?"

I batted my lashes. "Of our abilities of course. Let's see who can battle and hold out the longest."

He licked his lips. "You're on."

Chapter Thirty-Four

Erin

We made it back to Seth's place, having stopped at the liquor store on our way. I waited in the car while Seth ran in and grabbed a few bottles of god-knew-what and mixers. My buzz from the restaurant was still in full swing when we parked in front of his house.

"What the hell did you get? That's enough for a house full of people."

"I got a few things." A sly smile formed on his lips.

I rolled my eyes as he opened the passenger door for me. "So, chivalrous. What a gentleman." He chuckled and helped me out of his car.

"Always am, Snow. Always am."

"Nuh, uh. Not with me." I slurred as I swatted him off.

Seth shook his head as his eyes grazed the length of my arm that was in his gentle grasp. "I'd do it more, if you'd actually let me, Rin."

I turned my head away as heat rushed to my cheeks and mumbled, "If you say so."

He shoved the key in the doorknob and pushed it open, motioning for me to head over to the living room while he sorted through his haul, and mixed together a few concoctions.

I tapped away on my phone, pulling up notes from class on Leonora, hoping to review a bit before diving in and pulling off a twenty-five page paper over the next few days *without* losing my mind. The screen gave me nothing but a bunch of scribbled nonsense from a few classmates and a couple of vulgar drawings. I sighed.

This is going to suck major ass.

"Hey, no work tonight, Rin." I jumped, Seth's deep voice boomed from behind me. He reached over and plucked my phone from my fingertips, tossing it onto the floor, and replaced it with a large bluish-green drink.

"Hey! You could've cracked the screen," I whined. "Jeez!"

"But I didn't. Relax, Sweetheart. Try the drink, I think you'll like it."

I glared at him as he hopped over the couch, landing next to me; the thought of shooting a small fireball at him crossed my mind. I took a sip of the drink he handed me, my eyes widening. "There's booze in this? It's fucking delicious!"

He let out a low laugh, it reverberated through my bones, squeezing itself around the quickening muscle within my chest. "What do you think? Pretty good, huh?" Seth took a long pull from his, a smirk behind his glass.

"Why do you keep doing that?" I asked, taking another hefty gulp of my own bluish goodness.

"Keep doing what?" Seth arched his eyebrow and finished off his drink in record time.

"Calling me Sweetheart. It's weird."

He shrugged and got up, eyeing my cup. "You want another one?"

I knocked it back and handed him the empty cup. "You didn't answer me." I brought my legs up to the couch, tucking them under myself as I twisted toward the open kitchen.

He tossed some blue liquor into a cobbler shaker and followed it up with some clear-greenish liquor. I squinted and saw it was a flavored moonshine.

Oh, this is going to hit me hard as shit.

Seth dropped the top of the cobbler on and shook it. His arms flexing with the movement as he threw some oomph into it. I caught myself salivating.

"You'd make a killing as a bartender." It slipped out before I could stop myself.

He smirked. "Oh yeah?"

"One thousand percent. You'd rack up tips like crazy. And the ladies would be all over you." I laughed, ignoring the slight twang in my chest.

I blinked. From across the room, his eyes darkened. His mouth twitched. "What if I wasn't concerned about the 'ladies' aspect?"

"Well, considering you are a guy, who is above average height, rather attractive—as most women would think—and ooze Golden Retriever vibes, I'd say you're either in denial or pulling my leg." There was no denying the blush that overtook the entirety of my face and neck.

If any of this comes back to bite me in the morning, I'm chalking it up to being absurdly drunk.

He narrowed his eyes. "Golden Retriever vibes? I remind you of a damn dog?"

"Okay, first off, Goldens are freaking adorable so calm the frick frack down, Sassy Pants. Secondly, yeah. It's like, a guy who is super easy going, carefree, and like your best friend. Huge heart and super sweet. Like a Golden Retriever."

"So, you are comparing me to a dog?" He craned his neck towards me. His forehead creased, brows pushing together in confusion.

"Ugh, no! I just. I'm just saying you're a good guy and any girl would be crazy about you."

He paused, his gaze catching mine. "What about you?"

I froze. "I. I...Seth, you're my best friend," I stammered. His face fell.

"Yeah, best friend." Seth's shoulders slumped as he walked over, drinks in hand.

Fix it, Snow!

"Wait, Seth. That's not. That's not what I mean. I mean, obviously, I'm not blind," he perked up a little. "We've just been friends so long, best friends...I don't want to ruin anything." I grabbed my cup, my fingers grazed his, my eyes glued to his.

"How do you know anything would be ruined?" He tilted his head, his pupils dilated. The darkest depths of the ocean glimmered within them, drawing me in.

I can't.

"I...I...I'm not someone you'd want to be with Seth. I mean look at me. I'm average, if that. I blend in. Besides this past nightmare of a month, my nose is usually stuck in a book. I'm a mess and a half. I mean, hell, my own father went running in the opposite direction. I have zero friends outside of you," I wobbled my head a bit. "Okay, maybe you and Ashlin. And Libby and Derik seem to tolerate me. But that's it. The coolest thing about me is I can apparently spit fire and lightning from my fingers. And that's only recent. You could do better."

"What if I don't want to do better, Erin?" He paused, seeing the hurt on my face. He swore under his breath. "That's not what I mean," he ran his fingers through his hair, gripping it as he pulled it back. "What I mean is, you're more than that. So much more and I...wish you could see yourself the way I see you. The way the world sees you." His eyes desperately searched mine.

"Libby and Derik consider you family. Josh even likes your company. And his cranky ass can't stand anybody. Ashlin would be lost in the library stacks without you. Hell. *I* would be lost without you, Rin."

He took my drink from me and set it on the coffee table. His voice cracked as he reached for my hands, clasping them within his own. "You're smart. Beautiful. Your eyes shine like the sky in the early light. Your laugh, your presence, it lights up the room. You bring so much joy to so many people and you don't even realize it. Erin, you...you are so much more than just my best friend. I know you think I have some big brother complex with you but that couldn't be further from the truth." I waited with baited breath.

Seth...

He squeezed my hand. "And what happened with your dad. That wasn't your fault. You were fourteen. No one knows what the hell happened to him. No one. We've looked. My uncle, he looked, searched every nook and cranny before he died. That had nothing to do with you. And you didn't cause him to run off. That's on him. Not you. You are not to blame for his actions."

Tears welled, threatening to flood my eyes. "I don't know what to say," I whispered.

Seth moved closer and leaned in. He pulled me close as he rested his chin against the top of my head. "You don't have to say anything, Rin."

I nestled into his embrace as his fingers traced circles along my spine. "Thank you." I sniffed, my lip pouting.

He let out a soft chuckle. "Anytime, Sweetheart." He swiped his thumb across my cheek.

My lip wobbled.

Seth moved his thumb under my chin, tilting my face up towards his. "Rin, you really are drunk, aren't you?"

I quickly nodded my head as a sob escaped my lips.

His eyes softened and he reached his arms around me. "Why don't we head to bed? You want me to carry you to your room?"

I nodded my head and added, "Can I sleep with you, tonight? Please? With Libby not here, it... it feels empty in there." It was a partial lie. We've grown close over the last month and a half. I was getting used to being around her bubbly energy and I found that I missed it, even if just for a night. And...I didn't want to sleep alone. Not with everything in my system.

I didn't want to risk the fears and pains I shoved down threatening to make themselves known.

Seth hadn't responded. I pulled back, and looked up to find him staring at me. "Did I say something wrong?"

"No, Rin. Not at all," he paused; a faint smile grazed the corner of his mouth, almost sad. "You're always welcome, anytime you need."

Chapter Thirty-Five

Erin

It was like déjà vu. I awoke to eardrum-shattering snoring, only to realize it was Seth.

And I was laying in his bed. Again.

I panicked and threw the blankets off of me, terrified to find what might be underneath, considering the situation. I breathed a sigh of relief when I found myself in the same clothes as the night before, my black skinny jeans and long sleeve from training. I was just minus a hoodie and shoes. No panties or bra missing. I glanced over to see Seth still passed out, fully clothed and snoring like a motherfucker.

I nudged him and whispered, "Seth. Seth! Wake up," he grumbled and turned on his side to where his back was facing me. I nudged him with my foot. "Dude." I hissed. He responded with a groan. I huffed, frustrated and needed answers. I swatted the back of his head.

"Ugh, what? What's the emergency, can't a guy get some shut eye?" he grumbled.

"Seth!" I growled.

He flopped over, facing me, his eyes squinted, and glared at me. "What?"

"Did we sleep together?"

He blinked at me, processing. Then groaned and rolled back over. "No, Rin. You'd know if we slept together." He began snoring again within seconds.

I blew out a sigh of relief. "Thank fuck," I whispered under my breath. The thundering in my chest slowed.

I slid out of Seth's bed and crept to his door, slowly cracking it open. It creaked and I winced, looking over my shoulder to see if he was still asleep. He snored in response. I tiptoed my way out to the kitchen and scavenged through the pantry for the coffee grounds before dumping them in the coffee machine, set to strong brew. I might not get hangovers, but Seth sure as hell did.

While it brewed, I padded to the guest room and grabbed my laptop, determined to knock out some of my schoolwork revolving around Jensin's class. I pulled the notes up from the online course and browsed. I scrolled through pages upon pages, finding nothing worthwhile.

I gave up and clicked out of the notes. I pulled up my search engine and typed in Lady Leonora, not much hope lingered. "Where did Jensin even get this stuff from?" I mumbled.

The coffee beeped, signaling that it was done brewing. I poured myself a cup, adding in more creamer and sugar than was necessary, and stirred it as I scanned an article that had been published a few years prior, which delved into who this Lady Leonora was. I sipped from my mug.

> Lady Leonora, the woman who saved her kingdom. Humanity.

"Well that sounds a bit dramatic." I read on.

I stopped halfway through the article. "Wait a minute." I set my mug down on the island and leaned closer to my laptop. Rereading the excerpt in front of me.

> She was thought to be the answer. The one destined to rule them all. To wreak havoc. Her power emanated from her. Fire, light, ice, water, and the Earth. The elements bowed to her, and were hers to wield.
>
> The darkness threatened to take her. To use her to reign. To overtake the world as it was known.
>
> In her dying breath, she vowed to protect humanity. In all her power. She would live on. The innocent would be protected. The darkness would not prevail. She whispered a promise to her beloved on her dying breath, a sword thrust between her breasts, her blood oozing from the wound. Flooding her gown.
>
> She was the key to their undoing. And with her, the secret to how they would survive, died.

"Holy. Fucking. Shit."

I bounced on the balls of my feet. I'd grabbed eggs and pancake mix and set about making a large batch of breakfast. While I let the pancakes cook through, I sent out a mass text, asking Libby and Derik to come over. Even Josh.

The only one I'd heard from was Libby saying she'd be at Seth's within fifteen minutes. Nothing came through from the guys and Seth was still hunkered down in his room, passed the fuck out.

I flipped the last stack of pancakes and eggs onto the serving plate when Libby walked in.

"Good morning!" she said, chipper as ever, a smile graced her lips, spreading from cheek to cheek. She inhaled the aroma wafting from the kitchen. "Oh! You made breakfast! It smells amazing, Erin!"

"Yeap!" I attempted to keep the anxiety from my voice as she padded to the kitchen, sliding into one of the stools at the island.

She leaned her elbows on the counter, her white tank top perfectly accentuated her toned, tanned arms. She flipped her blonde bob to the side, waving her bangs away from her eyes as they glistened in the natural light flowing in from the massive windows that rested above the kitchen cabinets behind me.

"So, Erin, what's up?" Libby flashed me a smile, unaware of the information dump that was about to be plopped in her lap.

I set a plate of eggs and pancakes in front of her and passed her the syrup. She eyed me as she sliced and bit into her food. Curiosity danced within the emeralds of her face.

"I, uh. I might have a lead."

Libby's eyebrows shot sky high. Her fork dropped from her grip. "What!?"

"You can see memories too, right?"

Libby nodded, her mouth hanging open.

"If I give you my hand, can you sort through what I saw and found? Is that okay?" I asked, my voice growing a bit shaky in anticipation. Libby nodded and I held my hand out for her to take, letting her reach forward.

Her hand gripped mine and her pupils dilated, turning a light grey, the irises a pure white. Her shoulders jolted but she held firm. I searched her face, looking for any signs of pain or concern. Libby's lips strewn tight, a shade of blue tinged her lips. "Libby?" I called her name. Another minute passed and her head was thrown back on her shoulders. "Libby!" I hissed and leaped over the island, catching her before she toppled backward onto the hardwood. I was able to get myself underneath her in time and we landed with a loud thud on the ground.

Libby's shoulders shook, as she regained her focus, her eyes returned to their usual bright green.

"Are you okay!? I thought you said the visions with other people weren't as harsh?" I twisted her in my lap, even though she towered over me typically, and searched her face for any pain.

Libby brushed herself off, wriggled out of my grasp, and sat back on her heels. "You're as bad as Seth and Derik," she let out a tight laugh and dusted herself off. "But yes, I'm fine. They usually aren't that intense. Especially given what you showed me. It's odd."

"Are you okay?"

"Yeah, I'm fine, Erin." The tips of her mouth slanted upward.

"What do you think?" I asked. My gut turned as I awaited her response.

"I think we *do* have a lead on our hands. The real question is: What do you want to do about it?"

Libby listened as I explained my plan, my arms flailing in the air as I rambled. She kept her eyes trained on me, taking in every word. And agreed with keeping Seth out of the loop. It'd be better to keep him out of it for the time being.

Until we have what we need.

An hour later, Seth came out right as we finished. His hair was tousled, bags under his eyes, five o'clock shadow darker than usual. He mumbled a thanks as he grabbed a plate of food and a mug of coffee off the island then went back to his room.

We giggled as the door shut behind him, my gaze trailed him the entire way. My chest tightened, ached.

I will do everything in my power to protect you, Seth.
You and those missing people.

I sighed as I shoved a forkful of eggs into my mouth and prayed that I was making the right decision.

Chapter Thirty-Six

Seth

I sprawled across my mattress as the eggs and breakfast cakes hit my stomach, and thanked God that Erin knew how to cook. I chugged the mug of coffee and set the empty cup on my nightstand. I pulled one of the pillows from the side Erin slept on over my face, blocking out the sunrays filtering in through the overhead windows on the far wall of my room.

Why did I install so many damn windows in this place?

I breathed in deeply, relishing the peaches and cucumber that filled my nose. My head was pounding, a jack hammer beat against my eyelids. Erin's scent made it worth it, the warmth from her being in my bed still remained.

I sat up and dug into my nightstand, eyes squinted as the sunlight cascading along the panes of my bedroom wall once again pummeled my eyes. "Fucking hell." I hissed, as my fingers finally grasped the emergency Ibuprofen bottle. I popped three and swallowed them down dry. I fought the urge to gag as they crept down my throat. I fell back on the bed, pillow once again hiding me from the death-rays that peaked in.

Erin's face floated through my mind.

Her brilliant grey-blue eyes lit with laughter, her long brown hair swept into a ponytail, trailing behind her. Her laughter echoing around us in little wisps of gold, encircling her beautifully. They then flowed toward me, gripping my heart, my soul.

Erin's smile faded and tears took its place. Black rivers flowed from her sockets, dying the whites of her eyes, her pupils disappeared into the darkness.

"Erin!? Erin!" I reached for her shoulders and shook them, needing to bring her back.

Her face hollowed out, cheeks sunk in. Her mouth agape, cracks formed on her skin. The black pits that formed her eyes stared up at me, devoid of the brightness that was there only moments before.

Her voice came out crazed, strained. A bony finger, stripped of its flesh, lifted, pointing at my chest. "You. You did this to me." A screech escaped her, and she lunged forward, claws extended from her fingertips. I cried out as they pierced my chest and sunk into my heart. Blood spurted from the wound, her claws twisting in further before she yanked them out, taking my still beating heart with them. Flames licked their way through the entirety of my empty chest cavity, the pain forcing me to my knees. Salty tears raked down my face.

"Why?" I begged, metal began coating my tongue.

Her lips spread and her skin cracked further, nearly splitting her face in two. Sharp pointed teeth gleamed, ink dripped from them. She brought my heart to her lips and tore a large chunk of it out, gnashing it between her teeth; her dead eyes continued to look down at me as I withered at her feet.

"Rin, what...what did I do to you?" I sobbed.

The blood from my heart merged with the ink as it dripped down her chin. A maniacal laugh belted through her piercing teeth. Her skin split, exposing the tissue underneath, across her entire body. Her flesh began to melt, her bones with it. My half-eaten heart thumped to the ground. My stomach turned, wisps of gold and grey ripped from me. The pain was unbearable, far worse than my heart having been torn away. An emptiness enveloped me, my body chilled, my vision blurred. It felt as if...as if my soul had been torn from me, shredded to pieces.

I fell forward, head hitting the ground. Numbness overtook me. I dragged my strained vision to the puddle of flesh and bones that had been Erin.

Hovering over her, stood Erebus. He crouched down, his teeth flashed, and his tongue darted out, licking up the pieces of Erin.

His voice broke through the numbness, scratching its way along my bones. "I told you she was delicious, didn't I, boy?" He retracted his tongue, a large lump of flesh encircled within, and swallowed as he licked his lips.

"Now, it's your turn."

I bolted upright, panting, sweat coated my body from head to toe. I threw myself off the bed and ran into the living room, frantically searching for any sign of Erin. Nothing.

I ran to her room, slamming the door open, the doorknob crunched the wall as it hit. Her bed was made, clothes neat, everything was where she'd been keeping it. I steam-rolled my way through the house.

Where the hell is she?

The front door clicked, and I sprinted to the living room. "Erin?" I shouted, throwing any attempt at hiding the panic in my tone out the window.

Josh and Derik stood at the kitchen island, both wide-eyed. Derik arched his eyebrow. "Uh, where's the fire, dude?"

I panted, hands on my knees. "Have either of you seen or heard from Erin?"

Josh checked his phone, the definition of calm. "Yes, she and Miss Libby are out running errands. Something along the lines of 'girl time' as Miss Snow had put it," his attention moved to me. "Any particular reason as to why you are stampeding through your home like a rampant untrained horse?"

I opened my mouth to respond, and Derik swooped in. "Lover Boy probably got his rocks off in dream land, and wanted the real thing, huh?" He winked at me, and I forced the corners of my mouth upward.

I added a laugh for good measure. Josh rolled his eyes as he returned to his phone, scrolling. Derik eyed me but let it drop.

I slid onto one of the bar stools and nestled my feet behind the barred footrest, elbows leaning on the counter top. "So, what has you two waltzing in here this early in the day?"

Derik slid a mug towards me, it sloshed over the rim as I caught it in my hands. I took a sip, grimacing as the bitter cold brew slid down my throat.

I choked. "There's no way this practically turned to ice that quickly. Erin made it fresh this morning."

"Nothing gets past you, does it, Seth?" Derik retorted and grabbed his phone out of the pocket of his bedazzled jeans. He tabbed the screen with his thumb. "It's three in the afternoon, dude."

I flipped him off, glaring over the sage green rim. "Explains a lot."

I didn't even think I fell asleep. It felt so real.

I rubbed the center of my chest, a slight ache present. Derik quirked an eyebrow at me and I brushed it off, pointing my attention at Josh.

He tapped away on his phone, features devoid of emotion. His mouth formed a set line, his eyes bored. I could never figure the guy out. Always quiet, observing. Rarely partaking with our group unless a hunt was involved or intel was needed.

Until recently.

I narrowed my eyes at him.

"Any reason why Erin would text you instead of me?" Envy boiled in the pit of my stomach.

He snapped his smartphone shut as his stone-cold gaze met mine. "Actually, Mr. Draven, it was I who reached out to Miss Snow first. I had sent her a text message alerting my arrival. She simply responded," judgment shown in his eyes as they swept across my body. "Your jealousy is ill aimed, Seth. And not the best look on you."

The hair on the back of my neck rose. "Screw off, Josh. Why are you guys here anyway? You never answered me."

Jackass.

Derik responded first, "I wanted to pop over to dive into some more Demon and 'Key' hunting. I found a few things yesterday and wanted to run them by you. Plus, one of the girls texted me to come over. Not too sure about Chronically Cranky over here, though." Derik jutted his thumb in Josh's direction.

Josh rolled his eyes at the nickname. "Similar."

I leaned back in the stool. Arms crossed. "Alright. So, what've the two of you got?"

Derik sat in the stool next to me, bringing a bag of chips with him. He dug his phone out of his pocket and sat it in front of me.

"From what I found, it looks like the Demons can't just maim, procreate, and torture these humans at their whim to screw us all to hell—to an extent—it must be done on the night of the Blood Moon and coincide with The Key being brought forward and unleashed." He gulped.

Josh whispered, "To truly unleash the chaos and disruption in this world."

"And the next one is less than a month away."

"Shit." Lead hit the pit of my stomach. The vision of Erin overtook me, panic constricted itself around me.

"I texted Miss Snow and Miss Libby. They should return momentarily." Josh's voice faintly registered through the cackling as it rang in my ears. I nodded in response, rapidly blinking away the memory of Erin's molten flesh.

I shoved myself back from the island, knocking over the barstool. "I need to head out for a few. I'll be back. If they show up before me, make sure to keep everyone here." I ignored Derik as he shouted after me, asking what had happened.

I headed for my room and pulled out a dagger I kept hidden within a pocket on the underside of my nightstand. I strapped it into the waistband of my sweats, rammed my feet into my running shoes, made my way back down the hall, through the living room, and out the door. Derik and Josh's eyes burned into my back.

The leaves rustled around me as I crept through the trees. Afternoon had begun to shift into evening as I hunted my prey. I needed the distraction, an outlet for my anger—my fear. And a gym session wasn't going to cut it.

I needed to kill.

To rid the world of something vile.

My nostrils flared.

The tang of blood filled the air, guiding me forward.

Guttural laughter sounded in the distance. "This one is going to be delectable, brother. I called first dibs."

I heard a shriek echo further into the woods. The air stilled, as if hearing it as well. As if the forest felt the pain of the victim. A howl skirted through the trees.

The shrieking abruptly stopped.

I picked up my pace, the bitter taste of fear hit my tongue.

I came upon a clearing and ducked behind a wall of shrubbery as I took in the scene before me. Two Demons standing nearly seven feet in height each, had a human strewn and torn in half between them, fingers still twitching as the light dimmed from their eyes. Their throat had been gouged out, torso split from their lower half, entrails hung from their severed body. One Demon's back was to me, long hair jutted from its spine, elongated, pointed ears sat atop its head, a snarl erupted from its mouth as it bit down on the human's head, ripping it free. The damned thing had transformed itself into a wolf of nightmares. I fought the bile that rose from my stomach.

The second Demon ripped what little clothing was left strewn across the human's flesh on their bottom half. A forked tongue stabbed the human's center, a female. My heart ached. The Demon dove its tongue further within the human, until it erupted to the other side and tore her body in half once again. Anger rippled through me.

The human is already gone.

I gripped my dagger.

I need to wait.

The moment has not come yet.

I watched as the Demons devoured the human's body. Bit by bit. Until there was nothing left, and their bellies were filled, sated.

Now.

I crept forward, ears trained on the clearing and trees around me, listening for any potential surprises. There was no sign of any other Demons.

I sprinted, using my full Nephilim speed to launch myself forward as I drove my dagger into the wolfed Demon's back, directly aligned with its empty heart. I drew my blade back and ink spurted out of its wound. It turned swiftly, its body shook with rage, claws flailing, pawed feet tripping over themselves. I quickly stole contact upon its snout, reversing its memory as it collapsed. Black blood gurgled from its center as I leaped onto it, slicing down its core as I propelled myself into the air, landing on the shoulders of the second Demon. I twisted, snapping its neck and lodged my dagger into the side of it.

"Please." It panted, breath strangled.

I leaped down, landing next to the Demon as it plummeted to the ground, head lolled towards me as ink pooled from its mouth. I crouched down, its eyes darting, fear infiltrated their usual cocky demeanor. I ran the blade of my dagger along its sunken cheekbones as I let out a low laugh, ice laced my voice.

I leaned down to its ear and whispered, "Your survival went out the door the moment you set foot into my territory and threatened the people here." I sliced the dagger clean through its head, yanking it back as it split in two. Just like the woman they raped and murdered.

I looked to where they had feasted on the innocent life. Nothing but crimson blood and guts laced the ground where she had been. I begged that whatever awaited her, was peaceful and far better than what she had suffered.

I hung my head, arms draped over my knees as I sat, coated in the Demons' blood. The adrenaline continued to coarse through me. Erin flashed through my mind.

I have to protect her.

Chapter Thirty-Seven

Seth

I ran off the rest of the adrenaline as I sprinted through the woods and deeper into the thick of it. My anger and bloodlust having got the better of me. The hunt was needed, but I needed the information more. Time was ticking away. The humans grew closer to their deaths each day. Erin's potentially not too far behind. If she was The Key, that meant she'd be used to bring the Demons into power—domination. And it was unclear if that meant she too would be slaughtered and sacrificed once they were done with her. A growl escaped my lips as the image of how we'd found her in Erebus's lair loomed in my mind.

I tore through the forest, increasing my speed as the trees and brush rushed past me. The wind whistled through the woods, bringing with it the chill of the night. Images of Erin continued to haunt me. Her smile. The tears she shed. The distant brokenness that drifted in and out of her as she plastered on a smile the day we reunited after all those years apart. It hadn't reached her eyes. It took months—years—for the glimmer to return, the sunshine that had been buried deep within. Hours of running. Lifting. Goofing around. Dancing; endless coffee runs, late nights, painting, reading, and everything in between.

Then he took her. Erebus took her from me. And that light began to dwindle. She became haunted once more. The beautiful grey-blue depths of her eyes shone a little less. The hollows under them deepened. She'd become leaner, stronger than ever, and not just because of her Nephilim strength. Her training had gotten better. She worked at it constantly. But...I didn't know if it was enough.

I blinked and her dismembered body with dark, empty eyes flashed behind my lids. I barreled through thickets growling, an empty clearing before me. A dreary meadow, having seen better days. My dagger was at the ready.

An ear-piercing roar erupted across the meadow. A Demon came barreling out of the trees, deranged, and foaming at the mouth. I braced myself for impact as it ripped its way through the tall grass toward me, only for it to stop short, two figures slamming into it from the sides.

Silence.

Its roar bellowed through the clearing, the leaves on the surrounding trees shook as it fell to its knees. A third figure waltzed into the clearing. I blinked and the scorching red imploded through my vision once again.

"Erin? Libby? What the actual *hell* are you two doing out here? And with *him*," I growled deeply, the sound vibrated my chest. "Some fucking errands." I kept my feet planted, even as the thought of slicing Josh's throat for risking Erin's life flicked through my head.

Erin stepped forward in Josh's defense, arms outstretched, palms facing me. She jumped over the overgrown monster's arm and nearly face-planted in the process. "Seth, chill out."

My voice rose. "Chill out!? Erin, you aren't fucking trained enough to be chasing after Demons, let alone one that's the size of a freaking tank! You could've gotten yourself killed. What the fuck were you thinking? Did Josh fucking put you two up to this?!" I yelled, stomping a foot in his direction.

Erin planted herself directly in my path, throwing her hands on her hips as lightning crackled from the tips of her fingers, fire blazed in her eyes.

"You want to fucking try that again, Seth? How *dare you* fucking pull that shit when you're out here *alone* and by the looks of your ink-stained clothes, fighting the hellhounds without anyone else. So, don't you *fucking* dare sit there on your soapbox, you fucker," she struck her finger against the center of my chest, the lightning extinguished. "And don't you dare pin this on Josh. This whole thing was my idea. We weren't getting anywhere and after seeing Josh's methods"—Erin quickly flicked her eyes in his direction—"I thought it might be useful to have him in on this."

That was it. I fumed. "He answers to *me*, Erin. Not you. You don't have the experience necessary to go off on some Demon hunting escapade. And Libby"—I glared at her. She ignored me and eyed her nails—"should've said something to me about whatever this mess is."

Erin scoffed. "Oh, really? So, what? I'm just meant to sit on the goddamned sidelines while your ass goes out and risks *your* life behind *my* back? Or while you send Derik to do it for you? Really?" Libby's head shot up; her eyes narrowed. "Clearly you have a case of hypocrisy, Draven." My heart ached, a knife wedging itself in. She almost never called me by my last name.

"That's not what I meant," I grumbled.

"Sure as hell fucking sounded like it." Erin growled.

Josh clapped his hands. "Ladies and Mister Draven. I understand the lot of you would easily stand around all day insulting each other with various profanity but we must get a move on. I can only hold this creature for so long," he motioned to Erin and Libby. "Ladies."

Libby crouched down next to the Demon, not yet touching it. Erin did the same as she planted herself directly in sight of the Demon, weight on the balls of her feet. Josh yanked a dagger from its side and threw it in Erin's direction, she caught it without removing her attention from the Demon before her, its eyes slowly beginning to open.

At least she didn't slice her hand trying to catch it.

Ice crept into my bones as she began to speak, her voice hollow, deadly, cold. Something I'd never before heard from her. "Wakey, wakey, creepy ass Demon. We need some answers."

I froze. *Where the fuck did this come from?*

It blinked and a smile equivalent to that of a demonic toy, crept along her face. The grey-blue of her eyes darkened, her pupils narrowed. Her teeth were bared and her flames erupted from her palms. The Demon seemed to pale, before its own teeth flashed. "You vermin! You are trash, how dare you! You bow to *me!*" The Demon spat at Erin.

Her grin widened; a cold laugh escaped with it. "Might want to save your breath there, Demon. As it's limited." She leaned forward, elbows propped on her knees, and ran her dagger along its face, pushing it into the skin as she went, a thin, faint line of black ink trailing. My eyes widened. The Demon began howling, screaming; its body began to convulse. "Now you see, my friend over there," Erin pointed her dagger towards Josh. "He will make you absolutely miserable, your worst fears brought forward. Unless, that is, you cooperate and tell us what we need to know."

The Demon continued to convulse; a whimper fell from its mouth. Erin flickered her gaze to Josh, her head nodding. Her eyes then landed on me, fear lined the outer rims. I looked closer, her skin a shade green, as if she were on the verge of puking.

It's an act.

A terrifying one.

What's your plan here, Erin?

My attention snapped back to the Demon as its mouth foamed, body shaking, the ground around it moving from the vibrations. Erin's attention returned as well, her mask falling back into place. "It'll stop. All you need to do is answer a few questions for me and you'll be free to go back to your handler, Demon." The Demon screamed once again, piercing my eardrums as I fought the need to cover my ears, Erin and Libby's hands twitched as if fighting the same urge. Josh remained unfazed.

It roared out in pain. "Okay! I'll do it. Just please. Make it stop!" The Demon begged.

Erin snapped her fingers and the Demon's screams stopped, replaced by ragged panting. It moved to sit up, Erin wagged her finger. "Ah, ah." The Demon visibly shook.

What the hell did Josh show it?

The Demon stopped moving, eyes clouded and darting around frantically. Erin patted its massive head. "Good boy," the iced smile crept back into place. "Now, what can you tell me about the humans your lot took? And don't leave out any details." She sang a siren in the forest.

The Demon panted; voice trembled as he spoke. "I...they...we took thirteen of them. Eight females and five males."

"Yes, we are aware, go on," Libby added, her voice low, devoid of its usual singsong tone.

The Demon's clouded eyes shot in Libby's direction, not seeming to realize she was still there. "O-okay. The humans, they worked for a factory, all of them out here. That's how we found them."

"Why them though? Why did that have anything to do with you taking them?" Erin poked the Demon's face with her dagger, barely missing his eye.

"We searched for them," his voice became strained, as if fighting to speak. "We were searching for The Key. Erebus told us we must find these humans. The descendants. The descendants of some deceased human girl, he said her name was Leonora. That we would know. As their births would have fallen on the day of the blood moon."

"There are anywhere between two to four blood moons a year. Countless children are born on those days. Why these thirteen specifically? How could you know the difference between them, these *descendants,* and any normal human being?" Erin questioned him.

Interesting.

We've been searching for weeks...and never has anything been mentioned about these 'descendants.'

Or Leonora...

A vein in the Demon's neck twitched, his face wincing in pain as he ground out, "Their scents. The energy that radiates off of them. There was rumor that they were more than human, and Erebus ran with it. They all happened to be at the same place."

Erin's eyes narrowed. I stepped toward the Demon, shoving my foot down on its head before Erin could begin her next line of questioning. I let my voice drop, the promise of death rumbling from my throat. "Where does Leonora come into this then? What significance would her bloodline play?"

And how the hell is some assignment from a college history class tying into all of this?

The Demon whined. "All I've heard was a theory. I don't know. Erebus had told us of a legend. One that described this Leonora as a unique individual. A traitor to her kind." I pushed the heel of my shoe further, the Demon let out a wail.

"Out with it, Demon."

I snuck a look at Erin, she was beginning to shake, her mask falling. The Demon kept his clouded eyes trained on me; its neck twisted at an unnatural angle.

"She...she was a Demon, who chose the enemy. She abandoned the Demons, and in turn fell to become half-human as punishment by our ruler. Her father," the Demon sucked in a ragged breath. "She had been the strongest Demon of our kind and stripped herself of that power for an Angel. Her descendants...they were not of her bloodline but the bloodline of the thirteen Demons who followed her betrayal."

"Was she killed?"

The Demon's voice strained. "No one knows. Not even Erebus."

Erin scoffed. "Of course he doesn't. That's fucking convenient."

The Demon shook as his eyes darted back to Erin. "That's all I know, I swear."

"Where are they?"

The Demon's eyes began to bug out of their sockets as he wailed once again.

"Josh, stop it!" Erin shouted, shooting up to her feet. Josh's eyes widened, bordering panic.

"It's not me, Miss Snow. I swear."

"Then what the fuck is happening?" She shot down to her knees next to the Demon, clasping her hands on its shoulders in an attempt to shake it from its lying position.

"Erin, that's not going to do anything! He's convulsing!" I shouted as she frantically rocked the Demon's body back and forth on the ground. I lunged forward to pull her away, motioning for Libby to get back as well, when the Demon exploded. I threw myself at Erin, doing what I could to wedge myself between her body and the flying Demon carcass.

Black sludge sprayed throughout the meadow, dying the entirety of the area a deep ink. Scraps and chunks of Demon flesh lined the clearing. Several pieces clung to my back, slowly oozing down my sides as I pushed myself off of Erin, both of us breathing heavily. Libby's eyes were wide, the emeralds shining against the ink that coated her face and hair. Josh stood a few feet back, Demon flesh in his hair, black goo stained his white V-neck, his black blazer seeming to blend in.

"What the flying fuck was that?!" I shouted, to no one in particular. My eyes darted along the stained meadow, searching for the source.

"The flying part was the Demon," Erin quipped next to me. I turned my head, staring at her, my mouth hanging open.

"Really? This is when you decide to make jokes?"

She showed a small smile, her lip quivering. I let out a sigh. "It's what I do best." Her voice shook.

"That was fucked," Libby said, her singsong tone returned.

"Quite," Josh added, as he brushed the Demon chunks from his hair.

"Now what?" Libby asked as she sat next to Erin, tucking her knees underneath herself and wiping away a few fleshy pieces that snagged Erin's gear. Erin swatted Libby's hand away.

She's reacting...a lot better than I would expect...

Erin regained her composure. "Now, we find those humans," she flashed Libby a smile as she stood, pulling Libby up with her. Libby's back stiffened briefly; her eyes clouded for a nanosecond before Erin released her. A glint of mischief gleamed in the corner of Erin's eye.

My gaze narrowed.

What are you not telling me, Snow?

Chapter Thirty-Eight

Erin

(Earlier That Day)

> Hey.

Good morning, Miss Snow. To what do I owe the pleasure?

> I have a question and potentially a favor to ask you.

Go on, Miss Snow.

> I might have a lead, but I need help tracking down a Demon or two. Know anyone who might be able to help?

> Miss Snow, I request that if you are asking what I think you are asking, that you do not go wandering after one on your own.

> You may have improved your skills in training, but it would be foolish to charge ahead, alone.

I sighed and bit back the snarky remark at the tip of my fingers as I texted Josh that morning.

> I wasn't planning on going alone. I'm not that stupid.

> I didn't say you were, Miss Snow. Simply that it would be foolish. And you don't strike me as someone foolish. Now, what do you need from me?

> Libby is going to be with me but I need you to tag along as well.

> And since you seem to have a way about hunting down said Demons, I would greatly appreciate assistance in locating one.

> And questioning.

> I will assist. However, you must do the questioning. Not me.

> Why?

> Practice, Miss Snow. You are not the most intimidating individual.

>> Ugh. Fine. But one more thing.

> Yes?

>> Don't say anything to Seth. Or Derik.

> My lips are sealed, Miss Snow. I am at your service.

>> Great. Meet us in about twenty or thirty minutes.

>> If anyone asks, Libby and I are out running errands. Shopping or something. And keep Seth distracted.

>> He probably fell back asleep and hungover. Just come up with something. See you soon. Thanks.

"Alright, we've got coverage. I messaged Josh to help us out." I dropped my phone back on the table amid our leaning tower of literature.

Libby sipped on her iced coffee as we flipped through history books and an assortment of mythology texts; searching for anything else that might help us on our Demon interrogation, or anything we might be able to pull on Lady Leonora.

Libby tapped her nail on the rim of her cup, her forehead creased. "You sure you don't want to let Seth in on this, or Derik? They know what they're doing too, you know. And Seth would do just about anything to help you..." she paused; her eyes bore into me, "to help you out. This involves all of us."

I sighed. "I know." I ignored the slip, still not wanting to get my hopes up. In part because why the hell would someone like Seth want someone like me? But also, because of the slim chance of him actually seeing me that way, I wasn't going to risk that being his downfall, where he throws himself in the way of danger just to protect me. "But that's part of the problem. I want to keep him out of it. It's easier. And it'll keep him from feeling obligated to play hero, be overbearing, and keep me sidelined while he's risking his ass." I slouched forward.

"You have a point. Seth does kinda have to be the self-sacrificing guy. He really was cut out for this life, being Nephilim."

"No kidding."

I flipped through a few pages in the massive, worn, leather-bound book in front of me. I sent a small prayer to the gods, Angels; anyone who'd listen to give us a hint, a nudge, anything in the right direction.

Libby squeaked. I arched my eyebrow at her in question. "You, uh, you good, there, Lib?"

She pointed at the page in front of her, sucking down the last of her iced coffee. "Here!" I scooted closer, peering over the page. "It says that Lady Leonora had abandoned her family in pursuit of saving her people, saving humanity." Libby's eyes twinkled in the dim light of the library, her fingertip tracing the words in front of us.

"Interesting," I sat back in the hard wooden chair, mulling it over. "You know what I don't get, why would it be in a history book, versus like mythology or something? Saving humanity and powerful mumbo-jumbo doesn't really sound like something that Angels or Nephilim would allow to make its way into human textbooks."

Libby shrugged. "Well, I mean look at all the different legends that have made their way in our historical texts too. Probably under that same scope. What most humans see as myth, in reality is the very truth that reveals our history."

My phone dinged. I tapped the screen, and a text from Josh popped up.

> Seth woke up and is now out the door.
>
> Do you wish for me to pick yourself and Miss Libby up?

"It's Josh. Sounds like we're good to go. You ready?"

Libby nodded, snapping a picture of the text before gathering up her pile of books to take to the return cart.

> We're at the library on campus. We'll be waiting on the curb.

> I'll see you soon, Miss Snow.

I slid my phone into my back pocket and slipped on my padded jacket, having changed into my fighting gear before we left, being sure to hide my dagger within my jacket. My pile of books feeling light as I carried them behind Libby to the return cart.

"Let's kick this popsicle stand." Libby giggled as she looped her arm in mine, pulling a snort out of me.

At that moment, I realized just how much she was growing on me. And maybe, just maybe, if we survived this, I might have more than one best friend for the first time in my life.

CHAPTER THIRTY-NINE

Josh

Miss Libby and Miss Snow awaited my arrival at the curb in front of the library. They were speaking energetically as I pulled up.

Miss Snow seems rather animated today.

"Good morning, ladies. I hope I didn't keep the two of you waiting too painfully long," I said, as I quickly moved to open the rear passenger door for them.

Miss Snow stepped to the side, allowing Miss Libby to glide into the backseat ahead of her. Miss Snow grinned up at me, a mischievous glint to her eye. "You're actually right on time, Josh. Thanks for picking us up."

"My pleasure, Miss Snow. Now, where to?" I asked, sure to flash her a smile as I returned to the driver's side and started the vehicle.

Miss Snow's grey-hued eyes met mine in the rear view mirror. "Actually, I was going to ask you that. Where can we go for some live-action information hunting? That isn't that weird skyscraper." She visibly shivered as Miss Libby gave her an alarming look, her brows arching.

Ah, I wonder if Miss Libby is remembering her own experience.

She hadn't taken it as calmly as Miss Snow.

A smirk played along my features. "I know of just the place."

"Excellent!" Miss Snow forced a smile as she turned to face Miss Libby, taking in her concerned expression. "What? That's half the reason I asked the guy." She shrugged, dropping the conversation as she pulled out her phone, scrolling and tapping away.

I wonder, Miss Snow, what have you found?

"I still don't get why the hell you called him and not me." Seth glared over his shoulder in my direction as him and Miss Snow led our little group through the dense forest.

"Look, Josh answered my texts. And you were passed out. Plus, it's easier dragging him around than it is you. He's actually quiet." Miss Snow shrugged.

He hung his head, shaking it. "Rin, I literally came out and grabbed breakfast. Ya could've said something then."

She scoffed at Seth. "Considering how cranky you are when you wake up on a good, hangover-free day? No thanks. Anyway, we had it handled before you showed up. All covered in blood and guts. And speaking of," Miss Snow turned on Seth, causing Miss Libby and I to pause behind them. Miss Snow jabbed her finger to Seth's chest, "why the *fuck* were *you* out here and covered in blood and guts?"

"Well, we did just have a Demon explode all over us." Seth braced himself, hands reaching for Miss Snow's.

She growled in response. "You know *damn* well that's not what I mean, Seth. Out with it. Now. Or your ass is walking all the way back to your house."

He clicked his tongue. "I ran all the way here, so no big whoop."

Lightning pricked at her fingertips, sending a jolt through Seth, his body tensing in response. He yipped.

I bit back the smirk which begged to make itself known.

Tsk, tsk, Draven.

You waltzed right into that one.

Not the brightest, are we?

"You want to try that again?" she said through gritted teeth, her voice mirroring that of which echoed throughout the meadow when she had questioned the Demon. As if she would destroy the man's very being with a single thought.

Seth jaw clenched, his Adam's apple bobbing as he swallowed. "I needed to run off some adrenaline and pent-up frustration. I ran into a couple of Demons wreaking havoc. That's it."

She roared, "Two!? Two fucking Demons? Are you freaking kidding me, Seth? *Alone*? And there you were lecturing me. You fucking *hypocrite*," her pupils lit, her rage on the verge of escaping. "I'm not even going to touch the fact that it sounds like you went on a damn manhunt for no rhyme or reason other than to cause bloodshed. Even if it were for Demons. Aren't you the one who said we had morals?" Miss Snow had thrown her hands onto her hips, staring Seth down, even as he towered over her.

"Like I said, *I* can handle it. And the Demons. I came across them while they were...feeding."

Miss Snow's eyes narrowed. "Spit. It. Out. Draven."

Seems as if Miss Snow has quite the flame ignited within her today.

Seth anxiously ran his fingers through his onyx hair, blue irises casted downward, avoiding Miss Snow's. "They were feeding on a human, who when I stumbled on them, was still alive."

Her face grew a shade green, her eyes softened slightly, a pang twitched within my abdomen.

Interesting.

Miss Snow composed herself as she turned on her heel and stomped forward into the wooden abyss, Seth running after her and

Miss Libby following closely behind. They remained within hearing distance. I kept to the back, sending my senses outward, listening to the creatures rummaging through the undergrowth, searching for a safe haven from the nightmares which littered the forest.

The forest fell silent as we reached the alcove, hidden off the side of the two-lane road. Miss Libby and Miss Snow stood to the rear. Seth leaned on the front of the vehicle, resembling every bit of an infantile canine with its tail between its legs; Miss Snow's back to him, blatantly ignoring him.

This ought to be a rather quiet car ride.

I clicked the locking mechanism on the ring of keys in my pants pocket, unlocking the vehicle, allowing Miss Libby and Miss Snow to slip into the back seat, Seth to the front.

I strode calmly around the nose of the vehicle and situated myself into the driver's seat, turning the key into the ignition, and pulling out onto the dirt road. "Shall we?"

Chapter Forty

Erin

I avoided Seth until the end of the night. We all went back to his place; Derik was lounging around the living room when we walked in. The sunset streamed in from the kitchen windows, casting an array of reds, oranges, and purples throughout the open space, as it was the only light illuminating the house on the inside. Derik had greeted the four of us with a simple wave. Libby and I joined him, taking up spots on the floor. Josh stood to the left of the sofa and Seth hovered from the distance of the kitchen, moping.

Libby filled Derik in, unfortunately including the bit about me going off on Seth, before she lingered on the part about Derik having been sent on a hunting route slash protection duty; neither of them seeming to have the thought to let her know or have a buddy system in place, considering that's what we're supposed to do. Libby laid into Derik, leaving him in a similar state to Seth by the time she was finished.

I tacked onto the end of her verbal lashing, backing her up. "I swear, it's like the two of you are trying to get yourselves killed." I threw my hand in the air motioning between Derik and Seth, who had finally scurried his way to the living room, joining the rest of us. Josh had remained quiet, playing spectator. I eyed him.

"Josh, you know what, did *you* know anything about Derik's little tracking detail? Where Seth decided to have Derik play secret bodyguard on my way to work?"

He met my narrowed stare. "Yes, I was aware, Miss Snow."

Great. So all the guys were in on it.

We're not fucking helpless, you assholes.

"And any reason as to why you weren't *with* Derik? Or why Seth failed to tell me he had someone watching me?" I crossed my arms over my chest.

"I was occupied with other business matters at the time, my apologies. As for why he had not discussed it with you beforehand, I am unsure, Miss Snow." Josh adjusted his button up, flicking a lingering piece of Demon flesh onto Seth's hardwood floor.

Well. That's probably going to leave a stain.

You know what? Good.

Seth's mouth moved to chime in, and I turned my nose in the opposite direction. Silence followed until Derik came to his defense.

He reached for my shoulder and I yanked it out of range. "Erin, I get it, you're peeved, but he didn't say anything because he figured you'd fight it. And from the way you're reacting, he was right. I get it you're upset but get over it."

My nostrils flared.

You don't get it.

None of you do.

I met Derik's eyes with a cold glare. "I may have fought it, but the fact remains that I'm not some weak individual that needs protecting. I will not have you guys literally out there risking your lives and ultimately the lives and safety of the people around here. The people we're trying to protect and save, for me. I am nothing in the grand scheme of things. You pull shit like that, say something. Don't leave me to figure it out by my super-powered hearing to pick up the fighting and gurgling of Demons' having their throats ripped out on my way to campus. I was two seconds away from stampeding through the bushes when I heard you finish them off, Derik," I boomed, my voice growing louder with each word. I took a steadying breath, trying to calm myself. My jaw clenched. "I am not worth that risk."

My safety...my life is worth nothing.

Derik shot to his feet; his slate-blue eyes wild. "Oh my God, Erin. Get over it. Get over the whole 'daddy abandonment' issues. For fucks sake," his fists clenched at his sides as his body shook. "We're in this together. All of us. We're not fucking going anywhere, Erin. Dead or alive. We may not have been around each other a whole lot until recently, but we fucking love you. We are a damn family, Erin. *A fucking family.* And family helps each other, no matter the fucking risks. So lay the fuck off of Seth. Give it a fucking break," Libby went to his side, clutching his fist, and pulled him toward the front door, Josh only a step behind. The three of them left, the door slammed shut behind them, but not before I caught the tail end of Derik grumbling, "He cares about you more than you know."

I sat there, dumbfounded. My mind, blank. I stared at the front door, long after they left.

I felt fabric weigh on my shoulders, breaking my trance. My bleary eyes looked up to see Seth draping a blanket over me. He sat down beside me, crossing his legs, his shoulder brushed against mine.

He let out a sigh, the pain within it mirrored that which ached within my chest. Seth brought his thumb to my chin. As he lifted it, his glistening, ocean-deep eyes locked with my simple grey-blues. He rasped, barely above a whisper, "Erin."

My lip wobbled; a cry forced its way past my lips. Seth pulled me close, tucking me under his chin.

His mouth brushed against my hair as he whispered, "You are worth every risk, Rin. Every damned one."

I sobbed into his shirt, soaking it. He held me, whispering to me for what felt like hours, yet only minutes had passed. I pulled back, the salty tears continued to fall. Seth titled his nose, bringing his face closer, his eyes searched mine. I subtly nodded and closed the gap. Our lips clashed, meshing together. Soft and wet as they moved as an extension of one another, slowly.

The tears fell faster, the ache in my chest grew, clenching, afraid to let go. I gripped the front of Seth's drenched shirt and pulled him closer. His hand splayed on my back, his fingertips kneading my shirt as if fighting the urge to yank it off, to rip it. A moan escaped my lips; Seth growled in response. I leaned into him, pushing him onto his back. I nestled my legs on either side of his hips, straddling him. We both panted, our kiss deepening. Seth hooked his thumbs in the waistband of my pants, bringing my hips down closer to his. My hands ran down the length of his torso, reaching the hem of his shirt. I began tugging it upward, wanting, needing to run my fingers along his sculpted body. He grabbed my wrists, stopping me. I whimpered as he slowed our heated kiss and pulled back, one hand moving to cup my face.

No, please.

His eyes were clouded, emotion swirling within them as he gazed in mine. "Rin."

I placed my hand over his. Letting the question linger.

"Not like this. Not when you've been emotionally drained," he moved my hand, placing it on his heart. "When we do this, I want it to be right. Perfect." Every word vibrated my hand, shivers snaking up my arm, warmth filling the cracks within me. Bit by bit.

I need you.

My lip wobbled and he wiped the tears from my cheek. "Why?" I whispered, fear gripping me.

"Because Erin. You are far more important to me than you know." He moved my hand to his mouth, placing a kiss across each of my fingertips.

And you are far too important to me.

A final tear escaped and I blinked, taking in Seth's beautiful face. A small, hushed voice whispered in the far corner of my heart.

Mine.

Chapter Forty-One

Erin

The following week and a half flew by, with no repetition of the night that I broke down. Seth and I moved a comfortable distance around each, almost falling into a routine. We'd wake up at the crack of dawn, Josh already at his front door. I'd grab a few waters and protein bars for myself and Seth then we'd head to the field behind his house and train until noon. They had me rotate between my daggers and sword, as I now wore all three on my person at Seth's insistence. I'd emailed my professors and had my classes switched to online strictly and after spinning some tale for Ashlin, which still hadn't sat well with me, I was down to a single four-hour shift per week.

Unfortunately, that left my wallet suffering and my feeling like a burden to be in full swing, even though Seth more than assured me that it wasn't an issue. I broke my lease at my apartment, seeing as I wouldn't be going back for the foreseeable future. Financially, it made no sense to continue to pay the rent with me no longer dwelling there. So, two days ago, we loaded up the remainder of my belongings and shoved everything besides the rest of my clothes into a cheap storage unit, much to Seth's dismay. I'd told him to suck it up and he'd mumbled something about his house being open to me and my things, I only half listened, preoccupied with exhaustion.

In an attempt to make up and keep my being a burden to a minimum, I'd taken it upon myself to beat Seth to the punch on all things cooking and house related. He fought me on it, daily. Racing to re-rack and clean up the workout area before I could, same with his living room and the kitchen. I caved on him helping me cook, due to Libby and Derik popping in and out throughout the day. Even Josh hung around beyond lunch. And with so many grown Nephilim, each of us with the appetite of a horse—with the exception of Seth and Derik who matched several horses—there was a lot of food being prepared throughout the day.

The first day or two after my verbal lashing from Derik, we barely spoke or acknowledged one another. Until he'd handed my ass to me. He volunteered to spar with me, reverting back to hands only combat. He had me panting, flat on my back within seconds.

He reached his hand out and I swatted it away. Derik took that as a challenge and wrapped his hand around my swinging wrist, hauling me to my feet.

"I could've gotten up myself." I huffed, as I dusted myself off.

"I know. But I wanted to help you up. And honestly apologize for what I said. It was kinda harsh." He ran his fingers through his shortened, shaggy brown hair.

"It might've been harsh but do you honestly regret what you said?"

Derik chewed on his lip for a moment. "No, I guess not. But I could've been nicer about it."

"If you don't regret it, then don't apologize. It's fine. Otherwise, when it's for something you truly mean, it won't hold as much weight behind the apology." We walked to the edge of Seth's house, each grabbing a water.

"Where'd you hear that?" Derik asked as he sipped from his bottle.

I shrugged. "I heard it from an old teacher of mine. I used to apologize so much that she started taking points off of my assignments each time I would apologize unnecessarily."

"Huh, sounds kinda extreme."

I shrugged my shoulders. "Maybe, but it worked."

Things had calmed down between the two of us since then and that was the end of it.

In the afternoon, I'd go on a run, Seth not too far behind me. We'd sprint through the outskirts of town at our inhuman speed, increasing the pace day by day. I needed to continue to build my endurance, as well as nailing the frail attempt of escape if I were caught off guard by a Demon or two.

We would spend most of the day together, from sunup to sundown. Being around him to that level, I felt more at ease. But it didn't last long. Prickles of fear began to gnaw at the edges of my stomach. We were nearing the blood moon. The final countdown. And I was getting restless.

We all were.

My phone had beeped as Seth and I returned to his house after our midday run. I tapped my screen to unlock it while I snagged a toaster pastry off the kitchen counter, leaning against it as I tore the wrapper open. I swiped through my messages, most being automated spam texts, until I saw one from Libby. I paused, my thumb hovering. Biting into the pastry, I tapped on the message and opened it.

> Hey, I need your help with something. Can you help me?

I texted back, tapping away with my thumb, my other hand occupied with my snackage. Seth and Josh chatted about our training session from the morning. I zoned them out, not wanting to relive the embarrassment of tripping over my own feet after I finally took Seth down.

> Yeah, I'll grab the guys and we'll head your way. Where do we need to meet you?

> Oh! No, just you please. It's a surprise and I don't want to ruin it. :)

> Oh, okay. No problem, my lips are sealed.

She texted me the address and I copied it into the GPS on my phone as I sloshed down the rest of my pastry with some much-needed water and headed back toward the front door, grabbing my keys off the counter.

"Where are you going, Rin?" Seth asked while I passed him, popping a handful of nuts into his mouth.

"Libby needs help with something. Girls only! I'll see you guys later." I called over my shoulder, waving my fingers as I shut the door behind me, bouncing down the steps and beelining for my car.

The GPS had me winding through town and to the other side of campus. I pulled up to a small apartment complex, a little security gate at the front of the building. I parked in a spot marked for visitors, beeped my car locked, and walked up to the gate. A security guard posted at the entrance asked my reason for visiting and I gave him Libby's name; he waved me in.

Talk about a safe spot. Damn.

I hiked up the three flights of steps to the top floor, winded, and skimmed the hallway for apartment three-oh-nine. For as often and as far as I ran, I could not stand trudging up stairs. The silver-plated numbers shimmered from the bright hallway light. I lightly rapped my hand on the cherry oak door, and it swung open; the space beyond, completely doused in darkness. I stiffened, a knot forming in my stomach.

This...this doesn't seem right.

I drew one of my daggers and crept over the threshold, suddenly grateful that I recently heeded Seth and Josh's advice and kept my twin blades on me at all times.

"Libby?" I called into the pitch-black room. I heard rustling further in. I felt a switch as I ran my hand along the wall to my right and flipped it on.

And there in the center of the ivory carpet lay Libby, unconscious, her torso twisted and blood trickling from the top of her head.

The door clicked shut behind me as an eerie laugh sent ice through my veins, chilling me to my core.

"Well, we meet again, Erin Snow."

"Erebus." I growled.

Chapter Forty-Two

Erin

I jolted awake. My chest heaving, sweat slicked my forehead. I frantically searched the room around me, searching for any sign of Libby.

I blinked, the space coming into focus.

"What?" A wave of confusion struck me. I fumbled out of bed, rummaging for my phone and pulled up my GPS history. Nothing. The last thing in there was from a few weeks prior. My brows furrowed.

What the hell?

When did I fall asleep?

I clamped my eyes shut and counted to ten before opening them again. I was in the spare room at Seth's. A baggy shirt wrinkled and covering my torso, hung off of me. I felt along my thighs, neither straps nor harnesses still fastened around them. I shoved my hand under my mattress, anxiously feeling around for my daggers or sword.

Calm. We are here. The hum of my sword filled my mind, easing some of the building tension in my shoulders.

I let out a breath. "I'm getting really tired of these damn dreams," I said more to myself than my sword.

You do not rest well, that is true. Your tossing made it difficult for my sisters and I to slumber.

"You guys sleep?" I cocked my head to the side.

Not in the same way as you, but yes. And given the intensity of your training as of late, we require as much rest as we can gather.

A pang of guilt rushed me. "I'm sorry about that." I slumped against the side of my bed, head falling onto my mattress.

No need to apologize. It comes with the territory. Given your destiny.

"My destiny?" I cocked an eyebrow, as the lids of my eyes shut.

Why, yes. Only one other has had weapons such as us.

"Huh," I clicked my tongue. "You want to tell me what this grand destiny is?"

You already know part of it. The rest has yet to be decided.

"Well, aren't you cryptic," I grunted and pushed myself to my feet, groggily walking toward the bedroom door. "I'm going to get something to eat, I'm starved."

Wait...

I waved my sword off and padded into the hallway towards the kitchen. Only to stop in my tracks as I came upon Libby and Seth. Locked in a tongue tango. I choked back a sob. A crack splitting within my chest. "Seth?" I whispered, my voice wobbling.

Their eyes shot open. He pushed himself away from Libby, his deep blue eyes wide with surprise. "Erin?" His panicked eyes flicked between Libby and me. Tears welled in the corners of my eyes, threatening to fall.

I turned on my heel and bolted back into the bedroom, slamming and locking the door behind me. Seth banged on it from the other side, yelling my name. I grabbed my phone and sent out a text to the one person I knew who'd get me out of this then began shoving clothes into my school bag.

Tears streamed down my face as I reached under my mattress and grabbed my blades, my sword attempting to speak to me. I quickly hushed her, not wanting to listen and hear how stupid I was to believe there was something between Seth and me. As I piled my belongings into my bag, the photo on my nightstand caught my eye. It was from the night we all got wasted playing truth or dare. Seth had his arm wrapped around my shoulder, the goofiest grin on his face; drunken idiotic hope and adoration plastered on mine as I looked up at him. I grabbed the frame and threw it as hard as I could at the far wall of the bedroom, denting the plaster, and leaving a gash in the wall as the frame shattered and fell to the ground.

Good fucking riddance.

My heart shattered with it.

My cell phone beeped; the screen lit with the message that my ride was here. I hauled my bag over my shoulder, daggers poking out on the side, sword slung in the holster I clipped to the front. I got to my feet, not bothering with putting on shoes and stomped to the door, yanking it open. Seth stood. Blocking my escape. His eyes red and wet with tears.

Liar.

His hands reached for my shoulders. "Erin, please." His voice broke. I met his eyes with a dead stare.

My insides chilled, the frost coating my vocal chords. "Get out of my way, Seth."

His hands squeezed. "Erin, it's not what you think, please, let me—" I cut him off as sparks of electricity lurched forward, crackling their way up his fingers, and through his arms. He stumbled back, pain flickering across his features.

"You are worth every risk, Rin. Every damned one."

"You are far more important to me than you know."

Fucking horseshit.

I opened myself...for the smallest moment...

Libby reached for me as I barreled towards the front door and to my escape. I stared her down, letting my fire erupt within my irises as a warning.

I yanked the door closed behind me; the doorknob blackened and melted shut, my pain fueling the molten rage bubbling at my fingertips, not wanting either of them to follow me.

I reached the car waiting for me and tossed my stuff in the backseat not concerned with being polite. I stomped to the front and slid in, not bothering with fastening the seat belt. What would be the point when my heart was frozen? And soon...I'd probably die in our feeble attempt at protecting the humans...and the man who just broke what barely remained of my heart.

"Let's go."

A few days had passed since I'd seen Seth and Libby. The two of them kissing, swapping saliva, forever burned into my brain. I squeezed my eyes shut in an attempt to push the image away and felt a fist clench around my traitor of a heart. *I thought...*

I wiped the tears pouring from my eyes on the arm of my long-sleeve *heartbreaker* shirt. Talk about ironic. I grabbed this first shirt I could when I snuck back into Seth's place this morning. I wasn't ready to face him yet, so I asked Josh to shoot me a text when Seth left.

The text came through around seven a.m.

> Seth is leaving now. He just pushed his key into the lock and is heading down his front steps to his vehicle.

> Do you want me to come pick you up?

I blew a breath I hadn't realized I'd been holding.

> No, I'll drive myself over.

I hit send then added,

> Thanks though.

Josh had brought my car over the day prior, suggesting that it might be best so I would have access to leave his home if needed.

The whole trip took an anxiety-inducing ten minutes. I had no idea exactly *how close* Josh lived to Seth. Not that I'd known the guy that long but still. I made it to Seth's and after gaping at the damage I had done to the front, the handle melted into the burnt door, I rushed around the outside until I found a weak point in one of the windows and bashed it open.

I'll figure out a way to pay him back, or not.

I ran into the guest room, which for whatever reason had the door already flung open, and grabbed a handful of clothes from my bag. I ran back out and down to my car, flinging it out of park and into reverse. I was still surprised I didn't hit anything speeding my ass out of there.

I rested my chin against my hand, looking out the front window of Josh's house.

I still don't understand...I know we weren't...dating but...something was there. I could feel it. Like there was something building between us...and then he just...kissed Libby.

And it was a pretty damn passionate one based off of the two seconds I witnessed before bolting. It's not like he didn't know I was there.

After I'd gotten in Josh's car, I'd scrolled through my messages, seeing if there was anything that might've made sense or distracted me. Seth had apparently texted me the night before, asking to hold off on training the following morning so we could run through our defense plans against the Demons.

Did he want *me to see them? Was that his way of telling me he's not interested? That the other night hadn't happened?*

I felt the tears starting back up again.

Get it together, Snow. You have more important shit going on, like I don't know, stopping Hell's Angels from murdering a bunch of missing people?

"Ugh! Get it together!" I shouted. "This is fucking stupid."

"What is it, Miss Snow, that you find stupid?" I jumped, not realizing Josh had came up behind me. Or that he had returned.

"Nothing. It doesn't matter," I mumbled, still looking out the window.

"It doesn't seem like nothing. Do you wish to talk about it? I've been told I'm an excellent listener." His dress shoes tapped against the floor as he stepped into my peripheral vision and leaned against the eggshell wall.

I rolled my eyes. My head turned, still resting on my hand, and glared at Josh. Sending my best *leave me the fuck alone* look I could muster. "What's it to you anyway?"

Josh chuckled, light and throaty. "Well, you are currently squatting in my home. I've left it for the past few days but I would like to know the reason as to why I felt the need to provide you with shelter."

I sighed.

Oh, what the hell.

"Well. Do you want the short version or the stupid version?"

"Miss Snow, if it is something that has you this distraught, I wouldn't deem whatever the situation is as stupid. Potentially rather dramatic, but hardly stupid." He shot me a smile.

"Uh. Huh. Sure."

Dramatic, might be pretty spot on.

"Well. How much do you know about Seth and me?" I caught myself, there was no 'Seth and me.'

"Truth be told, I don't know a whole lot outside of the two of you having been childhood friends and that he seems to be a type of interest to you, based on how you've become rather flustered around him on more than one occasion."

A blush crept its way up my neck. "That's the basics. You've pretty much got that down." I leaned back in Josh's burgundy vampire-esc lounge chair and crossed my arms across my middle. "We've been friends for years, as you know. Best friends, actually. We've always told each other everything. I thought so at least, until he divulged this whole being a Nephilim thing to me. Which hurt. I mean I get why he couldn't tell me and why he waited so long but it still hurt. And now...with Libby...I...they both told me they weren't dating. That they were history and just friends now," I took a ragged breath. "But clearly, that wasn't—isn't the case. And I was just getting my hopes up. When Seth was clearly never interested." I blinked, another tear escaping.

"Have you always...cared for him this way?" Josh asked quietly, a hint of pity tracing his words.

"Yes. No...I...I don't know. I don't think so. But I noticed it a few months ago, around the time this whole Nephilim mess started. I chalked it up to hormones and changing. But it feels like so much more than that. I mean, I've had crushes before, dated a few times but none of it felt like this. When I saw...when I saw Seth kiss Libby...it felt like my heart split in two." I choked, tears free-falling down my cheekbones.

Josh brought his hand to my shoulder, squeezing it. "I'm sorry, Erin. I imagine that must be hard. A love squashed without ever having been explored."

I let out a half sob half laugh. "I'm pretty sure that's the first time you've actually used my first name. I really must be a complete wreck."

"Not a complete wreck, dear." The warmth from his smile hit me like a freight train.

"Prick."

"Yours, truly, Miss Snow. At your assistance." We both laughed.

I wiped the treacherous tears from underneath my eyes and pushed myself to my feet. "I'm going for a run." I needed to get out and stop moping about. I wasn't going to find these humans on my own sitting around and feeling sorry for myself.

"Would you like me to accompany you?" Josh asked softly from behind me.

"If you want." I felt his golden-flecked, piercingly blue gaze burn a hole into my back. Yet when I peaked over my shoulder he was gone. I shrugged and reached for the door handle.

"I'll be just a moment, Miss Snow." I jumped as Josh shouted from down the hall.

While waiting for him to come back out, I pulled my phone out of my back pocket and swiped up to find an absurd amount of unread notifications from Seth, with a few from Libby sprinkled in. I'd kept my notifications off from all contacts and apps with the exception of Josh and Ashlin, not that there were many from either.

I blew out a sigh and bit the bullet. I scrolled through the texts from Libby first, as there were far fewer to sort through.

> I'm so sorry, Erin.

> Erin, I know you're upset. I would be too. Please let me explain.

> It's not what you think.

> I'm so sorry.

> I know you probably don't want to see me right now but please call or text me. We need to talk.

The last one from her caught my attention.

> I might have found something on the humans. Call me ASAP.

I moved my thumb over the screen, to select the texts from Seth, and hesitated. Deciding I wasn't ready to conquer that hill yet. I tapped on Libby's contact in my phone and let out a breath, bracing myself for whatever she was going to say. I played the possibilities in my mind while I waited for her to pick up.

"Oh yeah, Seth and I have been dating this whole time."
"We were drunk."
"We didn't know you were home."

Okay that last one hurt a bit more, since I hadn't yet called Seth's place *home*. I hadn't even let myself consider that.

"Hello? Erin?" Libby answered, her voice hushed.

"The one and only. What do you want?" I snapped and chastised myself; reminding myself that I needed to be civil, let her explain. I needed the information about the humans.

"Look, I get you're upset but we'll deal with that later," Libby clipped. "I might know where the Demons are hiding them. Where they're keeping the humans."

My heart raced. This was it. "Spill. And leave absolutely *nothing* out."

My eyes widened and blood hummed in anticipation with each word. I bit back a growl when Josh returned, joining me in his foyer. Concern or fear flashed in his speckled eyes as they widened, his pupils dilating. I couldn't tell which and nor did I care. Sparks sizzled at my fingertips; fire began to rumble within my abdomen.

Libby finished, leaving me space to digest everything she had dumped on to my plate.

This is it.

I cast a dead stare at where Josh remained standing. "How quickly can you be ready?"

A beat passed before Libby responded, a fierce determination in her voice. "You tell me when."

"Now. We go by foot. It'll be quieter and attract less attention. Grab everything you need. And be prepared." I hung up, not awaiting a response and sent over where to meet. My lips pressed together.

"Change of plans, I presume, Miss Snow?" Josh said, a chill of ease in his voice.

I pushed past him, my shoulder ramming into his abdomen, and grabbed my bag from the pleated chaise lounge on the other side of the foyer. "Yes. Now turn around and don't fucking look. I catch you sneaking a peak and I will torch you."

"I am a gentleman, Miss Snow, I would never."

As if.

I rolled my eyes and tore through my bag pulling my fighting gear out: weapon resistant long sleeve and matching black padded leggings. I quickly threw them on, then slid into my jacket, fastening it; my arm and leg guards in place, making sure all the vital parts were protected. I strapped on my harness for my sword and the two for my daggers on my thighs before sheathing each blade. I grabbed a knife from the side pocket of my bag and slid it into my waistband, as an added precaution. I wrapped my long brown hair into a high ponytail and spun around, heading straight for the door, leaving Josh in my wake. "Do not follow me," I stopped at the bottom step. "And leave Seth out of this. I might be pissed, but this is bigger than that. I'm not letting him risk his life, when I'm what they want."

"Noted," he clipped.

I flipped him off then ran. Every minute I wasted, put those humans at more risk. I snuck another glance at my phone as I reached the forests dividing us and Riverside.

Time had flown by, and we were out of time. Tomorrow would be the night of the blood moon. It truly was now or never.

Chapter Forty-Three

Erin

Talk about a damned coincidence.

I reached the meadow where we had taken that Demon down and questioned it over two weeks ago. The black gunk was gone, as if it were never there. The trees towered over the landscape, bushes wedged in between.

The only real difference between then and now was that I probably wouldn't be walking away from this. It was still me and Libby. We just didn't have Josh with us.

I crouched down and pulled a granola bar from my jacket pocket, combing through an idea of how exactly Libby and I were going to manage this. I had no idea how many Demons we'd run into or what state the humans would be in and my ass had us running in there guns-a-blazing. Okay, swords and knives but all the same. If Libby got killed or any of the humans, it would be on me. I stopped mid-chew.

Shit.

I suddenly regretted telling Josh not to follow me, it'd been brash, and we could use the muscle. And if I died, he could at least get Libby and the humans to safety.

I rolled my shoulders, there was no point in dwelling on it now.

Footsteps crunched to the left of me, I whipped my head towards the sound, drawing my sword.

"It's just me." Libby emerged from the woods; hands drawn in front of her person as she neared me.

I stood and resheathed my sword. "Sorry, with where we're headed, I figured the possibility of stumbling upon a rogue Demon was pretty high, given my luck—" I bit my tongue.

Given my luck with stumbling upon things I shouldn't apparently.

Libby rolled her eyes, as if she knew what thought had waltzed through my head. She shook her head at me. "Understandable. Now, do you have a plan?"

"Minimal," I dusted the dirt off my pants. "I was thinking we wing it. Go after the bad guys, save the humans, and get our asses out of dodge."

Libby scoffed as a grin spread along the contours of her face. "I like your style. Let's go save some people."

We crossed the meadow and took off in a sprint. We headed deeper into the woods, the trees growing thicker; the sun dropping lower into the sky, casting us in fiery shadows as we ran through the undergrowth, our feet light, as we weaved through.

I felt my sword hum at my back.

"On your left."

I slid a dagger from my thigh as a Demon came barreling towards us. Its frame came into view, bulky, purple arms grabbing the air where I'd been a moment before. I dipped low, dodging, and struck my blade at its thigh, scraping it through to the bone. Black blood gushed from its wound. I pivoted, launching myself onto its back and wrapping my arms around its neck before I sliced my dagger across its throat, ink bubbling up in the Demon's mouth. I snapped the Demon's neck back as I jumped from its back and out of the way as its body came crashing to the forest floor with a thud. Libby stood to the side, gawking.

"When the hell did you learn to do that?" She hissed.

I kept my dagger at the ready and motioned for us to keep going. "Training has been paying off. And I might've snuck out on a few occasions to try my hand at hunting."

"And you were pissed at Seth," Libby mumbled.

I shot her a glare and she snapped her mouth shut. "Exactly why I kept it to myself." And Josh, as he'd been sending me leads, weaker ones, that he believed I could handle on my own for the time being. The silence between Libby and I grew.

Kinda helps when you get stabbed in the heart.

It's not so hard to beat the living shit out of a Demon or two when it's gone.

Wonder if that's Josh's secret.

"How did you know it was coming? I didn't hear or sense anything." Her head swiveled, on the lookout for more.

"My sword told me." I flicked my wrist toward the deceased Demon, a small flame spurted from the tips of my fingers, catching them on fire.

Libby's forehead creased as her brows pushed together in question.

I brushed her off and I kept my focus forward as we trekked up into the mountains. I took the lead, so that if we were attacked again, I'd be our first defense and in a better position to keep Libby safe. If Seth cared about her, especially in that way, I needed her to make it out of this. Even though I was beyond hurt, they were my friends.

"I'm sorry, Erin, but your *sword* told you?"

"Yes. Keep the judgment to yourself," I snipped. "I don't know why but my sword can talk to me, and I can talk to it." I shut the conversation down, my sword humming again, the twin daggers vibrating as well.

Where?

"There's several. They're narrowing in. Have your guard up and be on the ready. Back to hers. Now!"

"Back to mine, and weapons out. Now!" I hissed. Libby instantly jumped into position.

Can you sense where the strongest is coming from?

"No. That falls to you. I'm sorry."

How the hell am I supposed to do that!?

"How did you find us? Or your talents? It is all in the same. Quickly. You are running out of time."

I shut my eyes, slowly releasing my breath. My flame and lightning appeared behind my lids, aching to be used. Another sensation hid in the shadows, calling to me. I stepped towards it, and it jumped back. I tried again, this time slowly extending my hand. I held myself still, pushing down the growing anxiety in the well of my stomach as the Demons were closing in.

I won't hurt you.

It peaked out at me, and slowly reached for my extended hand. The sensation's form grew into a shimmering white blob as its warmth grasped my fingertips, my ponytail whipped around in a sudden gust of wind. An angelic voice rang through the crevices of my mind, caressing me.

"Home."

Home?

"Yes."

I am your home?

"Yes. And I am a part of yours."

What does that mean?

"That is for another time. Now, tell me, what do you need?"

Help me.

My eyes flew open as a pale demon launched itself through the air, aiming for Libby.

This one. The angelic voice cooed. I twisted, jumping and using Libby as leverage, and launched myself at the Demon. My dagger made contact with its neck, missing the jugular and nicking the side. Its blood spurted, before the wound healed almost instantly. I bit back the surprise, masking my expression and lining up for my next move, the Demon's attention fully on me and no longer on Libby. It growled as we circled one another. Another surge caught my attention.

"Libby to your right!" She leaped into action, quickly taking down the Demon as it came into view, her blade slicing through its middle.

I returned my attention to the Demon towering over me, our eyes locked, a cocky snarl ripped from its lips. Recognition flared in its yellowed eyes. "You're the one he's been searching for," he exhaled deeply. "Ah, yes. Just as delectable as Erebus had described. I shall have my fun with our Key before you fulfill your purpose." A shiver raked down my spine as I swallowed down my first encounter with Erebus.

"Do not falter. You are The Key. Be the key to his undoing."

I smacked my lips. "Oof, sorry to disappoint but you'll have to buy me dinner first, big guy." I could've sworn I felt the voice shake its head. I feigned boredom, taking a note from Libby and glanced at my severely chipped and neglected nails on my free hand, dagger in the other.

The Demon gawked at me and took the bait. He roared in pure ego-stricken offense. "How dare you not fall to your knees in fear. You should be begging for me to spare you." He puffed out his chest as he cackled.

I looked up from my nails and pursed my lips. "Eh. I've seen worse. Try again."

His eyes went wild as the Demon lunged forward, claws extending. His movement was fueled by rage; I took the opportunity and pulled my sword from its sheath, leaping high and bringing it down on the Demon's head. The blade slicing all the way down, splitting it in half, its entrails roping outward, and flopping to the ground. Its guts squashed underfoot as I stepped between the two halves.

I wiped the inked blood on my sword onto my leggings and slid her back into her harness. I extended my hands, palms facing the Demon's severed body and called my flames forward, burning it until nothing but ashes remained.

I am taking no chances.

Libby fought against two others, out maneuvering and slowly wearing them down. I readied to join in when another presence caught my attention.

I hissed. "Derik, what the fuck are you doing here?"

I'm going to kill Josh.

"We're a team, remember?"

I growled and jumped in to snatch another Demon that had crept in while I was briefly distracted by Derik's unexpected appearance. I made quick work, as it was a smaller Demon; it hadn't seen me and was hunting Libby. I kicked it in the center of its back and shoved my dagger into its stomach as it whirled on me, sending electricity through my blade and frying the damned creature from the inside out.

Sweet. I didn't know if that'd work. I didn't hurt your sister, did I?

"No, she is fine. But really? No thought, just went for it?"

Yeap.

"God help us"

I snickered at my sword and turned on my heel back to Derik. Libby finished off her Demons with a final thrust of her blade, taking their heads clean off. She wiped the sweat off her brow. The Demons' blood caked both of us.

Derik just gawked.

"What?"

"You. What the hell? You took that thing down like it was nothing."

I stared at him. "It was nothing. Now out with it, why the hell are you here? And how long did it take for Josh to blab?" I stepped closer, making sure to flash the dagger still in the palm of my hand, baring my teeth. Out of the corner of my eye I saw Libby step closer, ready to get between the two of us if necessary.

Derik threw his hands up in front of himself. "He texted me right after you left his place," Derik shot a knowing glance to Libby, who in turn shrunk back. "He said to tell you that you only told him to keep himself and Seth out of it and said nothing about keeping me out of the fight."

I mentally kicked myself in the foot for not thinking to include Derik in the 'do not tell' list. "You still should've gotten the message. So get. Obviously, I've got this handled."

"Maybe, but you really think the two of you can take on whatever is awaiting you? And get those people out? Are you psychotic?"

"Excuse me but we've been fine. And I have a plan." I narrowed my eyes at Derik.

"And what the hell is that? Cross your fingers that your stab-and-zing trick works on a bunch of Demons who are more powerful than you?" Derik was bent slightly, his face inches from mine, fuming.

"We were going to wing it, actually," Libby mumbled.

"I'm sorry, you what!?" Derik growled.

I bristled. "Dammit, Libby." I met Derik's death glare with one of my own, the fire in my eyes reflecting off of his.

"No. Don't you fucking 'dammit Libby', her. Erin, that's fucking idiotic. You could get yourselves killed. And I might be pretty freaking peeved at Lib right now, but I don't want her dead. I know you don't either. And do you have any idea what that would do to Seth?" His voice turned to a threatening whisper.

"Of course I don't want her dead. I don't want *anyone* dead, Derik," I kept his accusing glare. "Keeping the rest of you and those people alive is the fucking plan."

Derik's eyes softened with understanding. "Erin..."

Don't look at me like that, Derik.

I cut him off. "We need to go. If you're tagging along fine. But we leave. Now." I turned on my heel and slashed through the bushes and continued through the forest, Derik and Libby close behind.

Chapter Forty-Four

Erin

The sun set as we neared the mountain summit, I peeked behind me and sent a silent thank you that I wasn't afraid of heights. Derik on the other hand was greener than a tub of slime. Libby rubbed his back as they reached me. Derik stiffened at her touch and put a bit of space between them. Her face fell for a brief moment.

"Under different circumstances, this would be beautiful," Libby said, laced with wonder…and regret.

"Yeah," I sighed and faced the mountain once again. "How much further—" Muffled screams cut me off. I dropped to the ground, Derik and Libby followed suit. "Shit."

"That doesn't sound good," Derik whispered.

I smacked him on the back of the head. "Of course it doesn't, Dummy." I hissed.

I pushed out the sensation from earlier, the shimmering expanded behind my eyes as I pushed my feelers out for Demons. My brain whirled on overload from the influx of Demonic power. My sword chimed in first.

"Holy shit."

No kidding. My head hurts like a bitch. What do I do?

I felt the stares from my sword and the presence with the angelic voice on me.

"I would hope you knew what to do, as you are The Key to all of this, Miss Snow." My sword deadpanned.

Okay, yes. Charge in, slay the Demons, save the humans. I got that part. But is this the right spot? Are the humans here? And why the hell does everyone keep referring to me by 'Miss Snow'? Can that stop, please for the love of all things holy?

"Fine. Focus, Erin. Sense for yourself."

How?

"Focus."

Aren't you helpful?

I huffed, shutting my eyes. I dove deep within myself, beyond the flame, lightning, and the blob. My skin tingled and I found myself within the center of the summit. Surrounded by Demons of all shapes and sizes with humans, men and women, in their grasp. Thirteen. All thirteen were there. My chest welled with relief. I counted the Demons, and my hope deflated. We were vastly outnumbered.

I came back to myself, blinking my eyes open. "They're here," Derik moved to rush in, I clamped my hand down on his shoulder, keeping him in place. "They're here. But we're outnumbered. There's over twenty Demons out there Derik. We're royally fucked."

He swore under his breath. My ears pricked at the sound of Libby tapping on her phone.

"Libby what the hell are you doing?" I hissed.

"I'm calling for backup. We have a few guys that stay on the outskirts, you met them when we originally went to Riverside." I racked my brain trying to remember. I came up with jack squat.

"Fine," there was no point in arguing. "How long until they get here?"

"Within an hour or two."

Leaves crunched behind us. My body stiffened, alarms going off in my head.

A man's voice scratched behind us, "Well, well, well. Would you look at who we have here? It seems, our Key has come out to play."

Chapter Forty-Five

Erin

The Demon, an oversized blue-hued nightmare with spikes scaling its shoulders, muscles bulging from under its skin, veins pulsing, looked down at the three of us still crouched on the ground. I went to draw my dagger but Derik beat me to it, pulling out his and sprang into action.

I silently thanked him and pulled Libby with me as we ran for the clearing. "Erin, we can't leave him!"

I shouted over my shoulder, "You know as well as I do that Derik will be fine. Especially against the one. If we don't move now and get what surprise we can on them, we're fucked. Once Derik slays it, the others will smell its blood, alerting them all that we're here. You know how that works far better than I do, Lib."

"But, Erin, I can't..."

I whirled, stopping us in our tracks and braced my hands on Libby's arms. "Where did that strong, fierce Nephilim in the forest go, Lib? He'll be okay. You know that."

"But, what if he's not, Erin? I cheated on him, and I didn't even know it. And I haven't apologized. We haven't talked since you left and ran off to Josh. None of us are talking besides Seth and Josh." A tear ran down her cheek.

How did you not *know you cheated? And since when were the two of you dating?*

I shook my head, filing it away.

It didn't matter.

"Libby, listen to me," I held her eyes. "We're going to make it out of this. All of us. Derik, you, the humans, me," I bit back the wince at the small lie. "The only ones not making it out of here alive are those damn creepy assholes, do you hear me?"

Libby nodded. "I hear you."

I smiled as wide as I could. "Ready to kill some assholes?"

"Hell yeah."

We drew our weapons and crept up to the edge of the summit ahead of us. As we neared, one of my nightmares clicked. This was the valley. It was the same valley that kept appearing in my dreams.

"It was a summit this whole time," I mumbled.

"What?" Libby whispered.

"My nightmares. The dreams I've been having with that weird guy in them. This place. I've been here before."

"Is that a good thing?"

"We're going to find out." I spotted two Demons walking towards us, gloating about their latest meals and conquest. My fingers twitched as they grew closer.

The moment they were out of view from the others, we pounced. Silently, we leaped from behind, making quick work of slicing through their necks. Their heads toppled to the ground, blood pooling around their bodies. I pressed my hand to their chests and sent trickles of fire through my fingertips, burning down to their cores.

We moved quickly, picking our next prey. Three others headed our way, alarm crossed their features as the scent of the Demons' blood reached them. Their muscles tensed and anger flashed across their eyes. They raced toward us, nostrils flaring.

As they crashed through the trees, their bodies met our blades. I had my sword drawn, at the ready. As the first Demon, a grey-scaled one, ran through, I swung my sword out, slicing the Demon's torso right below the chest. He roared as blood spewed. He lunged at me, the other two catching sight of Libby.

The grey Demon extended his claws. They clashed with my sword, matching my every movement. The Demon hissed and spat at me, a spiked crevice opening across his bottom lip.

I cursed under my breath as my arm began burning. I glanced down to find that the spot where the glob had landed on my fighting gear, had melted away. My exposed skin was bubbling and burning, as if it were on fire.

I blinked back the pain and swung my sword above my head, bringing it down on the Demon's, almost missing my mark as the pain seared through my arm. My sword sliced through its skull diagonally. I dropped my sword, gripping my arm with my hand, biting back the scream clawing its way up my throat. I dropped to my knees, my vision blurring as I took in the melting flesh, the bone beginning to poke through.

"Fuck," I spat.

Someone dropped next to me. "Let me see, Rin," it was Derik. He pulled my arm into his lap as he examined it. "It's acid."

They can spit fucking acid!?

"No one mentioned anything about these assholes being about to spit *freaking acid*," I panted. "Can you fix it?" The pain was unbearable.

"Yes, but you're going to have to keep quiet. This isn't going to feel good," he rasped. Libby stood at the ready as she'd taken her Demon down.

I bit my lip, drawing blood as I fought back the scream. Not feeling good was a fucking understatement. Every part of me burned, like my flames were consuming me from the inside out. Guilt washed through me as I thought of the Demons I'd scorched.

"They deserved it."

Did they though?

"Erin, look around you. The pain they cause and the horrors they are trying to bestow unto this world. Yes they deserved it."

Alright fine, you're right.

Derik ran his fingers over the closed flesh once more. "Okay, you're done. It's rare that any of them can spit acid...but if any other sends fluids your way again, dodge, and cut them down immediately."

"No fucking shit." I panted. Derik stood up and reached his hand out to me, pulling me to my feet.

More Demons were beginning to take notice. A roar echoed through the forest. We readied ourselves as the trees behind us rustled. I groaned internally.

Fuck. Not again.

I stepped in front of Derik and Libby, sword braced.

Four men stepped out, none of them Demons. Recognition plagued me, however my memory failed me as I couldn't remember their names.

Libby spoke up, the bounce in her step returning. "You guys got here a lot quicker than expected. Perfect timing," she beamed and faced me, her hand extended to the four individuals. "These are the guys I mentioned. The ones you met at Riverside."

"Oh, yeah. Sorry, I'm bad with names," I nodded a quick apology and pivoted, aiming for the summit clearing. Making sure they followed. "Take down as many Demons as you can. Don't get yourselves killed. Save the humans and do not let them out of your sight." I rolled my shoulders back. I stepped into the open with the others behind me. I held my sword, drawn at my waist and cleared my throat. Mustering up every ounce of courage I could. The Demons' attention caught the hunger for destruction in their eyes. I quickly glanced around the clearing, only one human unconscious, the rest awake and barely clothed, blood and dirt caked onto their skin.

We'd get them out. I'd die to make sure of it.

I kept my expression neutral, and shouted, my voice calm, "Hey, Assholes. Heard y'all have been looking for some 'Key.' Well, today's your lucky day," I swung my sword in a loop, a smile spread across my face. "Here I am. Come get me." I silently apologized to my sword as I stabbed it into the ground and propped my elbow on the hilt, leaning against it and waved my other hand through the air. "Unless, of course, you're afraid of a few Nephilim." I stuck my tongue out at the Demons and anger pulsed through the air, electrifying it. The corners of my mouth twitched.

The Demons rushed at us, and we braced ourselves for the onslaught. The first one jumped in the air, claws drawn, and the bloodshed began. I sent out my feelers, searching for the strongest and fought my way towards them.

Roars and screams vibrated the Earth around us. Blood pouring from Demons as we took them down, their numbers dwindling. Another Demon raced towards me, I slammed my sword through its kneecaps and pushed it backward over the edge of the clearing, sending it plummeting to the base of the mountain. I watched as it fell to its death, its body splattering on the rock face.

I whirled in time to find a Demon racing to the edge, its wings spread, a human within its grasp. I launched myself towards them, a roar erupting from within me. "Let. Them. Go." Fire coursed through my veins, my vision narrowing in on my prey. A growl erupted from my throat, rumbling through the sky above. Lightning began cracking down, striking Demons where they stood.

Their bodies flambéed and scattered throughout the field. The dried grass surrounding the clearing caught aflame. Three Demons remained, fury graced their features. I ran, my sights on the Demon readying to take flight, sword drawn. I leaped in the air, twisting and ramming my blade into its neck, pulling it clean through as I landed on the ground behind it. Its head thumped to the ground. Black ink oozed from its severed neck. The human it held captive screamed. Tears streamed down her face. The Demon's body dropped to its knees, I grabbed the woman before it fell forward, crushing her. Libby dismembered the second Demon, a second human woman in her arms as they escaped. That left only one Demon remaining. One.

I spotted him across the clearing, the Demon who aided in my torture during my captivity—Asier. His demonic wings were shredded, his eyes wild as he frantically searched for a way to escape, I flashed my teeth. He was mine. "Stay here," I whispered to the woman, not registering anything beyond her flame-red hair and motioned for one of the Nephilim nearby to take her to safety. My sights trained on Asier.

I stalked towards him, licking my lips. His eyes widened in panic as they met mine. Recognition flashed in his narrowed eyes. I sprinted, drawing my sword once again. I was mere feet from him when he disappeared. "Too slow, Nephilim trash," I whirled around to find Asier behind me, dagger nails clutched around a human man's throat. "Move and I'll rip his throat out." Asier smirked. "And it'll be all your fault, Nephilim." Ice crept up my spine.

He's playing with you. A familiar male's voice echoed in my mind.
I can't let the man die.
Then don't. Win this.

I dropped my sword, it hit the ground with a clink.

Asier bellowed out a laugh, hair pricked along my skin. "You weak, idiotic creature. So easy to tame. To manipulate." He licked the human's neck as he shook. Fear encapsulated the man, his eyes wide, skin ashen. His bones visible beneath his tattered clothing, what remained of it.

I dropped to the ground, one knee on the scorched grass, the other supporting my arm as I dropped my head in surrender. "You win."

Asier cackled. "Excellent. You made this far too easy," his footsteps neared, crunching the dead leaves and twigs underfoot. He crouched in front of me. "You see, you are what we truly need. As we've already bed the human women and feasted on the men, their blood is within safe keeping, you vacuous, Nephilim. So they may have escaped but all we need...is you. And Erebus shall be *oh so thrilled* to have you in his chamber again."

I tensed.

I sent out my senses, finding the humans had escaped, taken by the Nephilim. I let out a breath of relief before noting my mistake. The heat from Asier's towering form disappeared. My head snapped up to find the Demon, his arms wrapped around someone's neck. My heart skipped.

Seth.

Everything stopped.

He slumped in Asier's arms.

The Demon moved to the edge of the mountain, dragging Seth's unconscious body with him, and tossed him over the edge.

I screamed, sprinting faster than I ever had before as I launched myself over the cliff after him. Tears streamed, floating in the air as we plummeted. I tucked my arms and legs in close to increase my speed. As I reached him, I pulled him into my arms, rotating us in the air so my back would hit the ground first giving him a chance at survival.

I held him close, clutching him to my chest, eyes shut as I braced for impact.

Please. Someone please.

Fly.

What?

The male voice echoed through the air around us.

"Fly dammit. This is not how you fucking die, Erin Snow."

My eyes shot open. The man from my dreams flew next to us as we fell. Time slowed.

"Fly. NOW."

I gulped. Begged and begged. Scrambled within and clamped my eyes shut. My body tensed. A burning pain erupted from my back; I screamed as my back arched. My skin ripped and my eyes shot open.

We stopped. I held my breath, my eyes darting side to side, stars erupting across the sky, the sun having disappeared. I gasped as I gripped Seth closer, refusing to risk letting him go.

We were floating in midair. My shoulders burned, as if strained. Wind gusted around us. I swiveled, turning my head to the side. Black feathers ruffled at the edge of my vision. I switched to the other side; the feathers were there as well.

My eyes widened. "No fucking way."

The man from my dreams floated down in front me. As I peered closer, I noticed that he too was suspended in the sky, white feathers spread behind him.

"Holy shit. You have wings," I swiveled my head. "I have wings. What the shit?" Panic began to well within my stomach, nausea taking over.

No one said anything about flying. Why...why am I flying?

"Let us get you to solid ground. At that point I shall answer your question." The man flapped his wings, large gusts of wind whooshing around them as he did so. He continued until he gracefully landed on the moss covered ledge below us.

I chewed my tongue and did my best to copy his movement, flapping my newfound wings downward. It was sloppy, I jostled Seth in my hold and lost the rhythm several times. I finally landed with a thump, almost losing my balance.

I laid Seth flat on the ground and checked his pulse, biting back the nausea. I counted with the beat of his heart and let out a breath of relief. He was alive.

I remembered the guy from my dreams and whirled around, drawing my knife from my waistband, and leapt to my feet; my sword and daggers remained scattered near the cliff hanging far above us. "Alright, what the fuck was that? And why the fuck do you keep popping up in my dreams? Actually, no. Who the hell are you and why are you here? Why am I seeing you now? Is this some kind of sick joke?" I rattled off question after question, panting. He just stood there, a bemused expression on his face. I stomped my foot into the ground. "Ugh! Can you at least tell me who the hell you are, for fuck's sake?" I threw my hands in the air, frustrated.

Silken honey, warmed from the recess of my memory, seeped into my bones. "That my dearest Erin, is Raphael, your Angel Guide.

And my brother." My eyes widened; tears blurred my vision. I turned, the world slowing down around me.

"Dad?"

Wings of Destiny
The Erin Snow Series by V. M. Pire
Book One
End

Acknowledgements

First and foremost, I want to give a huge thank you to my husband and my kids for all of their support and encouragement. There were so many times that I doubted myself and struggled. They were there with me every step of the way and I love you guys so so much and am so unbelievably grateful. I also want to say thank you to my best friend for pushing me and her continued encouragement even when that damned imposter syndrome would get the best of me. You're a fucking badass and I'm so freaking grateful to have you in my life. Thank you for putting up with my ass.

And to my readers, my street team, my betas, alphas, editors, artists, arc readers, book buddies and everyone I've met along the way, I couldn't have done this without you! Thank you so freaking much for your support and feedback and just everything that you all do! I couldn't have asked for a better support system!

#FBN (IYKYK)

V. M. Pire

About the author

With a love for coffee and her Chai Tea topped off with a double shot of expresso, V. M. Pire thrives off of the sass of her favorite books characters and is fueled by her anxiety and absurd levels of overthinking (not to mention awful dad jokes). She can pull random TV Show or Movie References out of nowhere, and belt out some of the cringiest songs known to mankind with those that she's closest too. All in all, she is chaos, a mess express with a million thoughts, who said screw it and decided to get her thoughts and ideas out into the world.

Also by

The Erin Snow Series
Wings of Destiny: Embrace Your Wings, Beware Your Heart
Wings of Betrayal (2025)
The Erin Snow Series Book Three

Social Media

FOLLOW THE AUTHOR AND STAY TUNED FOR UPDATES!

Follow the Author on Instagram at @author.v.m.pire
Follow the Author on Facebook at Author V. M. Pire
Follow the Author on GoodReads at V. M. Pire
Signed Copies and Merch:
https://snowpirebooksllc.myshopify.com/

Milton Keynes UK
Ingram Content Group UK Ltd.
UKHW051851151024
449634UK00004B/12